HUNTER of SHERWOOD
KNIGHT of SHADOWS

A GUY OF GISBURNE NOVEL
TOBY VENABLES

ABADDON
BOOKS

WWW.ABADDONBOOKS.COM

An Abaddon Books™ Publication
www.abaddonbooks.com
abaddon@rebellion.co.uk

First published in 2013 by Abaddon Books™,
Rebellion Intellectual Property Limited,
Riverside House, Osney Mead, Oxford, OX2 0ES, UK.

10 9 8 7 6 5 4 3 2 1

Editors: Jonathan Oliver & David Moore
Cover Art: Luke Preece
Design: Simon Parr & Sam Gretton
Marketing and PR: Michael Molcher
Publishing Manager: Ben Smith
Creative Director and CEO: Jason Kingsley
Chief Technical Officer: Chris Kingsley
Hunter of Sherwood™ created by David Moore
and Toby Venables

ISBN: 978-1-78108-162-4

Printed in the US

To Felicity and Alice,
who also set out on this journey,
and to little William,
who was born along the way.

I
ENGLAND

I

The Tower of London
5 November, 1191

THE GAUNT EDIFICE of the Conqueror's great keep stood skull-white against the dark winter sky. He could see it more clearly now, illuminated by the cold light of the waxing, three-quarter moon. Crouched low in the small, blunt-ended craft, he stilled the oar and allowed the boat to drift for a moment on the icy, ink-black flow of the evening tide. Drops of freezing water flicked his face as, with numb fingers, he hauled the oar aboard. In the near-impenetrable dark of the boat's interior, the damp, heavy wood jarred noisily against the thwart. He uttered a curse, his eyes darting to the shoreline. No movement; just the shifting, black mirror of the water, his own foggy breaths and the powdery swirl of fine snow that blew about him, its dusty specks glinting coldly in the moonlight – colourless ghosts of the sunlit motes of summer.

In the past hour, the sky had cleared to reveal a starlit canopy. It would get colder yet. His curious garb gave back almost no light – rendered him little more than shadow – yet he had hoped the moon would maintain its shroud a little longer to better mask what lay ahead. There would be no more snow, at least, and only the foolish or desperate would venture out on such a bitter night (he laughed to himself – which was he?). He had seen a few lingerers, further upriver: London's lost and helpless, or those hurrying to finish their day and reach their hearths – if hearths they had. But here, there was no life at all. Spitting length to his left, on the northern shore, a jagged fringe of dirty ice edged the lapping water, giving way to a pitch-black inlet. A blunt spur of water that thrust a full furlong into the land, but only upon the west side; the failed attempt at a moat, over which – though he could not yet see it – stood the stone bridge that led to the Tower's gatehouse.

Beyond it, where the bank resumed, the cold, curved stonework of the Bell Tower marked the southwest corner of the new outer walls that rose up from the riverbank ahead. On the bank, patches of virgin snow sparkled in the dim light like ground glass. No foot trod here – human or animal. There were not even the forked marks of birds.

He knew there should be guards upon the new battlements, but he also knew that they relied on precisely this assumption. In reality, night patrols of the riverside curtain wall were lax and erratic – especially after midnight, and all the more so since the dramatic siege of the past month. But now, the Most Hated Man In England having been ignominiously ejected, the crisis was thought to be past. The decimated Tower guards – stretched beyond the limit of their capabilities, but not dreaming of further assault upon the most secure place in England – were weakened, disorganised and complacent, a fatal combination. And while its thick walls and iron-strapped doors afforded *prisoners* no chance of escape, *information*, he had discovered, was not so easily contained. He knew, for example, that the nearest guard would not be on the parapet at all, but in the octagonal Bell Tower on the new outer wall's southwest corner, partly the worse for drink, and clinging to a brazier. They did not expect trouble. They could not even imagine what kind of trouble *could* threaten them. They did not expect him.

He turned his attention back to the grim turrets and stern, square walls of the White Tower, thrusting above the castle's new ramparts like cliffs of ice. It would be a different story there.

The great keep was visible all over London. By day, its whitewashed exterior shone blindingly over the mud and squalour of the city. By night, it loomed like an ominous phantom rising from the darkness of the boneyard. Everpresent, watching, warning. That had been its purpose from the start. This was no cathedral to inspire men to great deeds. It was a demonstration to all, of the Norman invader's fierce dominance over his newly conquered capital.

He had been dead a century, but, by accident or design, the White Tower had captured in stone many of that king's own qualities. It was implacable, grim – even brutal. It had sophistication of mind in its features, but little time for delicacy. It did not seek to hide its purpose. Even in its stark, simple beauty – the unfussy, towering pilasters, the simple, arched and slotted windows – it was practical, stern, plain. It did not do anything by half measures. Its stout stone walls – entirely square, entirely vertical – stood almost a hundred feet high, and were fifteen feet thick at the base.

Turning from the Tower's grim face, then, he took up the oar and let his eyes scan the gloomy, lifeless shores once more, glancing back briefly at the dark bundle of equipment in the boat – the crossbow, the thin rope, the slender steel grapple, its metal entirely sheathed in delicately stitched brown leather. The preparations had been thorough. But as he drew silently closer, the oar dipping in the near-frozen swell of the Thames, he watched the task grow more formidable before his eyes.

It was a calculated effect. The Tower was not only built to withstand brute force, but to crush and wither resistance before it even began; to inspire awe in the hearts of all who stood for the King, and sap the will of those who would stand against him. And this, he knew, was no empty threat. Its reputation went before it. A supreme symbol of royal power and military might, long envied across all Christendom, its walls had never been breached.

Until tonight.

II

JOHN BREKESPERE PEERED over the northern battlement of the White Tower and shuddered. The dizzying expanse of pallid stone stretched away beneath him, finally disappearing into an endless blank gloom – a channel of impenetrable black between the walls upon which he now stood guard, and the snow-capped edge of the outer wall floating in a sea of darkness beyond.

As he stared, and his eyes adjusted, he fancied he could just make out the ground of the inner ward far below, a dusting of light snow picking out its frozen ruts. He swayed, and drew back from the edge. He'd never been good with heights – a curious trait, given that he stood at least a foot taller than most men – yet somehow, the compulsion to subject himself to them had driven him to the edges of things throughout his whole life. It had been like that at Dover. Something – some morbid compulsion – had made him gawp over the dizzying brink of the white cliffs, even as his brain was screaming at him to back away. He'd stood there, toes on the crumbling edge, hair standing on end – or so it felt – swaying towards the yawning abyss, unable to banish the image of his great bulk cartwheeling down past cackling, shrieking birds, clothes whipped and tugged by the wind in a moment of tranquil suspension, before bursting like a sack of manure on the rocks below. He sometimes thought it must be the Devil taunting him with these desires, these terrifying pictures. Each time, he'd pull himself back – but the weird thrill of it haunted his nightmares.

These walls reminded him of those cliffs. He idly wondered if they had always been whitewashed like this, and whether the Conqueror had, in fact, meant to echo Dover.

As he stared out over the dim, barely perceptible lights of London, a bitter wind from the north shook his frosted beard and flung icy flecks against his face. One of the lights – ahead and some little way to the right, though weaker than the weakest star – was in all probability that of his own home. He briefly tried to identify it, as he had striven to do on countless other nights, knowing all the while that the attempt was futile. It was late, anyway; perhaps, by now, it was extinguished and his wife slept soundly there. He hoped this might be the case. They were so close, and yet he hadn't seen her for so many weeks. As the wind buffeted his face from the direction in which she lay, its frozen pinpricks stinging the half-numb flesh, he was suddenly gripped by a familiar, terrible yearning, pulling at his innards like a physical pain. His rational mind struggled to subdue his rebellious heart – but no sooner had the feeling gone than part of him ached for its return.

It had been hard for her, coming from the Holy Land. Not that it hadn't been hard for him, after the horrors of Hattin, after imprisonment, after the slow return to life. But he had been able to leave that behind – physically, at least – and had been granted a homecoming. She had left everything she knew for this land of soul-crushing winters and staring, suspicious, hate-filled eyes. Sosa was a Syriac Christian, as devout as any man or woman he had met. But when they looked at her here, he knew they saw only "Saracen" – whatever that meant. He wasn't sure himself any more. These things seemed so simple at a distance; far less so when seen up close. It was, he noted, often the women who were the most spiteful towards her. Perhaps they had lost someone to the crusade. Still, he found he constantly tried to reassure her that their situation was otherwise, wanting her to see the best in his fellow countrymen – hoping, somehow, that plain old good cheer could yet carry them through it. She would smile, and put a hand to his face, and kiss his broad brow, the light glinting in her beautiful dark eyes, and tell him she was happy. Yet he could not quell the growing conviction that he, and this whole great kingdom of which he had told her so much, had failed her.

Another deep shudder racked his huge frame. He was chilled to the marrow, and he needed a piss. He stamped his feet in a hopeless attempt to coax his benumbed toes back to life, passed his spear from one hand to the other, flexing his frozen fingers, and tried to think of something else.

It was Longchamp who had kept them apart, Longchamp who was responsible for all their recent woes.

John Brekespere had been recruited to the Tower guard over a year ago by William Puintellus, Constable of the Tower, as a personal favour to a knight named Geoffrey of Launceston. Launceston had also fought at Hattin – if briefly – with the advance guard of Count Raymond of Tripoli. Raymond's cavalry had charged through Saracen lines only to find themselves outside the fray, with the remainder of the Christian army encircled and overwhelmed. They had not returned to the battle.

It is said that the guilt of the survivor is the heaviest to bear. So it was with Launceston. From that day, wherever he could, he had sought to make amends by engineering advantages for veterans of Hattin who had gone through what he had not. John Brekespere did not know how Launceston had come to hear of him – perhaps those differences that made Sosa so stand out amongst the English had, for once, worked in their favour. Whatever it was, he did not tempt fate by questioning this stroke of luck.

Puintellus was a dour but supremely practical sort – lacking humour, but organised and fair-minded in his dealings with other men – ideally suited to the responsibilities with which he was charged. It was said he was more mason than soldier, but Brekespere liked and respected the constable. All the garrisoned guards did. It was Puintellus who had managed the building of the new walls, Puintellus who had maintained the security and daily life of the Tower – a complex enough task even without the logistical challenges of the building works.

Puintellus, however, was directly answerable to Longchamp. Norman by birth and upbringing, William Longchamp – Bishop of Ely, Lord Chancellor, Chief Justiciar – was the most powerful man in England. Personally appointed by King Richard to manage his realm – even though he knew little of its ways, cared even less, and spoke no English – Longchamp was monarch in all but name. Wherever he went in his diocese or the city of London, the people noted the vast retinue of servants and the menagerie of animals that accompanied him on his travels, and weighed the need for them against their crippling taxes. Where other, more subtle leaders would have sought to engender loyalties, Longchamp somehow succeeded in alienating entire populations, and inspired only resentment and hatred amongst the barons. To secure his position, he granted castles to his own relatives, and when faced with resistance from existing castellans, attempted to remove them by force of arms. It was Longchamp who was behind the project of improving and expanding the Tower's defences. Though this undoubtedly had the approval of the absent King, Longchamp clearly saw within it an opportunity to secure his own position at the heart of the realm, and to these ends had put Puintellus and his men under the lash.

In their struggle against this scheming usurper, the barons had found an unlikely ally.

Prince John was little loved in England. Of late, however, he had unexpectedly redeemed himself by rallying an army in defence of the beleaguered castles in the north. Few doubted that the prince – humiliatingly sidelined by his brother Richard – had an agenda of his own, but for now anyone was preferable to Longchamp. "Better the Devil you know," became a familiar truism.

John succeeded in halting Longchamp's territorial ambitions. For a time, there existed an uneasy truce. Then, the Lord Chancellor went too far. Seeing a chance to discredit and eliminate another potential rival to his authority, Longchamp had had his brother-in-law, the castellan of Dover, arrest Geoffrey, Archbishop of York. The archbishop resisted, was besieged in St Martin's Priory, then violently dragged from a place of sanctuary and flung into a cell on a trumped-up charge of treason. The fact that a holy place had been violated and the right of asylum rent asunder was an unsettling enough echo of Thomas Becket as it was – but this archbishop was also brother to Prince John and King Richard. It was all the excuse John needed to rid England of Longchamp for good.

What happened next burned hot in Brekespere's memory.

It had been a bright, cold day in October and all was proceeding as normal – the familiar buzz, if anything, lightened in spirit by the arrival of the sun and its banishment of the fog of previous days. The masons continued the works on the new walls and towers. Surveyors and enginers continued to scratch their heads over the issue of the moat – one of Longchamp's ongoing obsessions. Guards were changed, food was cooked and consumed, horses were stabled, groomed and shod. Everyone complained about the hours of work forced upon them. Nothing was out of the ordinary.

At the time the news broke, Brekespere was not on watch. He had just made the climb up to the west battlement of the keep to inform the duty guard that an inspection would be made later that morning (Puintellus liked to give the guards warning about surprise inspections, in spite of Longchamp's wishes to the contrary – or perhaps *because* of them) when he had spied a single figure approaching the Tower at a run. News. There followed a commotion at the gatehouse. The man was admitted, but soon disappeared from view, having crossed the outer ward in haste, accompanied by a watchman and two guards. Moments later, the whole place was in an uproar, its orderly routines replaced by urgent cries and frantic preparations. Still aloft on the battlements, Brekespere had called out to those below. Their hasty, half-heard replies were disjointed, the story – perhaps already third or fourth hand – confused and contradictory, but the nub of it was clear. A great army was coming. Prince John was marching on London.

Brekespere's guts lurched. Was it possible? Having restored Lincoln and taken the castles of Nottingham and Tickhill, had John's successes made him hungry for greater glory, and had he now set his sights on the greatest prize in the kingdom? Brekespere broke into a heavy run towards the northwest tower. Before he could reach it he saw, out to the west, a great throng surging towards the Tower precinct along Eastcheap – its progress rapid but disordered, a colourful entourage at its head.

By the time he had emerged from the keep into the inner ward, it had become clear that this rabble was not the expected army – which, he also learned, was many times its size – but Longchamp, fleeing ahead of it. The Chancellor was seeking refuge in the Conqueror's impregnable White Tower – the king's tower, *his* tower – with his entire personal guard behind him. As Brekespere strode across the courtyard of the outer ward, his eyes searching frantically for Puintellus, the gates were flung wide, and in poured a great mob of puffing, sweating humanity. Longchamp had arrived.

Never was there a more graphic demonstration of the scale of the man's vanity and the paucity of his wisdom. He had brought wagons laden with boxes, barrels, bolts of rich cloth, pieces of furniture and every kind of unnecessary thing, unidentifiable animals – some in cages, some cavorting on chains, often threatening to break free in the disordered crowd that swarmed after him. There were dogs in eager, darting packs, horses of all sorts – some laden, but many not – and more ladies and ladies' maids, pages and stewards, cooks and servants, grooms and standard bearers than one would have thought to find attending anything less than an Emperor. Behind this, his army – mostly mercenaries from the Lowlands, judging by their looks – trudged in a surly, seemingly unending torrent, their austere demeanour an absurd contrast to the foppish opulence and gaudy colours of Longchamp's entourage.

They flooded into the Tower precinct, crowding out the masons and labourers, crushing against the guards and each other, their hot bodies and rank, sweaty smell filling every corner of the keep until all were standing shoulder to shoulder with barely room to move.

And there was Longchamp himself. Defiant, enraged, he strode agitatedly back and forth, gaudily clad in what appeared to be some approximation of papal robes, with the ludicrous addition of a pair of baggy pantaloons in red and gold silk – a failed attempt to make him look like he had spent time in the Holy Land, although everyone knew he had been no further east than Paris. Flinging his arms about in fury, the gold adorning every finger flashing as he did so, he renounced John as a traitor in a language incomprehensible to most present, spit flying from his thin, pinched face as he did so. Evidently, he believed he could make a stand here. But it was a ridiculous gesture – one that everyone, right down to the humblest kitchen boy, could see was already doomed to failure.

And so it proved.

When John's army surrounded the Tower, the prince did not squander his energies by battering walls that he already knew were unassailable, and which, in any case, might one day be his. He simply waited, knowing what all those inside – except, apparently, their master – had known from the start: that in a matter of very few days, life within would become unbearable.

Longchamp sent out appeals to the people of London. He ranted incoherently from the battlements, demanding that they rise up in his defence. Few can have understood his words – but they understood the man and his predicament well enough. As one, they folded their arms and stood back to let John do his worst. John, meanwhile, had a dinner table set up within sight of the battlements, and made sure Longchamp could see how well he ate and drank while conditions within the overstuffed castle grew steadily worse. By the fourth day, all resistance had collapsed, and Longchamp emerged, purple-faced, humiliated – forced to surrender the keys by his own men, subtly spurred on by Puintellus.

What became of Longchamp and his guard after that, Brekespere never knew. Nor did he discover what happened to those of his fellows who had been foolish enough to express loyalty for Longchamp. He was simply glad to have been one of the survivors. Within days, they were forgotten. A stain that had been scrubbed out. A kind of normality was restored – the surest sign of which was the return of the suspicion and resentment with which the Tower's unexpected new master, Prince John, was regarded.

So, it was over. For now. Brekespere sighed a thick, cloudy breath, then turned and stared southwards, in the direction of the Thames. Between him and the opposite battlement overlooking the river, the twin pitched roofs of the White Tower stretched, several feet below the level of the parapet walkway. Beneath one of these – the left one, he thought – the prince now slept. He supposed he was grateful to their royal guest for ridding them of the weasel Longchamp. He just wished the prince himself would now bugger off so things could properly return to normal.

It suddenly struck him how much the roofs resembled coffins – huge, stone sarcophagi, built to contain giants, sunk side by side within the keep's walls. They brought to mind a half-remembered story from his childhood – one his mother used to tell, of a pair of titans called Corineus and Gogmagog who slept beneath London and would rise up to protect the poor people of the city when their need was greatest. Looking back, she often told him tales of noble giants – a tactic, he now realised, to make him feel more comfortable with his own large stature, but also, perhaps, to inspire him to worthy deeds. He wondered whether she now looked down upon those deeds, and whether they seemed worthy enough.

As he gazed, lost in thought, a fine, powdery snow – too cold to stick – blew across the angled, grey stone, forming an uneven, constantly shifting layer. As fine as flour. Brekespere snorted at that. In the first half of his life he'd seen enough flour to last an eternity. He turned and let his eyes wander past the barely perceptible speckle of lights across North London to the deeper dark beyond.

Here, he knew – though all was now invisible – the mud and stench of the city gave way to a pleasant landscape of tilled fields, level meadows and pasture criss-crossed by streams. Beyond that, just visible during daylight, spread a vast forest, its copses teeming with stags, does, boars, and wild bulls. And somewhere out there, an arrow shot from the hamlet known as Isledon, was his father's mill.

A pang of guilt pierced him, mixed with a stubborn defiance. Apart from the brief time when his mother had fallen into her final illness, he had not clapped eyes on the place since he had been a boy. In those childhood days, he had been known as John the Miller's Son, or, occasionally, John Attemille. Life had seemed simple then. His older brother would one day take over stewardship of the mill, and Young John himself had no responsiblities other than to perform such daily tasks as his father required. To what lay beyond – to adulthood – he gave no thought, although roaring around the countryside, he entertained vague, happy dreams of adventure, inspired by the knights and men-at-arms he occasionally saw passing along the great north road – the main thoroughfare carrying his father's flour into London. Armed with sticks, he and his brother would practise their fighting skills in the woods – until his size began to make the outcome a foregone conclusion, and his brother, increasingly resentful, gave up the good-natured sparring and took to belittling him in whatever ways he could.

One day, when he was fifteen, he had woken up to find his brother gone, and his father weeping. At no other time in his life was Brekespere to witness that, not even when his mother died. Young John never knew what had happened between his father and brother. His father never spoke of it. He simply became sullen and withdrawn, and immersed himself in the backbreaking toil as if it had become a form of self-punishment – now with Young John at his side. Gradually, daily routines changed. John's responsibilities grew. Then, one day, months later, John looked about him and suddenly understood that his entire world had shifted. His brother was probably dead; he was the son now. The mill – which he had never expected, and never really wanted – would fall to him.

Work continued. His father's mood brightened. Over time, Young John – gradually, grudgingly – came to accept his fate. A year after the disappearance, he had finally begun to embrace it, even regarding it as good fortune. A little older, and a little wiser, he now understood that this had brought him closer to his father than he had ever been – that, for the first time, his father had shown him the love and respect that he had not even realised was missing. The future, now, was set. It had a shape. He would take on his father's occupation, and with it the name "Miller".

Then the impossible happened. His brother came back. The boy who had run away to war returned a man – but he had not returned undamaged. He was nervous, with darting eyes, and prone to forced laughter, and although far humbler than John remembered, it was plain to see that it was not the humility of maturity, but the weak flickering of a ruined spirit, broken by suffering and terror. He had chased the adventure of which John had so long dreamed, and its realities had destroyed him.

His father did not hesitate. He forgave the errant son and reinstated him as heir to the mill, apparently without a second thought for the boy who had kept it going these past twenty months. It was, he said ecstatically, just like the gospel story. Young John, suddenly bereft of purpose – of everything he thought he had gained – could only nod stupidly. His mother looked upon the scene with a resigned but strangely melancholy look, which John could not fully interpret.

A week later, Young John met some soldiers upon the great north road, who told him King Henry was recruiting mercenaries. There was rebellion brewing amongst his barons, they said. John took the long-handled *guisarme* that his father used for lopping apples, and joined them.

When he went to London, they had called him John of Isledon. Then, as his travels took him further afield – far beyond where any had heard of that place – he became John O'London. He had fought against the king of Scotland under that name, until circumstances brought him up against several other Johns hailing from that city. Isledon and the mill all but forgotten, he fought in Normandy, Aquitaine and France and on into the Holy Land under an endless succession of nicknames, few of which pleased him.

"Brekespere" had been recent. It was acquired during a skirmish with some rabble on Old Fish

Street in which – thanks to his prodigious strength and uncompromisingly robust tactics (he had fought with a quarterstave as a boy, and so liked to use every part of the pole) – he had managed to snap his favoured guisarme clean in two. But, at last, he had a name he actually liked, and whose use he would encourage. It made him sound like a soldier, at least. Certainly it was preferable to nickname he had suffered under during so much of his time in the Holy Land: "John Lyttel".

He peered over the precipitous walls and shuddered again, shivering to his bones. He'd slope off to the dark corner by the northeast tower in a while and relieve his bladder. Nothing, he told himself, could possibly happen in those few moments.

III

THE OAR DIPPED silently in the icy black water as the punt slid unseen beneath the new walls of the outer ward. Directly ahead, a ship sat moored to the Tower's jetty – so close, he could already hear the muffled voices of the shadowy figures moving between it and the jetty's gatehouse. With a twist of the oar, he guided his small vessel to port, towards the yawning gap of the second inlet that cut into the bank between him and the mooring. Like its cousin further upriver, this had been an attempted moat, marking the original extent of the castle's outer walls. Longchamp's new fortifications had now stretched far beyond it, encircling and containing the ineffectual intrusion of this huge ditch – yet they were not complete. Here, at the point where the water pierced the land, there was also a break in the new curtain wall where the old moat passed through – a broad, unguarded opening which would surely one day be closed by stone when that particular engineering challenge was overcome, but which for now was open to the air.

The gap almost made it possible to sail a boat from the river straight into the midst of the outer ward, entirely bypassing the gatehouse at either the main entrance or the jetty. But temporary measures had been taken – a cluster of huge, sharpened wooden stakes driven into the mud and grit of the river bed all about the inlet. So closely packed and tangled was the forest of spikes that not even the narrowest boat or punt could hope to negotiate it, and the banks on either side were so narrow and so steep that it was assumed – quite rightly – that nothing could cling to them. But, tonight, at the inlet's edges, the still water about the stakes was frozen. It creaked in the swell of the water, extending a few feet from the bank, its edges glassy and frail. But, here and there, immediately beneath the mossy guard tower and the wall lining the inlet, it was just thick enough to support the weight of a man.

Crouched like a crab, he reached up from the punt as it drifted in close, grasping the green, slimy trunk of the nearest stake and using it to haul the craft forward. Slowly, he moved from one stake to the next. The rows of tiny spikes on the palms of his gauntlets gave extra grip, but his clumsy, leather-clad fingers dislodged icicles as he went. He winced as some clattered noisily into the body of the boat, others dangling on threads of green weed. He forged ahead nonetheless. Even if they heard him now, he doubted they would be able to see him. Guiding the punt steadily towards the corner of the bank, he finally felt the bow crunch against ice and shudder to a halt. Hastily, he lashed the craft to the nearest stake, slung the coiled rope and grapple over his right shoulder, uncovered the crossbow and heaved it upright. It was more than half his height, and suddenly, now weight was a more immediate issue, seemed far heavier than he remembered. But there was no time to question it now. He slung it across his back and stood up at the punt's blunt bow, feeling the tiny spikes that also lined the soles of his boots bite into the wooden hull. With his left arm wrapped around the slippery, stinking post, he placed his right foot tentatively upon the ice.

The ice creaked and gave. He stretched as far as he could, knowing that the ice closest to shore, immediately beneath the guard tower, would be thickest, if he could only make it that far. If he did not, he would not survive the river. He would sink like a stone, the cold water forcing the air out of him as he was sucked by his own weight into the freezing black. Before he could think further, he launched himself forward, grabbing for the next post. The ice dipped and bounced sickeningly, great cracks crazing its surface. He threw his arms about the awkwardly angled timber, feeling his spiked feet skid and almost slip from under him – then righted himself. He clung for a moment, his nostrils filled with the stench of river mud and dead fish, then slowly slackened his grip, allowing the frozen surface once again to take his full weight. There was a creak – but the ice held.

He could use the ice shelf to make his way undetected along the edge of the inlet, following the line of the old walls all the way into the outer ward. But there was something else to be done first. Turning back towards the river, he divested himself of crossbow and rope, and laid them carefully down on the frozen surface. Then, staying close to the bank, steadying himself on the frozen stonework of the guard tower, he inched gingerly around the delicate fringe of ice at its foot. It thinned dramatically closer to the flow of the river; he could already feel it splinter and groan beneath him. But he was within sight of the ship now. If it only held for seconds longer, it would be enough. Peering around the curve of the tower, he reached into the leather bag at his side and pulled out an almost spherical earthenware bottle, wrapped in sacking and sealed with wax. He threw off the sacking and weighed the bottle carefully in his hand, eyeing up the distance between him and the ship. He drew his arm back, and hurled it as hard as he could.

He did not see its flight through the air. But he heard its crash upon the the ship's port side, saw a great eruption of yellow flame that near blinded him, lighting up the mast and throwing the spidery rigging into sharp silhouette. There were cries of alarm, but he saw that his aim had been poor. Another earthenware globe was already in his hand, and this time the target was plain to see. The dark ball sailed through the air and burst against the mast, showering the deck with flame and instantly igniting the furled sail. He hurried back toward the dark of the inlet, one foot momentarily dipping into freezing water as he misjudged his footing and a slab of ice gave way. He didn't stop to think, but snatched up the rope and crossbow and ran across the bouncing surface of the ice, as if the fire on the ship had also ignited something in his blood. He vaulted a dark gap in the ice – a privy outlet in the wall, he supposed – almost losing his footing on the other side (if he fell now, would he crash through?), but already the ice was thicker, its surface here thickly layered with crunchy, frozen snow. He threw himself forward. Within moments, he was off the ice, clambering up the snow-covered, mud bank, and – black hood pulled about his ears – stepping unchallenged into the castle's outer ward.

Already, figures were dashing about: numerous guards, singly and in groups, armed with crossbows or spears; a fat, red-faced old woman hauling up her skirts to avoid the horse dung; a single knight, in a full coat of mail with sword drawn, striding purposefully towards the gatehouse; a bemused mason, covered head-to-toe in white dust and literally not knowing which way to turn; a gaggle of squires, some half-dressed or in the process of dressing, all engaged in what seemed a violent argument. None took the slightest notice of him.

On one side, immediately ahead and to his right, the west wall of the keep towered over him like a great white cliff, the toothed battlements flickering weirdly as they reflected the fire-ship's flames. Cutting across the hectic courtyard, he did not pause to look back at the entrance to the inner ward giving access to the keep's main door – about which, he had no doubt, a formidable band of armed men were now clustered.

Heading away from it, his head low and his back turned to the distant blaze, he pressed on against the prevailing flow of scurrying humanity towards the White Tower's northwest corner, a dark space from which no figure issued – a place he knew no one else would be going, and no one would be looking: the ward immediately beneath the Tower's north wall.

With his strange, black-cowled cloak, coiled rope and huge crossbow slung across his back, he cut an outlandish figure, even among the diverse residents of the citadel. But they looked through him and past him – all eyes straining towards the river, its leaping flames, and the deadly and immediate threat that must be close behind it. *Control the battlefield.* That's what his old mentor had taught him. That was the principle that had dictated his daring plan. All was now unfolding exactly as anticipated – but the greatest challenge was that which lay immediately ahead. Even with his hooded face so resolutely averted from this heaped mountain of stone, he could feel its daunting presence, the blank windows staring from that cold, monstrous face like the dead eyes of its maker. This was the closest he had ever been to the White Tower. Its walls now seemed more forbidding than ever.

He passed unnoticed between a long, low stone building and the corner of the keep, and was swallowed up by the blackness beyond. The darkness here was total. No lights burned. The cold light of the moon did not penetrate, nor the glow of the distant flames. He was in the Tower's cold shadow.

As his eyes grew accustomed to the inky black, he began to make out shapes over by the outer wall: a couple of wagons, a heap of rubble, a jumble of upended wooden planking – evidently for the use of the masons and labourers working on the new fortifications. This was, for the most part, a forgotten place. A dumping ground. Beneath his feet, the iron-hard ground was uneven, the ruts dotted here and there with brittle, icy puddles and dusted with undisturbed snow. The ground was also higher here than at any other point about the keep's walls. It was this fact that brought him here.

Upon reaching the halfway point of the keep's wall, he set his back hard against the stone, walked a carefully measured number of paces from it, then stopped and turned. He heaved the crossbow off his shoulder and slid the rope carefully off his arm, placing both upon the frozen ground. With the outer rampart to his back, and the White Tower's north wall filling the view before him, he finally straightened and allowed his eyes to wander over the soaring stonework, all the way up to the battlements. The air around him was still; the shouts and curses outside the quiet enclave seemed far distant. From somewhere wafted the dank smell of human waste. High above and to his left, he could now see a dim light in one of the upper windows. Now, so close to his goal, the seeming impossibility of the task struck him full force. Suddenly, he was painfully aware of every physical limitation: the cold sweat beneath his arms, the stiffness in his left shoulder, the smallness of his body before this unending slab of stone. He flexed his muscles and stretched his arms, as if pushing the thoughts from him. He could not let doubt get in the way of action. Not now. This was the lowest section of the keep's walls. The equipment was built for the task. He had prepared and tested everything a dozen times, and nothing now was any different from every one of those successful attempts in the forest. He need only keep a clear head, and repeat everything as he had done before.

Taking a deep breath of the cold, clammy air, he stooped, raised the crossbow on its end, and began to turn the windlass, leaning into it with all his weight as the bow reached its limit and the rhythmic, dull clicks of wood against metal slowed to a stop.

"Hey!"

At the sudden cry, he almost dropped the weapon. To his right, silhouetted against the feeble light from the courtyard, stood a figure of a man. By his outline, a tower guard, a conical helm upon his head, a crossbow across one arm.

"What're you doing here in the dark?" came the voice. It was jovial rather than challenging; even now, even here, he had aroused little more than bemused curiosity. He might have only moments before it coalesced into suspicion. A wave of something like regret, or even sadness passed through him as he laid the primed weapon gently upon the ground and turned towards the guard. The man before him had no idea what he faced, or what was coming. As he strolled towards him, he heard the man actually laugh, as if expecting to share a joke – or perhaps it was because the man had finally taken in his oddly macabre appearance. Then, as he neared, he could discern the man's features clearly enough to make out a frown just seconds before he smashed his forehead into the guard's face. The guard collapsed heavily, his helm bowling across the hard ground, a sound of laboured, sticky breathing coming from him as he slumped.

There was no time for internal debate now. Crouching on one knee, he hastily arranged the coiled rope to ensure there were no snags, then loaded the shaft of the metal hook into the crossbow. He set one end of the weapon on the ground, his right foot behind it, and raised it until the angle satisfied him. This was the critical moment: too high and it would fall short of the battlement. Too low and it would glance off the stone. At ninety feet, this was at the very limit of even this weapon's effective range; the projectile was heavy, the drag of the trailing rope severe. The rope had been made as thin as possible to reduce weight, but that also made it more likely to catch in the wind, or to become tangled in itself as it unfurled. If either happened, it would fail; and there would be no second chances. He held his breath.

The guard groaned and shifted where he lay. He would come to in minutes. But by that time, his quarry would be long gone.

Still not daring to breathe, he released the trigger. The crossbow thudded, recoiling violently against his foot. The bolt flew, the slender rope whipping freely into the air in its wake. For a moment he lost sight of it completely, and was gripped by panic. Then he heard a dull impact far above – the sound of metal against stone, muffled by leather. He pulled upon the rope. It gave, slackened suddenly, stopped again – then held. He pulled it taut, able now to pick out its curved line snaking up to the battlement high above and slightly to his left. Going hand over hand, he kept the strain on the rope as he hurried to the wall, then, in the moment of truth, put one foot upon the stonework, pressed the spikes in the palms of his gauntlets firmly into the rope's fibres, and allowed it to take his whole weight. He felt it stretch – but it did not give.

Slowly, he began to climb.

IV

JOHN BREKESPERE WAS tying up his breeches when the sky caught fire. A moment before, he'd been quietly relieving himself in the crook of the north wall and the northeast tower, contemplating the hot steam rising from the icy stone, when a distant, dull crash intruded upon his meditation. It was at once familiar and strangely incongruous. A cooking pot? A flagon of the prince's wine? He couldn't quite imagine it being either, at this time of night. He pitied the poor sod who'd let it slip, whatever it was. Then, as he'd finished, there had been cry of alarm from somewhere near the river, and before he could turn, the entire expanse of the stonework before him was lit by orange flame. He wheeled around, baffled, gaping across the sunken, pitched roofs of the keep to see huge tongues of fire leaping above the darkly silhouetted parapet opposite – so fierce he fancied he could feel their heat upon his face.

At first, he had the bizarre impression that the south wall of the White Tower itself was ablaze. Only gradually did he realise that the conflagration – whose roar he could now hear, as well as he could see the flames – was somehow situated on the river. The sound was now interspersed with distant shouts which grew rapidly in urgency and number, expanding from their point of origin until it seemed they were coming from every part of the inner ward below, and spreading like a flame up and along the adjacent battlements. Instinctively, fearing some kind of attack (Longchamp?), he roughly knotted the laces on his breeches and set off in a heavy, flat-footed run along the walkway towards the southern rampart. Glancing across to the west, he couldn't see any guards on the far side of the northwest tower. Nor could he see one at the southwest turret. All, he supposed, among the cluster of figures he saw arrayed along the southern battlement overlooking the river, starkly silhouetted against the glow. His big, numb feet almost skidded from under him as they made clumsy contact with the uneven, slippery stone. He wasn't made for running at the best of times, and the narrow walkway – its surface now turned to ice, and with a fresh dusting of snow – was hardly conducive to it, either.

The thin, worn soles of his boots lost their feeble grip again and he slithered perilously close to the edge, his arse clenching as he righted himself awkwardly with his flailing spear. *What a ridiculous way to go...* The thought came in such a bizarrely detached manner that it actually made him chuckle. *I survive the Hell's oven of Hattin, only to end my days slipping on ice and dashing my bloody brains out on the roof of the King's chamber.* For a moment the possibility struck him that, given his weight, he might crash right on through it. If he landed on their royal guest and survived, he thought that might be worse.

Finally reaching the southern rampart without either fate befalling him, he grabbed at the frozen wall of the southeastern tower for support. If it had been possible, he'd have hugged it. As he crept around it to join his fellows, some impulse made him glance back across the roofs toward the post he had just abandoned. He wasn't entirely sure what made him do that. Some movement or sound, he later thought. But there was nothing. Turning back, he jostled with his comrades, staring out over the blazing hulk of the ship, immersed in their various exclamations of bafflement and defiance.

Within this – though none spoke of it – was a sense of apprehension. Nothing was following in the wake of this inferno. There was no assault, no act of violence, not even a specific enemy that any could identify or respond to. All attempts to form a plan of action were frustrated before they began. They could only stand uselessly and wait for what happened next – if there was anything. Already, the possibility of it being a tragic accident was being entertained among one or two of the more optimistic men gathered on the parapet.

Nevertheless, an inexplicable and deep sense of unease was growing in John Brekespere's mind – something that nagged and nagged and shouted at him to return to his station. He glanced briefly back again. His vision, dazzled by the brightness of the flames, struggled to penetrate the gloom – but in that glance he swore he saw, in the flickering half-light at the edge of his vision, some dark *thing* slither over the battlement and crouch motionless upon the walkway. He felt his flesh creep, and the hair on the back of his head bristle. He lowered his eyes, blinked hard, trying to clear his vision, and looked back. Of the black shape, there was now no sign.

The impression had been fleeting, only forming fully in his mind once he had looked away. But the unsettling image would not leave him. Without a word, his mouth suddenly dry, he turned and began to walk steadily back to the north wall.

While the hazardous, headlong run along the eastern rampart had felt all too hectic, the return journey seemed almost supernaturally slow. It was like something in a dream – a weirdly still moment during which every possible explanation flitted through his mind. Rats. A raven. Something blown by the wind. One by one he tried to make the explanations fit what he had seen. But the shape was far bigger than any of those creatures, and the wind was now barely more than a breeze. With the attention of the world entirely elsewhere, he felt a sudden sense of dreadful isolation, and an inexplicable dread, as of some impending disaster. With each step, tales of the vengeful ghosts and malevolent demons that were said to stick to the stones of this place crowded his brain.

All this time, his eyes had been fixed on the walkway of the northern wall, scanning it for something – anything. But nothing had moved. Nothing was out of the ordinary. As he approached the northeast tower, he realised that his pace had unconsciously quickened, to the extent that, as he rounded its curving wall, he was almost breaking into a run.

The dark figure was suddenly inches from him – appearing so unexpectedly, as if out of nowhere, that he had to draw up sharply to avoid crashing into it. For a moment he balanced unsteadily on his toes, eyes wide, mouth open, staring straight into the shadowy features.

"Get down there and help with that fire!" barked the man, gesturing impatiently towards the northeast tower. John Brekespere flushed hot with embarrassment as recognition of the face sank in. Responding instantly to the voice of command, hoping to make amends by the swiftness of his compliance, he muttered feebly in acknowledgement and ducked away through the tower's low doorway, hurrying down the narrow, spiralling steps.

Shit, shit, shit... He cursed his own stupidity as his big feet stumbled clumsily down the cramped stone stairs, his spear clattering awkwardly against the curved wall. What an *idiot*. He'd been caught on the hop. For the first time in his life he'd abandoned his post without being ordered to do so – a cardinal sin – and had been found out. What had he been thinking? But a kind of relief washed over him too. He'd let his imagination get the better of him up there. After all he'd been through in his life, to be spooked by shadows... To his surprise, he found himself laughing at the thought. He'd get a bollocking for this, all the same. Maybe in all the confusion it'd be overlooked – though that depended, he supposed, on what happened next. And how forgiving the man on the battlements was. He just hoped that the knight – he must be a knight; that much was obvious from his tone – was fair-minded. In his experience, though, knights were rarely as fair-minded as they fancied themselves. So, who was this one again? Some part of him had instantly acknowledged the man's face as familiar. Now he thought about it, though, he couldn't quite place it. One of Prince John's men? If so, what was he doing up here? What was his rank? His name? His attire was rather odd, he now realised. The material of a strange sort. Not really like anything he'd seen before. Certainly not about the Tower...

As he descended the relentlessly turning stairs towards the foot of the tower, the growing doubts that spiralled around and around in his head were, he now understood, leading him towards a single, inevitable and ghastly conclusion. He was overwhelmed by a sick, hot feeling; a feeling like molten lead pouring into his stomach. The feeling that he had just made the worst decision of his entire life.

Before he could think further, the stocky figure of William Puintellus, red-faced and literally roaring with consternation, barged into him and past him and charged on up the ill-lit stairs. He was followed closely by a crossbowman named Thomas, who John Brekespere knew well, but for a confused moment struggled to recognise; the man's face was deathly pale, his eyes red-rimmed and swollen, his nose smashed, blackened and bloody, with everything beneath it from lip to waist glistening red in the dim glow of the flambeaux. In his white-knuckled, blood-flecked hands he clutched a crossbow, cocked and loaded. Once again that night, John Brekespere turned back to return the way he had just come, blundering behind his furious master and feeling sicker with each rising step.

On the battlements, at that part of the king's palace which John Brekespere was solely charged to protect, his worst fears were realised. Between the third and fourth merlon he could now make out a slim, dark protrusion hooked over the edge of the stone. Puintellus grabbed at it: a long, slender grapple to which was attached a rope, and which to

Brekespere's increasingly baffled eyes appeared to be made of brown leather. Puintellus, purple with rage, hurled the hook back over the battlements with a cry of disgust and, drawing his sword, ran for the northwest tower.

When they reached the king's chamber, the door was already open. Five more guards were approaching in haste from the other direction, but Puintellus did not hesitate. He barged on through, sending the heavy door crashing back on its hinges – then stopped so suddenly that both Brekespere and his bloodied comrade Thomas cannoned into the back of him. The three of them stood, wide-eyed, motionless, barely breathing, transfixed by the sight that met them. Into the back of them crashed the arriving reinforcements – then they, too, stopped dead, the heat from the chamber's log fire flooding past their still bodies as it was sucked into the cold passageway.

In the fire's flickering glow – dressed in a loose, green robe and seated in a chair that had been deliberately turned from the hearth to face the door – was Prince John, the flames glinting in his dark eyes, his hair hanging loose about his shoulders. His expression was unaccountably calm, under the circumstances. For, across his throat, its edge resting against the exposed white flesh beneath the neatly trimmed beard, gleamed the double-edged blade of a broadsword – and gripping it, looming over the prince like a great shadow, stood the Devil.

John Brekespere wondered how he had ever let himself think the intruder's appearance was normal. Here, in this ordered, serene interior, the figure now seemed outlandish. He was tall and broad-shouldered, garbed in a cloak belted at the waist, and hooded like the habit of some dark monk. Its material, Brekespere now saw, was thick – like leather – but of such a rich black that it seemed to render the wearer hardly more than a shadow, possessing about it a kind of velvety sheen, like the feathers of a crow. In the midst of this shadow, though hardly detracting from its nightmare qualities, hovered an entirely normal, human face. Its features were chiselled and handsome, but hard and impassive – as only those tempered in battle could be – and to Brekespere, still troublingly familiar. But there was one final, bizarre detail that completed the overall impression, that almost made Brekespere shudder to look upon: from the hood of this grim figure, silhouetted in the low glare, protruded two leathery, black points like shrivelled ears, looking for all the world like the tiny horns of some demonic creature.

Brekespere could only stare, his flushed, sweating face that of a man who was watching his life collapse in smouldering ruins before his eyes. The intruder had made no demands, nor given any clue to his identity or purpose. But of one fact Brekespere was now certain: that the prince would be killed before they could do anything to prevent it, his white throat slit open in one swift movement, the hot blood splattering upon the stones. Poor Thomas – eyes still streaming, crossbow ready but only half-raised – seemed impossibly torn between surrender and action, bereft both of orders or any independent grasp of what it was they faced. Even the normally pragmatic Puintellus stood stunned and useless, quivering with indecision, as if he, in turn, were awaiting some word from his royal master.

Word did not come. Instead, an entirely unexpected sound issued from prince's throat. A chuckle. Then a snort of gleeful amusement. And finally, a belly laugh – and a slow clap of congratulation. The dark figure withdrew the sword, placing its point to the floor, both hands resting gently upon the pommel, while Prince John, still applauding, rose from his chair.

"Good, *good!*" he said as his laughter subsided, and turned a small circle, beaming his smile alternately between the black figure and the stunned guards. He spoke in English, ensuring that the whole group could understand him. "You may stand your men down, Sir William," he added, and waved a dismissive hand. "Things are not as they seem." The clenched figures in the doorway visibly slackened. Weapons were lowered. Shoulders slumped. Brekespere seemed actually to diminish in size. But if anything, the draining of tension from the knot of men only allowed their utter bafflement to show through all the more. Puintellus, still flabbergasted, moved his mouth as though to respond – but no sound emerged.

Prince John's demeanour shifted abruptly, his features suddenly grave. "This is one of my men," he said, indicating the black-clad stranger. "He was testing your defence on my orders. He will provide you with a full account of his means of entry. You will ensure that it cannot be duplicated – and it goes without saying that any guards who allowed him to pass are to be punished." Puintellus shot a hot glance at Brekespere, who seemed to shrink further under the glare. "I leave that to your discretion, Sir William." The prince turned away from the crowded doorway, then, after an awkward silence during which none in it moved, turned back and added: "Well... Off you go, then."

Puintellus – glad, on some level, that things were nowhere near as bad as they had first appeared, but still deeply perturbed that they had happened at all – simply gave a nod of his head, and an awkward bow, and shuffled backwards out of the chamber, shoving the others with him. Brekespere had one last glimpse of the prince who had sealed his fate before the door of the King's chamber slammed in his face for the last time.

V

"You look a little better than last time we met," said John, pouring a generous measure of wine into a second goblet.

Guy of Gisburne pulled back his hood and loosened the clothes about his neck, sweating from his exertions and the heat of the fire. He had forgotten how much shorter John was than he. The prince had inherited his father Henry's squat build – certainly a far cry from his heroic brother's enormous stature. But John also had Henry's shrewdness and subtlety – qualities of which Richard had none.

"I have you to thank for that," said Gisburne matter-of-factly. Displays of gratitude never came easily to him. When he had first encountered the prince it had been a low period indeed. His nadir, he now realised – an abyss from which he may never have risen. That Prince John had seen potential in him even then was something for which he would ever be grateful. He accepted the proffered goblet from the prince's hand, noting as he did so that the prince's fondness for elaborate gold rings had not diminished – the one and only feature he shared with Longchamp.

"By the way," he said, gulping a mouthful of wine, "at the foot of the north wall is a large crossbow of unusual design. You will want to make sure it is safely recovered."

"One of Llewellyn's?" said John, charging his own cup.

Gisburne nodded. "And something you might not wish your enemies to possess."

John gave a sigh of mock exasperation. "I hope you're not overburdening him with outlandish requests. Special crossbows. Greek Fire..." He nodded his head in the direction of the conflagration on the river. "He costs me an arm and a leg as it is."

Gisburne supposed John meant this as a joke. The Counts of Anjou – John's father, Henry II among them – were notoriously tight-fisted, but for almost a year now he had been living at John's expense, and there had been no sign of penny pinching. Admittedly, his needs were few. During that time, he had performed various tasks at the prince's behest, and for the past six months had been training squires at Nottingham Castle with John as his generous sponsor. But none were made aware that it was the prince backing him – not even John's trusted ally the Sheriff had been burdened with that information. If anyone could guess it, thought Gisburne, he could. But the Sheriff also understood the need for secrecy.

The other knights at Nottingham were less understanding. At a time when social status was increasingly the measure of a knight, they regarded this rough interloper who had been foisted upon them – a man with no past, no family, no allegiances that they knew of – with open suspicion. He was a shadowy cipher. Something disconnected from their crude, but rigidly structured world. He had proven his worth, training the squires hard but fairly, and displaying modesty, pragmatism and a relentless vigour in his sparring with the other knights, and some warmed to him. When that sparring was organised into a contest – partly, Gisburne suspected, so one or two of them could have a proper crack at his skull – and he had doggedly fought his way through every one of them to emerge the outright champion, those bitter with defeat had reversed their good opinion. The process had proved a valuable point, nonetheless. Not to the other knights – Gisburne cared little what they thought of him – but to himself. It was really he who had been in training those past months. And now he was ready.

But ready for what? Gisburne sensed, from the drama of John's test, that what lay ahead was something momentous – but the prince was giving nothing away.

"What shall we drink to?" said the prince, turning to him with sudden cheer. He could be charming when he needed to be. "The King..?"

Gisburne did not laugh, nor did he raise his cup. It was also the first time he had ever heard John refer to his brother as "king" – even then, he had done so only in jest. That was John's way of facing difficulties, he had learned – through black humour. But Gisburne could not, would not laugh at Richard. John read the look in his eye, and withdrew the joke. "The future, then..." To that, both happily drank.

"You didn't warn anyone that I was coming tonight," said Gisburne, keen to know what this night was about, but feeling a growing conviction that John – often mischievous when allowed to be, and more often when not – would keep him guessing as long as possible. "Not even Puintellus."

"Of course not," said John, as if the suggestion were absurd. "What would be the good of that? A real enemy doesn't announce himself."

Gisburne was used to being unannounced. But it was a practical consideration that struck him now – a sudden, keen awareness that he was wearing no armour beneath his surcoat. Leaving his mail hauberk behind had been a necessity given the punishing climb up the Tower wall. And he had, naturally, shown mercy to his adversaries during this elaborate exercise – the unfortunate crossbowman's nose being the single casualty. But only now that he was past the moment of immediate action and allowed to reflect upon what had gone before did it come home to him that they would have shown no mercy in return.

"What if they had killed me?" he said – more a genuine query than an expression of outrage.

John looked faintly abashed, the smile still playing on his lips, then shrugged. "But they didn't... They weren't able to." He waved a finger. "That, really, is the point, isn't it?"

"I don't doubt another would take my place soon enough, even if they had." Gisburne's tone remained as matter-of-fact as ever.

"I think not... There really is no one quite like you, Sir Guy. Of that I am certain. As you should be – though I know you are far too modest to think so. I took a chance on you when we first met. And, unlike so many I could name, you have not disappointed me." He tapped his cup against Gisburne's and chuckled again. "Really, you are a most amazing fellow."

Gisburne said nothing. He had always found praise the hardest thing to take. As both drank, John wandered to the small, arched window looking over the Thames, the stonework about it still glowing orange from the flames of the blazing wreck.

"However..." John sighed deeply. "Did you really need to burn the ship? It had little to do with your mission."

"That's why I burned it," said Gisburne. "To ensure that everyone was looking the wrong way, at the wrong thing – which had little to do with my mission."

John chuckled gently. "Don't think I disapprove. Even this proves I made the right choice, as you will see. You have shown yourself to be quite the tactician."

"Control the battlefield," added Gisburne. "That's what Gilbert taught me."

"Gilbert de Gaillon..." The prince nodded slowly, regarding him in silence for a moment, his smile fading. "Best you keep that to yourself. At least for now. There are a select few of us who know the truth about his disgrace. But there are many who still bear a grudge." He turned back to the window, the light from the burning ship flickering on his face.

John gave a shrug. "It was one of Longchamp's, anyway. Shame about the wine on board, though. That was good stuff." He peered into his goblet appreciatively, swirling it around, then allowed a smile to creep back across his face. "You know, my father had the worst taste in wine of anyone I've ever met. To him, wine was just wine – there was no good or bad. He was also morally opposed to paying anything more than the minimum. So, everyone at court had to endure this wretched stuff that tasted like tar and vinegar. I think secretly he enjoyed inflicting it on them." He turned suddenly, returning to the present, and raised his goblet. "Here's to the last of the good stuff. And the last of Longchamp." With that, he drank deeply. Gisburne did likewise. John immediately recharged their goblets from the wine pitcher.

"This coat you wear," he said as he poured, looking Gisburne up and down. "This is new. I can't say it's exactly to my liking. A little... rustic for my tastes. Dramatic, though. And hard-wearing, I dare say."

"It worked for the horse," said Gisburne, flatly. Then, feeling he had on this occasion been rather too sharp, added: "Horsehide. From my father's destrier."

"Ah." John nodded, raising his eyebrows. "*That* horse."

"It's a reminder," said Gisburne, his expression dark. "Of what was taken. That such things cannot be taken for granted."

"And of those who took them?"

Gisburne did not want to acknowledge that, but knew it to be true.

"You have heard no more news of Hood, I suppose?" added John, casually. Gisburne felt his insides clench at the mere mention of the name.

"Rumours," he shrugged. "Stories. Nothing certain."

"Oh, there are stories..." said John. "The comman man about Nottinghamshire and Yorkshire speaks of little else. He is becoming – what do they call it? – a 'folk hero'."

"It's a pity they don't know him as I do," said Gisburne, his demeanour grim. "I have seen many who stole when they had to, but those who are thieves through choice are the lowest kind of villain – and Hood the vilest kind of thief. He steals the respect of others. He robs men of their good sense – misappropriates their friendship and loyalty and has them believe in a lie." He gulped agitatedly at his wine, feeling the anger boil in him. Once, a lifetime ago, he had himself been fool enough to believe in the man who now called himself Hood. "His creed is destruction," he continued, gruffly, "and he will lead those who follow him only to that end."

John narrowed his eyes. "You really are a curiosity, Gisburne. A man who distrusts authority, yet craves order. Who values the law of the crown, but rejects his king."

"I do not reject the king. I reject the man who calls himself king..." Gisburne fought to calm himself, aware that, despite John's sympathy for his views, what he was saying was treason, and the man he was now condemning, John's brother. "You know I cannot respect Richard after all I have seen. I know the chaos he leaves in his wake."

"As do I. All too well..." John's voice trailed off. "Little wonder that Hood gravitates towards him. We suffer under a similar curse, you and I." He regarded Gisburne coolly, his shrewd eyes narrowing again. "You know, you are the only man who speaks honestly to me. That is why I value you so highly. I don't believe there is another in England I would trust to hold a sword to my throat." He thought about that for a moment. "In the world, actually... And yet you never refer to me as 'My Lord,' or indeed by any honorific to which I am entitled. That could be read as disrespect." The playful glint had returned to his eye.

"A man is what he is," shrugged Gisburne. "Titles mean nothing."

"Including that of 'knight'? Wasn't that a title for which you once fought so hard?"

Gisburne faltered. "It was not the title I craved. It was... something else."

"You have heard, I suppose, that our... *friend* in the north – the one who holds sway in Sherwood – has allowed the rumour to spread that he, too, is a knight?"

Gisburne had not heard it. The news cut him to the quick.

"The story goes he is a nobleman whose lands were unjustly seized – by me, of course – and that this flagrant injustice drove him to rebel. His followers have latched onto it, caring little whether or not it is true – neither the folk nor the tale will be held back by a minor matter like truth. They paint him a loyal supporter of the absent Richard – who can do no wrong since he isn't here – and a champion of the common people. Poor fools!"

He laughed suddenly, and loudly. "It was my noble brother who bankrupted this land for the sake of his crusade, who drove up their taxes and then abandoned his kingdom, allowing all to fall into disorder and leaving the rest of us to pick up the pieces. To carry the blame." For the first time that night, there was a note of bitterness – almost desperation – in John's tone. He gave another hollow laugh. "That's our lionhearted king... The noble King of England! My God, he couldn't wait to leave!" As he spoke, his voice began to tremble and crack, his wildy gesticulating hands clutching into claws and his eyes widening with almost bestial ferocity. "Do you know how long he's spent here, in his entire life? Weeks. He doesn't even speak English. Never saw the point in learning the language of his own people. Little wonder he appointed an idiot like Longchamp! He only graced these shores at all so he could get crowned and claim it as a base possession..." John fought to rein in his rage, swigging at his drink. "No, dear Richard cared not a jot for this land, beyond what it could raise in cash. You know, he once said – and I swear these are his very words – that he would have sold London if only he could have found a buyer? They all laughed when he said that. Only I knew he really meant it."

The tirade over, the prince steadied himself with one hand on the back of the chair and and exhaled deeply. Gisburne had heard that all of the dynasty of Anjou had savage tempers. He did not doubt that applied to John too, given what he had seen – but he was glad not to have seen it in full flood.

The prince began to pace slowly, his tone once again restrained, controlled. "I have heard other curious tales from the north. Disturbing tales. I would value your opinion on them..." He stopped again, clutching his goblet before him in an attitude that momentarily evoked the sacrament. "They tell of the dead rising from their graves and terrorising the living."

Gisburne frowned. "Stories to scare children," he said, dismissively. He was not a superstitious man. Nor, he thought, was John. But there was no smile on the prince's face. "I've known my share of death," he continued, with a tone of steady pragmatism.

"Sent a good many on that journey. I've yet to see one get up again."

John nodded slowly, seeming to stare off into an imagined distance. "It is a sign of a kingdom in chaos. One in which natural laws are so overturned that the land no longer holds fast to the dead." He shook his head suddenly. "It matters little whether the stories are true or false. As with Hood. That people believe them... That's what matters."

"I can deal with Hood..."

John turned and flashed a charismatic smile. "That time will come. I know you used to hunt the forests of Sherwood with your father, and you shall again – for a more rewarding prey, this time. But Hood is the least part of my reason for bringing you here tonight." He gestured to the chair. Gisburne sat – silent, expectant. The prince paced before him, his eyes burning with a cold fire.

"In the coming weeks a certain artefact is to come into Marseille by ship. The skull of St John the Baptist, once a treasured relic in Antioch, girt with gold and encrusted with precious stones. The skull is a gift from the Templars to Philip of France. A peace offering, in a way – intended to buy off the French king's claims to Cyprus. It will arrive just in time for Christmas. Rather sweet of them, don't you think?" He paused for a sardonic smile, then resumed his steady pacing, his voice growing in intensity.

"Let me explain how this came about... Last June, Philip was on his way to the Holy Land with Richard – the pair of them united for once by the shared crusade. But like schoolboys they competed constantly. Unfortunately for Philip, this was a pissing contest he couldn't hope to win. If there's one thing my good brother knows how to do, it's outshine everyone else – especially where brute force is involved. He first captured Messina after Philip had failed to do so, and then – never one to pass up an opportunity – stopped to conquer Cyprus and had himself declared king. When he heard of it, Philip, who had sailed straight to Tyre, was piqued. Richard had used men and resources meant for their crusade. To add insult to injury, Richard then married Berengaria of Navarre, in spite of the fact that he was still technically betrothed to Philip's sister Alys, and had already claimed the territory of Vexin as her dowry. By the time they joined together to face Saladin, relations between Richard and Philip were, by all accounts, seriously strained.

"Then Richard, already bored by his new acquisition, sold Cyprus to the Templars. They understand its strategic importance, of course. So does Philip. And Philip has a claim, of sorts – that the island was taken by the crusading army of which he was a commander, and disposed of without his consent. He covets it – partly, I suspect, because Richard had the audacity to take it from under his nose and have himself declared twice a king. But also because he had the stupidity to then toss it away as a spoilt child does a toy. If Richard were wise, or in any way a politician, he might have recognised Philip's acrimony and the need to assuage it, if only for the unity of his precious crusade. But he is not. He never was able to put himself in another's shoes, or even see the point of doing so. And anyway, he was already off, chasing another bone. Another of those 'meaningless titles' of yours – King of Jerusalem, this time." He allowed himself a chuckle at that, then banished it with a sigh.

"He'll probably get it, or die trying. We'll see how that works out. The Templars, though… They are subtle. They understand that real power depends on more than the sword. And they are still smarting after the disaster of Hattin. To rebuild their web, they need a sound foothold in the Mediterranean, within striking distance of the Holy Land, and Cyprus suits them well – but they want their dominion to be unchallenged. And so the skull of my holy namesake makes its merry way to the French King."

John stopped before the fire, took up a poker and jabbed at a log, sending a shower of sparks up the chimney. It was a moment before Gisburne realised that John's tale was over – that it had ended before he was able to divine his own place in it. So, a holy relic was passing from the most powerful organisation in Christendom to one of its greatest monarchs. It would establish a peace, of sorts – a peace that, as far as he could see, was of as much benefit to England as anyone else, and was being created via a transaction in which no one in England or the lands ruled by Anjou played any part. Finally, he asked: "What is it you wish me to do?"

John looked him squarely in the eye. "I wish you to steal it."

Gisburne felt his blood freeze in his veins.

"The skills you have shown tonight," continued John, matter-of-factly, "all those will be needed if this is to succeed."

The flattery bypassed Gisburne entirely. "You… wish me to *steal* a holy relic?"

"Put aside its religious significance," John said, sweeping his hand before him. "The gold and jewels that it has accumulated during its life are greater than a king's ransom. Make no mistake; although this seems a noble and pious gesture – a benevolent gift – it is payment. Nothing more. Both sides know this, though none will speak openly of it."

In truth, Gisburne cared nothing for any holy power it supposedly possessed. He had seen plenty of such relics in his travels – saints with more bones than a team of oxen, pieces of the true cross sufficient to build a small ship, thriving workshops that did a roaring trade churning out both. He had also see men fight, and die, depending on them – enough to regard such talismans with ambivalence at best. But while defying a respected religious order ce ainly gave him pause – even if it concerned an object of dubious provenance – it was the notion of theft itself with which he struggled most. John pre-empted his objection.

"If it helps your conscience, consider this..." His voice was stern now, devoid of the calculated charm he so often affected. "I believe that Philip intends to use this gift to fund outrages in England; acts calculated to further destabilise the kingdom, to take advantage of a weakened realm and an absent king. Do not think of this as a mere act of thievery. It is a blow against those who would see this land engulfed by anarchy. Against the agents of chaos. Those who would rob men of their good sense."

The return of his own words startled him. Gisburne stared into the depths of the fire in thoughtful silence, weaving the threads of their whole conversation together and wondering if he was correct in supposing who one of those agents might be. If he was, then John's reasoning was unassailable.

"I have already told you more than you need," said John, as if pre-empting the question. "More than I should. But I tell you this so you may understand, and not judge me too harshly." He sighed deeply, resignedly, as if being judged too harshly were a curse he had to bear. "Tonight's little charade... Well, it was more than that. I needed to put you to the test. To push your capabilities to the limit. Not because I doubt your tenacity or resolve, but in order to ensure I was sending you on a mission from which you could actually return."

"Did I pass?" muttered Gisburne.

John laughed, the mischievous glint momentarily returning. "Well, you're here, aren't you?" He turned away again, towards the window. "I have sent many good men to their deaths. That is the lot of a prince. It would doubtless surprise the people of this land to know that it gives me no pleasure. I would have you return alive – or know, at least, that I had done more than send you to the scaffold. Tonight was a demonstration of this desire. And, by the simple application of a sword blade, that I trust you above all men."

After a moment's silence, Gisburne gave a single, solemn nod.

John smiled. "The skull is to be met at Marseille and escorted to the king's palace in Paris by a senior Templar named Tancred de Mercheval." John's eyes slid to Gisburne, as if looking for some flicker of recognition. But the name meant nothing to him. "Tancred is revered – feared – even among the

Templars. It is a measure of the importance of this transaction that the Grand Master of the Temple entrusts the task to him, even though there is little love lost between them. Tancred is... Difficult. A maverick. But once it is in Tancred's hands, there will be no wresting it from them. Only a fool or an army would attempt that – and you are neither." He looked at Gisburne in silence for a moment, as if awaiting an objection. None came. "Therefore, you must strike at Marseille, before the handover to Tancred is effected. And that means, I regret to say, that you have a long and difficult journey ahead of you... Arrangements have been made for you to stay at Dover Castle prior to your departure from England. There you will join a ship bound for Calais, where you will disembark disguised as a humble pilgrim, heading for Marseille."

"Disguised?" Again, Gisburne smarted at John's words. Again, John raised a hand in protest.

"I know you detest all this secrecy, this deception. But it is necessary. Our foes are masters of it, and we must become masters of it ourselves. If my information is correct – and my information is always correct – there will be other interests, other forces, looking out for this prize. Even within the Templars there are factions who abhor its loss. You must tread carefully, my friend. One day you will be able to step out of the shadows. But for now, that is where I need you."

"But... Dover Castle..?" said Gisburne.

"I know," said John, waving a hand with mock displeasure. "I am hardly their favourite prince..."

In truth, Gisburne would also have preferred a far less grand lodging place. What was wrong with a simple inn, with good food and honest ale?

"I have my reasons, however," said John, an inscrutable smile flickering across his lips. "On that day, its castellan, Matthew de Clere, will playing host to another guest who you may wish to meet. Think of it as a parting gift." Gisburne waited for more on the matter, but nothing came. "Don't worry – I will keep my name out of the arrangements, and it would certainly be best for you if you did not mention me."

"I'll need time to prepare," said Gisburne.

"You have two weeks and a day," replied John.

"And I will need to see Llewellyn."

"Then you are in luck," said John, triumphantly. "He is here. I find it useful to keep him nearby during trying times – which is, I must say, almost all of the time."

He moved to the door, and opened it. Gisburne stood. Outside, lurking hesitantly, was the bloody-nosed guard. "He'll be awake, of course – he always was a night-owl – and will be expecting you. He has a way of sniffing these things out. And I'm sure he can offer you a pallet for what remains of the night."

As Gisburne passed through the open door, the guard scrutinised his attacker with a kind of timid resentment, hastily breaking eye contact when he realised Gisburne would not. "He's ensconced in the enginer's foxhole," said John, "buried in the bowels of this place. The guard will show you the way."

"I know the way," replied Gisburne.

John stared at him in amazement. "I thought you had not set foot in the Tower until tonight. And most who have do not even know this chamber exists..."

"I contrived to make the acquaintance of a disgruntled mason," said Gisburne. "Sacked by Puintellus for being in drink. I bought him as many drinks as he liked at an inn in Southwark. In return, he etched a complete plan of the keep on the underside of a trencher."

John laughed and clapped his hands with delight. "Upon such trivialities are empires made and kingdoms broken..." The laughter faded. "Sleep well, Sir Guy. We shall not meet again until this matter is concluded." And with that, he began to swing the door shut.

"One thing..." said Gisburne. John stopped, his eyes glinting through the narrow gap. "The guest at Dover. The one you have contrived for me to meet. How am I to know them?"

"You will know them," said John. "And they you."

"May I at least be told who it is?"

John smiled. It was the smile of a man who had just played the winning stroke in a long and complex game. "Lady Marian Fitzwalter," he said, and closed the door.

VI

IT TOOK THREE attempts to find Llewellyn's "foxhole". The first had brought him to a dead end in a dank, airless vaulted interior that smelt of damp earth and vinegar and which was filled, as far as he was able to tell, with barrels of pork and salt fish. Next time, he'd have the informant mark the map on a piece of cloth, and keep it in his pocket.

As he wandered, the shadows gliding and leaping across the stonework at the passing of the smoky, sputtering tallow candle, he puzzled over John's final words. Lady Marian Fitzwalter... Every time he thought he knew the man, John found new ways to surprise him. How could he have known about Lady Marian? Gisburne had told no one. Not that there was much to tell, of course; Marian had never returned Gisburne's keener affections, nor even shown much interest in doing so. He wondered if John knew that too. She liked him, of course. They had always liked each other. She had even tolerated his later attempts at intimacy – tentative though they were – with good grace. But her tolerance, well-meant though it was, made him feel less like a man, and more like one of her dogs. Hatred would be better. At least then he would be the subject of some strong emotion.

Turning back on himself, he headed again into the store room with its ranks of stacked barrels. This, surely, was where the chamber should be – so his instincts told him, anyway. Then, just as he was about to abandon the place for a second time, the same instincts urged him to investigate a shadow deeper in the chamber. There, in a small archway, almost obscured by the barrels flanking it on either side, was a narrow door. He pushed on it. From inside, carried upon a heat like a desert wind, came the smell of sulphur and woodsmoke.

In one corner, a small furnace glowed. Before it stood an incongruously elaborate wooden chair – it almost deserved to be called a throne – and by its side a small rustic table bearing some scraps of cloth and broken pieces of charcoal. In the other, a huge flap of brown leather screened off a a tiny section of the room, its surface marked by silvery flecks of molten lead. Against one wall was a cluttered bench strewn with tools and pieces of shaped wood and beaten or cast metal; on the other, shelves packed from floor to ceiling with every kind of curiosity, from bottles of liquids and jars of coloured powders, to animal skulls, antlers and lengths of bone. And, in between, every inch of the cramped space was filled with sacks, barrels, boxes and chests.

"The crossbow worked, then," said a gruff voice. Llewellyn of Newport stepped out from behind a ragged flap of the hanging partition. Gisburne fancied for a fleeting moment that he could see smoke rising from his grizzled hair and beard.

"And the Greek Fire," replied Gisburne.

Llewellyn snorted in laughter, and slapped Gisburne on the arm. "I could tell that, even buried way down here. It has a distinct aroma. And it gets about." He grunted in laughter again, waving his guest inside and closing the door behind him. "If you only knew what I'd been through to perfect that recipe. Speaking of which..." Crossing the room, avoiding every obstacle with practised ease, he stooped over a sturdy leather bag near the chair, and extricated an elegantly shaped glass bottle, stoppered with beeswax. A smile creased his face as he cradled it in his hands, blowing off a little dust.

"You know what this is?"

"Does it explode?" said Gisburne. He naturally assumed that nothing in Llewellyn's possession was quite what it seemed.

"Monks made this. A heady brew. If ever you wondered why so many of them are unable to speak..." He chuckled, waving the bottle gently in Gisburne's direction. "I've been waiting for some excuse to drink it. I had hoped for something momentous, but your arrival will have to do." And with that, he placed the bottle on the little table by his chair and began rifling the shelves in a hunt for cups.

"My apologies for the mess," he called, his head half buried amongst bottles. "The previous tenant was French." He said this as if it provided the entire explanation. Gisburne thought better than to mention that it looked, if anything, slightly more ordered than Llewellyn's own workshop in Nottingham. As he stood, wondering where to put himself in the mayhem, he idly picked up a complex wooden model from the cluttered bench – evidently some kind of variant on the trebuchet – pulling back its arm and watching in fascination as its tiny pulleys pulled and tiny gears meshed.

"Please don't touch that," snapped Llewellyn, extricating himself.

"Do we make war on mice now?" Gisburne said, putting a rivet in the trebuchet's tiny bucket and firing it across the room. It clattered behind a long, low chest.

Crossing the room in two strides, Llewellyn snatched the device from him, slapped it back on the worktop irritably and threw a cloth over it. "The real one is bigger." As he turned, he gestured to the big chair by the furnace. "Sit. *Sit*. You look ready to drop."

Gisburne sat. Sure enough, as he did so a wave of fatigue suddenly broke over him. It was the familiar crash after the rush of battle. He didn't fight it – the time for fighting was past, at least for now – and instead allowed his body to relax for what he realised was the first time in days.

"So," Llewellyn said as he excavated a horn cup and blew into it. "I would imagine the prince has now revealed his mission, and you are in need of some tools to speed its successful completion. Correct?"

It was a fair summing up. "There is a catch," said Gisburne. "I need them in my hands in two weeks."

Llewellyn stopped for a moment, and looked at him steadily, a knowing look in his eye. "I might have one or two things that could be adapted to the purpose."

Gisburne stared back. "Do you already know the mission?"

Llewellyn pulled a dented, tarnished silver vessel from a wooden box, knocked it upside down on the bench a few times and then rubbed the lip on his tunic. "I know only weights, tensions, tolerances and reactions. Anything else is for others to worry about." He stood for a moment, a cup in each hand, an unconvincing look of feigned innocence on his face. Gisburne wondered if it had simply become a habit with Llewellyn to pretend to know far less than he actually did. "However," he continued with a shrug, "in judging those tensions and tolerances, it might help if I were to know who you will be up against."

"The King of France," said Gisburne casually. "And the Templars."

Llewellyn, who had now placed the cups upon the table and again taken up the cherished bottle, stopped as if struck by an arrow. He nodded slowly, his expression sombre. "A general piece of advice, then, from one friend to another... Templars are not like any other adversary. Oh, I know – I won't lecture you about their dedication, their ruthless efficiency. I know you've seen those up close. Just be aware: they have the best enginers of anyone in this world, Christian or Saracen."

"Better than you?"

Llewellyn did not succumb to the flattery. "Whatever ingenuities you may bring, whatever... surprises I can furnish, expect the same – and more – from them."

"They're still men."

"Yes. Men with wealth greater than kings. Men driven by a religious zeal more fervent than popes. Men with political reach beyond that of any emperor. They have no nation, yet princes fear them. They have a network of loans and debts stretching from here to the Holy Land that makes the wealth of nations appear feeble and archaic – and upon which some of those nations depend. They are a web – everywhere and nowhere – and answerable only to God."

"And yet, their flesh is no more resistant to the bite of a blade. Their blood flows no less freely. Their skulls are no thicker than any other man's." Gisburne thought for a moment. "All right, maybe their skulls are a little thicker..." But Llewellyn did not laugh. Not this time.

"Do you know of a knight named Tancred de Mercheval?" said Gisburne with a yawn, breaking the momentary silence. "John says he is a maverick." He saw what he thought was a flicker of alarm in Llewellyn's eyes, hastily suppressed. Then a smile creased the old man's features.

"So, it's 'John' now, is it...?" The smile faded away again, like a brief chink of sunlight peeking through cloud. "'Maverick' is one word for it. He was favoured by the old Grand Master, Gérard de Ridefort. The new one is less enamoured, and keeps him on a long leash for when he needs his dirty work done. But he controls him less and less."

"He exceeds his orders?"

Llewellyn took a deep breath. "There was a case of a heretic monk in southern France, harboured by his community. Tancred was dispatched to bring him to justice, but ordered not to kill him. The monk had preached that the Almighty was the God of Peace – that all killing was a sin. Tancred determined to prove him wrong. Since the whole village had protected him, he had every man, woman and child in it put to death. Then he let the monk go to contemplate the consequences of his actions. The monk hanged himself under a bridge two days later. So yes, you could say he exceeds his orders, though he would perhaps disagree. His orders come direct from God."

Gisburne considered Llewellyn's words for a moment. "Another lunatic," he sighed at length. "I've spent my life surrounded by them. Present company excepted."

"He is a formidable adversary, Guy," said Llewellyn softly. "One who plays by no rules but his own."

He regarded the exhausted Gisburne for a moment, looked as if he was about to say something more, then seemed to dismiss it. Sighing deeply, he stared at the bottle in his hand.

"You know, I think I may save this a little longer. To toast your safe return." And with that, he returned it carefully to his bag. Gisburne, by now too drowsy to appreciate the gesture, simply felt relief. He had already been plied with copious quantities of the good wine that Prince John had liberated from Longchamp. The fire in his blood from the assault on the Tower was now fully burnt out, and in its wake had left exhaustion. Now, with the heat from the furnace, his eyelids were drooping.

"We can't let this occasion pass without wetting our whistles in some way, however..." said Llewellyn, diving between a pair of barrels. "I know I have some wine here. The good stuff, mind..."

There was a clatter. And a clink. After a moment of huffing and grunting, Llewellyn emerged again, a cobweb caught in his hair, a cylindrical earthenware bottle in his hands. He pulled the stopper, sniffed at the open top, and gave a growl of satisfaction. "Burgundy's finest," he said, and turned to his guest with a beaming smile.

But Guy of Gisburne was already asleep.

VII

Dover – 20 November, 1191

THE RECEPTION AT Dover was as icy as the weather.

There had been no fresh snow that morning, but so cold was the air that the fall of past days sat everywhere in stubborn refusal to relinquish its numbing grip. A freezing wind blew from the sea – not gusting, not giving any hint of respite, but a constant blast – hurling the tang of the sea at his face. Even before it came into view he could taste its salt on his lips, already feel, in his mind, the queasy heaving of the ship that was to carry him across its leaden, foam-streaked swell the following morning. He wondered if the ship would even set sail in such weather. Brow furrowed in concern, he shuddered, urged his steaming horse on, and tried not to acknowledge the part of him that hoped it would not.

Then there was the castle itself. Glimpsed tantalisingly between the leafless, skeletal trees as his horse – crow-black against the white, snorting plumes of fog – had plodded the final few miles towards the coast, it at last loomed upon the misty horizon in all its monstrous permanance. Great, grey turrets thrust upward from the hill on which it sat. A stone fist clenched towards the continent. The gatehouse of England. As if on cue at Gisburne's creeping approach, the sun broke free of its prison of slate-coloured cloud and beamed down upon the awesome expanse of those forbidding walls. The great gates clanked and groaned. His horse whinnied and tossed its head as they parted, the cold eyes of the guards staring down from the castle's towers. "Easy, Nyght," muttered Gisburne, and gave him a reassuring pat. But he knew the animal was merely reflecting his own unease.

The vast stronghold commanding the clifftops had been Henry II's most ambitious project – at its centre, a square keep against which even the Conqueror's paled, surrounded by concentric walls and enormous ditches, with a succession of elaborately guarded gates and towers. It had benefited from the lastest wisdom in castle design, and Henry had spared no expense. It was said he built it, in part, out of guilty conscience, to welcome noble pilgrims who came to visit the tomb of Thomas Becket – Archbishop of Canterbury and England's newest saint, whose death Henry had, perhaps unwittingly, brought about – and had fitted it out with all manner of luxuries, including running water and sanitation. But none who set eyes upon it could fail to consider the warning note it sounded. This would have tested the ingenuity of Llewellyn to its limit – perhaps, even, was beyond it. Although its doors were flung open to Gisburne, and he able to ride freely in, this approach in the crisp light of that cold November morning somehow seemed infinitely more daunting than the nocturnal assault upon the White Tower.

From the moment of his arrival, the contempt in which Gisburne was held could not have been more obvious. The castle's Constable, Matthew de Clere, managed the opulent royal residence on behalf of the monarch. With Richard far away in the Holy Land, however, de Clere was its undisputed master, and lived like a king. He was also, Gisburne knew, an ally of Longchamp. Of de Clere, or any other welcoming face – beyond a haughty, sour-faced steward, and the sullen youth who led Nyght to the stables – there was no sign. At the feast, which commenced that morning in the castle's guest hall, and to which he was immediately and peremptorily ushered, he had been seated about as far from the noble castellan as decorum would permit – at the extreme end of one of the two rows of benches flanking the long, black-beamed walls. This placed Gisburne with his back so close to the doorway that another few inches would have had him sitting outside the chamber altogether. He felt only half arrived – had not, in fact, even been given time to change his clothes. He mused upon this as he was subjected to a lengthy and unnecessary wait within the hall – still dishevelled, sweaty and damp. A roaring, crackling fire blazed in the huge arched fireplace half way up the hall – but he was too far away to benefit from its heat, and merely shivered in the persistent, icy draught that was sucked in past the curtain that barely covered the doorway. This blew at his back with such unyielding vigour that the white tablecloth flapped about his knees and the flames on the iron candelabrum at his right shoulder leapt and guttered with every gust.

It was the position at formal table that Gisburne's father would have referred to as "one up from the dogs". Though the old man never said as much, Gisburne had a strong sense that his father – a knight of faultless record and high principles but precious few means, and entirely deficient in the art of flattery – had endured the position on many occasions.

It soon became clear, however, that his father's assessment had been an exaggeration. The dogs had by far the better deal. Whilst Gisburne froze in the unrelenting draught – and half way up the hall, a young knight, far too decorous to complain, suffered the opposite fate, roasting to a beetroot red just inches from the huge, arched fireplace – de Clere's hounds were left free to caper on the freshly strewn rushes covering the wooden floor. They gradually identified the most comfortable distance from the source of heat, padded in circles a few times and then lounged there as de Clere, on the high table at the head of the hall, tossed them some of the choicest cuts of meat from the platter in front of him. Gisburne, who had yet to be served – who was destined by his position to be last, and would therefore eat less well than any creature in the room, including the fleas in the rush matting and any opportunistic mice – swore that de Clere caught his eye as he did so.

Providing a sufficient number of servants to tend to every visitor's needs, however humble they may be, was considered the sign of a good host. It appeared that de Clere, deep in smug communion with an elite core of sycophantic guests for most of the evening, was not greatly concerned with the fate of those at the margins of his hospitality – or, if he was, had instructed his servants to deliberately withold it from Gisburne. On the table's end, by Gisburne's right elbow, the dish of grimy water in which he had washed his hands prior to dining still sat, perhaps intentionally overlooked.

To his left sat an aged, rank-smelling cove who avoided eye contact as if his life depended on it, and whose size suggested he had never let a crumb of food get past him his entire life. He was styled a knight, but Gisburne noted no scars upon him, and if there had once been even a ghost of decent physical condition, it had long since been engulfed in layers of fat. "There are two kinds of men who lack scars," Gilbert de Gaillon had once said. "Those who never fight, and those who afford their enemy no opportunity to do so." Gisburne had taken the point – and perhaps even this one had had his day once. But his apparent need to assert superiority over the lowest in the room – along with his general corpulence – suggested otherwise. It was some time before Gisburne realised that the odd rasping sound he could could hear, even over the echoing hubbub of the chamber, was his neighbour's laboured breathing. The only other thing to pass between them that day was when the knight, through great effort, rocked his enormous bulk to one side and broke copious wind.

As Gisburne toyed with the dregs of the soup – stone cold, by the time it came his way – and waited for whatever gristle was left of the mutton, he distracted himself by listening to the scarlet-clad musician seated in the corner opposite, who plucked with affected seriousness on a stringed instrument. A single musician, Gisburne noted – and tallow candles, and wine that was certainly not Longchamp's good stuff – but the most lavish burgundy and gold wall hangings that the king's fortress could provide. Behind the high table hung a great banner bearing the three royal lions, and either side of it tapestries depicting lively, stylised scenes of hunting – an activity about which Henry had been fanatical. De Clere obviously enjoyed luxury, as long as it wasn't at his own expense. The music plinked away against the rasp-rasp of his neighbour, the *pop* of the fire and the hum of the two dozen or so guests – a string of interminable French tunes that went nowhere, doubtless the latest thing from the court of King Philip. On the whole, Gisburne felt peasants understood music better.

It inevitably brought to mind the songs so beloved of Richard. He shuddered at the thought – though perhaps that also had something to do with the gale at the back of his neck. Richard – a prolific composer of songs – had a fine voice, and knew it (Gisburne pictured his doting mother, the redoubtable Eleanor of Aquitaine, applauding Richard's boyhood efforts heartily whilst the subtler talents of his brother, John, went utterly unnoticed). He had himself heard Richard sing on many occasions, and had found it instantly captivating. By the fifth or sixth verse, however, interest began to wane. By the twentieth, he was ready to cut his own throat.

De Clere himself cut a superficially impressive figure. He was tall, broad shouldered – every inch what was expected of a knight. Some, apparently, considered him handsome. Yet, to Gisburne's eyes, his forehead was somehow too high, his teeth too gappy, his lips too moist and petulant to warrant such praise. Scrutinising his face now, Gisburne was reminded of dough that had swollen rather ludicrously beyond its required size, his eyes two currants stranded in its midst. His wife Richeut (in a bizarre moment, Gisburne had thought she was being referred to as "Richard") was her lord's opposite, with mean, pinched features and an expression he supposed was meant as a smile, but which looked like someone had just farted in her face.

She also looked oddly familiar, in ways that troubled him. It was not until part way through the evening – when Gisburne overheard an initially baffling reference to Longchamp, and was moved to picture Richeut with a beard – that he realised Matthew de Clere's wife was William Longchamp's sister.

John had been at pains to distance himself from the arrangements for Gisburne's stay here, ensuring that the introduction had been made through an untraceable – and deniable – chain of intermediaries. But de Clere clearly had his suspicions. He must also have been stung by the events of the past months – the growing hatred and ultimate ejection of Longchamp, who secured this place for him, but whose patronage had turned to poison. Then there was the utterly humiliating episode of his brother-in-law's bungled escape from England after his rout in London. The tale of the weasel Longchamp being caught in a dress – looking, by all accounts, like a bad approximation of a cheap Parisan whore, and rumbled by the misguided gropings of a randy sailor – had given the whole of England occasion to guffaw. Longchamp had been let go, to slink back to Normandy – blown on his way by gales of laughter, no doubt. After such universal ridicule, what further – or worse – punishment could possibly be inflicted? England was glad to be rid of him – but it was likely to keep the good folk of the realm clutching their sides for weeks to come. And it had happened in Dover. Assuming de Clere's wife had not been born with that peevish expression (although Gisburne was certain she had) it was not difficult to imagine how she might have acquired it, nor de Clere himself.

Gisburne was startled out of his reverie by a dish of mutton, which arrived at his left hand with an unceremonious thud. Or rather, it arrived at his neighbour's right. As this gentleman was clearly senior in both years and status – to the extent that talking to the shabby knight at the end of the table was either beyond his aged capabilities, or beneath him – it was Gisburne's duty to serve him from the dish placed between them. Since the man was the size of a barn and had shown nothing the entire evening but the back of his oily head, Gisburne decided he could go hang. He hacked away whatever morsels the already well-picked bone had to offer – occasionally imagining his knife blade plunging into his neighbour's blubbery flesh – and fought the childish urge to make furious, obscene gestures behind Sir Fatarse's idiotic head.

It was at that moment, as Gisburne had accepted his complete invisibility and abandoned all pretense at etiquette, that de Clere addressed him from the far end of the hall. Or so it seemed. He had for some time been deep in conversation with the esteemed personage to his left, a large man with a face like a ham and an unpleasantly self-important expression. Dressed, Gisburne thought, somewhat in the manner of a Flemish bureaucrat, an absurdly overstated gold chain hanging beneath the folds of his wobbling, porcine neck. Gisburne had no idea who this man actually was – had not, in fact, been granted the courtesy of an introduction to any of his fellow guests – nor had he been party to the conversation that prompted de Clere's unexpected comment. Their host had, without warning, raised his voice to the extent that all present could not fail to overhear him, and, gesturing limply in Gisburne's direction with the point of his eating knife, had said: "Our guest at the far end of the table was squire to Gilbert de Gaillon, I believe..."

Surprised, mid-mouthful, the clamour of the table suddenly falling away, Gisburne looked up to see all eyes upon him – some in pity, others outright disdain. Richeut de Clere's nose wrinkled up further than he thought possible. For a moment, he was unsure whether the comment was even meant to invite a response, but before his thoughts could cohere, de Clere's whine filled the silence. "Let us hope that he is one day able to creep out from under that shadow." There was laughter at this, then the thrum of chatter resumed as each member of the assembled company turned back to their neighbour, and their meat.

Gisburne continued to be ignored by most of the assembled company for the rest of the evening.

The one glimmer of light in this unrelenting gloom was Marian.

Seated close to the high table, on the same side as Gisburne, she had caught his eye briefly as the feast had been about to begin, and then had all but disappeared from view behind her fellow guests. In that moment, however, she had shot him a smile of such warmth that it hit him like a breath of summer air. All thought of winter was banished. Every trace of the hostility and meanness about him melted to nothing. The joy that rose up in response was total and unrestrained. Its power shocked him.

She was even more beautiful than he remembered. Her lips so finely curved, and so ready to laugh; her hazel eyes sparkling but also curiously sad; her gestures so disarmingly open, so honest. She was just so... alive. All the more so in this frigid and sterile company. Like a spring bloom in winter. He found himself actually thinking those words: *like a spring bloom in winter...* Gisburne did not regard himself as sentimental – far less a poet – yet here he was, somehow reduced to the moronic dribbling of a lovestruck adolescent. He had forgotten what this was like – had buried it deep in some part of him that was resigned to perpetual winter. Now it had sprung up, as fresh and green as ever it was, and he had fallen to his knees before it.

If John had meant this to present some sort of opportunity for Gisburne, however, the evening did not appear to be following the prince's plan. Marian's tantalising proximity – and unbearable distance – became a kind of torture. He would lean forward to catch a glimpse of her, as casually as he could, then someone else would lean in – reaching for a jug of wine, or turning to engage their neighbour – and obscure his view. Each man who did so, he wanted to kill. But he knew his anger arose partly because it so accurately reflected the one-sided nature of their relationship. She did not miss him, he was sure – did not yearn to catch a mere glimpse of him, had no inkling of the torment that she inspired. Yet he hungered for more, like a deluded beggar wishing soup from a stone. And he knew that if this were all he had – if it were this or nothing – he would accept it, and all the agony it entailed.

Why she affected him so, he could not understand. Others had lips as full, or eyes as bright, or cocked their heads in just that way. Many had more than hinted at a willingness to return affection. But, for all their beauty and charm, most had meant nothing to him. They were not *her*.

He had not seen her for over a year. Even then, it had been fleeting. That had been almost at the nadir of his fortunes, as he had been heading north to see his father for the last time. He had not seen the old man for six years – not since they had fallen out over Gilbert. But this time, Robert of Gisburne was dying. His lands had been seized and sold by Richard, his heart all but broken by the fate of his only son, whose quest to become a knight had ended in disgrace and failure, fatally tainted by the blackened reputation of Gilbert de Gaillon. Robert's reaction to the affair all those years before had been harsh – and young Gisburne, by this time a man as well as a son, had not stood for it. He had hotly defended his old master – even castigated his father for allowing himself to believe the worst of his old friend. For reasons that were so trivial that Gisburne could now barely recall them, things had escalated, and taken an irrevocable turn. Gisburne sensed, even as it was happening, that both had struck deep into the others' territory, doing violence to defences that had never before been challenged, and which afterwards could never be rebuilt. In retrospect, he understood the old man had only meant the best for his son, and in time both would come to feel the gnawing bitterness of regret. But by then, it was too late. He was then a world away, steeped in the blood of battle, fighting for pay under a foreign king.

His return, and their final reconciliation, had barely been in time. Robert's mind had turned. There would be moments of clarity – then he would call out for his long-dead wife Ælfwyn to bring ale, or ask Guy where his little sister Adela had got to. Adela had died when Gisburne was seven years old, and she four. The pain of this confused collision of memories proved almost too much for Gisburne to bear. He had stood before the mightiest armies, had been battered by combat in a dozen lands, had lived through the Hell of the most damaging, scarring conflict of his age – which, even now, was spoken of only in hushed tones. Yet fighting his father's phantoms to reach the rapidly dwindling places in the man's mind where sanity had not yet been overthrown was the hardest battle he had ever fought.

There was more – far more – that Gisburne wished to have said. But during those grim weeks, it had been Marian who had been the shining light. Her sympathy – he did not dare use the word "love" – had been total, unconditional, given without judgement. She had always been pure of heart, thinking of others before herself – he used to make fun of her for it when she was a child, and he the older, more worldly-wise teenager – and of that she had given freely.

As a young boy, Gisburne had a special attachment to Marian. Everyone could see it. Perhaps it was because she had been the same age as Adela, and he felt some compulsion to keep this little, pretty creature safe from the world – to provide the protection he had been unable to extend to his sister.

His father and Fitzwalter had long been friends, and when the younger Gisburne went to Normandy to train with de Gaillon, it followed that he would visit Marian's family, who also spent their summers there. In time, both fathers came to regard them as a natural match – even though, Gisburne had to admit, Marian could have attracted someone of far higher status than he.

Then came the rift.

Fitzwalter had come to admire Richard. Gisburne's father could not stomach the idea of Richard as a future king. Their conflicting loyalties divided them. Contact between Gisburne and Marian withered.

One day he met her and found she was a woman. But her youthful idealism had not faded. It had found a cause. She had grown to become a passionate champion of the wretched and the suffering – if anything, with more fire in her belly. Part of him still dismissed it as naivety. Yet there was a part of him, too, that admired her dogged refusal to accept injustice in the face of an unjust and chaotic world.

There had been a time in Poitou when they had quarrelled over exactly this. They had not seen each other for nearly five years. Gisburne was then serving as a serjeant in Henry's army, during the old king's last struggle against his son, Richard. Richard eventually emerged the victor, and Henry died, leaving his errant son the throne.

Perhaps driven to greater cynicism by this turn of events, he had told her she would always be let down by life if she had such high expectations of it – always disappointed. But what would the world be, she said, without people who earnestly believed things could be better?

The quarrel had been politely resolved, but left a bitter taste. He had been too high-handed, too familiar – trying to speak to her as if she were still the same silly girl and he the overconfident older boy. Now he thought back, it had been patronising and arrogant in a way that was not like him at all. But what had seemed so dismissive had, in fact, been desperation – desperation to recapture something he feared lost. Afterwards, he knew for certain that it was.

When they met again – his father dying, his fortunes at their lowest ebb – hope had been unexpectedly rekindled. She seemed, quite suddenly, to give more of herself to him than she ever had before. It was not until long after that he began to understand why. He was the underdog. The wretched. All this time he had craved her love – but all she really had to offer was compassion.

Immediately after, as he headed north to his dying father, she had departed for Normandy. Now, she was returning to England just as Gisburne, once again, was heading in the opposite direction.

"My lord Gisburne..."

Gisburne started at the sound. He had been slouched in his seat, chin on one hand, eating knife in the other, stabbing into the soggy slab of stale bread before him in a state of irritated detachment when the voice – familiar and close – snapped him back to the present.

Marian stood before him.

It was considered bad form to move from your place during a meal. What was the point of all that hierarchical seating, after all, if people just got up and wandered about? Nevertheless, the host could always dictate otherwise. And here was the catch.

King Henry, who had abhorred laziness, could hardly sit still for more than a few minutes at a time. Even when he managed it for brief periods in court, he would be doing something else – reading, or repairing his saddle for the next day's hunting, or both – much to the frustration of any bishop or baron who was attempting to converse with him on matters of state. At formal feasts, he would spend most of the time standing up, or pacing about, which provided his guests with the opportunity – perhaps even the obligation – to do the same. Amongst those who had loved Henry, the fashion had persisted. Clearly, this was a matter of great distaste to de Clere. Such liberties, even when taken by a king, were a crude throwback. It was all a bit... Saxon. But in a land where the living monarch was absent in both body and spirit, a dead one could still hold sway.

With her head slightly bowed, and her hands clasped before her, she appeared every inch the demure, modest lady. So different from the Marian he had known as a youth. And yet... Did the mere fact of her standing there, on the other side of this narrow table, not suggest a certain, familiar independence of spirit? He wondered at her words, too. "My lord"? She must be pulling his leg, surely – just as he used to pull her pigtails. He certainly wasn't a lord, even less was he hers. Just considering the possibility made his heart thump, his brain teem and his face flush with heat.

"My lady Marian," he managed to stammer. If she was mocking him, he would give as good as he got.

She stood for a moment, eyes on him.

Her dress was blue-grey, her veil and wimple white, topped with a simple circlet of silver. The look was plain – plain enough, almost, for a nun – but if anything it only threw the beauty that it framed into greater relief; the curve of her breasts and hips, the curling wisps of auburn hair escaping the veil about her face, the natural, unaffected grace with which she bore herself. She had always been beautiful – and in recent years had become beguiling – yet stood before him with a familiar, unselfconscious ease. Ever since he had known her, Marian had seemed to have a complete disregard for her own beauty, and a blissful lack of awareness of the effect it had on others. It was yet another reason Gisburne would lose his wits over her.

Her eyes widened and a mischievous smile flashed across her lips – the smile of the girl he had always known.

"Have you been avoiding me?"

"Not at all," he protested. "It is unfortunate that... matters... have taken me away from you." He winced at his own words. *Away from you.* That was too much.

But Marian did not wince. She cocked her head to one side, knotted her brow into a frown of sympathy, and, leaning forward, placed one slender hand on his. "My poor Guy..."

He stared in a kind of disbelief at the smooth, pale fingers wrapped about his own dark-skinned, rough hand, and resisted the urge to crush them to his lips. At the same moment, he seemed to become acutely aware of everything else in the hall: the eyes now upon him, some surreptitiously; the other guests – mostly women – who had taken Marian's lead and escaped their immediate neighbours to enjoy more promising company, whether with humans or hounds; the piqued expressions of the de Cleres, who now exercised a blank refusal to even look in Gisburne's direction, as if to do so would impart something like approval.

"I was so happy to hear of your knighthood. So proud!" She squeezed his hand tighter at this. Her voice became a whisper. "Not before time. It is shameful, the way you have been treated. But God rewards the good." With more presence of mind, Gisburne might have questioned her undying faith in God's influence on earth, citing all the good men he had known who had gone unrewarded or died in a ditch whilst those less worthy survived and prospered. He might also have wondered whether she would feel as proud knowing it was Prince John who had dubbed him a knight. But, in that moment, he was utterly lost in the feeling of her breath against his cheek. She drew back suddenly, flashing another smile.

"So, tell me – are you bound for the Holy Land?" There was child-like wonder in her voice. But rather less concern than he would have liked. Another image tore at his insides: Marian, proudly waving him off, likely to a martyr's death. If the situation were reversed, he knew he would clasp her to him and beg her to stay, even if it offended God himself.

"Not to the Holy Land," he said. "But on a pilgrimage." The words almost caught in his throat, but her eyes widened in delight at them. He felt wretched.

"Return soon," she said. "We need more good men in England." *That's all I am*, thought Gisburne. *A good man*. He had striven his whole life to be exactly that – yet sometimes, it felt far from enough. How good was he, anyway? He couldn't hope to satisfy her purity of expectation. His pilgrimage was a bitter lie.

But there was also something much deeper, much more fundamental. In spite of the fact that he had fought the most bitter battle of his life against Saracens on the parched plains of the Holy Land, he knew he'd convert to Islam on the spot in exchange for her.

"I will do what duty and conscience demand," he said, with a bow of his head – then, casting his eyes towards the de Cleres, added: "It does indeed seem a world turned upside down."

Her eyes flashed with a sudden passion – passion that he knew was not for him. "I'm always saying it!" She straightened, let go of his hand, raised her voice so it could be heard. "You know, there is a man in the northern shires outlawed simply for making a stand against the iniquities of the corrupt officials there. A good man before God made a criminal, whilst those with dubious loyalties squeeze the ordinary people for ever greater taxes."

A murmur ran around the room in response. Gisburne's blood ran cold. Was every part of his life doomed to be infected by Hood?

Marian's brow knitted into a frown again. "Such a man should not be outlawed. He should be applauded, for doing what duty and conscience demand, as you are so proud to do." She turned, and cast what to Gisburne seemed a challenging look towards the de Clere's. He had never felt more proud of her – nor more sick at his situation.

Several guests, taking her words as their cue, literally applauded in support. Voices rose above it.

"Someone needs to stand against John and his cronies," muttered one.

"They scheme while the King is absent... taking advantage of his divine mission," came another.

"It's not just treason," trilled a woman. "It's blasphemy!"

Gisburne gazed about him at the eyes of his fellow guests, struggling to comprehend how his status had shifted. Because of his association with Marian. Because of his association with Hood.

"I do not believe John is a bad man," said Marian, as the sound lulled. She did not believe anyone was bad – just desperate, or unfortunate, or misguided. "But if men like Hood can bring him to his senses, then I shall cheer them."

This time, a cheer. Gisburne felt himself trapped in some kind of Hell. A Hell of truths he could not utter. That the taxes were not John's. That Richard was a monster. He wanted to shake her, to make her realise. But he could not jump to John's defence – not in this company. And there was something else he feared even more. Their fathers had fallen out over exactly this. He could not stand to lose her over it – what little he had of her.

"There are those of us who still stand for justice," he said. It was the best he could muster. And it was at least true. But the assembled guests eagerly murmured their approval, and Marian – misconstruing its meaning entirely – continued her impassioned speech.

"Robin Hood is a symbol of the stout English heart," she said, her voice now quavering with emotion. "Of all that is right and good in this land. The spirit of the Lionheart!"

All cheered and clapped. Even the de Cleres now made a reluctant show of approval. As Gisburne looked around in disbelief, he realised that they were also applauding him – that by some strange sorcery whose mechanics he could not fathom, he had become

Hood's proxy in this chamber. A fleeting incarnation of something deemed heroic. Marian, the wielder of this magic, beamed at him, eyes filled with pride for the man he knew he was not.

How could he tell her that everything Hood possessed – his title, his reputation, the loyalties of those around him – he had stolen? How could he begin to explain to one so untainted by cynicism, that this symbol of the stout heart of England had no heart himself – that the black space where it should have been was a chaotic void that threatened everything they both believed right and good? How could he hope to convince her of any of these things, when he was sent by England's detested prince to steal the head of the baptist of Christ from the most respected holy order in Europe?

He gazed at Marian in the midst of momentary triumph and unending torment. He marvelled at her, at her beauty, her purity of spirit, her faith in him. And he felt sick. False. A lie. In this moment, he felt every bit as untrue and fabricated as Hood. Yet lies had won her over, and would continue to do so. The truth risked driving her away. Most miserable of all was the realisation that this thing so precious to him, which he had fought so long and hard to attain – and to which Hood attached no value – was already falling so easily into the outlaw's hands.

The company had hushed. All eyes were upon him again. It suddenly struck Gisburne, with a kind of horror, that they expected some utterance from him. He looked from expectant face to expectant face. He clenched his teeth, and raised his goblet.

"To King Richard," he said.

VIII

DEJECTED, TIRED, FUZZY-HEADED from an excess of bad wine, Gisburne sat upon the frozen, mildewy bed and stared at the gear strewn about the dingy interior. This was the first time he had seen it all together. He had kept it lean – he was used to that – but the baggage brought here ahead of his arrival, including the extra items Llewellyn had provided, would be a challenge for one horse to carry. He told himself it would look better when it was packed.

For a while he occupied his mind by visualising the process, much of it now so familiar that it was second nature. Some modifications would be necessary for this trip, of course. His sword he would stow wrapped and out of sight beneath his saddle, in the Saracen fashion. Likewise his shortsword, which was of the single-edged type the Saxons called a "seax". The leather bag containing his mail hauberk could hang behind as it always did. In truth – embarrassed though he was to admit it, even to himself – it was not really a knight's hauberk at all. The knight's mail that Gisburne was entitled to wear covered the body from head to foot, but he had grown so used to the serjeant's shorter haubergeon and the greater freedom it afforded that he had never managed to give it up. It was less weight to carry, at least.

There was the addition of the helm, of course – a present from John. A "great helm," he had called it. The latest thing. It covered the entire head and looked like a bucket, but Gisburne had immediately seen its worth. That, too, would hang in a bag, away from prying eyes.

There were clothes, of course – his gambeson, spare garments, blankets. Bags of coin that he had distributed amongst his baggage so as not to be easily found, mostly sewn into a spare gambeson. Food and drink, and feed for the horse. A pilgrim's staff. That was as much for effect as anything. Likewise the broad-brimmed hat, of the type he had seen so many pilgrims wear.

Then there was the box. Fashioned from thick, dark wood with steel clasps and lock, its lid perfectly square, its body slightly longer than it was wide, hinting at an interior large enough to contain a human head, it was not so easy to disguise. But it was an essential part of his plan. As were the three earthenware bottles, bound together and carefully wrapped in sacking and straw.

He sighed deeply. He was impatient to get on, to get out of this place and over that churning stretch of water; for it to be just him again. Simple. Self-contained. His destiny back in his own hands. With his horse. And his sword. On his road. These things, he understood.

Somewhat against expectation, Gisburne had been lodged in a private chamber for the night. In theory, this was a high honour. What soon became clear, however, was that de Clere had achieved the mere appearance of granting Gisburne the finest hospitality the castle had to offer, whilst in fact keeping him as uncomfortable as possible.

It also meant he was kept far away from the rest of the Constable's esteemed company. They would have to sleep wherever they could about the guest hall. The most exalted might be granted a private guest chamber, with a fire all its own (the pig-faced Fleming was the one who looked to have been lined up for this particular privilege).

Gisburne had never really understood the attraction of castles. The necessity, yes. Their defensive capability, certainly. He could perhaps even appreciate their value as symbols of status, much as he detested such display. But as places to actually live, he could hardly imagine anything worse. Perhaps in the summer – or in southern Spain, perhaps, or Palestine – such a places could ineed be pleasant. A boon, even, with their cool, airy interiors. But an English winter turned every one of them into damp, dark, freezing, inhumane dungeons – and every one of their inhabitants into prisoners. None but the most low and desperate would countenance living in a stinking, clammy cave. Yet the high-born of England clamoured to build such conditions for themselves, at huge expense.

Doubtless this castle was a miracle of its age, and perhaps its master found some comfort in it with his running water and new-fangled sanitation and proximity to a fire and servants to stoke it throughout the night. But the blank cell in which Gisburne now found himself – set in the furthest, most windswept extremity of the mountain of stone – would give a flagellant pause. There was no curtain at the window, and certainly no such lavish commodity as glass – only a shutter with a bent latch, which rattled incessantly as the wind and sleet howled through the yawning gap. There was no privy – although the whole place smelt like one. There was no hearth for a fire – not even, in this God-forsaken corner, a nearby chimney flue from which some residual heat might be gained. Despite all the unwelcome ventilation, the walls ran with moisture, and the bed was so damp and cold that getting in between its covers seemed about as enticing as sliding naked into a freezing duckpond. Such a place might well keep out an army with all its ramparts and moats and murder holes and walls within walls – but there was more simple comfort to be had in a serf's hovel.

He thought back over the excruciating experience of de Clere's feast, and shuddered. His triumph there had been short-lived. A toast, another cheer, then all had begun to melt away again into a generic murmur, the moment passing away as quickly and completely as a warm breath in a gale. Or a spring bloom in winter.

He was glad of it, except that it also meant the passing of Marian. She had smiled warmly, and grasped his hand – the simple contact again making his heart pound against his chest – then moved away to converse with others with exactly equal warmth. Marian gave generously of her heart to everyone. And equally. He began to believe he would never have the greater share of it. She was now preparing for bed somewhere within these walls, watched over by her chaperone. He tried to push such thoughts out of his head, and began checking over his gear again, ready for the morning. It wasn't neccessary, but it would keep his mind occupied, at least.

He realised it was *inside* that he was feeling unprepared. In spite of his recent training, he was tired; in spite of his recent good fortune, dispirited. His left shoulder ached. It always grew stiff in cold weather – had done so since the trials of the Holy Land – and the climb up the Tower wall had hardly helped matters. He reached for his sword – his father's old blade – and drew it from its scabbard. It was solid, reassuring. It reminded him of his father. But there was something else, too. Without fail, every time Gisburne's fingers closed around the grip of a sword, a vision of his old mentor flashed into his mind. He allowed himself a private smile. It was a very specific memory.

HE WAS TWELVE years old, and had just arrived in Normandy after the most awful experience of his life – his first sea voyage, during which he had vomited everything his stomach had to offer within minutes of leaving Dover, and then, in spite of that, had carried on vomiting for whole of the rest of the day.

His stomach muscles still ached and his legs still wobbled from the heave of the ship as he stood beneath the castle of Fontaine-La-Verte. The weather was bright and warm – late spring or early summer – and before him, on a wide expanse of grass, dozens of figures were shouting and laughing and milling about. Riders tilted at sacks suspended from ropes, or practised turning their mounts back and forth around barrels with their hands on their heads, using only the pressure of their knees; younger squires sparred with wooden swords and shields, while some older ones – not far off knights themselves – fought at the pell or duelled with blunted weapons in roped rings, attended by knights who sometimes took up swords, maces or axes against each other to demonstrate proper technique. Among them, boys of all ages ran about, fetching water or lances or leading horses for their masters, weaving in and out of the brightly coloured tents dotting the edges of the field. From one corner came the rousing sound of a pipe and drum, and in another a great pot steamed over a fire, from which a long trestle table lined with benches stretched into the patchy shade of the gently swaying oak trees.

Guy stood, entranced, his baggage still hanging off him – all his nerves and homesickness, for the moment, quite forgotten. He had been late coming to this world – most here would have been pages by the age of seven or eight – and he envied the ease with which these boys inhabited it, many much younger than he. Guy's father – a poor knight, who, as he often pointed out with somewhat bitter humour, owned "less land than most yeomen" – had schooled the boy himself until he had found a knight-mentor for him. That was an old friend from past campaigns, who Guy had apparently once known as "uncle". He loitered, with no clear memory of that man, and no means of recognising him.

A noisy flurry of activity caught his eye not far from where he stood. Two older squires, surrounded by perhaps a half dozen more, were engaged in a ferocious duel. Occasionally the combatants disappeared behind the spectators, the only sign of them the glinting blades flashing over their fellows' heads. It became a kind of music: long phrases beaten out without pause, followed by a tantalising moment of respite, then the theme would be taken up again, with variations and shifts of tempo. Then they would again dance nimbly into view, side-stepping or parrying the relentless barrage of crashing blows with battered shields. The sheer danger of it thrilled and appalled him. He could feel every blow in his gut. He knew they would be fighting with practice or tournament blades – their edges filed flat so they could not cut – but a strike with one of these could still break a bone or crush a skull. And yet, with its movements and rhythms – swift, agile, fluid – the combat also possessed a curious, abstract beauty. One in particular – the taller, more slender of the two, in a yellow gambeson – whipped his sword around with such flow and grace that he made it appear weightless, a natural extension of his arm. He had an unusual grip – his forefinger hooked over the sword's cross-guard. Compared to Guy's own clumsy efforts with his father's blade, such lightness of touch seemed miraculous.

The boy's blade flashed. The other stumbled and fell, rhythm broken. Victorious, his fallen opponent at sword point, he threw off his helm to reveal a shock of sandy, sweat-streaked hair as those about him clapped and cheered. In that moment, Guy knew his one goal in life was to emulate this older boy.

"You are intrigued by his technique?" Guy turned to see a knight beside him – solidly built, hair cropped short, his expression serious. The man seemed ancient compared to the youths upon the field. Guy was not expecting to be spoken to by a knight, and uncertain of the correct form of address. To compound his confusion, the man had addressed him quite matter-of-factly, almost as if he were an equal. Guy nodded. He was sure that was wrong, in any company, but it was too late now for pleasantries. The old man nodded in return and grunted. He looked away again, as if scanning the clouds.

"I knew a knight by the name of Osbern who favoured that hold. He said it afforded better balance, and more control over the angle of the blade. A Flemish mercenary changed his mind at the battle of Alnwick." Guy frowned at that. A knight take the advice of a common mercenary? The old man saw the question on the boy's mind and allowed a flicker of smile to pass his lips. "The mercenary was with the opposing army. During the assault on the camp of William the Lion, his axe hit the knight's blade, slid its length and instead of stopping against the cross-guard stopped against Sir Osbern's forefinger. He lost the finger. Then his sword. Then his life. You will not be following his example."

The old man – although he was, at the time, only 35 – then introduced himself as Gilbert de Gaillon. Gisburne would be under this man's tutelage for the best part of the next ten years, first as page, then squire.

In those early days, Gisburne had known nothing of the battle de Gaillon had mentioned, nor that William the Lion was the rebellious king of the Scots. He later learned that the Scottish king had been successfully subjugated by Henry, imprisoned in the Conqueror's old castle at Falaise in Normandy, and was made to sign over his kingdom. The treaty of Falaise had lasted until 1189 – when another royal Lion named Richard, hungry for money to fund his crusade, had sold William back his castle, title and feudal rights in exchange for 10,000 silver marks. Richard had been unable to find a buyer for London. But he had, at least, managed to sell Scotland.

A RAP ON the door snapped Gisburne back to the present. His fingers tightened on the grip of his sword. It was not the tentative knock of a servant, nor the jaunty knock of a friend, or even the peremptory knock of an official. Two knocks of exactly equal force; indistinct, cryptic, unreadable.

He hauled the door open, sword still in his hand. Before him, and perhaps a foot shorter than he, stood a man several years older than himself, a flickering tallow candle between his fingers, his dress nondescript, his stubbly, half-lit face round and expressionless.

"I'm your new squire," he said, matter-of-factly. Gisburne looked the curious figure up and down, uncertain for the moment quite how to respond. His instinct was to guffaw. Instead, he let a frown crease his brow.

"Aren't you a little old for a squire?"

At that, the man's facial expression subtly shifted from inscrutable to withering – as if Gisburne were something he had just stepped in, and the smell had just reached his nostrils. Gisburne sensed more was to come, but was in no mood for it.

"You've made a mistake," he said. "I don't need a squire." And he swung the door back towards the man's face before the other had time to speak. Its heavy oak stopped against the man's boot, and was shoved back open again with surprising force.

The little man glared at him, drew his foot back from the door frame and flexed it with a wince. "I'd prefer it if you didn't do that again. We have a long road ahead of us and I need both my feet."

Gisburne, who'd already had more than he could take on this day – who felt he could well do with a whipping boy on whom to vent his frustration, even one as old as this – advanced on the man, sword still gripped in his fist. "Listen – I've no idea who you are, nor who put you up to this, but believe me, I'm in no mood for jokes. A knight chooses a squire, not the other way around. And the day I choose you is the day Saladin himself rides into Heaven on the back of a pig." He attempted to slam the door again. It was stopped with a palm.

"It's at the request of your employer," hissed the little man through the gap. He reached inside his tunic and thrust a folded parchment at Gisburne's chest. Gisburne did not need to read it. It bore the seal of Prince John. This was no mistake. Whether the strange creature before him was meant as a helping hand, or a challenge, or was simply some kind of cosmic curse, Gisburne could not yet say. But one thing was certain: John's wishes trumped his own. A knight chose a squire – but only at his prince's pleasure.

He stood in silence for a moment, absorbing the fact that he was stuck with this irritating little man. That every part of the journey ahead, as he had imagined it, would now be different. He hated partnerships – had hated them for a long time. Since the Holy Land. Since *that*. He worked alone. But he also trusted John. Though ill-served by those around him, he had more wisdom in his little finger than

Richard had in his entire being. And infinitely more humanity. He would not have made such a decision lightly. Gisburne knew he must at least try to accept this – to have faith in his master's judgement.

There was one irritation he found harder to put aside. It centred on a single word. *Employer*. Of all the words this squire – his supposed servant – could have chosen... as if he was no more than a common tradesman. But what pierced his pride most was that, for much of his life, this had been true. Until John had found him, he had fought for whoever would take him on, selling his muscle and sinew and basic craft to whoever would pay – no different from a blacksmith or carpenter. Except that when he had done his job, people were dead. In all that time, during the dark years when he had struggled daily to regain the respect that had been lost, he had rarely faced this simple fact. What had kept him going was the belief that he was a man on a quest. A knight expectant. A knight in the shadows. Now, the plain truth struck him almost as comical. He had been a labourer with a sword, earning his bread from day to day, drifting from place to place – no status, no prospects, no future. Against all the odds, that perseverance had paid off. But he was keenly aware that it had come about by no more than a stroke of fortune, and that fortune's wheel had more often turned against him than in his favour. Everything he had hung by a thread.

He took a deep breath, and – as so often in his life – asked himself what de Gaillon would do. There was no question; he would work with what he had, and keep his complaints to himself. "Well then..." he said, softening his tone. "I suppose you have a name? Can you at least tell me that before we both die in this draught?"

"Galfrid," said Galfrid.

"Galfrid..." repeated Gisburne with a slow nod, as if trying it out for size. He was about to announce something along the lines of "I accept you into my service out of respect for my lord" when Galfrid pre-empted him.

"The ship for Calais leaves on the morning tide," he said, deadpan. "Have your accoutrements ready by first light."

Gisburne stared in amazement, irritation swelling inside him once more. Shouldn't he be telling this Galfrid to do that?

"I'll send two boys to help bring it down to the courtyard," Galfrid added. Then, without another word, he turned on his heels and was swallowed up by the dark.

Gisburne slammed the door shut, and wondered how on earth he was going to make this work. Who would this man be taking orders from? His knight, or his prince? If Galfrid would not take orders from him, the challenging days and weeks to come were going to be impossible. Perhaps he should just tip him over the side somewhere between Dover and Calais.

Fully clothed, his horsehide coat wrapped about him, he climbed into bed, admiring as he did so the tenacity of the lice that managed to thrive within it. He lay for a long time, then, thinking of Marian and watching a drift of sleet forming beneath the window, the stink of piss in his nostrils.

IX

GISBURNE DID NOT need the servants. They stood idly by, watching in awkward silence as he loaded himself up, then headed down to the yard where his horse was waiting. It was largely habit. He was used to trusting no one, relying on no one. But also, today, it was partly pride – a note of defiance. That he should feel the need to defy a squire – that he had one at all – seemed absurd. But there it was.

When Gisburne arrived in the inner ward, weighed down with his gear, he found Galfrid already waiting. By him were two stable hands, and two horses – a pair of sturdy rounceys. As Gisburne neared, the snotty-nosed stable boy arrived with Nyght. A look of incomprehension crept over the youth's face as he saw the assembled company. Panicky looks darted between the stable hands, as if some dreadful misunderstanding had occurred for which they would likely get the blame. Galfrid looked at Gisburne's mount, back to his own, then to Gisburne.

"You're not taking that with you..." He nodded at Nyght.

Gisburne held Galfrid's gaze, uncertain for a moment whether the man meant it as a question or a command. The stony face gave no clue. He lowered the last of his baggage. The ground was icy, but too cold to be wet.

"It's the latest thing," said Gisburne. "It's called a 'horse'." Galfrid's eyes narrowed at that. "It's a long way to Marseille. I don't intend to walk."

"I have already made provision..." began Galfrid.

"Well, I prefer mine," snapped Gisburne.

"These are better over distance."

"He's a good horse."

"I can see that," said Galfrid with a nod. The conciliatory air withered as swiftly as it had bloomed. "As will everyone else. It won't do."

Nyght stamped and snorted and shook his head, as if taking personal offence at the comment. "Won't *do*?" fumed Gisburne.

"He's too good."

Gisburne's annoyance boiled over. "So, I'm to ride some nag now, am I?"

"When did you last see a pilgrim riding a courser?"

"When the pilgrim was a knight."

Galfrid fell silent. There was a logic to the response, though it was not logic that drove Gisburne. It was defiance. And pride. And perhaps something more. A knight – a *chevalier* – was not a knight without his horse. He'd sooner give up his sword.

Galfrid moved in close to Gisburne's face, his manner suddenly impatient, his voice lowered to an irascible hiss below the hearing of the stable hands. "We are crossing the lands of the King of France. Enemy lands, in all but name. We do not especially wish to announce the fact that we are a knight. It prompts unwelcome questions. And please – spare me the 'a knight's not a knight without a horse' speech..." He turned away, seemed to try to compose himself, but failed. "Or perhaps you would prefer me to blow a trumpet fanfare as we disembark at Calais and shout 'Hurrah for England and bollocks to King Philip'?"

Gisburne felt a strange satisfaction at the outburst. The little man was human after all. "The horse stays," he said flatly.

For a while they held each other's gaze in silence, then Galfrid let out a deep sigh, seeming to deflate. "So be it," he said. He came in close again. The earlier ire had quite gone, but a quiet intensity remained in his voice. "But know this: if we be captured, we can expect no protection – least of all from our master. We will be denied. Condemned, if necessary. We have only each other for protection now."

"Nyght is also my protection," said Gisburne. "And I his." It was a moment, Gisburne could see, before Galfrid grasped that he was referring to the name of his mount. "He is not merely 'a horse'. Nor 'a knight's horse'. He is *my* horse. And he has proven his worth. You have yet to do so."

Galfrid stood in silence again, as if digesting Gisburne's words, then nodded in resignation.

Gisburne loaded up his horse in silence. Throughout all his earlier adventures as a mercenary, no matter where he had found himself or who he had fought for, Gisburne had never presented himself as something other than he was. People took him as they found him. Sneaking around, going in disguise, *stealing*... Those things went against the grain. To Hood, it was second nature. But not to him. No, not to him. Yet he understood that he would need to adapt his ways. To become something new. He could even see, he grudgingly admitted, that there might be some good sense in Galfrid's words – not that he was ready to yield to a superannuated squire just yet. "One must adapt to stay alive, but one must stay true for that life to have purpose." That was one of de Gaillon's many maxims. As with all of the old knight's pearls of wisdom – most of which were now permanently set in Gisburne's brain – it was easy to recite, but excruciatingly difficult to live by. De Gaillon had a maxim for that, too. "Only the unremarkable man lives easily."

At the moment he thought this, his leather-sheathed eating knife jumped out of the leather satchel that his impatient hands were wrestling in place behind his saddle. It fell, bounced and turned a somersault on the hard round. The knife evoked an unwelcome memory. The real reason thievery set his teeth on edge; the reason part of him still feared it. He did not want to think about that. Only de Gaillon had known that truth, and he was long gone. Gisburne scooped up the knife, flung open the satchel and shoved both it and the memory deep down where they belonged.

And yet, his change – his transformation – had already begun, with his assault on the Tower, with his preparations for this quest, with the contrivances that Llewellyn had prepared for him. But somehow, when he was dealing with inert matter – wood and metal, and solutions to practical problems – the ethics seemed of little account. Perhaps the trick was to focus on these – or think in a similar way about people.

"What wood is this?" said Galfrid, his earlier irritation quite gone. "It's heavy." Gisburne turned to see the little man hefting his pilgrim's staff – a sturdy length of wood that stood just below shoulder height. The top eight inches were wrapped round with cord to serve as a hand grip, and had a bulb of polished iron at either end of that portion – each about the size of a hen's egg, but spherical – the topmost forming a solid head to the staff.

Gisburne snatched it from him and tucked it beneath his bags. "Since I'll be carrying it, you don't need to worry." He saw Galfrid's eye wander next to the wooden box, and whipped it away before the squire could settle on it. He hung it over Nyght's left flank. It was not ideal – he would need to secure it more tightly, to stop it bouncing against Nyght's hip – but there would be time for that.

Galfrid had meanwhile produced a wrinkled apple from somewhere, and took a slice off it with a knife as he looked Gisburne up and down. "You're wearing that, then, are you?" Gisburne looked down at his black horsehide coat, then back at the squire.

"Yes," he said acidly. "Does that meet with your approval?" One of the stable lads stifled a laugh.

"It is... not so bad. Strange, yes. But practical. And one can't imagine a knight would wear such a thing. Which is good."

Gisburne sighed and turned back to his horse, beginning to wonder if there was anything upon which his unwelcome squire did not have an opinion, or the need to have the last word. Beyond his right shoulder, he heard the stable hand's snigger finally break loose. He really would be glad to be rid of this place.

There remained only the earthenware bottles. Gisburne had looked all over his tightly packed saddle and bags, at first refusing to admit that they could not be accommodated. He now eyed Galfrid's more leanly packed horse. "Since we are of an accord – and you of such a practical bent – I'm sure you won't mind carrying these."

To Gisburne's surprise there was no word of protest, no grimace, no sigh of contempt. Galfrid took them without hesitation and strapped them firmly to his saddlebags.

"Your own personal supply?" he said.

"Don't drink it," warned Gisburne.

"So, what's in the box?"

Gisburne wondered how long it would take him to ask. The squire had tried to sound casual, but without success.

"I'll be keeping that by me," Gisburne said. For the first time, fundamental questions formed in his mind. Just how much did Galfrid know of this mission? Everything? Nothing? Was there perhaps information this man possessed that he himself did not? Such questions were the reason he worked alone. Working alone, the matter of trust was simple: you trusted no one. There was no need. That would be another painful adjustment on his part. Weighing these thoughts, he looked Galfrid straight in the eye, and from a great effort of will, spoke without guard or affectation. "Do not touch it. Do not try to open it. And after we are successful in Marseille, it is to be guarded no matter what. Understand?"

Galfrid nodded, for once accepting his new master's word without question. As they moved off in silence, Gisburne resolved to discuss the details of the mission with Galfrid at the first opportunity – to share what he knew. He hoped Galfrid would do the same. The trust had to begin somewhere. But it would not be quite yet – he would wait until they were in France and safely on their way.

"So," piped up the squire as they wound their way down towards the harbour. "You're a knight... And you called your horse 'Nyght'?"

"Yes," returned Gisburne, irritably. "What of it?" But Galfrid simply nodded slowly to himself, and crunched on another slice of apple, and gazed out over the gently heaving expanse of grey ocean.

Gisburne had the feeling this was going to be a long trip.

II

FRANCE

X

Limousin – April, 1177

IN HIS SIXTEENTH year, Guy of Gisburne knew for the first time that he was about to die.

He was no stranger to death. He had certainly seen enough of it for his intellect to grasp that it was often a real and immediate threat – a hovering, everpresent possibility. But what he encountered on this day was something new, something more. It was the absolute certainty that, in that moment, his end was upon him and his existence on earth was about to be snuffed out.

When they rode into the sheltered courtyard of the farm, he was feeling the sad euphoria following his first taste of defeat. The farmhouse where they had retreated to lick their wounds seemed to him an oasis – a sprawl of a building sheltered by large and ancient trees, miraculously untouched by the events of recent months. Dismounting, he and the other squires set about feeding and watering the horses and seeing to the needs of their knights. All were exhausted. But many had the same, strangely desperate feeling of joy at having survived. In some, it manifested as a slightly manic good humour. There was banter between the older squires – usually at the expense of the younger. The usual social division that existed amongst the squires – between the French-speaking sons of the wealthy nobles, and the small band of poorer, English-speaking boys who were habitually put upon by their loftier peers – was today forgotten.

Among them, however, one stood apart. His name was Eadwyn, squire to a knight named William of Tempsford. Gisburne watched out of the corner of his eye as the boy – not much younger than he – tended to his master's horse. Sir William had not been on it – not since the routing of the army at Malemort. It was, Gisburne knew, almost a certainty that his master was dead, and that the squire now was without a knight. Gisburne was sure someone would take him under their wing, though. That was the way of things. For now, however, no one seemed keen to look him in the eye.

While de Gaillon and the knights took up residence in the farmhouse, the squires camped down wherever they could. Gisburne had been lucky. He had been with a large, rowdy group that taken over the small barn across from the main building. The others – mostly English, mostly poor – would have to make do with whatever shelter they could find outside.

The barn had the sharp tang of dead mouse about it, but he was too dog-tired to care. It was shelter, and peace, and safety. It had a bed of straw and it reminded him of home. For now, nothing else mattered.

It was not Gisburne's first battle in support of his knight. De Gaillon was in the service of a petty baron who had pledged support to Duke Richard, and for almost a year now had been engaged in bringing other, more rebellious factions within the Angevin realms into line. Very soon, it had become clear to the young squire that his childhood notions of war were entirely wrong. When he had imagined battle as a child – stomach down on the mud of the yard, using acorns and twigs for soldiers – he had pictured two armies drawn up against each other in impressive formation; each of a single mind and purpose, charging in response to the heroic cries of their generals, and one side being swept before the other in the epic clash, before finally fleeing the field as the cheers of the victorious rang in their ears. It was an image of discipline and order – in which, through titanic struggle, a wider sense of order was restored.

There was indeed discipline amongst the knights and soldiers with whom he had served. A more powerful, palpable discipline than he could ever have imagined – made all the more immediate by the threat of chaos that constantly snapped at its heels. He now knew – because he had seen them up close, had looked into their death-haunted eyes – that those impressive ranks maintained their shape only by the continual exertion of an iron will. He had also seen that will fail. He had seen armies lose structure, command, sense of direction. He had participated in victories that seemed more like defeats, had been in skirmishes where he no longer knew which side was which or what bearing its outcome had on the wider battle – if it had any. He had been in situations so hectic that it had not even been possible for him to tell whether they ended in victory or defeat, or indeed what the difference was between the two.

Afterwards, when the smoke cleared, Gilbert de Gaillon would explain to him how and why they had won. Then, it would seem to make sense once more.

But today, he had observed something quite different. It was not just the defeat of an army. It was the collapse of all order.

Every mile Gisburne was able put between himself and that morning's disaster was a relief – one so deep, so all-pervading, that it seemed to throb within him like a longing. He was in no doubt that, somewhere back there, the dreadful conflagration still raged. Thinking of those grim, life-sapped figures – their tarnished, blood-drenched weapons, the dark look in their eyes like lamps gone out – his heart ached with gratitude at being alive. At *feeling* alive, at being vital amongst those walking corpses. On the road back, he had even caught himself muttering the words *"Thank you, thank you, thank you..."* over and over in time with the pounding of his horse's hooves upon the dry mud road. To whom or what this gratitude was directed, he had no clear idea. He had never spoken aloud to God in his life, nor had any sense that anything out there would listen to his pleas. But today, the need to express it – even to a blank, indifferent universe – was urgent and overwhelming. And sometimes, perhaps, expressing it was enough.

Not a word was uttered between them as they rode. And yet, as mile piled upon mile with no slackening of pace, that relief was magnified by a further realisation. If this small band of battle-hardened knights – men who he had known eat and even sleep whilst conflict raged nearby – had felt the need to retreat this far, then the horrors they'd left behind must be terrible indeed. Gisburne felt vindicated by it. Less alone in his fears, and more connected to the men he so respected. It was one of those moments when he began to believe he could be one of them.

But it brought, too, a kind of creeping dread.

It was a dread founded on no one simple, graspable object – nothing that could be contained or defined. It was a dread of madness. Of a world infected by chaos. Of a dark creature that had been loosed upon it – murky, shifting, insubstantial, but a monster all the same – one that could not be tamed or destroyed, and which would stalk him to the ends of the earth.

That was what he had seen when their army had been routed at Malemort. It was not so much the battle that had horrified Gisburne – though that was bloody and bitter enough. It was the chaos that came after.

In his training, Gisburne had been schooled in much more than the practical techniques of fighting. He had also learned of the many types of men who engaged in it – the components of an army. There was the knight, of course – the model of courage and honourable conduct. The archer – low in social status, but of such strategic importance that he could sway a battle. The serjeant – a respected fighting man said to be worth half a knight, but often, in the thick of close combat, worth much more. There were endless divisions and subdivisions, encompassing all classes, from the loftiest prince to the most lowly footsoldier.

In his rather more intense education on the battlefield, he had learned about another kind of fighting man. The mercenary. Although anyone from a knight to an infantryman might be a mercenary, and the practicalities of combat were exactly the same for them as for anyone else, they were a separate species – one that made young Gisburne, a knight aspirant, uneasy. He was uneasy with the concept of fighting for pay. He was uneasy with the mockery this made of the concept of loyalty. And, when he finally encountered them, he was uneasy with the natures of the men themselves. Some were men who had lost all notion of honour, if they ever had it. Others were victims of ill fortune – outcast by their community, or forced to make a living by the only means they knew how. A few, he was sure, were probably criminals. Yet, even amongst their own kind, there were classes who were regarded with suspicion, or contempt, or fear.

Most terrifying of all he had enountered were the "rotten". Gisburne didn't know what the nickname meant, nor how it had been acquired. But it seemed fitting enough.

His first sight of the army of Brabançon mercenaries fighting for Richard under the command of William of Cambrai stayed with him forever. The "rotten" were protected from head to foot in leather jerkins, armed with staves and weapons of steel and iron. When not hired by kings or dukes, they went about in bands of thousands and reduced monasteries, villages and cities to ashes. None could stop them. None dared. They had no fear. Believing it no sin, they committed violence and adultery, openly proclaiming there was no God. Fugitive rebels, false clerks, renegade monks and all who had forsaken God joined them. These were the men who, on this day, had formed the greater part of Richard's army.

Malemort should have been a simple action: the suppression of a rebellious population. But such was the wrath of the citizens that they smashed Richard's assault. When William of Cambrai – leader of the "rotten" for the past ten years – had been killed, the cohesion of his army evaporated. And there was Hell on earth.

When he was ten years old, Gisburne had shot an arrow at a wasps' nest that hung high in a tree at the edge of the pasture. His father had repeatedly warned him away from the spot. But he was lost in a game, shouting out commands to his imaginary army and issuing threats to their enemies. He cursed haughtily at the wasps and fired an impulsive shot. The last thing had he expected was for it to hit. But not only had it done so, it had knocked the whole nest to the ground. He remembered being incapacitated by a kind of cold dread, standing rooted to the spot as a furious, buzzing cloud rose from the vibrating, papery ball. The sound made him feel sick. But as he looked on in horror, he began to realise that the wasps swarming about the nest were paying him as little attention as they would a tree or gatepost. He was a little distance from it – and, in his state of shock, he had remained completely still. Perhaps it was this that had saved him. The thought paralysed him further. Every muscle tense, he watched for what seemed a lifetime, unable to move, the hectic army wheeling about the air above the besieged nest until its armoured soldiers finally began to settle, regrouping, repairing, crawling all over its surface, obscuring it in a seething, shining mass of buzzing black and yellow.

It was then that the idea came into his head. When a knight was down, he was vulnerable. That was when you dealt the death blow. You should not flinch from it. The thought terrified him. But as he stood, the compulsion to act on it grew. He fought to overcome that fear – to conquer it, and to conquer his enemy. Thinking these things, he drew the wooden sword from his belt, raised it high over his right shoulder, and crept towards the nest.

For another agonising moment he stood over the heaving, poisonous globe, uncertain whether he could do the deed, yet unable to go back, wasps whining about his head.

Before he knew it had happened, his will had reconnected with his muscles. The sword crashed down. The nest split in two. Black beads of venomous rage exploded in every direction. He fled, the throb of mad fury behind him – ran and ran until his legs could take no more, until the angry whir of vibrating air had faded into distance – and, with his heart thumping against his chest, flung himself into a cornfield and collapsed in a heap. He lay there, panting hoarsely, gradually becoming aware of the dozen or so stings on his arms. He laughed at that – at the boldness of his victory, the genius of his escape – and began to wonder how long wasps might hold a grudge. If they could recognise him. If they would come after him.

A long time after, he crept back to the battlefield. He was not prepared for what he found. It seemed the colony had gone insane, attacking anything they could find. He found dozens half-dead with their stingers stuck in pine cones, in the gnarled bark of trees, in the nearby bulrushes. Hundreds floated on the surface of the pond about a trio of dead frogs. Not far from the nest, he found a grass snake writhing, a few clinging, deranged berserkers still stabbing at it. Further out, on the grass, stiff and contorted, a crow lay dead, more of the striped creatures stuck to its blue-black feathers like jewels. And everywhere on the ground, others crawled, exhausted, their purpose lost, their lives spent. Only the nest itself was completely free of them. It lay, burst open like a conquered castle, utterly abandoned, as if now cursed – a shattered relic. No birds sang. But there was a stranger sound. In the next field, his chestnut pony, maddened by the crazed insects stinging its head and eyes, had careered into the fence and impaled iself. It lay groaning and close to death.

Gisburne lied to his father. The nest had fallen, he said. To his surprise, his father took it calmly. Years later, he learned that the old man had seen the arrow embedded in the tree bough – where it remained ever after – and had guessed exactly what had happened. But he was simply glad that it was only the pony, and not his son, that had died.

His father had told him that, most likely, the king of the nest had perished, and, leaderless, they had gone mad. The horror of the destruction that he had unleashed haunted him long after.

Today, it came back to him afresh. He had watched as the mercenary army had been smashed open, its furious survivors dispersed. The images of destruction that followed burned in his brain.

As he attended de Gaillon at that night's meal, he had been finally moved to ask a question which had long troubled him, but which he had thought too stupid to put into words. "What is the difference between victory and defeat?"

De Gaillon almost laughed – the grim, ironic laugh that emerged when things were so bad they were absurd, and which, bit by bit, was becoming the only laugh he had. "You're more tired after a defeat," he said, with no expression in his voice. Then he snapped a morsel of meat from his knife point, chewed on it with little relish, and added: "But both can kill you." He forced himself to swallow.

Gisburne was surprised by the cynicism. De Gaillon was a realist – sometimes, brutally so – but he was not one for giving up. Not ever. After a time, perhaps aware that his reply was inadequate, he sighed and paused in his eating again. "What a battle really is," he said, pointing with his knife, "is a world brought to the brink of chaos. The purpose in fighting a battle – and the primary objective of a knight – is to bring it to a conclusion, to restore order, as rapidly and decisively as possible. To establish peace. The ultimate enemy is not the one who stands opposite you on the field. It is in here." At this, he tapped the side of his head with the blade of the eating knife. "And it is out there." Here, he gestured all around. "It is the chaos that threatens to overrun us when our guard is down. The enemy of peace. The enemy of happiness."

De Gaillon had made similar pronouncements before. At the time, Gisburne had not fully understood them. But today, he did.

It was not long before Gisburne realised the ghastly mistake he had made in his choice of bed. The straw that had seemed inviting from a distance revealed itself to be musty and thick with crumbling rat droppings. With the doors closed, and nowhere for it to go, the acrid stench of decay that seemed to seep out of the creaking fabric of the barn concentrated and closed about them with sickening intensity. Something had died in here, and was still here – a mouse, a rat, perhaps something bigger. The boys outside in the ragged tents – or even just sleeping in the open of the cool night air – had by far the better bed.

But none complained or made a move. He certainly would not be the first to crack, the first to admit defeat. He'd had enough of defeat today. And besides, his own flesh was too exhausted to answer his commands. And so he lay, aching, his heart thumping, his brain teeming – almost feverish – until finally he drifted off to the chorus of snorting and shuffling, the reek of sweat and dead rodent in his nostrils.

He could not be sure what woke him. Later, he supposed it must have been the sound of the barn door being opened. It might have been the light itself. In the dark of the night, the cool glow – of a moon almost full – seemed startlingly bright in the part-open doorway. He blinked sticky, blurry eyes, not wanting to stir any more than necessary. The moonlight formed a white halo about something in the doorway – a figure, in silhouette, standing motionless. Even before he could properly focus his eyes, he recognised the shape: a knight. The helm and armour were unmistakable. In the figure's hand, a sword, unsheathed. Gisburne forced himself up on one elbow, his brain telling him to wake – but something terribly wrong about the scene, something definite but as yet indefinable, made his heart shrink and his limbs weak.

All at once, the knight-figure raised the sword and a wavering voice rose to fill the thick silence within the barn.

"*Veni, creator spiritus*!"

The whole room seemed to shift as one – bodies jerking into life, unfolding and disentangling from themselves and each other as the reedy, uncertain tones seemed to gather strength. Gisburne had immediately recognised the hymn so beloved of knights and crusaders – the call to the holy spirit to fill the soul, to steel the body for battle. He looked on, baffled, as the figure stepped in amongst them, and one of the older squires nearest to the door – Gisburne recognised him as Jonas – struggled to his knees in gruff indignation. Then the impossible happened. The sword swung and struck the still kneeling squire on the neck. Gisburne heard metal bite into bone, felt something wet strike his face. The squire jolted violently, legs straightening in a ghastly convulsion, and collapsed back onto his fellows with a horrid gurgling sigh, his head – Gisburne could see, even in silhouette – at a disconcerting angle.

All Hell broke loose.

There were shouts of alarm as bodies surged and limbs flailed, each boy trying to clamber over the others, some still bewildered from sleep. Gisburne struggled to gain his feet – was jostled and elbowed in the side of his head – but stood in time to see the sword fall again. And again. There were cries of agony now. The blade swung about, striking flesh and bone and teeth, sweeping closer as the wavering voice was raised in song, struggling to drown out the desperate cries of the boys. Gisburne felt the air move as the sword whooshed past his face. He tried to step back, found he could not. And then he knew. He would die here, in this barn. He would never see his father again. All things not yet done or said were hopeless dreams that he had mere seconds to contemplate.

The blade swung through the air. Something struck his head. He fell, a strange calm descending as he did so. It was inevitable. Unfair – wretched – but inevitable. All was lost. Now he would know if there was a God.

But he did not die.

There was a muffled sound, as if his ears were stuffed with cotton. A singing note in his head. Then a blaze of light. One eye registered nothing – but the other saw clearly.

Gilbert de Gaillon had burst in, half-dressed, sword slung about him, mace in one hand, torch in the other, his face more gaunt and skull-like than ever in its flame. The attacker turned and froze, his voice dying away, the light revealing the full horror of the scene – blood and gore everywhere about the barn's filthy floor, bodies hacked, some moving, some now no more than meat for the flies, boys of all ages crushed and cowering against the barn's interior, and in the centre of it all – dressed in his lost knight's spare armour, the white surcoat spattered head to foot in blood – the wild-eyed, bereft figure of Eadwyn.

Without hesitating, de Gaillon struck him full force across the side of the head.

He spun full-circle and fell dead among the clumps of blood-sodden straw and rat bones, two of his teeth rattling against the far wall.

Gisburne put his hand to his head. The tip of the blade had caught his brow as it flew, and cut a vertical gash that parted his left eyebrow and the flesh beneath, blood blinding that eye. He blinked, sight returning. No more than a yard from him, one of the other squires fell to his knees, laughing.

"Thank you!" he cried to the barn's web-strewn rafters. "Thank you!"

"What are you doing?" barked de Gaillon with unexpected ferocity.

"I am giving thanks to God!" cried the lad. "God protected me. Now I know He loves me!"

With a sudden, gruff sound in his throat, de Gaillon clouted the boy with the back of his hand, sending him sprawling across the bloody floor.

"Imbecile!" he said. "Do you think God loved them any less?" He gestured towards the heaped, bloody bodies of his fallen comrades. "That they *deserved* this? If God protected the pious, then the world would be replete with good men and we could all lay down our swords. God is not so simple – and He certainly doesn't waste His energies on the likes of you. Now get out of my sight."

And he kicked the flabbergasted squire out of the door.

The hand that de Gaillon extended to him, that raised him up off the ground, was perhaps the most welcome human contact that Gisburne had ever known.

He knew, that day, that the natural order of the world was chaos, and that overcoming it lay in the hands of men.

XI

Northern France – 23 November, 1191

GISBURNE DIDN'T SEE the rope until it was too late. It was the sound that made his muscles tense, the split second before impact – the crackling of the half frozen hemp cord whipping into the air before him, then the deep thrum as it pulled taut, and a spray of ice crystals on his face. Then came the impact that took the air out of his chest. By the time he knew what was happening, he was already falling.

They were riding fast. That was the bad luck. Gisburne had been pushing hard since Calais. The weather had been cold, even for the heart of winter, and the frozen ground tough going for the horses. But there had, at least, been no more snow. The roads were passable, and the ground just pliable enough to give decent grip. So, he had pushed their advantage. It also meant he didn't have to suffer Galfrid's conversation quite so much.

Gisburne had been determined to reach Lucheux before nightfall. The promise of a good inn and sweet hay for the horses – which, in turn, improved the prospect of reaching Amiens the day after – had them racing against the failing light.

The good luck was that it was Gisburne, not Galfrid, who went first into the low ravine. Had the smaller man been riding ahead, the rope would have caught across his throat. At a gallop, that meant a broken neck – or as Gisburne had seen happen once before, decapitation. Instead, it had struck Gisburne across his right arm – which he had raised instinctively – and across his collarbone. That meant, at least, that he was not dead before he hit the ground.

If there was one thing a knight learned, it was how to stay on a horse. How to cling to its back like a limpet, no matter what the terrain; how to face lance and sword and wield weapons in both hands at full gallop. But before Gisburne's brain could make any decision on the matter, his body had known what to do. It had known that, no matter what, it was going no further, and that the beast upon which it was sat was not going to stop. Instinctively, his legs relinquished their grip. His arm flailed and caught around the rope. Nyght leapt ahead. For a moment he swung in the air, hearing Galfrid's horse thundering to an abrupt halt behind him. The rope sagged, stopped, then gave completely, and he crashed to the hard ground. A gurgling cry of pain and anger issued from somewhere nearby as he did so – but the moment was too confused for him to tell where.

Gisburne lay still, framed in an icy crust of snow, dazed, struggling to catch his breath. He twisted feet and hands, trying to feel past the numbing cold for wrenched muscles or broken bones. The wind was knocked out of him, but there was no pain. That was not conclusive – pain was not always quick to come with the worst wounds – but it was a start. Had he tried to stay mounted, it would have been far worse. But now, he was down. That was not so good. A mounted knight was a near invincible force. Unmounted, he was still a formidable soldier. Flat on his back, with no weapon, he was as good as dead.

Before he could move, the man was already on him, a sword point at his neck, the other hand curled up in a resentful claw, its fingers bloody and raw, its palm lobster-pink and shiny from a fresh rope burn. His whole being quivered with pain and anger, snotty nostrils flaring as he snorted like an animal. "I *got* you!" The sound seethed through broken teeth. The man was stocky, dressed in muddy layers that had the stink of months of wear on them. The face atop this mound of rags was round and sweaty, his hair plastered to his head as if slick with pig grease. "I got *you!*"

Gisburne tried to get himself onto one elbow. The man put a reeking, ragged foot on Gisburne's chest and pressed him hard against the crunching snow, his eyes wide, his teeth bared.

A smile broke out across the stranger's face. He began to laugh. It became wild – erratic – bursting out between the words "I got you! *I got you!*" He spoke with growing intensity, as if each repetition of the weird chant were imbuing him with some magical potency.

Gisburne stared along the sword blade in a strange state of detachment, its cold point resting in the hollow at the base of his throat. Curved. The weapon was badly notched along its edge, but ended in a hilt that glinted gold. Only by degrees – and with some incredulity – did Gisburne realise he was looking at a *paramerion*, a Byzantine weapon. How such a blade came to be in the hands of this wretch, God alone knew.

Other details impressed themselves upon him. He was still alive. His hands were free. The man's right foot was on his chest. The man was now one-handed. And he had his right forefinger hooked over the sword's guard. He almost smiled at that. Somewhere, some part of him was also beginning to wonder where Galfrid was.

"What're you going to do now, eh?" The pig-grease man leered over him, then winced, as if a pain were suddenly asserting itself. He stared at his own bloody, filthy hand for a moment in appalled fascination – then, in response to some instinct, licked it. Gisburne almost heaved. "I'll have your bollocks for this, you basta..."

He did not finish the sentence. Gisburne grabbed his foot and pushed it upward. The man flailed backwards, the blade flying away from Gisburne's throat in a futile attempt to right himself. Gisburne, still clinging to the foot, gave it a sharp quarter turn to the right. There was a *crack*, and a piercing shriek, and the man completely overbalanced, hopped uselessely, then bowled over onto the ground, somehow avoiding his own blade.

Gisburne was on his feet. Nyght was trained to return to him, and within seconds Gisburne had him by the reins and had pulled the nearest thing to hand – his pilgrim staff – from his pack.

"Stop! *Stop!*" It was not his attacker. Nor was it Galfrid. The voice was weak, fearful. But the figure behind it, he now saw, had a drawn bow aimed directly at his chest. Gisburne at last understood why Galfrid – whose horse snorted and stamped just behind where he now stood – had made no move.

Pig-Grease heaved himself to his feet, leaning on his ludicrously exotic blade, his eyes blazing like a furnace. He winced as he put weight on his right leg.

"You don't know what you done," he growled, pointing his sword. "You got no idea..."

His companion with the bow, meanwhile, had not the means to hide his nerves, and visibly shook. Gisburne even fancied he could hear the shaft of the arrow rattle against the bow. His face was also in stark contrast to the other – as long and thin as a coffin board, with nervous, beady eyes and a mouthful of yellow teeth like carpenter's chisels. Many times Gisburne had had occasion to compare someone to a rat, but never had the similarity been so literal.

In the tense stillness of that moment, Gisburne sensed movement at the very edge of his vision. Galfrid's hand was reaching slowly for one of the earthenware vessels on his saddle.

"Not the bottles," hissed Gisburne.

The bowman switched his aim to Galfrid. The little man froze. Gisburne fancied he saw a scowl on his squire's face.

They stood like that, a gleaming sword pointed at Gisburne's chest, an arrow aimed at Galfrid's heart, waiting for what would happen next.

Pig-Grease took a deep breath, seemed to gather himself. A smile creased his features. "Now... Let's try that again."

As he spoke, he eyed up the gear packed about the horses. His gaze settled on something.

"What's in the box?" he said.

XII

THEIR ARRIVAL AT the port of Calais had sounded a warning.

Gisburne – never the best of sailors – had inwardly rejoiced at setting his feet on dry land again. In Sicily, he had experienced the great *tarides* – ships built to carry forty horses with their knights, squires and equipment. When he recalled that memory, he could still feel their horrible, long, heaving motions, and the corresponding heaving motions they inspired in his own belly. It was a great relief, therefore, that their vessel on this occasion had been far humbler; a small but serviceable tub – swift and unfussy with only the adaptations necessary to carry a half dozen mounts. A large hatch opened in its port side, with a ramp upon the quay leading directly into the hold. Nyght had not travelled by ship before, and, feeling the queasy rise and fall of the gangplank, balked several times before he would be led into that dark interior. Gisburne coaxed the animal as best he could, given his shared misgivings. Inside were six makeshift but stoutly built stalls, three fore and three aft, each with canvas slings that went under the horses' bellies to steady them.

The stallion had whinnied and stamped as the ship slipped its moorings and England slid away from them. Gisburne patted the animal on its glossy black neck, then, making his way to the deck, spent the voyage clamped to the ship's side, staring resolutely out to sea.

Calais itself had the feel of a town unable to cope with the number of people it contained. The whole place was abuzz, thronging with travellers – most of them, it seemed, Englishmen. They treated it as their own, laughing and shouting to each other in their own tongue, making purchases of hot food from the barrows and stalls that clustered about the quay, buying provisions for the journey ahead or striking deals with merchants from France and further afield, the cold air thick with the smell of roasting chestnuts, sour wine and fried fish. Some of the foreign traders bartered and haggled in French, but many also had the good commercial sense to speak in English, and it was this language that dominated. Several of the English, it seemed, had come with the express purpose of buying large quantities of wine to ship immediately back home, and barrels of the stuff were piled high at the quayside. Here and there, individuals had been persuaded to sample the wares, the thought perhaps being that a drunk was more easily separated from his money. Gisburne couldn't help wondering whether the wine they quaffed on this quayside bore any relation to the wine they found in the barrels when they reached Dover.

Weaving amongst the merchants, the drinkers, the costermongers and the swindlers were the pilgrims. Some – generally the more modestly dressed – were evidently delighted by their lively surroundings. Others – those more ostentatiously clad in the richest fabrics or the most meagre sackcloth – looked upon this orgy of common commercialism with queasy distaste, or haughty disapproval.

One other thing had boosted traffic through Calais of late. War. Richard himself had passed through here with the core of his army on his hasty journey to the crusade. There had been a steady flow of armed English or Anglo-Norman knights ever since, and here and there, French knights and other surly representatives of the crown looked on warily, resentfully, a little too keen to make trouble – perhaps imagining some future time when this Little England would seek to assert itself more fully.

"You!" Gisburne and Galfrid, leading their packed horses from the quay, had not advanced a hundred yards on French soil when the shout rang out. Galfrid's furtive gaze had confirmed that it was indeed meant for them.

"Keep walking," he had said, his hand gripping Gisburne's elbow.

"Hey!"

Gisburne shot a glance behind them. A long-haired knight in a bright blue surcoat – obviously French – pushed his way towards them, a younger, beardless facsimile of himself following at his shoulder.

"Keep walking..." murmured Galfrid. "If questioned, say nothing..."

"You there!"

The cry was tinged with irritation this time. They did not stop. "Say nothing..." sang Galfrid, as if it were a monk's incantation.

A gauntleted hand landed on his shoulder, turning him around. "What's the matter with you? Are you deaf or stupid?"

"Is there a problem?" said Galfrid in his best French, and with the impressively-wrought air of an innocent. Almost, Gisburne thought, that of a simpleton.

"Whose horse is this?" the knight barked in Gisburne's face.

"This is my master's horse, as you see..." replied Galfrid.

"Have I developed a squint? I was talking to him, not you." He returned his attention to Gisburne, looking him up and down with an expression of repugnance. "This is a knight's horse. How did you come by it?"

"And what's in the box?" said the younger knight, less convincingly. He circled behind them, looking their horses and gear up and down. Probably a token gesture – an insecure youth asserting himself, thought Gisburne – but he didn't like the direction things were going. Galfrid's eyes widened, still pleading with him to say nothing.

"You're trying my patience..." The knight drew his sword. Galfrid leapt forward, his hands in a supplicatory gesture.

"Now, now – no need for unpleasantness. I'm sure we can all..." But before he could finish the sentence, from behind them came a sharp, metallic *snap*, and a cry of pain. Gisburne turned in time to see the younger knight recoil from the box, the forefinger of his ungloved right hand – beaded with a neat row of fresh, bloody punctures – going instinctively to his mouth.

"It bit me!" whined the young knight in disbelief. "The damn box, *bit* me!" His face looked suddenly flushed.

"Idiot!" said his older cousin, and with obvious exasperation shoved his comrade to one side, then Galfrid to the other. "You!" He slapped Gisburne on the side with the flat of his sword. "Who do you think you are, dolt?" His sword slapped again – harder, this time.

Before his blade could make contact a third time, it was snatched clean out of its astonished owner's grasp. Gisburne's free hand grabbed the knight by the throat and pulled him with such violence that he twisted and collapsed onto his knees. Gisburne stood behind him, the stolen blade across his throat, a space suddenly clear about them in the crowd, faces staring. "I am a knight," he hissed into the man's ear. "*Dolt...*"

"What is this?" The new voice – as heavy with authority as it was with age – boomed from an imposing man with greying beard and drooping moustache. His surcoat was of identical blue to the others – less gaudy in its cloth, but far finer in the making, its hems subtly embroidered with gold. The gawping onlookers stepped aside for this one as he strode past. He stopped before Gisburne and narrowed his eyes. "Who are you?"

Gisburne straightened up, and made as if to speak – but before he could utter a word, Galfrid again thrust himself between them. "My lord de Belleville..." He bowed low before the old knight. "This man – my noble master – is Bernard of Ickleford, second cousin to Balian of Ibelin, benefactor to the nuns of Ventnor, and loyal knight to Richard the Lionhearted of England, en route to the Holy Land to join his King in the pursuit of the Lord God's justice."

De Belleville stared at Galfrid in amazement. Gisburne tried hard not to look like he was doing the same. He released his hold on the knight, who staggered to his feet, shooting Gisburne an aggrieved and murderous look.

"Is this true?" demanded de Belleville. It was a moment before the knight realised the question – and de Belleville's indignation – were meant for him. His mouth opened, but no sound emerged.

"I am sure your man had every good reason to accost my master with a drawn sword," continued Galfrid. "These are trying times for those without the wisdom to fully understand them – though your own wisdom and compassion are well known, my lord." He bowed low again. De Belleville visibly softened before the flattery.

"He wouldn't speak," blustered the knight. "Can he not speak for himself?"

Galfrid, fearless, stepped up to the knight's chin. "He has – *had* – taken a vow of silence, raising his voice to no other than God until such time as Jerusalem is returned to Christendom."

"And *you* made him break it, imbecile!" barked de Belleville, striking the knight sharply across the head with his gauntleted hand. "You are lucky this man did not take your life, as by my reckoning he still has every right to do!" He then turned back to Gisburne, his expression full of remorse.

"Please accept my apologies, Sir Bernard. This man will do penance for his outrage." He glared back at the knight. "We are sworn to protect pilgrims, and respect our betters – though there has been shamefully little evidence of either today."

He turned his attention to the younger knight. "And where were *you* while all this was going on?" But the man merely shivered, and looked oddly distant, a sweat breaking out on his forehead in spite of the cold. "Gah!" exclaimed de Belleville, and turned from both in disgust.

Gisburne bowed his head, and offered up the knight's sword, hilt first. De Belleville took it.

"Go in peace, with our humble blessings," he said. "And, when you see your great and noble King, please tell him that Gervaise de Belleville sends his humble good wishes. We pray for his success, and hope he remembers us well." He shot another hot glance at his knights. "And also that he forgives us our failings." With that, he bowed low. Uncertain how else to respond, Gisburne bowed back.

Galfrid, seizing the advantageous moment to make an exit, began to push through the circle of knights. "Gentlemen..." They parted under de Belleville's stern gaze to allow the pair to pass.

They walked rapidly away, resisting the urge to look back.

"You *know* him?" muttered Gisburne when they were thirty yards distant.

"I wouldn't say 'know'," said Galfrid. "Know of. And it would hardly have helped matters if he had known me."

And what would he know, if he had known you? wondered Gisburne. "So, do you 'know of' many people?"

"A few."

"And... 'Bernard of Ickleford'?"

Galfrid sighed, as if having to explain something very obvious to someone very stupid. "Gervaise de Belleville is a profoundly pious man. So I gave you the name of his favourite saint and a place so small that he could not possibly know it or anything that might contradict my claims. He also fought alongside Balian, and hero-worships Richard."

"And the nuns?"

Galfrid shrugged. "I heard he liked nuns."

Gisburne tried not to let his smile show. The little man might have his uses after all.

"Tell me one thing," said Galfrid. "You weren't about to divulge your real name back there, were you?"

Gisburne's lack of response told Galfrid all he needed to know. He sighed deeply. "Just as well you'd taken a vow of silence then... Perhaps that was just wishful thinking on my part."

"I'm not a liar, Galfrid."

Galfrid's tone acquired a sharper edge. "You're no thief, either. But you'll have to learn to be both if we're to get through this. It's my arse in the fire, too, remember."

Gisburne decided there and then to share more of the truth with Galfrid. If nothing else, he could test his response – see if it met with a knowing look, or surprise, or perhaps merely the pretence of it. Though whether he would be able to detect anything beneath that unflappable façade was another matter.

"You know what this is all about?" said Gisburne.

"A treasure," said Galfrid. "That's all." His tone made it clear he neither expected nor needed more.

"A skull," said Gisburne. "The skull of John the Baptist."

Galfrid's eyebrows rose. "I wish you'd said earlier. There's one of those in a church in Kent." He thought for a moment. "So, we get the skull. Skull goes in the box..." There was another thoughtful silence, at the end of which he added: "About that box..."

Gisburne stopped, and went to the unassuming wooden casket that hung behind Nyght's saddle. At least, he had thought it was unassuming. It seemed, however, that at least one knight of France thought otherwise. Avoiding the row of six small steel spikes now projecting from just beneath the locked lid, Gisburne reached underneath, and pushed against an iron catch until there was an audible click. The spikes retracted into their holes and blended into the box's simple decoration. He took Nyght by the reins again.

"It's better you don't know," said Gisburne, and led his horse on.

Galfrid gave him a look. "Are you quite sure about that?" He gazed back towards the quayside where the crowd had closed about the blue-clad knights. "Our friend back there – the one who it... bit. He didn't know. And by the time we left he was looking decidedly... ill."

"He'll be fine," said Gisburne.

"Fine..."

"After a week or so, anyway."

"And before that?"

Gisburne shrugged. "In a few minutes, he'll start to think he's on fire. Then he'll collapse, expelling the contents of his stomach, bladder and bowels. Then he'll lose the use of his legs and he will become temporarily blind. And probably bleed profusely from his nose. If he doesn't choke to death, then he will probably start to hallucinate. And his whole body will be racked with violent cramps. Just for a few days."

Galfrid nodded slowly, thoughtfully. "And if *I* had happened to take a look at the box?"

"I told you not to touch it. You just have to trust me, Galfrid. I am your master, after all." He thought for a moment, then added – in a way intended to be conciliatory – "It's not in my interest for you to be out of the game."

"Hmm," said Galfrid, looking somehow not quite convinced. He cast another glance back in the direction from which they had come. "Well, then... Perhaps we'd best get a move on. Before the collapsing and vomiting and hallucinating."

At that, Gisburne had nodded. "Perhaps."

And then they had mounted their horses and put Calais far behind them.

XIII

"THROW IT DOWN there," barked Pig-Grease. "Then all the rest."

Gisburne made no movement. He could just throw down the box, he supposed. Let it bite again. But giving anything up to a thief – being dictated to by one – stuck in his craw. "A good fighter denies his enemy everything," Gilbert used to say. "When he's ready to fight, frustrate him. When he is unprepared, attack him." Gisburne had lived by this advice. He had also seen men die for ignoring it. And he had not yet got the measure of this enemy.

Impatient, Pig-Grease crept forward, his feet crunching on the icy snow. Nyght stamped and snorted, making him jump back. Rat-Face turned his bow on Gisburne again.

"My horse doesn't like you," said Gisburne.

The man's eyes blazed. "I don't give a shit what your stinking mare thinks!"

Nyght tossed his head, reared up and brought both front hooves down with a thud. Clearly he did not appreciate being mistaken for a mare.

There had been hundreds of mercenaries let loose over the years – soldiers taken on for a campaign, then set adrift when no longer needed. If these bandits were such men, they were dangerous indeed; if they had *killed* mercenaries to acquire their weapons, perhaps even more so. But Gisburne had seen many of those forbidding soldiers – had been one – and he did not see such men before him now.

"Jus' give it!" bellowed Pig-Grease, jabbing his sword at Gisburne. But even as he spoke, his eyes were taking in the quality of the horse, processing the possible reasons for it, and shadows of doubt were already beginning to cloud his face.

The sword clearly deserved – and had once had – a scabbard. But there was no scabbard to be seen – nothing but a wide, crude belt from which hung all manner of things: a broken-tipped knife, a small war hammer showing a bloom of rust and encrusted with filth, the wrapping around its grip half gone, and what looked to be a brace of whole rabbit skins. A killer would have taken the the scabbard as well. A scavenger, then. Or a thief.

"I give you nothing," said Gisburne. "If you want it, you'll have to take it."

"Then one of you dies." Pig-Grease swung his sword point towards Galfrid. "Him..." Rat-Face immediately turned the bow on the little man.

Clever, thought Gisburne. Out of his depth he might be, but he was quick thinking; resourceful. Pig-Grease knew now Gisburne didn't fear him. Perhaps had him pegged as a knight. So now he was exploiting his sense of chivalry instead – his supposed duty to protect the weak.

Gisburne's eyes flicked to Rat-Face. Even from where he was, he could see the bow was poorly looked after. Its shaft was darkened and battered, the bowstring likely worn of wax, and damp right through. The wood too. Assuming Rat-Face's arm didn't give out, or the bow snap in half from being drawn so long – or rather half-drawn, as it now was – its power would be diminished. It would still kill one of them at this range, of course, if the aim was good, but he now knew three things.

These men didn't know what they were doing, which meant their skills were poor. They preyed on those they believed weaker than themselves, which meant they feared a fight. And they had no idea what was about to happen to them.

"Kill him, then," said Gisburne, with a shrug.

"What?" The exclamation came simultaneously from Pig-Grease and Galfrid.

"Kill him," repeated Gisburne, more forcefully this time. "Then I can kill you." He pointed at Pig-Grease, then turned to Rat-Face. "And then him." Rat-Face's left eye twitched. There was little doubt that Gisburne could move faster than he could loose a second arrow – if he even had a second arrow.

It was Gisburne's turn to take a step forward now, his pilgrim staff clutched in his right fist. Pig-Grease flinched, sword still extended. Rat-Face switched his aim back to the knight, the arrow rattling against the yew of the over-tensioned bow. Gisburne thought he heard him whimper.

"Let's get this over with," said Gisburne, and took two sudden, decisive steps. Pig-Grease lunged at him with a roar. Gisburne sided-stepped and whipped the staff through the air in a broad arc.

The staff did not parry the sword blade. Nor did it hit the attacker's body – but struck where the sword's curved blade and cross-guard met. There was a sharp *crack* of impact. The sword went singing sideways through the air and sank into snow, its blank outline printed on the surface. Its owner staggered, seemed ready to rally, then stopped and stared stupidly at a second, tiny dint in the snow a couple of yards from him – its edges red-stained, a fine, dotted trail of crimson linking him to it. It took a moment – and the sight of the fresh red blood melting into the white immediately before him – to comprehend what he was looking at. At the bottom of the bloody hole was his freshly severed forefinger.

By the time he knew it, the air was split again, and the iron head of Gisburne's staff cracked across his temple. At the same moment, Galfrid spurred his horse with such violence that, even carrying all that weight, it reared high in the air, then thundered forward straight into the bushes where the cowering Rat-Face was watching his comrade fall. He yelped, panicked, tried to scramble backwards and fell, his arrow flying uselessly, pitifully into the air. Galfrid dismounted with surprising agility, kicked a rusty carving knife out of the whimpering clod's hand and snatched up the bow. It was still oddly bent about the grip. Had it been kept under tension any longer, it would have snapped in two. Galfrid broke it across his knee and flung it aside. "If you'd had a father, he might have taught you something about bowmanship!" he spat, then backhanded the man across the chops with such force that it flipped the thin man over onto his face. He lay that way, face down in the snow, sobbing, while Galfrid divested him of his remaining weapons, a look of distaste on his face.

XIV

PIG-GREASE'S CEASELESS, INCOMPREHENSIBLE ranting was getting on Gisburne's nerves. He'd seen it many times among men whose lives had disappointed them – who felt God, or the cosmos, or something owed them a favour. Whatever their bitterness towards the world, he couldn't see how shaking their fists at it would help. It was a waste of energy. "A bitter adversary is at war with himself," de Gaillon would have said, "and therefore has to fight on two fronts." De Gaillon had a saying for just about everything.

At first, as he and Galfrid had prepared their bonds – tying them back to back with their own rope – Gisburne had simply ignored it, as one ignores a spoilt child, hoping the fire would burn itself out. But Pig-Grease's bile seemed to flow from an infinite resource. Rather than simply put up with the noise, Gisburne had taken instead to delivering a lecture on their attackers' tactical shortcomings.

"You see, the first problem," he said, "is that you put yourselves in your own trap."

"I said this was a bad place for an ambush," whined Rat-Face.

"Shut your head!" rasped Pig-Grease. It was the first coherent thing he had said in some time.

"Actually, it's a good place for an ambush," continued Gisburne. "If you were on those rocks up there" – here he pointed towards the ridge above with his knife – "you could have picked us off with a bow – even a boulder – and there wouldn't have been a damn thing we could have done about it. But you were too afraid to kill us. With your own hands, anyway. You hoped the rope would do that work for you."

Galfrid lifted Pig-Grease's hands, which were tied in his lap before him. Pig-Grease struggled hard to pull them away, but the elderly squire held them in an iron grip, wrinkling his nose at the bloody stump where the forefinger used to be. "This won't hurt," he said, then sprinkled some brown powder onto the raw flesh from a small leather flask. Pig-Grease howled in agony. Expressionless, Galfrid turned away to tend their horses.

"Putting yourselves down here was the big mistake," continued Gisburne. He shook his head, and tutted. "Rocks on either side. Nowhere to run. And you have no horses. Even if you shot one of us, the other could ride you down. Trample you into the frozen ground." He shook his head again in dismay, and pulled the bonds tight about the pair. As he leaned in closer, Pig-Grease spat. The stringy phlegm stuck to Gisburne's shoulder.

"I'm a fair man," he said. "But you're seriously trying my patience." He stalked away and plucked the paramerion from its outline in the snow. Rat-Face wailed with anguish as Gisburne advanced towards them, closing his eyes and hunching into his shoulders as if somehow believing he could make himself disappear. But Gisburne strode straight past, thrusting its blade into the hard ground some thirty paces from where the two sat. "If you can crawl this far, you can cut your bonds before your arses freeze," he said. "By which time, we'll be long gone. If you can't, well... You'll have plenty of time to think on your errors."

Pig-Grease roared at him – spitting words that were either in another language entirely, or so warped with rage that they were rendered unintelligible. But there was little doubting the intent.

"Be thankful," said Gisburne, heaving himself into his saddle. "Others will come. Worse than us. They may not be content for you to simply lose a finger. So, if you want to live, I suggest you pick a new profession." Then, just before finally turning away, he added: "And sell the sword. It's worth more than all of us are carrying."

"Why did you spare them?" said Galfrid as they rode away.

"Because they were weak idiots," said Gisburne.

"But they still might prey on someone weaker. Some poor pilgrim."

Gisburne shrugged. "Maybe. Maybe not."

"My God," said Galfrid. "You actually think one or other of them has a chance. That they might reform their ways..."

"There's a possibility," said Gisburne.

"You're an optimist!" Galfrid chuckled. Then guffawed. It was the first time Gisburne had seen him laugh. It might have been a good thing, had it not been at his expense. "You believe men are good!" He hooted with laughter again.

"No," snapped Gisburne. "But everyone deserves the chance to be so. What of it?"

"Somehow, I never had you down as the type."

"I make no apology for not wishing to kill those weaker than me. I'm a knight. Not an executioner."

Galfrid pondered that for a moment, his laughter subsiding. "Don't you *always* kill those weaker than you? Those you have managed to defeat or subdue? I mean, in practice, don't they have to be weaker, in order..."

"Enough!" said Gisburne. "If I want a philosophical debate, I'll ask."

He almost found himself adding "I don't debate with squires," but he bit the words back. That, he realised, would have made him sound like the kind of knight he hated. He salved his conscience with the thought that *this* squire would try the patience of a saint.

They rode in silence for a moment before Galfrid spoke again. "I notice you weren't so protective of my existence." There was a pinched tone to his voice as he repeated Gisburne's words. "'Kill him, then'..."

Ah, so that was it. Feeling hard done by. Gisburne was damned if he was going to be made to feel guilty about that. "He was never going to loose that arrow," he protested. "It's like I said. If he'd meant it, he'd have pinned us from up there in the rocks. You saw his eyes. He was no killer."

"That's an optimist's view," said Galfrid matter-of-factly.

"I'm not an optimist," said Gisburne. "I'm a realist."

Galfrid sighed and shrugged. "Perhaps I'm no great loss."

On that, however, Gisburne refused to be drawn.

"Do us one favour," said Galfrid, eventually. "Put that bloody box in a sack." Then he geed his horse into a gallop.

XV

Paris – 29 November, 1191

THEY COULD SMELL Paris before they could see it.

At least three times the size of London, the infectious, burgeoning sprawl of humanity, with its crooked roofs and spires thrusting into the grey fog of woodsmoke hanging above, was an awe-inspiring sight to the approaching pilgrims. But the reek of its clustered humanity had been growing in their nostrils all the previous day.

The day had proven hard going – the weather dry, but with a bitterly cold wind blowing in their faces. It was not by the gusting wind that the stink of the city had first announced itself, however, but the Seine. Their approach had seemed to involve endless crossings back and forth across the meandering river, using ferries of ever more perilous construction piloted by ferrymen of dubious reliability.

One vessel, whose rope bindings were coming adrift, listed so alarmingly as it plied its treacherous course that Gisburne was convinced, half way across, that they and their horses were doomed to be pitched into the icy, open sewer. Another benefited from an operator who flatly refused to to move until more passengers came along, forcing them to huddle in the bitter wind for hours until this became the case. Without exception, they grew increasingly decrepit and more ridiculously overpriced as the distance from Paris diminished.

Soon, the long-threatened snow had begun to fall and darkness enveloped them, and – when literally close enough to smell the French capital – they had finally been forced to seek lodgings several miles short of their goal.

They had limped into a ragged gathering of huddled dwellings just off the thoroughfare. Gisburne, having expected to dine well that night in one of the world's greatest cities, had expressed the gloomy opinion that their chances of a decent meal now looked slim. "I'd eat mud if it was hot," Galfrid had said. Gisburne thought he had also attempted to smile, but that his face was simply too frozen to adequately express anything other than cold.

They sought lodgings at a low, hump-backed building with a flag outside that indicated pilgrims were welcome. Inside, the welcome was rather less evident. The fire was meagre, and around the cramped interior sat a few gloomy, exhausted-looking patrons who looked upon the new arrivals with an expression that seemed part pity, part plea for rescue. Too tired to argue, Gisburne and Galfrid sought out the patron to secure shelter for the night. Reassuringly rotund, with gap teeth and sunken, piggy eyes, he turned out to be a jolly fellow indeed, greeting them like long-lost friends and promising them the finest food and lodging for miles around. When it came, however, the ale was watery, the bread as hard as wood, and the grey, greasy stew that accompanied it barely edible. It had evidently seen meat of some kind, though of that there was now no visible sign. Beneath the sour tang of onions that had begun to rot was another strangely rank aftertaste, like dead fish. Gisburne did not want to think about why that was.

"About that mud..." said Galfrid, with a despondent air. Gisburne shot back a look that was half smile, half grimace, and forced down another spoonful of the filthy, lukewarm concoction.

Gisburne had been trying to be more conciliatory to Galfrid since Amiens, three days earlier. Whilst there, Galfrid had insisted – actually *insisted* – that they visit the cathedral. Gisburne had refused. His preferred plan was to keep to the outskirts and not touch the centre of the city at all.

"But it's what pilgrims do," Galfrid had said, making no attempt to hide his frustration.

"It's not what we do," Gisburne had replied.

"And do you want everyone to know that?"

Gisburne had not been convinced. "Galfrid – no one knows. No one cares. We travel. We rest. That's all. Our destination is a long way off, and I aim to get there before spring."

Galfrid had sulked for the rest of the day, gazing elegiacally at the cathedral's distant towers as they passed, and making Gisburne – much to his own annoyance – feel like a father who had been forced to discipline a demanding child. He also felt guilty. That annoyed him, too. It was too late to back down; it had been a point of principle, and his reasoning was perfectly sound. But perhaps he had grown too used to his own company in the past few years, too used to pleasing only himself and doing things his way. He had never asked for help, never wanted this companion on his journey. But now he had him, like it or not. And, while this strange little man seemed to adopt a gloomy air as a matter of course, Galfrid had never actually complained, but for this one point. He had done everything that was needed and more, and matched his master's pace in terrible conditions without batting an eye. Gisburne wondered if he had pegged Galfrid all wrong. Perhaps this man he thought to be a cynic was pious after all, and he had offended his religious sensibilities. He didn't think so.

Gisburne pushed away the remains of the putrid stew and looked around furtively. He was tired to the bone, but there was a niggling sense of frustration that wouldn't let him rest just yet.

"Do you suppose there's anywhere around here where we can at least get a decent drink?" he said.

"There are always those bottles of yours," replied Galfrid.

Gisburne simply smiled, and shook his head, as Galfrid knew full well he would. Then, without another word, both stood and prepared to plunge out into the night.

There were times when Gisburne was surprised by his own optimism. The prospect of anything out in this bleak, freezing night seemed slim, and as they trudged on past the few dwellings, the wind and snow lashing their wrapped faces, even he was on the verge of giving up and heading back to the paltry hospitality they had just left. It was better than nothing – better than being out in this. But some impulse drove him to follow the turn in the road ahead, to at least satisfy himself that there was nothing beyond it.

The few dwellings having been left behind, the way was now flanked by dark, dense trees which seemed to promise nothing but mile upon mile of disordered nature. As they rounded the bend, however, they saw not the expected expanse of forest, but another clearing, and more buildings, and among them, not far ahead, a long, low roof beneath which an encouraging light glowed. From it, as if in response to their wish, and gusting on the merciless wind, came the sound of raucous, drink-fuelled singing. Gisburne and Galfrid looked at each other and actually laughed.

The inn was the Heaven to the Hell of their own bleak lodgings. The fire blazed, beer, cider and wine flowed, and hot bodies crammed every corner. The air was thick with the smell of sweat and the damp fur of the dogs that cavorted about the straw-strewn floor, tempered with the sharp, yeasty tang of spilt ale, and the aromas of seared meat, warm spices and woodsmoke. In one corner, about a crude, circular table of absurdly large proportions, sat almost a dozen knights, and about and between them, a similar number of fresh-faced lads of various ages – squires – who the knights were evidently trying to get drunk. This company, Gisburne was sure, had been the source of the singing. The song had now abated, but someone – Gisburne could not see who – was playing a jaunty tune on a whistle-pipe. Hands beat time on the table tops, joining the clamour of talk and laughter.

Both looked around in wonder, pulling off their wrappings and squeezing in to find a space about a barrel, with upended logs serving as stools. By the fire, Gisburne now saw, spiced wine was steaming in a pot. They had two cups and a jug brought to them, and supped and smiled stupidly as the warm, sweet brew flowed through them. The irony of the situation was not lost on the pair. Not only had they stopped short of their goal by only a few miles, they had fallen short of this, far more generous accommodation by mere yards. Not that it mattered now.

Gisburne eyed the party about the big table. He was wary of groups of knights away from the duties of service or war. Too often, they seemed to feel a lack when these things were not present, and sought to fill it in ways that were troublesome. And he had seen even good men – who, when encountered alone, were as gentle and honourable as one could wish – turn oafish and rowdy in the company of others.

He had been wondering if such was the case with this group, and had resolved this night to remain as unobtrusive as possible, just in case, when a cheery shout went up amongst them. They clapped and roared words of encouragement, and up onto the table was hoisted a gangly lad – a squire who could not have had more than eleven summers on him. His face was flushed and embarrassed. But there was no fear in it. He took a deep breath. The knights fell suddenly silent, and the boy raised his clear voice in song.

It was a tune Gisburne had heard many times before, one he knew only as *Por mon coraige*; an old song favoured by knights. It told of one leaving all he loved to fight in other lands. The beautiful, simple melodic lines unfolded, piercing the din of the tavern, and as it reached their ears, each within fell silent, one by one, until the only sounds were the pure notes rising and falling, the crack of the fire, and the wind that buffeted the rooftop. Around the table, the knights – men who had undoubtedly survived unspeakable horrors and hardships – stared into their drinks, lost in memory of all they had won and lost, tears coursing down their faces. When he finished, and let his head drop, there was a moment of silence when even the wind seemed to abate. The cheer that followed shook the rafters.

After their return, Gisburne and Galfrid settled down for the night on pallets in a cramped, dank room that played host that evening to three other travellers. Gisburne lay a long time in the dark, listening to the grunting and farting of his fellow pilgrims, the sharp, sickly tang of dead mice in his nostrils. The smell – perhaps spurred on by the presence of the knights in the inn – had evoked a powerful memory. He rubbed the scar on his brow – the flesh had begun to itch, as if itself remembering.

THEY REACHED PARIS a day – or, at least, part of a day – later than Gisburne had wished. The advantage to their late arrival in the city was that they had arrived in daylight. Galfrid had been dismissive from the start. "It's like London," he'd said, "but more cramped, more filthy and with worse food."

Gisburne's first impressions were of a city at once brand new and in a state of advanced decay. The wind was gusting from the southeast that day, and carried before it the full stink of the hectic, noisy, heaving hive of grandiose squalor. But, as they approached from the northwest, it seemed that that there was no corner where some building was not taking place. Around the entire metropolis, as far as the eye could see, were massive, half-built walls, punctuated by piles of sand or gravel and heaps of stones. The snow was trampled and tracked by hundreds of hooves and wheels that constantly came and went. Around every edifice, teetering scaffolds crawled with men who toiled ceaselessly with chisel and hammer while, about their heads, wooden cranes and windlasses swung and creaked under the weight of fresh masonry. Before the walls, to the south, as they approached Porte St Honoré, the landscape had been scoured and scraped of every living thing for miles around, and from this barren patch of bare, frozen earth, grit and icy puddles – broken and heaped and dug with vast ditches – rose massive, round towers and more thick walls of stone. A fortress fit for giants. Galfrid – who seemed to know everything about everything – informed Gisburne that this was the king's new palace and royal arsenal. He had always envied London its Tower, and now meant to raise something even more grotesque. Gisburne asked if the palace had a name. Galfrid, with a snort of what may have been contempt at the French powers of imagination, said they simply called it "*L'Oeuvre*" – "the work".

Philip, it seemed, was a fanatical builder. Gisburne knew – because it was the one part of Paris for which Galfrid showed any enthusiasm – that in the heart of the city, on the Île de la Cité, the great cathedral of Notre-Dame was also being raised. Philip had paved the main streets that crossed the city from north to south and from east to west, too, and built vast new markets at Halles Champeaux. Another of his innovations was the gallows of Montfaucon north of Paris. The criminals who were hanged there were left to rot as a warning to others, and in deference to the status of the dead, the place had become a public dumping ground for all other foul and stinking waste that the river could not carry away.

At Galfrid's suggestion, they found lodging for themselves and their horses away from the centre of the city. Galfrid wished to continue on foot – to see the cathedral, he said – and this time, Gisburne resolved not to deny him this one pleasure. The cathedral was next to the current royal palace – the supposed final destination of the skull – and that was something Gisburne wished to see for himself. And so he donned his pilgrim hat – which he abhorred – and took up his staff.

As they advanced, the signs of innovation melted away, and the dingy, fungal maze of streets closed in about them.

Streets gave way to alleys, alleys to nooks not even wide enough to turn a horse. Up above, the teetering upper floors of the houses leaned in so close that Gisburne calculated one could easily piss from one open window to that opposite. And as the byways narrowed, the number of people grew. More than Gisburne had ever seen. Jerusalem had been populous – always bustling – but it was nothing like this. On every side, dirty figures shoved and jostled – young men, old women, children – occasionally regarding him with weary, blank eyes. Gisburne fought through the grim tide, oppressed by it. He felt like a knight's pell, a straw-stuffed obstacle to be struck and kicked about. People of all ages begged or tried to sell them useless or rotting wares – things that, for the most part, looked as if they had just been picked up in the street. Mud-caked harlots plied their trade everywhere one looked, some with an almost evangelical zeal. On more than one occasion Gisburne had to physically repel them, and saw one strapping woman – with hair like Medusa, the muscles on her bare arms like whipcords – literally drag a cleric away to her lair.

About their legs, rats, dogs, fowls and the occasional pig – all the same dun colour as the trampled slush and mud, and all scrawny – darted and fought with each other over unidentifiable scraps, some with the intention of making a meal of their rival. Here and there were dead creatures – or parts of them. Once or twice Gisburne saw figures lying in the ordure at the street's edge, the throng stepping over them on their hurried way. Whether they were alive or dead, he had no idea. Once, along a descending alley, a band of dark-eyed men with sticks came by, and the people stood aside. Gisburne and Galfrid did likewise, though what their purpose was, they never discovered.

If white was the colour of virginity, then Paris was a whore. In past days there had been a generous fall of fresh snow, but almost nowhere was it the good, honest white it was meant to be. Where feet, hooves and wheels passed – which was nearly everywhere – it had been churned and trodden to a grey-brown, icy sludge, its hue varying according to the neighbourhood. There were strict rules about what could and could not be emptied into the city streets, of course, but in this chaos – this abyss – enforcing anything was a virtual impossibility. In streets close to the river where certain trades predominated, one could tell the nature of the work not only from the dominant stink – a year-round feature, especially notable in summer – but from the distinctive colour of its effluent, thrown into even sharper relief where it stained the few untrodden patches of snow. There was grey snow outside the blacksmiths, red where the butchers had their shops and slaughteryards, yellow in the rows of tanneries clustered along the north bank of the Seine. Down one side street, where the snow was relatively untouched, Gisburne saw that it was blue. What had caused it, he could not guess. And everywhere, no matter what the trade, was the yellow-brown splatter of emptied chamber pots – 100,000 of them in continuous use in this one city, and tipped out of windows God knew how many times a day. If it was true what they said about the effect of cities on one's guts, this was a frequent occurrence indeed. Eventually, all this – excrement, urine, blood, offal, and the chemicals from tanning and dyeing – would find its way into the river, the same river from which the city's water was drawn.

Gisburne tried to visualise such an extraordinary quantity of shit, but found he could not. In the countryside where he grew up there had been muckheaps of almost legendary size, but they were specks in comparison. Surely, one day, the city would simply consume itself. He gave it ten years.

At last, the human tide flowing through the street drained into open space – the bank of the Seine opposite the Île de la Cité. Here, the general tumult was joined by the protests of horses, the rumble of carts and the cries of the traders whose stalls stood across the bridges.

Beneath the arches of the Grand Pont, great millstones turned day and night, driven by the open sewer of the Seine, grinding grain into flour for the next day's bread.

Galfrid gazed across the bridge – packed with merchants hawking their wares, and hectic with every kind of noble, knight, ruffian and trader – to the royal palace beyond.

"Well," said Galfrid. "That is where the skull is *supposed* to end up..."

Gisburne scanned the terrain from beneath his broad-brimmed hat. Back towards the Rue St Denis, his eyes came to rest on a small group of figures in white, red crosses emblazoned across their chests.

"Templars..." muttered Gisburne. He regarded them with a mix of respect and caution. The military order of monks known as the Knights Templar paid no taxes, passed unhindered through any borders and were answerable to no king. They were a formidable force – their coffers deep, their influence wide. It was wise to tread carefully where Templars were concerned.

"'Poor Fellow-Soldiers of Christ and of the Temple of Solomon', to give them their proper title," said Galfrid. He looked at Gisburne, then gave a shrug. "Although 'Templars' is shorter." Then something caught his eye. He squinted sideways at them, trying not to look too much like he was looking. "And these are not just Templars..."

Gisburne followed Galfrid's gaze, trying to obscure his own look under his headgear.

"You see that red ribbon tied about their left arms? That is the mark of Tancred de Mercheval. The White Devil."

"So, he is here," said Gisburne. "To see the King, I suppose?"

Galfrid shrugged. "Perhaps. Or simply heading south from Castel Mercheval. To collect his prize. And getting the lay of the land as he does so. And before you say it, no, we could not carry out the robbery here."

It was exactly what Gisburne had been thinking.

"It's tempting, I know. A city in chaos. A smash and grab raid. I don't doubt there would be a way we could snatch it. But what then? Their obstacles would also become ours. We'd never get out of the city alive."

"There's always the sewers," said Gisburne, wryly.

Galfrid simply gave him a withering look, as if the idea did not warrant serious consideration. "The streets *are* the sewers," he said. "This isn't Jerusalem."

Gisburne decided to let it go. He nodded towards the knot of men. "Is Tancred one of them?"

Galfrid laughed. "No..."

"So, why do they call him the White Devil?"

"They say he died and came back."

"How?"

"You'll know when you see him," replied Galfrid, and would say no more.

The Templars were momentarily swallowed up by the throng – but now, something else caught Gisburne's eye. Something at odds with everything around. A vision.

Swaying above the jostle and din, hoisted by an unnecessarily handsome quartet of green-liveried servants, was a litter. It had evidently just traversed the bridge, and was heading away from the royal palace towards Rue St Denis. And seated upon it, gazing with languid expression upon the hoipolloi of Paris, was one of the most beautiful women Gisburne had ever seen.

She was a uniquely bright thing in all this grim chaos. Her cloak was a marvel of blue silk with an ermine lining as white as fresh snow. Over a white chemise decorated with flowers, she wore a tunic of green silk, also completely lined with fur, body and sleeves. To enhance the beauty of her neck – which was, Gisburne had to admit, considerable – she had placed a clasp on her chemise that permitted an opening of a finger's width, through which one could glimpse the pale curve of her breasts. The clasp itself was a masterpiece of craftsmanship, gold and shaped like the sun with a bright yellow stone at its centre. On her head – framing her rosebud mouth, her shapely nose, her large, limpid green eyes – was a wimple of white picked out in gold, and about her slim waist a belt fitted with a golden buckle. A single tendril of red-gold hair escaped the wimple's edge, as if refusing to be contained.

She stifled a yawn, cast her eyes momentarily in Gisburne's direction, and for an instant their gazes met. She looked hard at him, then turned swiftly away.

Gisburne heard Galfrid's voice in his ear. "That is Mélisande de Champagne, daughter of the Count of Boulogne, granddaughter of King Stephen of England."

Then, as if in answer to the question that had sprung unbidden into Guy's mind, the squire added: "And wife of... no one. Yet."

Gisburne gazed as the litter wove its way onward through the crowd, momentarily lost.

Without warning, something heavy cuffed his head – so hard he staggered where he stood, his hat bowling onto the ground. The blow was swift and brutal. While it didn't feel as though it had drawn blood, it had about it the unmistakable heft and clink of metal. A familiar image leapt into his rattled brain. A mailed gauntlet. The hand of a knight.

"Filthy cur!" barked a voice.

Gisburne righted himself and turned to face his aggressor. Behind him stood four tall, broad-shouldered men. At their centre, and scowling at him from within a mane and beard of flame-red hair with a face of astonishing pinkness and appalled expression, like a freshly castrated hog, was his accuser. All wore the mail of a knight, a familiar white surcoat, and a red ribbon about the left arm.

Tancred's men.

Gisburne knew the elite military orders well. He had stood alongside them in battle, seen them fight and die. But he immediately recognised the type of knights that now faced him. The worst kind – men trained to fight, raised on dreams of battle, who yearned for nothing else, and yet were denied it. He knew they hungered to be in the Holy Land, suffering any deprivation or hardship as long as they were able to kill for the Christian cause. He knew, too, that for men such as this, the Christian cause was perhaps not their primary motivation, but a convenient excuse. His mentor, Gilbert de Gaillon, had warned against loving combat for its own sake. "It is a means," he would say, "never an end. One who fights for the sake of fighting has forgotten why he does it. Such a man dies soon, and for the most desolate of reasons – for no reason at all."

To Gilbert, the very height of stupidity was to engage in a battle that did not need to be fought. But some, Gisburne knew, could not help themselves. Away from the fight, they felt useless. Impotent. They hated it – hated themselves – and so turned their hatred outwards, seeking conflict with everyone and everything around them. Such men would find a fight, or make one. Through all his battles, from the castles of France to the scorched plains of the Holy Land – battles in which the enemies had at first seemed clear – Gisburne had come to understand that the real threat to order came not from without, but from men such as this. They were the destroyers of peace, the agents of chaos. The ones who lusted all the more for battle when peace was upon them.

"How dare you gaze upon a lady thus?" The response that first sprang to mind – that he would look at whatever the hell he liked, in whatever manner he liked – remained behind clenched teeth. Instead, he said something he had never before said in his life.

"Peace be with you, brother." And with that, he turned and walked away. He heard Galfrid sigh with relief as they went, picturing the throng closing around them as they plunged back into the current of human traffic.

Within moments, a rough hand spun him back round, and the ham-coloured flesh of the Templar was in his face once again. The quest for anonymity – the hoped-for dissolution back into one of the greatest concentrations of humanity in Christendom – had not been successful. Nor, Gisburne saw, could it ever have been. Around the Templars, even where the crowd were hard-pressed one against another, all maintained a fearful distance, eyes carefully averted.

"'Brother'?" spat the man. "I'm not your brother. Do I look like the bastard son of a pox-ridden whore?" Gisburne felt Galfrid's restraining grip on his elbow. But it was not needed. Various possible responses – many accurate, none particularly diplomatic – flashed through Gisburne's mind. But, using all the will he could muster, he kept his mouth resolutely shut. Teeth clenched, straining to contain his outraged spirit as if it were a breath that had been held too long, Gisburne smiled weakly, gave a slight bow as if in obsequious apology, and turned once more.

Gisburne had not gone two paces before a hand in the back of his belt stopped him dead. The remaining Templars – four in all – circled around him like dogs. He and Galfrid could go in no direction now that was not physically barred by their persecutors. His persecutor rounded on him.

"We're not done."

"You're making a mistake," said Gisburne. He felt Galfrid tense beside him.

"You dare question *me*? I didn't mistake the filthy look in your eye... *pilgrim*." He spat the final word as if it were the grossest insult – but Gisburne could see a flicker of uncertainty in his eye. He looked hard into it.

"No, the mistake is what you're doing now."

Involuntarily, the Templar's face fell. Gisburne, implacable, did not move, did not break eye contact, did not even blink. He could see the fear in in this man's soul – could see the gnawing self-doubt that he had suddenly and inadvertently revealed, making the knight, even now, consider defeat. Gilbert de Gaillon's words drifted back into his mind as they always did on such occasions. "Battles are first fought in the mind," he would say. "One who believes he may lose is already half-defeated."

Breaking away, as if suddenly aware that this strange pilgrim had seen too deeply, the Templar covered it with a raucous laugh. His fellows joined in as he turned to face them, then completed the circle back to Gisburne, his confidence visibly rallying at the sound. So, this was a man whose strength came not from within, but from without. It needed reassurance. He was weak.

"So what is it we have here?" he bellowed, far louder than he needed to, coming so close to Gisburne's face now that he could feel the man's spit hit his face as he spoke. "A *fighting* pilgrim? Oh! Pardon me, I have mistaken you, Sir Knight...?" He bowed low, his voice fluttering in a girlish mockery of apology. Gisburne felt Galfrid's grip tighten on his elbow. The man straightened. "Well, I knew those Hospitaller bastards were desperate, but *you*...?" His fellow Templars guffawed. "So, is there fight in you, *pilgrim*?" He poked Gisburne hard in the chest as he spoke. "Is there?"

"There won't be a fight," said Gisburne in a monotone. Galfrid relaxed his grip.

The Templar frowned, simply bemused this time. "Oh? I suppose you mean to assault me with your piety. Do you mean to persuade me to throw down my weapons and follow the path of peace, when mighty Saladin and his godless minions could not?" His comrades giggled like boys at the absurdity of this suggestion.

"Not exactly," said Gisburne, and smashed his forehead with unrestrained ferocity into the

Templar's nose. He felt the crunch as it flattened against the red face, saw the disbelief as its owner reeled backwards, the previously flushed face instantly paling – but for the gush of crimson that cascaded from its wrecked centre, clashing grimly as it drenched the coppery beard. Gisburne was vaguely aware of a drip of something on his own face as he braced himself for his next move – his enemy's blood, he supposed. Before the knight could regain his wits or his fellows recover from shock, Gisburne had rammed the iron head of his pilgrim's staff full force into the Templar's unguarded stomach, then, as he doubled up, had whipped it around and cracked the wood across the back of the man's skull. He went down like a sack of grain.

Two of the Templars already had their swords drawn. Galfrid's hand went instinctively to his belt – but neither had anything larger than a knife on them.

"Grab this!" cried Gisburne, extending the pilgrim staff towards him.

Galfrid did so – then looked startled as Gisburne pulled at it.

"Hold it fast," Gisburne said, and pulled hard again. It clicked, and the top eight inches, around which his fingers were clasped, came away from the rest of the staff. Two short metal bars sprang out to form a crosspiece. Then, in one swift movement, Gisburne drew out three feet of double-edged steel blade. Galfrid, suddenly understanding why the damn staff had been so heavy, looked in astonishment at the slender sword, then at the wooden scabbard in his hand. He had the less favourable end of this stick – but it was better than nothing.

Gisburne did not wait to defend himself, but hurled himself at the nearest of the Templars. Ill-prepared, the Templar flinched and raised his blade in reflex, stepping back as he did so. Gisburne whipped his blade around and smacked it into the knight's exposed ribs. It would not penetrate his mail, Gisburne knew – but being struck with a length of steel would still give him pause for thought. If the knight's blade hit him, however, it would be a different story – but for a coat of horsehide, he was completely unprotected.

He felt a rib crack, and the man doubled in pain. Gisburne brought the pommel of his staff-sword down on the man's head and sent him sprawling as the second knight advanced on him. But Galfrid's stick was already swinging. Its solid end caught the Templar square in the teeth with a sickening crunch, ensuring his apple-eating days were over.

The other two had their swords drawn, but they stood back – wary, now, of their adversaries. Gisburne was suddenly aware that a large ring had formed about them in the crowd, some gawping with thrilled delight, others at its edge looking trapped, and like they would rather have six or seven people between them and these men with drawn weapons. Deeper into the crowd, the litter bearing Mélisande de Champagne swayed dangerously as its servants fought to distance her from the fight.

Gisburne drew his blade back over his shoulder, ready to strike. "Do you concede?" he said.

They said nothing. But they did not laugh, either.

"Take them," said Gisburne, and lunged forward.

"It's all right for you," said Galfrid. "All I have is a stick!" But it was no time for arguments. He whirled it around his head in a great arc, and charged at the other.

Gisburne's opponent was wily. He appeared to stand firm, only side-stepping at the last moment. Gisburne, sword raised for the attack, found himself charging empty air, and began to fall. It was a simple but effective move – the knight would now swing around and strike Gisburne full force in the back or neck, killing or crippling him instantly.

But Gisburne knew the training. He had fought countless battles, and he had read the move. As he fell, he twisted his body, letting his blade swing out and up. It connected as the knight's own sword was flashing towards its target, striking his hand with the mid-point of the blade and sending the Templar's sword flying into the startled audience. As Gisburne hit the ground, he heard the Templar howl and saw him leap about, clutching his right hand. It was mail clad, but he wouldn't be playing the lute any time soon.

Galfrid, meanwhile, had succeeded only in keeping his opponent at bay. His whistling, whirling staff was far longer than the knight's sword. The knight – who swore under his breath in some Germanic tongue – couldn't get close enough to strike, and edged backwards, occasionally hacking at the stick in an attempt to parry and dislodge it.

He was waiting for Galfrid to tire. Gisburne could see that unless a decisive move was made against him, the Templar would succeed in disarming Galfrid in moments. He also realised that the knight, moving gradually closer to where he now lay, was entirely oblivious to him lying on the ground. So Gisburne drew his eating knife from his belt and stabbed the man in the foot.

When Gisburne regained his feet, the knight was hopping comically. With one push, he toppled him over. There were a few laughs from the audience. Someone clapped.

Gisburne and Galfrid looked about at the circle of amazed faces, their dazed and wounded opponents already beginning to stir.

"I suggest we run away," said Galfrid.

"Agreed," said Gisburne, snatching up his hat. And they barged their way into the crowd and headed back towards the maze of streets.

"So much for not drawing attention," said Galfrid as they ran. "Thanks to you, I didn't get to see the cathedral!"

"It's only half a cathedral anyway," said Gisburne. "Come back when you're eighty. They might even have the front door finished by then."

And so they made their way up the Rue St Denis and disappeared into its anonymous side streets, both unaware that their progress was being followed by the green eyes of Mélisande de Champagne.

XVI

Auxerre – 4 December, 1191

BEFORE THEY HAD reached Courances, Gisburne knew that Nyght would go no further.

The past few days – and especially their eventful flight from Paris – had taken it out of the poor beast. And it wasn't just his horse that Gisburne was thinking of. Galfrid had been right; Nyght's gait was not suited to long distance travel, and now his master's arsebones were suffering.

As they sat in yet another inn on yet another endless road, he thought of his poor raven-black courser, now many miles behind them, and of his poor arsebones. They were recovering now, thanks to the chestnut palfrey he had been riding. But those pains were as nothing to the pangs of guilt he now suffered – and the looks of "I told you so" from his squire. That horse had saved his life. Both of their lives. And how had he thanked him?

A platter was slammed on the table top. The gruff old woman – half Gisburne's size – glared at them both. "Ham," she said, and stalked off.

The place had felt unpromising from the the start: an otherwise empty and seemingly little-frequented place on the outskirts of Auxerre with a hatchet-faced patroness who slapped the bowls and platters upon the table top as if personally insulted. But they were in no mood to be choosy. The previous night they had been forced to camp in the woods, and it was something Gisburne wished not to repeat. They had managed a fire, but it had seemed every bit as reluctant to be there as they, and it had felt to Gisburne that he spent more time nursing the damp, smouldering branches than actually sleeping.

He had also had an uncanny feeling that they were being watched. On one occasion, he swore he could see a shadow moving among the trees. A vertical shadow. He knew every kind of beast that lived in the forests, but there was only one that walked on two legs. It was not until the next day, when he had finally confided in Galfrid, that the squire confessed that he, too, had thought there was something – or someone – watching them.

But tonight, at least, they had a bed and a hot meal. The food, when it came, far exceeded the expectations inspired by their surroundings. The bean soup, thickened with bread, was flavourful and deeply satisfying, the ham smoky and delicious. There were pickled vegetables too, and although there was no wine – that was too grand for this humble place – the ale was good. Gisburne took another slice of ham with his eating knife. It was the very same one with which he'd stabbed the Templar. He'd killed a man with it once – through necessity rather than choice. It was a fact that slid through his mind every time he used it to cut meat. But he would not change it. This knife was hard won. It had been with him since he was a boy – since that time with de Gaillon. The time when everything changed. He stabbed a chunk of ham and raised it to his mouth, glad now they had the place to themselves.

Just five days before, they had been sitting in a very different inn somewhere in Paris. It had been a bustling, jolly place run by Greeks who practically accosted people on the streets – pilgrims, mainly – and hustled them inside. The perfect place to lose themselves after the fight with the Templars.

Once inside, however, Galfrid had mostly complained about having to pay tourist prices. Gisburne could tell he had been rattled by the encounter, and he had learned in recent days that a grumpy Galfrid was a difficult thing to deal with.

"Can't you just be happy to be alive?" Gisburne had said, and knocked back his drink. The wine was fair, the bread and cheese decent enough. And he was famished. The fact that they'd paid over the odds was of little consequence.

"What I'm not happy about," he said, "is that we were almost dead." Galfrid looked at his plate, sulkily. "You might at least have told me about the staff."

Gisburne shrugged and hacked at the bread with his eating knife. "Now you know."

"That was one of Llewellyn's, I suppose?"

"You know of Llewellyn?" Once again, Galfrid had managed to surprise him.

"I know of a lot of people," he said. "But that's not going to be a lot of use if you keep getting us into fights. We can't keep trusting to luck."

Gisburne narrowed his eyes. He didn't get them into any fight. And it wasn't luck that saved them. But he decided to let it go.

"Templars aren't what they used to be," he said. "Not if they're taking the likes of that red-bearded cur."

"Fulke," said Galfrid. "He is Tancred's red right hand."

Gisburne drank deeply from his cup and stared at Galfrid, amazed once again. "Is there anyone in Christendom you don't know?" he said.

Despite his good humour, he cursed the ill luck that had caused them to blunder into their foe. He especially did not like the fact that Fulke now knew what they looked like.

His fears were realised as they were leaving Paris the next day.

They had set out early that morning, heading south, out of the city. It had turned colder, and fresh pinpricks of snow were falling. Snow was not so bad – at least, not when it was like this, with flakes too small and too compact to stick to their clothes. What he did not want was rain. Their thick woollen cloaks would hold it off for a time, but no matter how they wrapped themselves against it, they would eventually get soaked through. As long as they were moving, and their bodies generating heat, they would get by. But if they stopped for any length of time, they would freeze.

These were the thoughts occupying his mind when Galfrid jolted him out of his reverie.

In the road ahead were five mounted men.

All were in full armour, helms upon their heads, three with maces and poleaxes, two with couched lances. Gisburne did not immediately recognise the one at their centre without his Templar surcoat. But as they neared, he saw that it was their red-headed friend from the Grand Pont. At first, he supposed the other four must be his Templar comrades. But gradually he realised – from their build, from their grim demeanour – that they were not. They were mercenaries, hired by Fulke for this act of revenge. Perhaps he had not wished to involve his fellow knights. Perhaps they had some greater sense of honour than he. But it was this that told Gisburne they meant to kill him. Plus, of course, the fact that Fulke had put off his Templar colours – an act forbidden by the Temple, which insisted its knights wear the cross at all times. As Gisburne knew well, one did not go in disguise unless one was going to commit a crime.

So much for the Templar's sworn duty to protect the pilgrim, he thought.

"What now?" said Galfrid. Gisburne, who had happily taken on such odds on foot, and would do so again, knew that to do so with knights on horseback was suicide.

"Evade them. Outrun them," he said. "That's our only chance."

"But they're blocking the road," said Galfrid. The men were now drawing their horses into a line. "And I think they're preparing to charge."

"They are," said Gisburne.

"So what do we do?"

"What they don't expect," said Gisburne. "We charge first." And with that, Nyght leapt to the gallop at the point of Gisburne's spurs. Galfrid's normally placid horse reared in alarm, and with a great cry he charged after his master.

Gisburne had drawn not his sword, but his pilgrim staff, which he whirled around his head, its five foot length roaring in great arcs as he thundered towards the mounted men. He knew Nyght would not willingly career into another horse. He trusted their mounts to have the same wisdom – but the men would try to put everything in his way.

What happened next was a blur in Gisburne's memory. There was a clash. Something glanced off the pommel of his saddle. The staff connected jarringly with metal. He realised that he had got past the riders without being struck, and that one of them was unhorsed by his blow. Now all they had to do was ride for their lives.

Then he saw Galfrid's horse, riderless. He wheeled around. Galfrid was alive, and running, but a moment away from being ridden down by one of their attackers – and now Fulke and one of his hired killers were heading for Gisburne.

Galfrid darted left, into the trees. Clever move, thought Gisburne. Amongst the trees, the man on foot had the advantage. An idea struck him. He turned his horse and, flattening himself against Nyght's back, plunged into the forest.

One of his pursuers – not Fulke – tried to follow and immediately struck a branch. Gisburne heard him fall heavily. He tried to turn Nyght about, looking for Galfrid, but could see nothing of him. Then there was a whistle from somewhere above. Gisburne rode towards it. Down from a tree swung Galfrid, dropping onto Nyght behind Gisburne.

He did not wait. Spurring his horse, he wove his way through the trees back to the highway, and rode for his life.

XVII

GALFRID HAD SAT for what seemed like hours by the foot of the cross. He was frozen to the bone, and certain Gisburne must be dead.

After their encounter on the road, Gisburne had finally stopped at the roadside calvary, the sound of other hooves having long since faded. Galfrid had slithered off Nyght's back, pale, exhausted, and struggled to straighten himself. By some miracle he was uninjured, but the ride had nearly killed him. Gisburne, however, had shown no signs of dismounting.

"Wait here," said Gisburne.

"Wha–?" Galfrid was not even able to articulate a complete question before Gisburne turned his horse and rode back the way he had come. *Wait here*. For what? For how long? For a few moments? Or until Gisburne had ridden to Marseille and completed his quest? The man had given him no clue. As the morning had crept past and Galfrid's arse had become indistinguishable from the frozen rock upon which he was perched, he began to wonder if Gisburne had gone back for his horse or his gear. It made a kind of sense. But only an idiot...

As he had thought it, he had heard the sound of hooves. A single horse. He hid himself – then saw Gisburne astride Nyght, his flanks packed with additional gear. His gear.

"I got lucky," said Gisburne. He dismounted, hauled Galfrid's rescued gear off Nyght's steaming back and dumped it in the snow at his squire's feet. "But no horse. And I'm afraid we lost the Greek Fire."

Galfrid frowned deeply. "The Greek Fi–?" His eyes suddenly widened. "The earthenware bottles..."

"One of Fulke's men must've tried to open them," said Gisburne.

"I was carrying *Greek Fire?*" stammered Galfrid.

Gisburne nodded. "Only enough to destroy a ship."

"And all these past seven days this was sloshing back and forth just inches from my privates?"

"Inches wouldn't make any difference," said Gisburne matter-of-factly. "You'd need to be thirty feet back at least. But don't worry. It was perfectly safe."

"So I see," Galfrid slumped back down on the cold rock, the risk of piles suddenly forgotten, shaking his head in disbelief. "And how did our Templar friends find it, safety-wise?"

"Two were burnt to smouldering heaps where they stood," said Gisburne. "One lay wailing on the ground, thrusting a smoking stump into the snow. He offered little resistance. Of our red-headed friend there was no sign."

"Most likely he fled," said Galfrid, "believing it the work of the Devil..."

Gisburne shrugged, continuing to sort through their gear.

"...and who's to say he isn't right?" added Galfrid under his breath.

"They weren't the only casualties, I'm afraid," said Gisburne, holding up a pair of Galfrid's breeches with the seat entirely burnt away. "But most of it seems intact."

"It could've been worse," admitted Galfrid, kneeling amongst the salvaged remains and carrying out a rapid stocktake. Several items were scorched – some severely enough to abandon. There was no sign at all of his leather flask, nor of the pouch of provisions. He thought of his flint and steel – then realised they were still upon his belt. What else was missing, he was at a loss to say. It would become clear over the next few days. But his sword was here, and his mail, and his collection of knives. Even the pigskin pouch – sold to him by a Spanish merchant who had claimed it made him immune to the thievery of Saracens – still containing its hoard of silver English pennies. With these things, he could make his way in almost any circumstances.

"The loss of the Greek Fire is bad..." said Gisburne gravely. "It will affect our plans."

"*Our* plans?" said Galfrid with a raised eyebrow. "You never actually shared this plan with me. And how come it only becomes *our* plan when it's going wrong?"

Gisburne ignored him.

Galfrid chuckled to himself, surveying the strewn accoutrements, mentally calculating the most efficient means of packing them onto one animal. In spite of everything, seeing the gear spread out, he now felt oddly touched that Gisburne had gone back. His master may have stowed bottles of Greek

Fire between his legs, but nothing could take away from the fact that he had risked his life for Galfrid's sword, some silver pennies and a pair of his burned breeches.

"Well, we are alive," he said brightly. "We still have our weapons. And our wits. And" – he patted Nyght – "this finest of horses." He allowed himself a look of genuine affection, then hastily extinguished it.

"So, are you going to tell him he has to carry this lot, or am I?"

XVIII

THEY HAD LIMPED on for a few more miles before Gisburne had found a solution to their problems.

Their saviour was named Boussard – a blacksmith with a red face and curly hair as black as pitch. As Nyght had staggered into the village, his energies clearly spent, they had seen Boussard by his forge, stripped to the waist but for a leather apron in spite of the freezing temperatures. It was always summer at Boussard's forge.

Their need was clear. Boussard said he had horses, but they were his own, and he could not be persuaded to part with them at any price. Nevertheless, he promised to send his eldest boy to a neighbour who he knew could provide them with what they needed – excellent animals, from a farmer he trusted. Gisburne, impressed by Boussard's love for his own horses, offered him a large sum of silver there and then to take care of Nyght until their return. Boussard was taken aback, and at first reluctant to accept, but Gisburne was insistent. Finally the blacksmith relented. And so it was agreed. In the back of his mind, Gisburne considered the possibility that they would never come back. If that were to happen, Nyght would at least have found a good home.

Two more days passed before they were able to ride away on a pair of good palfreys. During that time, Boussard had proved himself the most naturally generous of men, seeming happy to keep plying them with his own food and drink as long as they regaled him with tales. His kindness moved Gisburne. These were plain folk, whose lives were hard. They had nothing to gain from their generosity, and every reason for witholding it. Thus, when it came, it meant more than the most lavish gift from a prince.

Gisburne thought of this as he watched the gruff old woman remove the remains of the ham joint, and shuffle back to the table with a wooden bowl of dried fruits. Doubtless there would be those who found her ways coarse. But there was love in the food she set before them.

Galfrid gave a great yawn and stretched his toes towards the glowing fire. They would sleep well tonight.

XIX

SOMETHING JARRED GISBURNE from his slumber. He could not be sure what it was – whether a sound or a movement. He was not even conscious of hearing it. But there had been something. Like any seasoned soldier, he could sleep through all manner of uproar and noise. But there were subtler sounds to wh ch he was sensitised, as a mother is to the cries of her babe.

He lay on his bed, not moving, barely breathing, listening to the night. A drift of cold air struck the back of his head. He turned it slowly. As he did so, he realised that the shutter at the window was open, its opening a pale glow of moonlight. Had Galfrid done that? He could hear his squire's soft breaths in the darkness. If he had done it, it had not been recent. But it could not have been long, or the room would be frozen.

As these thoughts formed in his mind, he seemed to become aware of something at the periphery of his vision. Something in the blackness of the room. A shape. Not moving, but not belonging. Realisation slowly dawned.

A dark figure was standing over the bed.

He leapt to his feet, grasping his shortsword. The shape moved swiftly, silently – evading him, and momentarily passing before the open window.

He saw a figure – small and slight, clad entirely in black, even its head wrapped about with swathes of dark material. He swung at it. It seemed to slide away from him like a shadow.

Galfrid was awake now, and on his feet. They had it cornered, one on each side. But as Gisburne advanced, sword in hand, it seemed to bend, then spin around, and what he believed to be a foot struck him in the side of the head, sending him sprawling. He righted himself just in time to see Galfrid's knife kicked out of his hand, then Galfrid himself grabbed, spun and flung to the floorboards with a *thud* that shook the whole house. Then, as Gisburne watched, helpless, the thing seem to somersault up and out of the open window, its shadow shooting across the floor as the window frame emptied and it was gone.

Gisburne stood, stunned and speechless as Galfrid, winded but apparently otherwise unharmed, hauled himself to his feet.

"What in God's name was that?" said the squire, panting.

"I don't know..." Gisburne crouched and saw in the gloom that their gear had been disarrayed. Searched. But why?

"The way he moved... The way he fought..."

"I've never seen anything like it. Except..."

"Except...?"

Gisburne hesitated, not wanting to use the word. "Hashashin. I saw them on three occasions. But I've never heard of them operating further west than Palestine."

"But they're killers. If they'd wanted us dead..."

Gisburne nodded. "We'd be dead already."

"They had every chance. As we slept..."

"Whoever this was, they had some other object in mind." He turned over the strewn gear in search of a clue. Something that was missing. Taken. But nothing seemed to be. Galfrid's stash of silver pennies – a small fortune – had been rifled, but ignored. The only thing that was missing, as far as Gisburne could see, was any apparent motive.

Galfrid read Gisburne's thoughts.

"They were disturbed before they could take anything, perhaps," he said. But this was blind optimism. Gisburne was, by now, realising the truth, and it made his blood run cold.

"They were after information," he said. "About us."

"But why us?" said Galfrid. As soon as he uttered the words, his face fell. "They know."

Gisburne mulled it over, his expression grim. "The fact that they are interested in us at all... It suggests so."

"That shape. In the forest..."

Gisburne nodded. "We are being watched. Followed. And we must assume they know of our mission."

"But how could they?" Galfrid's bemusement was entirely understandable. Only a handful of people had ever known of it, and their loyalty was beyond question.

"I don't know," said Gisburne. "But whoever or whatever they are, they know of us. They know of the skull. And they want it for themselves."

III

TEMPLARS

XX

Angoulême – 17 April, 1182

GISBURNE WOULD NEVER forget the screams of the women. The sound seared into his brain, like a brand on cattle hide. He knew, too, that he would never banish that image from his mind – the terrible look in their eyes as they had been dragged from their home. One – the younger, darker-haired of the two – had looked right at him just before she was flung to the ground in the dung-strewn yard. It was a look of pleading – of hopeless, tragic desperation – but also of accusation, and of hatred. A look that shamed him to the core. She was raped there and then by three of the Duke's most respected knights as he and a dozen others stood by.

Some watched in silence as it happened. Others, their blood still afire from the day's fighting, cheered. The Duke himself – who never actively participated – laughed and clapped along with his knights' exertions. Turning from the spectacle with a feeling of nausea, Gisburne found himself staring numbly at the towering, broad-shouldered figure of the Duke. He stood a full head above his fellows, his ruddy, heroic features as incongruously handsome as ever, despite his generous, bronze-coloured locks – several shades darker than his coppery beard – being lank and sweaty from the heat of his helm. Richard the Lionhearted. Count of Maine. Duke of Aquitaine. Prince of England. And his master's lord.

As Gisburne gazed, five more knights dragged the other woman to the barn – her flushed face streaked with tears, her wimple, dislodged but still tangled in her chestnut hair, flapping in the wind. What became of her, Gisburne never found out.

It mattered little, in the scheme of things. By nightfall they and their menfolk would be dead, their land scoured of its crops, their livestock slaughtered to be consumed by noble knights who would laugh as they tore at the steaming bones around a fire. By morning, what remained of the farm would be burned to the ground. Then the knights would be gone, on to the next conquest. Gisburne had seen the pattern repeated many times whilst on campaign. He had watched as whole villages had been razed, the knights, serjeants, squires and infantrymen falling upon them like the swarming plague of Egypt, consuming all of worth, and destroying all else they could not eat, drink or carry. Many times, no one had been left alive to tell or remember what the place had even been called.

He should have left that farm courtyard when de Gaillon did. It would have been natural, even expected, for him to do so. But somehow his feet had not moved, and for Gisburne to make a separate show of leaving once Gilbert had gone seemed too bold a statement. He was only a squire. True, he would soon be dubbed a knight – he would embark on his twenty-first year within a month – but even then he would be a knight of little standing, and poor means. Knighthood, founded upon honour and prowess, was fast becoming the preserve of the rich.

Gisburne had forced himself to face such things – even immersed himself in them – in the belief that he must somehow become hardened to the reality of war. Over the years, several wiser than he had told him it would get easier to bear, but in fact, it had got worse. Especially of late. He feared he was a failure – too weak to become a knight. But it was not, he had begun to realise, the stress of battle, nor the gore of combat that repelled him. It was something else entirely. In the farmhouse that day there had been at least three children, whisked inside by the womenfolk as the knights' horses had thundered into the yard – two crying boys and a little girl mercifully too young to grasp what was happening. Gisburne had not seen them since. He hoped, for their sake, they were dead. But all at once, as he stood there, that thought – and the pragmatic ease with which it had come – sickened him. It seemed to open a floodgate for all his pent-up revulsion. He physically retched – felt a sudden, wild impulse to flee, in the vain hope of leaving behind the anger and loathing that boiled up in him – then an urgent, crazed desire to turn all of its mad violence on his fellows. But he did neither.

His master, Gilbert de Gaillon, had turned and left as soon as the coming events had become clear. That it would unfold so was, in part, predictable – actions in keeping with custom. Knights on campaign lived off the land, billeted themselves where they saw fit and left nothing that their enemies might use as a resource. The spoils were also their payment. But

Gilbert's tolerance for the deeds of this particular army had worn thin in recent weeks. If the excesses of Richard's army were extreme even to such a seasoned old soldier as de Gaillon, thought Gisburne, then they must be cruel indeed.

Richard was a ruthless leader, as well as a fearless one. He had led his first army into battle whilst still only sixteen, and by the age of eighteen had already earned his lifelong epithet 'Lionheart'. That was just seven years ago, during the campaign to crush the barons in Aquitaine who had rebelled against his father, Henry II. Henry had sent him on the mission as a punishment, but taking enemy castles soon proved Richard's greatest talent – and became his chief amusement. While others contented themselves with the tiltyard and an occasional game of chess, Richard regarded the whole world as a board upon which to play his games. Blind to self-doubt, but afflicted by the restlessness so typical of the Angevins, he was continually questing for greater challenges: larger armies to subdue, cannier opponents to outwit, thicker walls to crack with ever-bigger siege engines. The fact that the doomed castles in Aquitaine belonged to knights loyal to him – that the recent failed rebellion had been his, and against his own father – troubled his conscience not at all. It would put things right with the old king. Then he could seek out new and greater battles.

This he had done. He did not need to look far. Where Richard was, battle naturally followed. After he'd suppressed his former allies in Aquitaine – and literally made his name – new uprisings erupted in Gascony. This time, they had the support of Richard's own brothers, Geoffrey and Henry the

Young King. They were also a personal attack on Richard – directly inspired, it was said, by the growing cruelties of his reign as Duke.

Richard was to face his greatest test at Taillebourg. There, the rebels held a seemingly unassailable position – a famed fortress that commanded the entire valley, perched on a dizzying crag, inaccessible on three sides and so formidable in construction that it was considered impregnable. Richard simply ignored it. Rather than break his army against its walls, he set about destroying everything else he could find, first cutting off all supply lines and avenues of escape, then razing the surrounding lands with such savagery that the appalled rebels felt compelled to ride out and attack. Once in the field, their advantage was lost. Richard crushed their army in one hammer-blow, and, following the retreating rabble through the gates, slaughtered the remaining defenders and tore down the castle.

Few in the region dared challenge him after that.

When Richard's wrath was next turned upon troublesome barons in Angoulême, they appealed to Philip II, King of France, for help. Richard was unfazed. There was nothing he liked better than fighting those who had the audacity to call themselves "king". He acknowledged no one his superior – not kings, not emperors, not his own father, and especially not his elder brother, whose birthright he refused to recognise. Richard was second only to God – and even God, it seemed, was formed in Richard's image.

For young Gisburne, it had been a baptism of fire. In his few years, he had seen more action, and greater horrors, than many would see in a lifetime.

Gisburne had been eight years in the service of de Gaillon, all told, first as a page, then as squire. It had been a ceaseless round of bloody battles. In theory, de Gaillon was King Henry's servant on the battlefield. In practice, he had spent most of the years that Gisburne had known him at the beck and call of Richard.

De Gaillon's loyalty to Henry was unshakable. After the years of anarchy under King Stephen, it had been Henry who had restored the dukedom of Normandy to England, and England to order. Time and again, de Gaillon had impressed upon the young Gisburne that nothing could be achieved without order or discipline. But there was something more. Though it was only ever hinted at in de Gaillon's conversations, Gisburne sensed that he owed Henry a personal debt of gratitude – that, somewhere in the distant past, Henry may even have been directly responsible for saving his life. If de Gaillon served Richard – and he did so with full vigour, when required to do so – it was only because it pleased Henry; and, increasingly, he served under sufferance. Were his allegiances to be tested, there was no question which way they would fall – a fact that doubtless had not escaped Richard. Richard was crude and ruthless, with a simple view of the world. But he was not stupid.

At first, Gisburne had regarded Richard as a great hero – the perfect knight. He was courageous, physically powerful, strong of will, swift of thought and unhesitating when action was required. He was pious but also down-to-earth, and capable of good cheer in the most dire situations. He knew how to speak to his soldiers, and, mostly, they loved him.

He could also be capricious. In the bitter weather at the beginning of the new year, when his soldiers' spirits were flagging, he had hired a party of Flemish bagpipers and drummers who instantly transformed the mood to one of jollity. Richard had them play before battle, too, the harsh, stirring sound seeming to pull his men together as one, and to steel them for the task ahead. Then, after three weeks, Richard suddenly dispensed with their services, saying their hearts were no longer in their playing, and that if they weren't with him they were against him. The dozen or so men were suddenly adrift, in hostile lands, a hundred leagues from their homes and unprotected by the Duke who had hired them. But, to Gisburne's great surprise, this too buoyed up the army.

Richard had an uncanny knack of catching the mood of his men, but only gradually did Gisburne realise that Richard's supposed affinity with his troops wasn't empathy, or love, or paternal care. It was only that his intolerance matched their own. Many regarded him as a great man, and an inspired leader, nevertheless.

This was an opinion de Gaillon had neither challenged nor supported, although he once commented to Gisburne that he had learned "the best and the worst" from Richard. In retrospect, Gisburne saw that de Gaillon had been allowing him to make up his own mind – that only this way would he come to a complete understanding. And come to it he had. Now, when Gisburne looked at Richard the Lionhearted, he saw only a spoilt boy, at war with his own boredom.

No one around him seemed to see it. Or if they did, none showed it. Not even de Gaillon. Not until two days ago.

*   *   *

IT SO HAPPENED there was a particular rebel knight who had particularly irked Richard. None knew quite why – Gisburne did not even know the knight's name, since Richard refused to utter it, and others did not dare. But so riled was the Duke by the knight's behaviour – his defiance, his lack of respect, his refusal to die – that his downfall had become a personal quest. Then news came that he was hiding out in a local fortress. This fortress – an ancient rampart of mouldering wood – turned out to be so dilapidated as to be almost indefensible. At first sight of Richard's army, its ragtag inhabitants immediately surrendered. The nameless rebel knight was not among them, and Richard had been denied even a token fight. He slaughtered every one of them in frustration.

Afterwards, once his wrath had dissipated, it had occurred to him that some of the prisoners might have taken valuable information to their graves. By way of compensation – and so as not to look like a complete idiot – Richard took a company of men to a nearby farm to interrogate those there instead.

It was clear from the start that the action was pointless. The farmhouse had already been ransacked by enemy forces. The farmer – who had nothing left to give, and everything to gain from cooperation – clearly knew nothing of value. But it was no longer about that. De Gaillon and Gisburne had watched in silence as the man was tortured with hot irons and had his fingers broken on a stone with his own hammer. When that yielded nothing of value, Richard nodded to his captain to try a different approach. "Fetch the boy," he had said.

And out was dragged a young blond lad of no more than eight years.

At this, de Gaillon boiled over, a wordless exclamation of outrage and disgust bursting from him.

Everything stopped. Richard turned slowly, his eyes narrowed.

"What's that you say, de Gaillon?"

"I said nothing, my lord." De Gaillon did not lie. But as Gisburne looked at him, he saw his mentor's legs and clenched fists were shaking.

"Then what is it that you think?" Richard's tone and his look were like ice.

It was not fear that shook de Gaillon. It was an anger that swept all fear before it. Gisburne had witnessed it before, when mindless stupidity or needless cruelty on the field had driven his master to an almost ungovernable rage. Then, it had been those of lower rank who had been the object of his wrath. This time, it was his lord.

What happened next was one of the bravest things Gisburne ever saw. De Gaillon breathed deeply, as if suddenly resigned to something. The shaking ceased. Then he looked Richard squarely in the eye and said in a voice that was clear and strong: "I think that if the Saracens treated their own people in such a fashion, we would condemn them as savages – and we would be right to do so."

There was a stunned silence. A dangerous silence. Richard glared at de Gaillon, his face like stone. Then, his face reddening, he turned, drew his sword and advanced on the still-kneeling, bloodstained farmer. The blade, with all of Richard's strength and fury behind it, swung in a huge, sweeping arc and struck off the farmer's head with a single blow. It bounced with a wet thud and bowled across the muddy yard. The boy's cracked voice rose in a terrible, screeching wail as the man's headless body collapsed forward, spilling blood like an overturned keg.

Richard sheathed his sword. "We move on," he said, his voice expressionless. And with that, the noble knights had departed, leaving blood and chaos in their wake.

When Gisburne had gone to de Gaillon after that encounter, something seemed to have changed in him. He was sullen, silent. Gisburne could not immediately place the mood that hung over his master. Then he knew; he had the air of a condemned man. Finally, he had looked at Gisburne with a gloomy, glittering intensity in his eyes. "If anything happens to me," he had said, his tone urgent, "look to your own safety first." Gisburne had started to protest. De Gaillon had put his hands on Gisburne's shoulders, his face suddenly pained, suddenly old. "This is no time for sentimentality. Though it goes against everything you know, if need arises, you must put yourself at a great distance from me. This is the loyalty I ask. Tell me you will do it." Bemused, Gisburne could do no more than nod. Then de Gaillon had looked as if a great weight was lifted, and sank again into a long silence.

IT WAS THIS that slid through Gisburne's mind as the latest horrors were being perpetrated, the screams of the women shredding his nerve-ends. This and something else de Gaillon had once said to him, which came unbidden into his mind. "You must understand," he said, "that war is a brutal business. A terrible business. There is no war that is not a disaster. It is necessary, perhaps, but a disaster nonethless. Some become hardened to its brutality. It sticks to them like dirt – is carried with them from the battlefield. They fail to shake it off; they no longer even notice it. Soon, it becomes a part of them. Others get swept up by the actions of these men, believing them bold – so much so that they forget to ask themselves why. You must understand that these things are so. And you must resist them as fiercely as any enemy."

And it seemed then that something changed in him, as what he saw now mingled with his memories. His shame became resentment. His resentment, anger. In spite of all de Gaillon had said, he wished no further part of this thing he saw before him, no matter what.

And so he turned and walked away.

XXI

THE NEXT MORNING, they were roused early. The news Richard hoped for had come. The rebel knight and a dozen of his men – desperate, starving and half done, by all accounts – were hiding out in the forest to the north. This was their land. They knew how to use it to their advantage, and would fight to the end. But that end was now within Richard's grasp. A company of forty knights, serjeants and squires rode out to hasten them to their doom.

The ride through the forest was tense, the mood expectant. Smoke had been seen rising from the woodland ahead. They even fancied, at times, that they heard the distant whinny of a horse. There was no other sign of men. But instinct told them they were close.

At the edge of the trees, Richard called them to a halt. Ahead of them, beyond the clearing, was a small, wooded ravine, where the road narrowed and the banks rose sharply on either side. The Duke advanced his horse two steps, narrowed his eyes, and scanned the dark cleft and the foliage framing it as if somehow able to penetrate its depths. Satisfied, he drew his horse back.

"De Gaillon," he said, matter-of-factly, and pointed towards the shadowy path. "Ride ahead there and check the lie of the land."

De Gaillon followed the gesture, and gave a snort of derision. "If anything in this land lies, it's that ravine." A handful of the knights stifled laughs at the comment. Even Gisburne could see it was the perfect place for an ambush. But Richard's expression remained stony.

"Then go and wrest the truth from it." De Gaillon's half smile faded. It was no joke. The Duke meant it. He held Richard's hard gaze for a moment, then nodded curtly.

"My lord..." He pulled his horse around, gesturing silently to several of his fellows.

"No," said Richard, stopping him with a raised hand. "Alone."

De Gaillon stared at Richard, not quite comprehending the request. Then realisation dawned. He looked bleakly from face to face, and several of the other knights avoided his gaze. Richard lowered his hand, and turned it in a gesture towards the ravine. "Well?"

De Gaillon frowned, his horse stamping impatiently. "Alone..." he said.

"What is it?" said Richard calmly. "Are you afraid?" Gisburne saw de Gaillon's teeth clench at the suggestion.

This was madness. Richard meant for him to ride alone, unsupported, into that place. Why would Richard do something so stupid? Gisburne looked about him, waiting for someone to speak up, to point out the folly of this action, but none did. De Gaillon caught Gisburne's eye for a fleeting moment.

Something like an apology seemed to pass across his face – then Gisburne, with a rush of horror that churned his insides to mud, realised what was happening. What was about to happen. But it was too late. De Gaillon had turned his horse and was riding for the ravine. Gisburne, his eyes smarting, went to follow – he belonged at his master's side, no matter what – but a knight's hand on his horse's bridle stopped him.

None spoke as de Gaillon was swallowed up by the shadows. A strange silence followed. Then a shout. A clash of metal against metal. A shriek of pain. Gisburne looked from the Duke to his knights and back in panic and disbelief. But Richard, staring ahead, did not move. There was another cry – a different voice, this time. Then further clashes. Then silence.

"Come," said Richard. "Sir Gilbert needs our aid." And he spurred his horse. The entire company thundered into the ravine, then, weapons drawn. All but Gisburne. He sat – breathless, paralysed, impotent, his horse stamping in frustration – listening to the sounds of slaughter as Richard's knights destroyed the rebels.

De Gaillon had not called out, but Gisburne knew before the charge that he was already dead. His heart turned to stone in his chest. So often he had imagined this moment – the loss of his master in battle. It was an everpresent possibility, one he had rehearsed over and over in his mind. But for it to happen like this... He felt desperately unprepared. Sick. Bereaved. Betrayed.

In a daze, he watched Richard and his knights return. They parted, rode around him. Then

Gisburne rode alone into the ravine to recover his master's body, his own life seeming to slide into the abyss.

No one ever said he was outcast. But back in the camp, all shunned him. No eyes met his. He felt as if a ghost. Any hope that a new master would take him on to allow the completion of his journey to knighthood – a journey which only that morning had still seemed tantalisingly close to its end – was extinguished. The knights – even those de Gaillon had called friend – turned their backs. The other squires avoided his gaze, and dropped their heads guiltily when he was near. When food was prepared, one younger squire – who liked and admired Gisburne, and had perhaps thought him a fine example to follow – forgot himself, and brought him a bowl of soup. Before he reached the place where Gisburne sat, well away from the others, a knight gripped his arm, took the bowl from him, and tipped its steaming contents onto the earth.

The atrocity was not acknowledged. There was no mourning. And this, perhaps, was the worst of it. To die – that was bad enough. But for your death to go unremarked, to mean nothing... It felt like a dream – one in which his mentor of so many years had never existed. One from which he could not wake. The disconnection from the world was brutal and complete. De Gaillon was gone. He was a knight expectant no longer. Without a knight as master, he was no longer even a squire. He was nothing. No one.

It was a squire's duty to arrange proper burial for his knight. But he could not hope to return him to his home in distant Normandy. Not on his own. He knew no wife now waited there, and no children.

And there were no other relatives or lovers, as far as he knew. Of his friends he knew nothing, save those with whom he served – and they had abandoned him. This was the lot of the dedicated soldier, then – to end his days alone, unloved. For a day Gisburne sat with the slashed and beaten corpse propped against a tree, his head in his hands, weeping.

He toiled all the following night, burying de Gaillon in a secluded glade. The only other attendees at the graveside were the bats that flitted silently about Gisburne's head.

He marked the place with rough stones, then rode off into the north, no longer knowing where his road would lead.

XXII

Vézelay – 6 December, 1191

THE GREAT ABBEY church of St. Mary Magdalene
rose out of the mist like a white finger pointing at
the heavens. It was a welcome sight – a glorious,
uplifting vision that seemed to justify all the trials
that had preceded it. It seemed to have come upon
them suddenly, as if appearing from nowhere, the
hill on which it sat rising dramatically from the
rolling Burgundian landscape as if the earth itself
was striving to be closer to God.

Galfrid was happy. The snow had turned to
freezing rain, the wind battered them, whipping
their sodden, icy cloaks in their faces, and the pace
since Auxerre had been punishing. But Galfrid was
happy.

It had not been so when Gisburne had first revealed
his intention to divert westwards. It was worse still
when he outlined the reason: to effect a meeting
with an old friend, since they would be within a few
days' striking distance. Galfrid became impossible.
Nothing Gisburne could say would pacify him. The
diversion ·was a waste of time, he said. They had
already lost two days before Courances. This trip –

this "social call" – would put unnecessary strain on their fresh horses. They should continue straight to Pouilly-en-Auxois with all possible speed, then due south for Lyon – especially now they knew they had a shadowy rival. Gisburne – sorely tempted to say that this was *his* mission, and to Hell with what a squire thought about it – had instead painstakingly explained the need. This old friend – from Gisburne's days in Normandy, his days with de Gaillon – was someone with whom he had to consult. He had knowledge essential to their success. Galfrid had dismissed the necessity out of hand. Knowledge, he said, would be of little use if they missed the ship.

Then he had found out where Gisburne intended for them to go, and he was transformed. His objections melted away; he picked up his pace. Gisburne didn't think he had seen him in such high spirits, not ever.

Vézelay. The word had worked like magic on him. Here, on this imposing hilltop, were housed the holy relics of Mary Magdalene, making it perhaps the most significant site of pilgrimage in all of France – a starting point for pilgrims on the Way of St. James to Santiago de Compostela. Here, too, Bernard of Clairvaux had preached the Second Crusade in 1146. And here it was, in 1189, that the newly crowned King Richard and King Philip of France had chosen to meet, bringing together the English and French armies before departing for the Holy Land on the Third Crusade.

Why the so-called "eternal hill" exerted such a fascination for Galfrid, Gisburne could not guess. For Gisburne, however, Vézelay meant only one thing: Albertus.

Albertus was a scholar and physician who had seemed old even when Gisburne was a boy. Then, Albertus had been part of the community of Fontaine-La-Verte, tending the wounds of the many knights and squires who trained there – until he was drawn into Richard's wars. Disillusioned, worn down by the needless bloodshed, the cruelties and the endless lust after destruction, he had retreated to the abbey at Vézelay and taken the Benedictine vows of poverty, chastity and obedience.

Gisburne suspected that a key factor in Albertus's disillusionment had been the fate of Gilbert de Gaillon.

When de Gaillon had been betrayed by Richard, and Gisburne made an outcast, it was to Albertus he had turned. Albertus was the only one who understood. The only one with the backbone to stand by him. Not that there was much Albertus could do. But for Gisburne, understanding was enough. When all around had suddenly ceased to acknowledge him, it was as if he had stopped existing. As if it was *he* who died that day, in that shadowy ravine, and now walked the earth as a phantom beyond their reach – invisible, insubstantial, incorporeal. So disconnected was he that he had, in the days and weeks that followed, felt his grip on his own sanity loosen. But Albertus saved him. It did not require much – perhaps Albertus was unaware quite how important his role was – but it had restored some sense of reality, and provided Gisburne with catharsis – a means to mourn. Gisburne had no words to describe the relief he felt upon finding someone with whom he could talk about his mentor. Talk he did, all day and through the night, laughing, crying – by the end, all emotions were spent. But he was back in the world. He was real. De Gaillon was real. And his death was no longer a dream. His sense of desolation had transformed into something more fruitful: anger, and thirst for justice. Looking back, Gisburne now understood this was something Albertus had tried to warn him about. That impulse had led better men than he astray. Gisburne had not listened – but came to an understanding on his own.

He had returned to England to find his mother Ælfwyn had died two months prior. Instead of welcoming him, his father had berated him for lingering with Albertus in Normandy. Then a vicious argument had erupted about the death of de Gaillon and its aftermath. The perpetrators of the terrible betrayal had been quick to spread their version of the story. So powerful was it, that it seemed even his own father had been infected. His faith in his old friend had been shaken, his confidence in his son's valour almost destroyed. As the accusations flew and the words grew sharp, he had called Guy a coward. Without further word, Guy turned on his heel and walked out, intending never to return. Penniless, bitter and hungry to vent his rage, he joined a band of mercenaries headed south. That road had led him far further than he had ever wished to go – to the brink of utter destruction, and to the gates of Hell.

"Wait here," he said to Galfrid as they dismounted before the basilica. Galfrid, who clearly was not listening, simply gazed up in wonder at the towering grey-white west facade.

He flagged down one old monk, who went to fetch another, and finally a cadaverous young brother with thick black eyebrows appeared, his face a picture of indignation.

"What is this?" he said. Gisburne judged his accent to be Spanish.

"I'm Guy of Gisburne. I wish to see Albertus," he said.

The monk raised his large eyebrows. "Indeed! I was not aware you were expected..."

They were not expected. Gisburne had not had the opportunity to send any message ahead. Knowing little of monastic ways, he had rashly assumed that since this was Albertus's home, he could receive them when he chose. But, as the officious Spanish monk insisted on telling them, in tremendous and unnecessary detail, such was not the case. There were strict routines which could not be interrupted. The abbot ruled absolutely, and his rule was strict. Probably they would have to wait. They might be sent away altogether. He made sure, too, that they were absolutely aware of the annoyance and inconvenience their visit was personally causing him.

"What if I were ill?" said Gisburne. "Seriously ill?"

The Spanish monk frowned, his manner softening somewhat. "Then as physician, Brother Albertus would come to your aid."

"I'm ill," said Gisburne. "Seriously."

The monk stared at him blankly, having no idea how to take it. Choosing to ignore it rather than try to assimilate it into his narrow view of the world, he finally spoke again.

"I shall enquire. Meantime, you may spend time in quiet contemplation in the basilica." And off he scurried.

Gisburne found Galfrid already inside, awe and delight on his face. It was a look that had begun to appear even as they had approached the abbey by the long, sloping road up to the peak of the hill. It was the expression of a wonderstruck child. And now, finally, Gisburne understood. The desire to see the cathedral at Amiens. The frustration of not getting to see Notre-Dame. His sudden change when he heard that this was their destination.

This cynical, world weary squire just loved cathedrals.

Gisburne stood by him in silence for a moment, allowing his eyes to wander about the huge enclosed space, across its high, curved ceiling, the soaring, rounded arches on either side atop the rows of columns in alternating bands of white and coloured limestone, each with its own biblical scene – some elegant, some humorous, some gloriously grotesque – carved into the capital. Then on to the high windows above the altar, where the relics of Mary Magdalene were kept. Through these daylight now streamed, illuminating the translucent tiers of arched white stone, layered one upon the other, with such a glow that they appeared carved from ice.

Gisburne felt a stillness descend as he did so. He had never lingered in such places. He had never been a religious man. But now, he felt humbled.

"Do you... believe, Galfrid?" he said.

"I believe in places such as this," came the hushed reply. Gisburne nodded, feeling he understood. Galfrid looked at him. "You?"

He shrugged. "I've sent prayers up from time to time. In my youth, mostly. But it always felt like yelling into a void. I knew not to expect an answer.

In time I came realise it was merely an affectation."
Gisburne wondered why he was suddenly telling this man such things – sharing thoughts he had shared with no one before. He only hoped they weren't offending whatever religious sensibilities his companion might have, aware that they could sound cynical – even heretical. But when he glanced across, he saw Galfrid nodding slowly in agreement.

"That's a sound philosophy. A soldier's philosophy."

Gisburne looked back to the cathedral ceiling, wondering what battles Galfrid had seen in his life. Perhaps he had something in common with this man after all. "I don't doubt there is a God in Heaven. But I am not arrogant enough to believe that He makes time to listen to my pleas. Nor that He should be relied upon to effect change. Chaos threatens all around. It is up to us to create from it some order." His eyes roved around the interior of this impossible structure, the work of generations, whose toil and determination had somehow transmuted dead stone into a weightless, soaring wonder – a work raised not by God, but by ordinary men. "I believe we can do it. No, I know it. That is what I feel here. I look at this, and know we can do it."

"God must've gave us free will for a reason," shrugged Galfrid, and flashed the briefest of smiles. He turned his eyes heavenwards again, becoming momentarily lost in the same vision. "It always seemed to me... He's like a father. Nurturing us when young and stupid, then, gradually, letting us have our head. Make our mistakes. And there comes a time when we can no longer run to Him, but must rely on our own strengths. When He can help us no

more. All children must be let go at some point."
Gisburne looked at Galfrid in quiet amazement. It
was the longest speech he had ever heard him make.

"Why did you never become a knight, Galfrid?"
said Gisburne. "You're twice the man of many
knights I've known." For the first time, almost to
his surprise, he found himself addressing his squire
in unguarded tones.

"Couldn't afford it," he said. "Then I realised I
simply preferred being a squire. So a squire I resolved
to stay. I'm *arma patrina*," he said. "I offer my
service and lend assistance where I can, to whatever
masters may benefit from it. And those Prince John
chooses. So far, I have been lucky."

"How am I shaping up?" said Gisburne. He found,
to his surprise, that he wanted to know. Somehow,
what Galfrid thought of him had begun to matter.

"We'll see," said Galfrid, a faint smile on his lips.

XXIII

ALBERTUS GREETED GISBURNE with a cackling laugh and a hearty hug. He had not changed in the slightest – he was as thin and wiry as ever, with the same stoop, his lean face still as wrinkled as a dried apple, his eyes as keen. He was completely bald but for a kind of haze of white fluff that still clung to his head – but his steel-grey eyebrows and nasal hair were luxuriant. "My boy! My boy!" he cried as Gisburne's arms wrapped around his almost nonexistent frame, and asked a seemingly endless round of questions aimed at establishing all the facts of Gisburne's current life.

His cell was not the sparse chamber Gisburne had expected of a monk – every space was crammed with manuscripts, scrolls and piles of parchments. "I'm not supposed to own anything," said Albertus, somewhat guiltily. "So I call this a library and myself its keeper. Now, what brings you out this way?"

"John the Baptist," said Gisburne.

"St John the Baptist?" Albertus looked back at Gisburne in some astonishment. "You know of the solar alignment?"

Gisburne looked at Galfrid, then back again. "I'm afraid not..."

"Ah!" Albertus laughed. "Excuse me jumping ahead – or trying to. Not many know of it. It was a secret trick of the masons who constructed the basilica. At noon on midsummer's day, the sun beams through the southern clerestory windows at such an angle that it creates a path of light the full length of the nave." He chuckled. "It's quite a thing! Midsummer's day is the Baptist's feast day, you see. But this is not what you wish to ask me?"

Gisburne and Galfrid exchanged looks again. "My enquiry is more concerned with holy relics... The skull of John the Baptist."

"Ah..." Albertus's expression darkened somewhat. He nodded slowly. "Of course, of course... Silly of me."

"I need to see it," said Gisburne. "Or an image of it, at least. To be able to recognise it. It is of utmost importance to me..."

"Well..." Albertus turned to a pile of books and parchments next to his pallet, and plucked one from the very top. "I suppose you mean the one from Antioch...?" He placed the manuscript on Gisburne's lap. It was already open at the right page.

Gisburne looked. There was a coloured illustration of startling detail and strange beauty – parts were gilded, the gems picked out in red, blue and green, indicating the astonishing craftsmanship of the piece, but at the heart of it, staring back up at Gisburne with its long-dead eyes, was a human skull. Across the domed forehead, apparently etched into the bone, was a short phrase in Latin – *Ecce Agnus Dei* – and beneath the illustration, in a lavish hand, the words: SANCTUS IOHANNES BAPTISTA.

"It is decorated all about with gold and precious stones," explained Albertus. "There are gilded rays encrusted with rubies and garnets about the neck, symbolising the Baptist's blood."

"There are others? Like this?"

"Oh, there are always others," said Albertus. "One Baptist. Several skulls. You know how it is... But none, I think, quite like this."

"And this is completely accurate?"

"Completely. Drawn from life by an Armenian monk."

"So I would be able to identify it from this, were I to see it?"

Albertus raised a bushy eyebrow. "Will you see it?"

Gisburne smiled. "That is my hope. I wish to be sure it is... the right one. What with all these skulls about."

Albertus nodded sagely, looking as if he wished to ask further questions, but did not wish to press Gisburne to supply the answers. Gisburne sensed it. But Albertus deserved at least some explanation. He trusted him with his life.

"It is being sent by the Templars to the King of France," he said. "A gift. A diplomatic gesture. It is my task to... To..."

Albertus held up a hand, and smiled. "Say no more."

A question formed in Gisburne's mind, then – one that, thus far, he had not thought to ask even himself. "This skull... Could it be genuine?"

Albertus, nodded slowly, and cocked his head. "It could. But if it is, why would such pious and acquisitive men as the Templars be content to part with it?"

"I have heard," said Gisburne, tentatively, "that it is payment, and nothing more."

"Maybe," said Albertus. "Its value is great." He frowned. "But let me venture another thought... In ancient times, Herod Antipas, who executed the Baptist, suffered a terrible defeat at the hands of Aretas of Nabatea, and afterwards died in exile. According to Josephus, his ill luck was brought upon him by the ill-judged execution of the saint. It is said the skull – this skull" – he tapped the page – "has the power to bring down a tyrant. A more cynical man than I – a more political man – might suggest that this gift is also meant as a warning. A reminder to the King of France to remember his place, and that he, too, can fall."

Gisburne sat forward, a frown creasing his brow. "Another question... Might there be interest in such a skull from... Saracen quarters?"

Now it was Albertus's turn to frown. "Saracen? Do you believe there to be such interest?"

Gisburne and Galfrid looked at each other. "Perhaps. Might it be possible that agents of Saladin would wish to take it?"

"Or destroy it?" added Galfrid. "To deny it to Christendom?"

Albertus shook his head – a gesture more of dismissal than disagreement. "John is honoured as a prophet by Muslims. I do not believe they would wish it destroyed. And if they wanted to take it for themselves, why not when it was at Antioch all those years?"

Gisburne nodded slowly.

"Guy, forgive me," said Albertus. "Are you saying there are agents of the Sultan *here*, in France?"

"I can't be certain," he replied with a shrug. "It's possible."

Albertus went as if to say something more, hesitated, then continued. "Maybe I should not ask this," he said, "but perhaps you can enlighten me as to why there is so much interest in skulls of the Baptist of late? You are the second in the past two days to come asking about it."

Gisburne's blood ran cold.

"Who?" he said, sitting forward.

"Of course, I did not tell them quite as much as..."

"Who?" interrupted Gisburne. "His name... Can you describe him?"

Albertus began to laugh. "Him?" he chuckled. "It was the daughter of the Count of Boulogne. Mélisande de Champagne."

XXIV

Marseille – December, 1191

THEY WERE NO longer in France.

The principal port of Provence, Marseille was a hectic collision of cultures – influenced by the French, ruled by a Catalan count, a fiefdom of the Germanic Holy Roman Empire, and crammed with representatives of every nationality, every race and every creed. It had always been trade that brought them – the drive that overruled all other considerations. Of late, however, it had been war. Crusade. Richard's crusade.

Gisburne had worn his mail hauberk since Vézelay. Above all else, he meant to be prepared. There were a few too many unknowns. A rebel Templar. A shadowy assassin. And now a scheming countess. The odds were no longer such that he wished to put his faith in a wide-brimmed hat. His pilgrim staff – the fine piece of work by Llewellyn – he had given to Galfrid, who received it with great delight.

Now, out of the jurisdiction of the French King, Gisburne was fully a knight once again, the detested pretence dropped. Galfrid, nonetheless, appealed to Gisburne not to draw attention, and there was clear wisdom in his words. Gisburne kept his armour concealed beneath his riding cloak, and swore he would not.

The promise lasted less than two hours.

The ride south from Vézelay had been hard. The day they had departed, the temperature fell. The wet, partially melted snow froze to a hard crust. Where it was compacted, it turned to solid ice. Then a fine dust of powdery snow fell upon it, making it more treacherous still. The going made their horses hesitant and jittery; the sky above – resolutely flat and grey with the continuing threat of snow – oppressed their mood. One morning they awoke to find the sky had emptied, covering the land in a thick coat of white. It cheered Gisburne. Fresh snow meant better traction, and the skies were clear and bright. They set out that day in good spirits, the virgin snow glittering about them, dazzling white in the sun. So changed was the mood that Gisburne merely laughed when he saw Galfrid wrap a length of transparent black muslin about his head to shade his eyes, and took no heed of his squire's advice to do the same. He joked that Galfrid looked like a Bedouin, and that he had mistaken the snow for desert. Within an hour, his head was splitting from the glare, his eyes swimming with dancing swirls and dots. Galfrid wrapped Gisburne's head as he had his own, and said he would buy him a camel.

It was several hours before Gisburne stopped feeling like he had a poleaxe in his skull. He had taken to closing his eyes for short periods, riding behind Galfrid, knowing his horse would follow. It was while he was doing this – perhaps because the loss of one sense made the others sharper – that he detected a curious odour. It was familiar, but oddly out of place – and it seemed to be following them about. It seemed, in fact, to be coming from him.

"What's that smell?" he said, sniffing about, and shifted in his saddle.

Galfrid gave him that "Can you be more specific?" look.

"Sharp. Like..."

"Vinegar," said Galfrid.

Gisburne sniffed at his mail. It seemed to be coming from that. From the metal itself.

"Vinegar?"

"It's good for cleaning the links," said Galfrid. "The mail had grown a sheen of rust in this weather. So I took the liberty. As your squire."

Gisburne had served with a man who swore that he had only avoided dysentery on campaign by virtue of the fact that he washed his hands in vinegar on a regular basis. The fresh, sharp smell, he said, cleansed the air of miasmatic vapours and kept at bay other foul, disease-laden odours. It seemed to work. He was never ill. He stank permanently of vinegar, however, and earned himself the nickname "Pickle."

Against the odds, they had made the journey in eight days. They arrived in the city mid-afternoon, dishevelled and exhausted, their horses in a state of collapse. But they were ahead of the skull's arrival. They found lodgings, stabled their animals, then ate and washed and headed to the harbour. They would scout their surroundings for an hour or so, keeping their eyes and ears open, then head back to sleep. That, at least, was the plan.

The harbour was crammed with vessels: Scandinavian knarrs, Byzantine galleys, English cogs, French hulks, Italian galeas, Templar tarides, fishing vessels of every shape and size. Most were for trade, but some were for war – for it was from here that Richard had departed with his army. Invigorated by the recent crusader traffic, the harbourside and packed streets all around were abuzz with activity – much of it illegal, immoral or lethally dangerous.

At first sight of the sea, Gisburne had upped his pace. "There's something I have to do," he said. Galfrid had to break into a run to keep up, hurrying along beside as Gisburne walked right up to the harbourside, took his pilgrim hat in one hand and flung it, spinning, far out into the the water. "I hate that fucking hat," he said.

While he was still staring out to sea, Galfrid tugged at his sleeve.

"Don't look now," said the squire. But Gisburne did look.

"Well, well..."

On the harbourside, less than thirty yards distant, stood three Templars. And about the arm of each was the red ribbon of Tancred de Mercheval. A growl escaped Gisburne's throat.

"You've got to get past your hatred of Templars," said Galfrid.

"I don't hate Templars," said Gisburne. "I just hate *those* Templars." And he began to work his way closer to them.

The knights were deep in conversation with a family of pilgrims – husband, wife and young daughter – but from the look of things, it was one-sided. One of the knights had in his hand a bag that looked to contain coins, which the father of the group – angry, but also clearly terrified of these men who were twice his size – was trying to grab. The knight whipped it out of his reach, and the others laughed. The father raised his voice.

"This is unacceptable!" he said, shakily.

"What do you mean?" said the first Templar, with faux innocence.

"We were seeking passage to the Holy Land," said the father, his voice desperate. "A ship."

"You wanted to hire a vessel," said the knight. "And we gave you a vessel." He gestured into the water below, where, Gisburne now saw, a leaky rowing boat – its timbers green and half rotted – sat moored. The other Templars stifled laughs.

"Please," said the father, "that's all we have..." And he reached for the bag again – to no avail. His hand caught the side of the Templar's face. The Templar shoved him.

"That's it..." said Gisburne.

"You're not going to–" began Galfrid. But it was too late. Gisburne was striding towards Tancred's men. "Here we go again," muttered Galfrid.

Gisburne waded in between the Templar and his prey and poked the man in the shoulder.

"Give the man his money back."

The Templar stared at him in amazement, and then he and his fellows burst out laughing. "What's this?" he said, looking Gisburne up and down. "Perhaps we'll just toss you in the harbour, and you can all swim to the Holy Land."

Gisburne threw off his cloak and drew his sword. "Try it," he said, put his blade at the knight's throat, and relieved him of the bag of coins. His comrades drew their own blades. They were not laughing now. The first Templar leapt back suddenly and went to draw his own weapon. Before it was eight inches out of its scabbard, Gisburne kicked him in the balls, grabbed him by the surcoat and hauled him forward. The knight went sailing past Gisburne as he stepped deftly aside, flew off the dock, crashed through the rotten hull of the flimsy boat and sank like a stone in the scummy water.

The second man went for him. Gisburne parried the descending blow with his sword, their blades biting notches out of each other as they connected with a jarring impact. Gisburne pushed, whipped his blade hard about, forced his enemy's sword point down to the ground and then put his foot on it.

The knight had two choices – and only a moment to decide. He could watch as his blade was snapped in two, or he could let go of his weapon entirely, save the blade, but render himself defenceless. He chose the latter. As he stood gawping at Gisburne, waiting impotently for his adversary's next move, his eyes swung to the right.

Gisburne turned to find the third Templar was almost on him. But before he could land a blow, there was a sharp *crack*, the mother of the pilgrim family shrieked, and the Templar pitched forward onto his face and lay still. Behind him, pilgrim staff in both hands, stood Galfrid.

"I lend assistance where I can," he said. Gisburne grinned.

The second Templar had already regained his weapon and had it poised above his head when something made him stop. His face paled, the fight draining from it. He froze, and stared, as if suddenly petrified.

The third, who had already stirred and was climbing to his feet, did the same, terror in his eyes.

Gisburne turned, following their gaze, and saw Tancred de Mercheval. He strode towards them from the rows of market stalls, a second grim-visaged knight at his shoulder. Galfrid had said Gisburne would know him when he saw him. He was right. Gisburne almost recoiled at the sight of him.

He was tall, his head and chin roughly shaved, the skull coated with a greying stubble. Though he might have been considered fine featured in his youth – even handsome – the face that Gisburne imagined plump and rosy before being aged by a decade of war and penitence now appeared grey and gaunt, its cheeks hollow, its taut complexion more reptilian than human, its cold eyes as devoid of emotion as those of a dead crow. But it was not any of these things that struck Gisburne through with horror. It was the narrow, pale scar that ran diagonally across his face, from his left brow to a point on his chin, just beyond the right corner of his mouth. De Mercheval had, at some time in his life, suffered a terrible wound – evidently from the blade of a sword or other edged weapon striking him in the face. The blade had cut the flesh cleanly, taking away a portion of his nostril and part of the tip of his nose and – as Gisburne now saw when Tancred grimaced at the sight of this debacle – knocking out one tooth on the right side of his upper jaw. The flesh had healed, leaving little more than a thin white scar. But it had done so in such a way that the two halves of his face no longer met quite as they should. They had slid out of alignment along the neat, perfectly straight axis, and stuck that way, the overall effect one of weird distortion, as if his face were half underwater, or glimpsed in a cracked glass.

That he had survived at all was a miracle. Perhaps Templar skulls really were tougher, thought Gisburne.

Tancred looked at the cowering pilgrims, then at Gisburne, then at his own men. "Who instigated this?" His voice was like ice. Gisburne could have sworn he saw the knights trembling. The second of them spoke up, stuttering. "It was meant only as a joke. It's a misunder..."

Without hesitation, Tancred drew a dagger and stabbed the man in the eye. It was carefully judged. Not a wild or impulsive strike. Just enough to blind, but not enough to kill. His knight howled in agony, blood and vitreous fluid streaming from the wound. The pilgrim's child screamed.

"Now you will always remember your mistake," said Tancred. He turned. "Ulrich?"

The large, shaven-headed knight at his side stepped forward.

"Get him to a physician."

Ulrich nodded, gripped the gibbering knight's arm and dragged him away.

Tancred turned his cold eyes on Gisburne. "Bloodshed in a holy cause has the Lord's blessing. Go in peace, Sir Knight."

Gisburne, horrified by what he had seen, looked for a moment as if he was set to take the matter further. Before he could do so, Galfrid intervened, taking the money pouch from Gisburne's hand, putting it back into that of the whimpering pilgrim, and dragging Gisburne swiftly away.

XXV

THEY SAT IN a packed inn, a jug of wine between them, drinking in silence. Outside, the light was beginning to fail.

"Well, now you know," Galfrid had said.

"Yes," Gisburne had replied. "Now I know. The White Devil..." And he nodded slowly, deep in thought.

That had almost been the extent of the conversation when an overly coiffured herald entered the establishment, scanned the room, and wound his way towards them through the throng. Gisburne, the edge of his good manners – and his patience – knocked off by drink, looked the effete fellow up and down.

"Before you ask," he said. "I don't dance."

The herald's face flushed with displeasure, but he chose to ignore the comment. "A noble lady wishes to grant you an audience," he said. Gisburne exchanged glances with Galfrid. The herald looked from one to the other, then added, pointedly: "Alone."

He did not say which noble lady, but Gisburne would have known even if the man had not been wearing the green livery of Mélisande de

Champagne. What she wanted with him on this night was anyone's guess. But what was certain, he realised with sinking heart, was that she, too, now knew his purpose.

"I go with my squire, or not at all," he said.

For a moment, the herald looked bereft. He had not prepared for this eventuality.

"Don't be an idiot," said Galfrid with a sigh, and pulled the jug of wine towards him. "I'll be here if you need me."

The herald did not speak as they walked. Without looking back, he led Gisburne through an endless succession of crowded streets – past roaring drunks, toiling fishermen, and bad minstrels, running the gauntlet of whores plying their trade and religious fanatics plying theirs. But the expected gravitation towards some more grand or fashionable end of the city did not take place. Instead, little by little, the crowds thinned and the buildings shrank, grew shabbier and less numerous, until finally they dwindled altogether. They passed outside the walls of the city, and beyond its tattered edge, street gave way to road, and road to track.

As they walked, Gisburne again felt his heart beat faster. Not at the mission ahead, he realised, but at the prospect of meeting Mélisande. It would be no hardship to look upon that face again. She excited him. But in that, there was also danger. He was so close to his goal now. It could not be jeopardised – not for anything.

He had begun to feel a sense of unease as they moved on into the hills, the city and its glimmer of lights now entirely at his back. As they progressed along a winding, gritty path that seemed to lead nowhere, his hand went instinctively to the pommel of his sword. If he were arranging an ambush, this would be as good a place as any.

Then he saw it. A camp of several tents and wagons around a central fire – a mobile, makeshift village, bustling with life and activity, aromatic with the smell of woodsmoke, spices and roasting meat. The herald led him straight to the largest of the tents, opened the flap, and gestured for him to enter.

There, on a bed strewn with cushions, in green silk with a white wimple, leaning upon one slender arm, was Mélisande de Champagne.

The interior of the tent was opulent, the influence of the Holy Land everywhere evident. In its centre, a brazier maintained a steady warm temperature, while upon a thick Arabian rug, food was set out on silver platters – fresh bread, dried fruits and nuts, spiced eggs, poached fish, cheese, pickles and preserves and hot roast goose. Two male servants were in attendance, one of whom was filling the hostess's cup with wine as Gisburne approached.

She stood as she saw him, fingers clasped, smiling sweetly. "Welcome, Sir Knight."

She was even more beautiful than he remembered. It was not, he now realised, the beauty of bland perfection. Her nose was perhaps a little too long, her green eyes perhaps a little too large, her chin perhaps a little more pointed than a sculptor would deem fit. But, taken all together, animated now by a living spirit he at once recognised as equally imperfect, equally captivating, they far surpassed any piddling work of art. She stepped forward, extending a slender hand. A dim memory of courtly behaviour stirred in Gisburne's head. He bowed, dropped to one knee, took the countess's proffered hand and kissed its back. As he did so – mere inches from the close-fitting, fine silk of her gown, her warm skin scented with orange, spice and rosewater – he was keenly aware of the shabbiness of his own dress, of the rough stubble on his face against the smooth white of her flesh. She did not let it linger.

"I'm so glad you could come," she said brightly, as if it were a perfectly ordinary social occasion. He smiled unconvincingly as he stood. "Pray, be seated," she said. Gisburne did so, in the only place available – on the edge of the large, low bed. A cup was placed in his hand and filled with wine, a silver platter arranged with morsels of food introduced into the other. He felt his stomach rumble, and hoped she did not notice. She raised her cup. He raised his in turn, and they drank. "Now," she said. "You must tell me all about yourself. About all those brave battles you have fought, and the fair maidens' hearts you have won..." Her eyes glittered as she said it.

Gisburne stared, momentarily dumbstruck. The situation felt unreal. *She* seemed unreal. And if there was one thing he was absolutely sure of, it was that this delicate creature did not want to know the realities of either the battles or the women.

"There is little to tell," he said, awkwardly. Then added: "...that is fitting for a lady." She smiled. Her large eyes narrowed and slid sideways. And, with a gesture that Gisburne barely registered, the servants were dismissed.

She watched until they were quite gone, than gave a great sigh, pulled the veil and wimple from her head and flung them to the floor, shaking her gold tresses loose. "God, I hate those things," she said.

She evidently saw the surprise upon Gisburne's face. "Sorry, does my informality shock you?"

It was not, in fact, the informality that shocked him. It was the change. Somehow it seemed, in the removal of her headgear, that this wan, fey creature had torn off a disguise and revealed a quite different being beneath. Even her voice had lost its breathy sibilance, and was now something far plainer, far richer, far more complex. "As a child, my father let me run wild in the woods and fields," she continued. "I'm still that same girl at heart. But *they* do not approve." She gestured vaguely towards the entrance of the tent. He supposed she meant the servants. Though why the thoughts of a servant should matter to her was beyond him. And if they were meant to be her chaperones, then it was a pretty poor job, leaving her alone in a tent with a rough-looking knight.

She sighed, sipped her wine, slumped a little on the bed, kicked one foot.

Gisburne cleared his throat. "I am curious..." he began.

"Yes," she said with a smile. "You are."

He pressed on, unperturbed. "Curious... as to why I am here."

She lounged back languidly, pulling idly at her hair, her chemise parting to reveal the curve of her breasts. "I wished to meet you." She shrugged.

So, that was the game. He could play that. But he wasn't about to do so by her rules.

"Perhaps you should call back your servants," he said, nodding at the small handbell by her left side. She looked suddenly crestfallen. He smiled politely. "I wouldn't wish for there to be accusations of anything... improper."

She sat back up, a different kind of smile on her lips. For a moment, the spoilt girl was quite gone. In her place, yet another persona. Something tougher, more formidable. A knowing woman.

"What else of worth is there to do on a winter's night," she said, "but something improper?"

Her being, and her voice, had subtly changed again. Gisburne felt in the presence of an adversary, and a worthy one, at that. An equal. But whether this was the real Mélisande de Champagne – if indeed she was ever to be revealed to him – remained to be seen.

"Well, since decorum is cast aside," he said, "let's speak plainly. Why am I here?"

She sat up, her eyes not moving from him. "You have no idea?"

"None." It was a lie. He knew it had something to do with the skull. But he did not wish her to know that he knew. Not yet.

"I saw a knight come to the defence of some poor pilgrims," she said. "And I admired it."

"Then you are one of the rare few. What exactly was it you admired?"

"Are you fishing for compliments now, Sir Guy?"

"I never fish," he said. "I prefer hunting."

She raised an eyebrow. "A man after my own heart." She put down her cup, plucked a sliver of roast goose from her platter with nimble fingers and popped it into her mouth. "I admire fortitude. Strength of will. Strength of purpose. It's something I look for in people. All of those who serve me have such qualities."

Gisburne cocked his head to one side. "Is that a job offer? Or a proposition?"

Her smile faded. "You are very forthright for a supposed gentleman."

"As you are for a lady."

Her eyes narrowed this time. But there was something playful in them – a hint of the wild girl. "Perhaps you are not a gentleman at all." Her tone was gently chiding, but also inviting. Suggestive.

Gisburne thought to say something, but bit his tongue.

"Aha..." She smiled, as if in triumph. "I see you are a gentleman after all."

"Your offer is most kind. But I have a noble master to whom I am loyal."

It was here that anyone else might have asked who that master was, but Mélisande did not take the bait. *She knows,* thought Gisburne.

"A pity," she said, putting another shred of goose flesh in her mouth and licking her fingertips delicately. "I believe you would have fitted in rather well."

He could see what she was doing now. Anyone could. Resisting it was another matter. He'd had a good quantity of wine before coming here, and while his mind was sharp, his resistance was weak. In spite of himself, all this flirting and game-playing was starting to get the better of him. To Hell with the skull. To Hell with John. Why should he not jump into this countess's bed, whether she means it or not? In his head, he laughed. The impulse passed. It was wild fancy, no more than a pleasant image to toy with. But with it – with its denial – came impatience.

"I suggested we speak plainly," he said. It was his turn to sound chiding this time. "But I do not believe you are doing so."

"You do not think me plain?"

"Very far from it."

"Well, if plain is your preference..." She looked away, as if in appalled disappointment, and sipped at her wine.

"Stop playing games," he snapped.

She turned and stared at him in silence for a moment.

"Am I playing a game?"

"You know it. We both are."

Something flashed in her eyes. Perhaps panic. Whatever it was, it was swiftly conquered. "And the object of this game?"

"There is only ever one object with a game," he said. "To win."

There was a long hesitation before she spoke again. "And the prize?"

It was time, now, to put pretence aside. "A skull," he said. "Set about with gold and encrusted with jewels. Such as the one you saw represented in a manuscript at Vézelay not ten days ago. Such as the one that arrives here within the week."

She stared at him, searching his eyes, for once lost for words. He could see her calculating, plotting, weighing up – suddenly realising she had not the advantage in this game that she had thought, desperate to make a move that would somehow re-establish it.

He did not give her the chance. "Who do you work for?" he said.

"Work?" She said it as if it was a dirty word.

"I have a master and so do you. Who is it?"

Outraged, she reached for the bell. "How dare..."

Before she could touch it, Gisburne's hand enclosed her wrist. He held it firm, his face close to hers.

"Not entirely a gentleman, then?" she said.

"It depends," he replied.

"On what?" There was challenge in her tone. He released his grip. She looked away, affectation suddenly gone from her face. "I have heard of such a skull. The head of John the Baptist, lately out of Antioch. En route now to the King of France, brought there by the knights of the Temple."

"You would know that, of course," said Gisburne, "having been at his court not three weeks ago."

A frown flickered across her forehead and was gone. "And how would you know it?"

"Perhaps I read it in your face."

"And what else do you see there?"

"Your father is Count of Boulogne, loyal to King Philip, and an ardent supporter of the Templar cause. You would therefore wish the skull to reach its destination safely." He shrugged. "Or that is my guess. Faces can be deceptive."

Her eyes studied him intently, seeming to grow in confidence once again. "As a loyal subject, and a dutiful daughter, perhaps that is indeed what I would wish. But children can rebel against parents. And subjects may move against their king."

The words stung Gisburne. He thought of Richard rebelling against his father, of John's wish to see Richard fall.

"But let's suppose you are correct," she continued. "And suppose, too, that the Templar entrusted with its transportation through France was, shall we say, unreliable..."

"Tancred?" She did not reply. "What is your part in all this?"

"My part?" She pressed her open hand to her breast in mock humility, a gesture of almost absurd theatricality. "I am a mere woman. And a woman's part is never her own. It is always in the hands of another."

Gisburne stared. Then broke into a laugh. *Oh, she's good. She's very, very good.* He raised his cup. She gave a sly smile, and raised hers.

"To John," she said, sweetly. Then, after a pause, added: "The Baptist."

She stood suddenly. "Now, we are done. I must to bed. And, sadly, you must leave." With that, she rang the bell. Immediately, her servants appeared. Gisburne stood, bowed, and turned to leave.

"Beware of Tancred," she said, her back to him. "He is not what he seems."

And then he walked out of the warmth of that charmed tent and back into the cold night.

XXVI

THERE WAS SOMEONE waiting at the city gate.

When Gisburne had left the tent, he had caught the eye of the herald who had delivered him here. He expected, he supposed, that he might also be required to show him back, and in truth Gisburne – his brain tired and fogged by drink – would not have minded some guidance through that maze of streets. But the herald did not stir. Evidently, he would have to find his own way.

He had been contemplating Mélisande's words as his feet crunched in steady rhythm along the stony path, trying to fathom her purpose. But what had seemed merely curious when he had left her tent became more vexing and raised more questions the longer he thought about it. He decided to dismiss it from his mind, at least for tonight. It was still early, but he just wanted sleep. He was pondering this, and the fact that he would likely have to bribe the porter, when he saw the three cloaked figures ahead, lurking in the gloom some distance from the gate, their heads bowed.

He knew at once it was trouble. As he neared, and the tallest of them stepped up to him, he saw why. The man had a bloody bandage across one eye, and through the slit in his cloak Gisburne glimpsed the surcoat of a Templar. It was the knight he had fought at the quayside. The knight Tancred had half blinded. It seemed he wished to settle the account, and had brought two friends to ensure the bill was paid.

Gisburne was in no mood to pussyfoot. "Your master told me to go in peace."

One-Eye looked at him with unadulterated hatred. "He would not have done so had he known you went disguised as a pilgrim."

That, Gisburne supposed, was a fair point. How One-Eye knew it was another matter. Unless he had been comparing notes with Fulke, and drawing his own conclusions. "I've no idea what you're talking about," he said. "Now, let me pass."

The knight blocked his way, his companions – serjeants – stepping up beside him. "Don't think me such a fool. I have a good idea what you are and why you are here, even if my master does not."

"I find that hard to believe," said Gisburne. "That you had a good idea, I mean."

The knight growled – almost comically – and drew his sword.

Gisburne, exausted, tried to stifle a yawn, and failed. "Please," he said, one hand raised in apology. "Can't this wait until tomorrow?"

One-eye stepped forward, his face contorted with rage. "Tomorrow?" He laughed. "Tomorrow will be too late for you. The skull will be in our hands. And you will be dead!" And with a roar he went for him.

Gisburne, his reactions slowed, drew his sword just fast enough to parry the knight's first blow. But as he did so, One-Eye's head jerked convulsively. His eyes seemed to drift in different directions. And instead of drawing away to strike again, he kept coming – his whole body pushing towards Gisburne, falling onto him. Gisburne stepped back instinctively – defensively – and to his amazement One-Eye fell face down onto the ground, limp and lifeless, an arrow in his temple. Gisburne stared at him in astonishment, then back up at his companions, their expressions incredulous.

Fssssst. Something zipped through the night air. The serjeant to Gisburne's right convulsed and fell to his knees, an arrow in his chest. The second serjeant looked about in panic, his eyes scanning the distant trees. He was already backing away.

Gisburne looked him in the eye. "Better run," he said. The serjeant did so.

Gisburne turned just in time to see, some hundred yards distant among the shrubby trees, a small, dark figure, its face covered, leap upon a black horse and make off into the night.

XXVII

"So," said Galfrid. "Our shadowy assassin strikes again."

To Gisburne's amazement, he had still been sat at the same place in the same tavern. But he was glad of it. The encounter had woken him up, and the information it provided fired him with a new sense of urgency, and a need to talk.

"As long as he's on our side, I don't mind," said Gisburne. "Whoever he is, he saved my skin." Gisburne's manner was dismissive, but he knew this was a lie. He was not only being watched; he was being protected. And he had no idea by whom, nor their purpose. Question continued to pile upon question.

"And you say the Templar also knew? About your interest in the skull?"

"A shrewd guess. Perhaps I have been a little too... obvious... in my actions." He looked guiltily, almost sheepishly at Galfrid. "I'll work on it. But the man said he was no fool, and he was right. Though still foolish enough to let slip one other important piece of information." That fact he had yet to impart to Galfrid. He wasn't sure how. It somehow seemed too big, too momentous. He felt his heart race at the thought. But Galfrid would now ask; he had opened that door to him.

But Galfrid, for once missing his cue, did no such thing. "And Mélisande... How much does she know?" asked Galfrid.

"Everything. Or so we must assume."

Galfrid sighed. "This is fast becoming the worst kept secret in Christendom. Why did she want to see you anyway?"

Gisburne spread his hands. "To sound out a rival. To get a look up close." But, in truth, this, too, remained a mystery. If her goal was simply to safeguard the skull, and protect French interests, why not simply kill him? And why feed him information? The whole business made him uneasy. "She warned me not to trust Tancred."

"Were you likely to do that?"

"Hardly."

Galfrid nodded. "Our plan?"

"The plan has changed," Gisburne said. "The loss of the Greek Fire saw to that."

Galfrid leaned forward. "You know, you never actually told me what that plan was. But if I were you, right now I'd be considering intercepting the ship before it even reached Marseille."

Impressive, thought Gisburne. He nodded slowly. "The ship will hug the coast, put in where it can – especially in winter, and especially overnight. If we know where, we can get to it whilst it's at anchor."

"If we know where, and *when*," said Galfrid, somewhat gloomily.

"Tonight," said Gisburne. Galfrid almost choked on his drink. "The Templar. He told me.

Tomorrow it arrives in Marseille. Which means tonight it makes its last stop on the coast."

Galfrid stared at him, struggling to take the information in. "It's early. Ahead of schedule. Are you sure?"

"Absolutely. This is our one chance, Galfrid. After today, it passes into Tancred's hands."

"And you say the Templar *told* you? Why? Why would someone do that?"

"Because it's the sort of idiotic thing a man says when he thinks he's about to kill you," said Gisburne impatiently. He leaned forward, his eyes afire, his voice hushed. "This is it, Galfrid. This is what we came for." It had been six weeks since he stood before John at the Tower of London and received his orders. Six hard weeks, during which this had seemed a distant dream. But now, suddenly, it was upon them. He felt a strange thrill – one he had not felt in years. The thrill – and trepidation – that one felt before a battle.

Galfrid swallowed hard. "Do we know where?"

"We can find out," said Gisburne. "There's someone I need to see. Mamdour. An old friend. He trades here now. If anyone knows, he will."

Galfrid's eyes narrowed. "Would I be right in thinking Mr Mamdour is a foreign gentleman? A... *Saracen* gentleman?"

"Nubian, actually," said Gisburne. "And I trust him."

Galfrid thought a moment, then nodded.

Gisburne tensed his muscles, felt his heart pounding.

"Prepare the horses," he said.

XXVIII

The coast of Provence – December, 1191

THE TEMPLAR SHIP was already lying at anchor when
they arrived. "A business associate tells me two
Templars came asking for good wine and fresh
meat," Mamdour had said. "It was to be ta˙ en to
a bay along the coast, to arrive before tomorrow
night. They call the place the Bay of the Cross. It
is a day's sailing from here, at least. Two days by
wagon. But a determined man with a good horse,
he could get there in a few hours. A man determined
like you." He had smiled knowingly as he'd said it.
Gisburne had tried to reward him for his help, but
at that, Mamdour had looked mortally offended.
"Stay alive," he had said, and, grinning widely, had
thrown his arms around Gisburne and clapped his
hands on his friend's back.

Gisburne and Galfrid had ridden southeast,
cutting across country in a wide arc before doubling
back to the cove. The final approach they had made
on foot, and now – huddled among the rocks of
the cliff – looked down upon the small but bustling
encampment on the white stretch of beach. A fire
blazed at its heart, casting long, shifting shadows

beyond the neat row of tents set back from the ocean's edge. Gisburne counted six horses, and perhaps two dozen men milling about, most of them armed knights. Distant sounds of laughter and the rasping drone and mournful melody of a hurdy gurdy drifted on the air. And there, in the still waters of the small, sheltered bay, with the moon and stars of the clear night sky reflected all about, sat the vessel – small, high-sided and shallow of draught. A fine, new ship – swift and manoeuvrable – but not one for a heavy sea.

"Do you see any guards aboard?" said Galfrid, squinting into the gloom.

"I see no one at all." There was a note of surprise in Gisburne's voice. Clearly the Templars were confident in their abilities – they had every right to be – but he had not expected them to be so complacent. He could hardly believe his luck.

"And you're certain the skull will be on the ship?"

Gisburne scanned the beach again, looking for signs of something under guard. But there were no clusters of men. No tent that had more security than any of its fellows. The ship itself clearly made the best strongroom.

"I'd stake my life on it."

Galfrid looked like he was going to say something, but stopped himself. Galfrid hardly ever stopped himself – but Gisburne knew what its gist would have been. He *was* staking his life on it. If he was wrong, their quest would likely end here.

Gisburne had dressed lightly, his mail hauberk stowed in a bag upon Galfrid's horse, and now, creeping back from the cliff edge, he began to throw off the remainder of his clothes. Stripping down to his hose, he slung a bag across his chest, tucked a slim crowbar in his belt and slung his shortsword across the small of his back. He shuddered as the cold metal touched his skin. Temperatures here were nothing like those they had left behind in the north, but it was cold enough when half naked. The sea would be colder still.

"You're only taking the shortsword?' said Galfrid.

"Have you ever tried swimming with a broadsword?"

Galfrid clearly had not. He looked as if he thought swimming of any kind an abomination.

"Bring the horses up as close as you can," said Gisburne. He gestured to his pile of clothes. "And pack everything on them." He took a deep breath – a last look at the relative safety of this bleak crag. "When I return, we'll need to get away fast."

"How will I know when you're clear?"

"You'll know." And with that, crouching low, he stalked eastward along the clifftop, finally disappearing from Galfrid's view through a cleft in the rocks.

The climb down to the cove was treacherous. To avoid being seen, Gisburne had headed east of the beach to pick his way down through the rocks on the headland. Here, Mamdour had assured him, was a path – although it proved a path fit only for a mountain goat. There were great gaps, and drops of six feet or more, and occasionally jagged shadows into which he was forced to slither, with little idea how deep they went. In one place, he disturbed a huddle of birds that screeched and flapped and flew at his face. He clung to the rock a long time after they had fled, sprawled, motionless, the birds' fishy stink in his nostrils, certain he had given himself away. But there were no shouts from down below. No sudden mobilisation. No signs of alarm. The same breeze that carried their sounds to him carried his away from them. Finally he dared to move again, feeling the crust of birdshit crumbling beneath his fingers.

A sailor had once told him that the Mediterranean waters in the winter were warmer than the seas of England in summer. Gisburne focused hard on this thought as he slipped from the barnacle encrusted rock into the freezing, weedy water. From above, the sea had looked as smooth as black glass. Down here, less so. He flexed his left shoulder to relieve the stiffness in it, then, suppressing a shiver, he pushed himself off.

Gisburne had been a strong swimmer since childhood. But it had been months since he'd swum last, years since he had done so in the open sea. Even then, it had not been through choice. Now, the salty swell lapped in his face. The bag and his hose dragged, and the sword felt like it would pull him under. But he relaxed into the swim, and found his rhythm. The lapping waves gave way to a deeper swell. The shiver passed. There were some pockets of almost tepid water, and some that were ice cold. But he felt the warmth of the exertion flow through him. And so, in the moonlight, he advanced slowly, steadily towards the twin torches that glimmered like eyes upon the ship's high stern.

He had no formed no plan for getting aboard. He had neither grapple nor rope. There was, in any case, no means of throwing them from the water, nor any crossbow here capable of projecting them.

Lacking any other method, he had resigned himself to a painful climb up one of the anchor ropes. Now, he saw that they were not ropes, but thick chains. The Templars had spared no expense. As the dark timbers loomed like a creaking, heaving wall silhouetted against the moon, the dipping chains spreading from the hull like a spider's legs, the climb seemed impossible.

Then he heard a sound he knew. The hollow *thunk* of wet timber knocking against wet timber in a steady rhythm. As he drew nearer still, his eyes penetrating the deep shadow at the stern, he saw it. A small boat bobbing in the water, tethered to the ship, and above it – as if left for his convenience – a rope ladder stretching up to the deck. There was no one to see Gisburne's smile. He swam between the ship and the boat, gripped the rope, then began to haul himself up out of the water.

XXIX

HE HAD ADVANCED no more than two paces on the ship when he realised he was not alone. He froze, dripping on the deck, bare feet tensed against the boards. The snort sounded again, from his left, louder this time. He took another tentative step, and there he saw him. A Knight of the Poor Fellow-Soldiers of Christ and of the Temple of Solomon, fully armed and mail clad, ready for battle – slumped, drunk and asleep. On one side of him, an opened earthenware bottle; on the other, a gnawed animal bone stripped of meat. The gentle purring rhythm of his snoring was broken by another snort and a splutter. He shifted, nudging the bottle, which toppled and rolled across the gently swaying deck. Gisburne stopped it with his foot, and righted it. Then he drew his shortsword and advanced towards the sleeping guardian.

In the flickering light of the flambeau upon the gunwale, he could see the man's face. He looked as peaceful as a babe, a glistening trail of drool upon his short beard. Gisburne raised his weapon, and prodded the man firmly with its point. He spluttered and shifted again, but did not stir from sleep. Gisburne doubted whether the man would have been roused if a whole company had leapt aboard on horseback. He left him to his dreams.

The night air felt strangely warm now, the effect of emerging from the cold water. It would pass. He hoped to be back in the water by then. But there was one small thing to be achieved first.

Looking along the length of the deck, he spied a square hatch standing proud of the planking, some three-quarters of the way between him and the mast. On a ship of this size, there would be a hundred nooks to secrete the skull. But his gut told him – with the certainty of knowledge – that this was the place. He knew he was close – could smell it, taste it. Feel it in his bones. All these weeks of travel and hardship, and now, just yards away... Muscles tight, a strange thrill rising in his belly, he made towards it.

A shadow loomed suddenly before him: another knight, tall, armoured, sword drawn – not sleeping, not drunk. They stared at each other in silent amazement for a fleeting moment – but Gisburne was the more prepared. His blade swung and flashed in the firelight, the blunt back edge striking the man hard across the temple. He grunted, staggered, stumbled into the gunwale on the starboard side – and tipped right over the edge. There was a dull plash as his body hit the water.

Gisburne again stood tense, motionless, looking nervously to the still slumbering guard, then back at the shore. The knight had plunged overboard on the side facing shore. Even if they had not heard, anyone looking from the beach in that moment would have seen it.

But there were no voices raised. No sudden movements. The breeze brought only the familiar sounds of laughter, and the plaintive whine of the hurdy gurdy.

Gisburne hurried to the hatch. It appeared to have no lock. Llelwellyn's words came back to him – warnings about the Templars' ingenuity. Sheathing his shortsword, he gripped the edge and raised it, slowly, tentatively. It offered no resistance. He felt around its rim. There were no catches or wires. Nothing out of the ordinary. Could it really be they had simply put it in the hold of a ship, like a sack of flour or a barrel of salt pork?

He lifted the hatch completely. The impenetrable black of the hold's interior stared back at him. Creeping to the port side, he released a flambeau from its bracket and again peered into the gloom.

The space was large, and but for one object, appeared entirely empty. Some twelve feet immediately below the opening, sitting in glorious isolation at the centre of the hold, was a solitary wooden chest, of the right proportions to contain a human head.

His flame glinted on its hasp and hinges. Gisburne felt his heart beat faster in his chest.

There was no ladder, no stair, no rope. No indication at all of any means of access. Could it be entered elsewhere, below the deck? There wasn't time to find out. He freed one end of a line from the mast – the thickest he could find that wouldn't bring the yard crashing down upon his head – and was about to lower it in to the gloom when something made him stop. At first, he thought it was a trick of the light – an illusion concocted by his straining eyes. He held the flambeau lower, and moved it from side to side. There was something in the air down there. Something between him and the box, barely reflecting in the light. Lines, or something, like...

A hand grabbed his hair and yanked him back from the opening. He sprawled. The flambeau skittered across the deck, its shadows jumping weirdly. Towering over him – still drunk, but fired up for the fight – was the slumbering guard, a heavy, spiked mace raised and ready to plunge down into Gisburne's skull.

Gisburne launched himself head first and with all his weight at the knight's unprotected midriff; the Templar gave a great wheeze as the impact knocked the wind out of him. He collided with the mast behind him, and then vomited several pints of hot, sour smelling liquid over Gisburne's back. In a fury, Gisburne grabbed the knight by the surcoat and hauled him away from the mast. The material ripped, but the knight, still winded and now overbalanced, staggered awkwardly, fell to one knee then pitched forward right into the open hold.

The guard had made one fatal misjudgement, opting to take on Gisburne before raising the alarm. But it was not this that occupied Gisburne's mind in those moments: it was the cry the knight had uttered as he fell – a cry not of pain, but of fear. And also the other, stranger sounds that had accompanied his plunge – a flurry of bursts within the hold, one after another, like a flapping or hissing, before the body hit the timbers with a bone-cracking thud.

Silence followed.

Gathering himself, Gisburne recovered the still-lit flambeau and crept towards the hatch. Then, he understood. Far below, curled around the box, lay the knight's body, stone dead. It was bristling with crossbow bolts, and all about it, criss-crossing, caught up in his flailing limbs, was a tangle of fine threads – triggers for the deadly trap into which Gisburne had almost lowered himself.

So much for Templar complacency.

But there was now nothing between him and his prize. Lowering the rope into the gloom, he swung himself down, flambeau in hand, burning away what remained of the web of taut threads as he went.

His feet touched the floor. He knelt before the box, his pulse racing. The hasp was sturdy, but not impenetrable. It would yield. He looked around for somewhere to put the flambeau, and jammed it upright beneath the dead knight's chin. Hardly dignified, but the man was past protesting. Then he drew out the crow, inserted its tip beneath the hasp, and pushed.

With a harsh metallic sound, the hasp broke.

Gisburne did not wait. He flung the lid of the box open. Nestled within was a bundle of blood-red silk. His fingertips went to it, felt the curved, cold mass inside the bundle, then impatiently parted the wrapping.

Gisburne had often heard of people gasping at the mere sight of something, but had never thought it real. It belonged to ballads and stories, or to play-acting children. But now he heard himself gasp – felt the involuntary intake of breath as the thing was revealed.

It was just as Albertus had described. Just as the manuscript had shown. But no description could do justice to its grim, otherworldy beauty. As he drew the flambeau closer, he felt his face light up with the warmth of reflected gold. Gemstones glistened and cast coloured light all about, as if not merely reflecting it, but magnifying it tenfold. And from the heart of this splendour, haloed by the wealth of centuries-old kings, the hollow, lifeless, bone-rimmed eyes of the Baptist stared up at him, into him – the eyes that had looked upon Christ, staring into his soul out of some timeless abyss.

A sound in the darkness made him start. A click. Then another, from his other side. And then a third – directly before him, this time.

Raising his torch, he saw in the fluttering light that the hold was not completely empty of other objects. There were several more boxes of wood and iron, spaced equally around the central one, and pushed back almost to the walls. Each was barely large enough to hold a cat, but those he could see appeared to have metal grilles at their fronts which were hinged open, like small doors. He thought, with an odd detachment, that whatever was meant to go inside must need air. There was a fourth click behind him. He whirled around just in time to see the grille of the last remaining box flip open.

A sudden feeling of dread gripped him. He felt a cold sweat condense upon his skin. A sound in the shadows – unidentifiable, almost imperceptible – made his flesh crawl as if in response to some deep instinct, some nameless horror. Every fibre of his being yelled at him to get out.

Then he knew why. In the light, he could see something moving... Glinting. Black, like obsidian. Almost too late, he recognised the shapes that scuttled towards him in the dark.

Scorpions. Hundreds of scorpions.

The floor darkened about him as they swarmed forward. Desperately, he heaved the skull out of the box and tried to shove it into his bag. The neck of the sack wouldn't open. The metal resisted the wet material, sticking to it. He wrestled with the skull awkwardly, almost dropped it, finally forced it in and slung the bag over his shoulder.

Something touched his bare foot. He kicked it away with a shudder, slammed the lid of the box and climbed on top of it.

As he looked down, lowering the flame, he saw with horror that the horde of shiny creatures was flowing about it on every side, their legs clacking against the boards, against the box, against each other. He had recognised the type – an Arabian variety, highly venomous and extremely aggressive. Gisburne felt his toes clench and draw back from the edge of the box as they piled up against it and crawled over the arms, face and neck of the guard. They picked at the exposed flesh, began to devour it. As the blood flowed, more joined the frenzy. But the body on which they teemed was also slumped hard against the box upon which Gisburne's naked feet stood.

One of the milling creatures had already found its way onto the box. It sensed him, stopped, arched its back, its sting quivering. Gisburne kicked it to the far wall with his big toe before it could move. But more were coming.

He had to get out. But now he could not reach the rope. It hung at least three feet distant from his outstretched hand – too far for him to reach even with his shortsword. Had he been wearing boots, he might risk stepping on them. He might survive one or two stings, but any more would paralyse him. Then they would eat him as he lay there, still alive, tearing off shreds of his flesh as the burning poison coursed through him like acid.

He had to jump. If his hands failed to meet the rope in the dark or slipped on it, he would fall among them. But he could not hesitate.

He gripped the flambeau between his teeth, crouched low, and sprang for the rope.

One hand caught it. The other flailed and grabbed. The rope gave under his weight. He lifted his feet as they dipped close to the writhing mass of horny, stinging tails.

He hauled himself back up the rope, the flambeau in his teeth, and flung himself onto the deck, panting. As he watched in silent horror, the starved creatures swarmed over the body of the guard, until every part of him was obscured by their clacking, black bodies. With a shudder, he dropped the torch into the open hatch, slipped over the port side and plunged back into the freezing water, leaving behind a rising trail of smoke, and the horrid sound of scorpion bodies popping in the flames.

He did not look back. He did not think beyond the need to keep swimming. The skull hung heavily about him, seemed to want to drag him under. But he kept swimming.

He was about a hundred yards from the shore when shouts went up in the Templar camp. Then he saw, reflected on the rocks, the glow of flames, and all Hell broke loose on the beach.

He tried to look around, swallowed water, gagged and coughed. Two boats were already in the water – but they were not heading his way. All their attention was now focused on the ship, on trying to rescue the skull which they believed was about to be consumed by fire. Little did they realise how far it was from that fate, submerged beneath the waves.

If he could just keep going... It felt as if the skull was pulling him down, sinking like an anchor, the strap of the bag dragging, cutting into his shoulder. He almost laughed at it – the idea of the Baptist pulling him under the water. It was strangely appropriate, but he wasn't ready for that baptism just yet.

He grabbed at the rocks. A wave thrust him hard against them, and he felt the barnacles grate the skin off his elbow. The pain was distant – as if someone else's. With his heart thumping, a new thrill rising in him, he scrambled ashore, the flames of the ship now leaping high into the night air.

The climb back was quicker than his descent. His limbs moved without thought, hand and foot moving from rock to rock. The skull no longer seemed to weigh upon him. Nothing did. He felt light as air – as if he could float up the cliff. It hardly seemed possible that the mission had succeeded. Yet it had. He had done it. And they would not catch him. He was not yet to safety, he knew, but they would not catch him. It was something that he felt, beyond conviction. It was a certainty. A fact.

Galfrid's hand grasped his as he reached the top, and hauled him the last few feet.

"You really don't like ships at all, do you?" said the squire, trying and failing to hide his relief.

Gisburne simply laughed – a full-throated, hearty laugh, such as he had not experienced in years. He did not stop to pull on his clothes, but flung himself upon his horse and thundered off with Prince John's prize, closely followed by Galfrid, so buoyed by his success that he did not even pay heed to the single dark figure on horseback, some distance along the road.

IV

MÉLISANDE

XXX

Hattin, The Holy Land – 4 July, 1187

GUY OF GISBURNE stared out across the shimmering, heaving plain and knew all was lost.

Exhausted from lack of sleep and water, his soul crushed by the lifeless desolation of that rocky slope, he blinked against the ocean of heat and dust generated by the seething multitude of Saracen soldiers surrounding the doomed Christian army.

With a sick and aching heart, hands shaking, he hauled off his helm and flung it down into the grit. Saracen arrows still whistled and hissed above and about them. But he no longer cared. His brain felt cooked, the helm's metal as hot as a baker's oven. He would have at least some relief before he died.

But there was no relief. Blinking hard, he staggered and stumbled against the big man to his right, steadying himself with a handful of the oblivious soldier's sweat-reeking tunic. The big man turned his bearded face – a face shrouded with the curious calm of defeat – hooked his hand under Gisburne's arm, and hauled him up.

Gisburne looked, but said nothing. Thanks were superfluous. Absurd. The bearded man knew it. He gripped his spear and turned back to the horde, as if only waiting for them to make their final charge, and finish him.

Gisburne screwed up his bleary, bone-dry eyes in an attempt to clear his vision. They burned as if rubbed with hot sand. Not even tears were left now. His head swam. Somewhere overhead, he had the strange impression of a great, swirling cloud of black birds – but could no longer tell whether this was delirium, his failing sight, or some worse, dark thing.

Meanwhile, from the boiling, tempestuous sea of blurred approximation stretching away before him, unexpected, hallucinatory details leapt and flashed out with horrible, piercing clarity: iron-tipped lances glinting like stars; streaming yellow banners and standards red as anemones; feathered bows blue as birds; crescent swords and Yemeni blades polished white as streams of water; an ocean of hauberks glittering in the sun like the carapaces of a million gilded beetles. And all about, drums beat, weapons clashed, chargers whinnied, voices screamed and cursed, trumpets blasted out their taunting, triumphant calls – a demonic chorus of sounds so great, so incessant and so endlessly multiplied that all merged into one terrible, throbbing tumult, creating in his feverish mind the weird impression that this teeming army were somehow a single gargantuan beast – great Leviathan, whose vast engulfing shadow had come to stamp out the dwindling band of Christian knights.

Immediately about him jostled a dispirited, disordered rabble of infantry, lips swollen and cracked from thirst, their supplies of arrows and crossbow bolts almost exhausted, their fellows fallen at their feet. Among them were unhorsed knights, their mounts abandoned in prickly, arrow-stuck heaps, and here and there dusty, riderless horses bucking and snorting wildly in panic, foam flying from their mouths. All clung to this bare, sun-baked pinnacle of grey rock like ants to a mound, scurrying uselessly in the cold shadow of the great wave that was about to claim them.

He, too, wished only for it to be over now. But their enemy was denying them even that. The Frankish army had been twenty thousand strong at the onset of battle. How many remained alive, huddled here on this high ground, Gisburne could not guess – it seemed to him he had already seen ten times that number broken against this lifeless rock. And yet, when a gap had opened between the two armies as the Christians withdrew up the hill, the Saracens had not pressed home their advantage. In that gap, now, defiant Saracen cavalrymen wove incessantly to and fro, swinging their blades with wild-eyed fervour, and now and then, crouching low, small boys darted out across the disordered field, collecting arrows to bring back to their masters. Gisburne understood their restraint. The crusader army was in a state of collapse from thirst – cut off, now, from every source of refreshment – and he knew that Salah al-Din would have camels bringing his men a constant supply of clear, fresh water from nearby Lake Tiberias. They had no need for haste. They had only to wait.

The momentary ebb of the tide had revealed the full horror of the battle. Beyond their ragged line – and some way within it – the dry, ash-grey earth was littered with the hacked limbs and torsos of the fallen. They were scattered in pieces, lacerated, disjointed and dismembered, cast naked on the field of battle – tunics torn off, bodies cut in half, ribs smashed, stomachs disembowelled, throats split, spines broken, heads cracked open, eyes gouged out, teeth knocked in, hair coloured with blood. Gisburne had seen rivers of blood running between the rocks. They were soon sucked up by the thirsty desert, leaving its dust stained red.

This place upon which they had been forced to make their final doomed stand was called The Horns of Hattin. Already there were those calling it The Horns of Satan, and wondering of what great sin they must be guilty to have deserved such a fate. Death, when it came, would be a relief.

If there was indeed a Hell, Gisburne could not imagine it was worse than this.

They should have stayed at Saffuriya. There had been good water there. The wells at Turan – the supply upon which they had depended, once committed to this folly – had been inadequate for so large a force of men. Others along the route had been poisoned or filled in. And so Salah al-Din's plan had been slowly revealed.

Control the battlefield. That was what Gilbert de Gaillon used to say. He would sometimes give the example of a wild boar. You could not guess what was in its head. You could not tell it where to go. But you could close one escape route and leave another open. This, Salah al-Din had done. Gisburne was vividly reminded not of a boar hunt, but of the chasing down of deer – of powerless animals herded into a killing zone. It was not battle they had marched to, but slaughter. Worse, by the time they were committed, they'd realised they were marching into a trap. But then, there was no going back. The means of retreat was closed off. They could only move forward, deeper into the jaws of the beast, knowing that this was exactly what Salah al-Din wanted.

Gisburne had no doubt that it would make for a tragic but stirring tale some day. Whether any would remain alive to report what actually happened was another matter. It had begun with the attack on the town of Tiberias by Salah al-Din's forces. The great army of King Guy of Jerusalem, mustered by royal decree, was then at Saffuriya, two days' march away across a waterless desert.

KING GUY WAS by nature a cautious man – not one to hurl his men into danger, nor to ignore other possibilities than conflict. The King had not always proven popular, but Gisburne admired these qualities in his namesake. He had also learned from Osric – one of the squires who had attended upon their masters during the councils of leaders at Saffuriya – that Raymond, Count of Tripoli, had argued vociferously for staying put. Salah al-Din clearly wanted to draw them out by attacking the town of Tiberias. And what their enemy wanted was what their enemy must be strenuously denied. Raymond said this, knowing that his own wife, Eschiva, was in Tiberias.

There were those who read Raymond's circumspection as weakness – even cowardice – but Gisburne knew it was simply a different kind of courage. A better kind. It was easy to win respect

as a warrior, to impress the impressionable by
roaring into battle. Richard the Lionhearted had
proved himself an expert in that – but in truth one
did not even require competence for it, merely a bit
of luck. It was far harder to do so as a statesman
or peacemaker, no matter how skilled one was.
And there was clear strategic wisdom in Raymond's
words, which King Guy – more subtle than most of
his contemporaries – had understood. This, despite
his past history with Raymond, for when Guy – then
Guy de Lusignan – had been installed as King of
Jerusalem by his supporters, it had been the Regent,
Raymond, Count of Tripoli, whom he had ousted.

That last night at Saffuriya, Gisburne had slept
soundly, believing, from what Osric had told him,
that wisdom would prevail.

But, come the next morning, everything had
changed. For reasons that Gisburne did not know or
understand – which, perhaps, would now never be
understood – King Guy had listened to the hotheads;
to Templar Grand Master Gérard de Ridefort, to
Reynald de Châtillon. Gisburne shuddered at the
thought of Reynald – at the memories he evoked.
They had advocated a rapid dash across the desert
to relieve Tiberias. It could be done in a day, they
said. He later heard that a key lever in de Ridefort's
argument had been the money that King Henry of
England had given for the campaign – money that
had, in fact, bought Gisburne's services, among
others. The Templar's implication had been that
if they did nothing, this money – already spent
– would be wasted, thus causing mortal offence
to the English King. Whether this had been the
deciding factor, Gisburne did not know, but it was

a sly argument. In truth, had Henry himself been here, he would have seen far greater risk of waste in committing his army to a forced march across a dry, unprovisioned wasteland to a battleground of his enemies' choosing. Henry would have stayed at the sweet, fresh wells of Saffuriya, and forced Salah al-Din to come to him.

But the hotheads had prevailed.

They had done exactly what their enemy wished of them. In doing so, they had also allowed their enemy to deny them what they most wanted: water.

They did not reach Tiberias in a day. The march had become a descent into an abyss. All that day, as the lack of water had begun to bite, Salah al-Din's cavalry harassed them until nightfall. At night, thirsty and demoralised, camped on a plain amongst stunted trees, they had lain awake listening to the drums and distant jeers of their enemy. When they set off again next morning, hoping to reach the wells at Hattin, Salah al-Din had lit brushwood fires along the route of their march, blowing choking smoke into the crusaders' faces. Saracen warriors – so close they could see their expressions – taunted the thirsty Christian soldiers by pouring water onto the dry ground about them. The Christian army carried before it the Holy Cross as divine protection – the very cross upon which Christ himself died. But Gisburne would have traded it on the spot for a fresh well, or another thousand knights. Several nobles and serjeants deserted to Salah al-Din; the news spread as rapidly as the brushfires, plunging the whole army into yet deeper despondency.

And that was the moment Salah al-Din had chosen to attack. Cavalry clashed. Blood and arrows flew.

Decimated, the Christian forces had retreated to the high ground of the Horns. And now here they stood, in this lull, contemplating their inevitable fate.

So deep was Gisburne's despair now that it gripped him like a sickness.

MOMENTS BEFORE, ONE of their number – a yeoman who, two days prior, Gisburne had heard conjuring loving, longing images of the lush, green pastures of his farm in Kent – had suddenly and completely lost his wits, scooping up handfuls of the ash-grey dust and grit and shovelling them into his mouth until he gagged and retched, only to repeat the process, laughing and moaning like an idiot. For a moment, those around could only stand and stare, their resolve utterly drained – until a doughty, toothless old soldier called Bowyer stepped forward, and, with no more emotion than one would spare for an ox, raised his mace and felled the man with a blow across the temple. The yeoman twitched in the dust. Bowyer stove in his skull with a second blow, straightened then turned back again to contemplate his own doom. Gisburne was sickened – but also relieved. He wasn't sure, in that moment, whether to detest Bowyer for the act, or detest himself for lacking the resolve to do the same.

None spoke. The big man next to him – Gisburne thought his name was John – let his head droop, and a long, shaky breath escaped him. It almost sounded like a death rattle.

Tongues were parched, brains exhausted almost beyond the capacity for thought, but this, Gisburne knew, was not the reason for their silence now. He had seen men find inner reserves in worse states. He had seen soldiers shout and sing and laugh in defiance when they were so badly beaten and wounded it seemed impossible that they were alive.

This was different. It was the silence of defeat.

He yearned for some familiar sound then – any sound – was almost ready to batter his fellows into some response. When people roared and shouted in battle, even if it was to mask their terror, you at least knew they had some spirit left. But when *that* silence fell... That's when you knew you had lost. Gisburne had seen it before. The colour draining from faces, the resolve falling from limbs. It was as if their lives were already leaving them – as if they had come to some realisation that their end was upon them, and that no matter what they did, they would never witness another new day – never kiss another woman, never eat another meal, never see another place beyond the wretched field of corpses. Such men were finished before the fatal arrow or sword point struck, already picturing themselves food for the birds that circled patiently above their heads. Spirits flown, their very ghosts crushed. Red stains in the dust. "Battles are first fought in the mind," Gilbert used to say.

In this chaos, from the left of him, came an impossible, utterly incongruous sound.

Laughter.

It was not, as one might have expected, the laughter of madness, or cynicism, or irony. It was a rich, full-throated, belly laugh – something as alien to this place as the cool sound of trickling water. A laugh Gisburne had heard a thousand times – perhaps tens of thousands of times. It had been a constant presence at his side for over a year now, from Sicily to Thessalonika and on into the Holy Land. On innumerable occasions in the past, that laughter had lifted Gisburne's spirits when things seemed lost. Now, it chilled him to the bone.

Gisburne turned and stared dumbly at the familiar face next to him, its white teeth flashing in the sun.

Robert of Locksley laughed at everything. At danger, at pain, in the face of his own death. No, that was not quite true. He did not believe in the possibility of his own death. He seemed somehow charmed – capable of shrugging off the most extreme hardship. Even here, where the summer sun hammered down upon them and men felt their tongues splitting from lack of water, Locksley could be heard to comment on how the climate was good for his bowstring, giving his arrows extra range and power. It should have been infuriating, yet time and again, Gisburne had seen it lift men from the depths of their own despair.

"Well, what a merry ballad this will make," Locksley said. And he laughed some more. "I've a mind to make a better ending of it."

The big bearded man – the one called John – looked at Locksley with an expression of wonder, as people so often did. It was the very same expression Gisburne had once worn himself.

"Do you really think we can?" said John.

"Well, I certainly don't intend to die here. Do you?"

John received this as if it were a revelation – an entirely new possibility that had not crossed his mind. "No." he said. "No, I don't." And something real seemed to change in him. In spite of himself, Gisburne marvelled at it.

This was Locksley's great skill – apart from his genius with a bow, of course. As a bowman, he was formidable. The truce Gisburne had struck with him in recent weeks – a truce struck mostly with himself, and of which, in truth, Locksley was barely even aware – had been a wise move. Pragmatic. Only a fool would refuse to make the most of so keen a weapon. But that didn't mean Gisburne had to like it.

"Boy!" called Locksley. "I need arrows." But the boy, as if deaf, remained motionless, cowering behind the rock which he somehow imagined would afford some protection, his thin arms clutched about his knees, his face expressionless and empty.

Locksley sighed – the kind of sigh ordinary men gave when they found a fly in their drink.

"One more shot, then I am spent – for now," said Locksley, for once a note of frustration in his voice. Gisburne noted the phrase "for now". Locksley could not – would not – conceive of a future that did not include him. He was utterly irrepressible. "Well, no one can say I'm not spoiled for targets." He placed the arrow upon his Welsh longbow – as long as him – his still-keen eyes scanning the field. "Who shall we send this message to, Master John?" And he laughed once again. It was a laugh of unrestrained delight. Of unlimited possibilities.

At its sound – entirely unbidden, entirely unexpected – Gisburne felt a surge of raw emotion. Of hope. Of defiance. He thought to resist it, knowing the nature of its source. But today he did not care, any more than a drowning man gave a damn about who built the raft. Locksley had reminded him he was alive. That there were still things to do, that he mattered. He did not care if it was misguided or a delusion – did not care that he knew it to be both these things – he just knew he needed it. And he saw the effect it had on those around him – how they were emboldened by it, returned to life. He knew why Locksley inspired men as he did; but for a moment, he felt all the love and admiration for this man that had once also inspired him.

He was not dead. Not yet.

He blinked hard again, his eyes clearing. They alighted on something in the tumult, as if drawn to it. All at once, fully formed, an insane idea entered his head – a notion so audacious, so stupendous, he felt his scalp bristle and a thrill rise up in him. He felt himself about to laugh. With his left hand he grasped the arrow that Locksley was preparing to draw, and – eyes wide – pointed a shaky finger out across the heaving ocean of men. Locksley flashed him a look of almost homicidal annoyance – no one, *no one,* interfered with his draw... But then, following Gisburne's fevered gaze, he broke into a broad, white-toothed smile.

Off to the left of them – in the southwest, where the two armies were closest – a tent emerged from the boiling mass of the Saracen army, its long yellow banners whipping and flapping in the wind. Below, framed within it, but clearly visible even to Gisburne's bleary eyes, was a tall, distinct, figure. It was clad in a russet *kazaghand* – an armoured jerkin – picked out with gold. From the jerkin rose a silvery mail coif, which surrounded the bearded, hawk-like face, its eyes intense with concentration. Above that – making the tall figure taller still –

sat a conical yellow cap from which was draped, almost to the length of a cloak, a shawl of pure, nearly blinding white.

Salah al-Din.

"D'you think you could hit that?" Gisburne's mind reeled so violently at the possibility that he physically staggered, suddenly seeming to see the whole battle – the entire war, the future of every man here – turning upon this one moment.

It was an insane suggestion. The target was at the very limit of even the Welsh longbow's range. No bowman alive could hope to hit anything so distant with any accuracy. But that was the kind of challenge Locksley lived for.

He grinned wide at the suggestion. "I can," he said. He braced his left foot upon a rock, squinted at the figure framed in the yellow tent, and sniffed at the air, as if measuring the breeze. Then, with the leader of the Muslim world in his sights, he lowered his arms and upper body, and began to draw the creaking bowstring.

XXXI

THEY TAUGHT YOU to aim for the chest. Then, if your aim was not true, you would still likely hit something. But Locksley was never much of a one for rules. In fact, as Gisburne had noted time and again, to him, rules were like a red rag to a bull. Locksley took pleasure in doing the exact opposite of what was expected – in proving the rules wrong, or merely defying them for his own perverse satisfaction. Gisburne had met plenty of men who had no respect for authority, or who resented it, but Locksley's defiance verged on the pathological.

He had something else about him that the men responded to, though. Something more than charisma or charm – although he had barrel-loads of those too.

It was luck.

No matter how bold or foolhardy his actions, fortune favoured him – far more than any one man deserved, never mind a careless, amoral rogue such as he. It was as if he was somehow indestructible in both body and spirit, and in turn imbued those around him with a kind of boundless confidence – the feeling that if they simply stood near this charmed man, they would not, *could* not come to harm. It was this that had brought him to Gisburne's attention, back when they had first met in the pay of William the Good, Norman king of Sicily. That, and the fact that this lowly archer had, in the space of only a few weeks, somehow gathered his own loyal retinue about him – an army within an army, formed about a locus of natural authority. Such things were not always welcome where authority was supposed to go hand in hand with status, whether blessed by nature or not. But Gisburne respected him, to such an extent that he chose not to question the fact that this common bowman spoke to him – a mounted serjeant, worth half a knight, so it was said – as an equal. Whatever it was the man had, you couldn't fake it. And it got results.

Gisburne's cool pragmatism, natural caution and orderly mind had also apparently intrigued Locksley. Though complete opposites in just about every way, they had gravitated towards each other, ultimately forming a kind of unspoken partnership. Men flocked around Locksley, and Gisburne commanded them as if his own company – though he always knew it was Locksley to whom they really belonged. Locksley himself had no commander, and never would. Yet the bond had endured through the madness of Willam's bloody invasion of Thessalonika, and the doomed assault on Constantinople that followed. It had held firm as, time and again, they had watched whole companies perish around them to be replaced by new blood, and was made stronger as they two, out of all of them, somehow survived every extreme they faced. So formidable had they proved as a fighting unit, that when Locksley took to horse and affected the hauberk of a serjeant – and even began to address knights in a familiar manner that Gisburne himself would never have presumed – his employers let him have his head. When William's crazed dream of conquering Byzantium had finally come to a shuddering halt on the banks of the Styrmon, the pair had headed south, seeking new employment in the Holy Land.

They had found it almost immediately in Reynald de Châtillon.

When they had left the carnage of William's campaign, the cracks had already begun to show. It had been at Gisburne's instigation. The sacking of Thessalonika – after which as many as seven thousand Greeks lay dead – had sickened him. He knew, too, that William's luck was running out, and that theirs could not last much longer. He had also begun to realise that Locksley, fired by their successes, believed himself somehow untouchable. The man feared nothing. That was the source of his strength, but such beliefs were also dangerous. Gisburne had watched as Locksley had hurled himself ever more recklessly at his fate, and seen the delight in his eye as each time he had again come through unscathed, as if more deeply convinced of his own immortality. Where before it had spurred Gisburne on, now it began to unnerve him.

Locksley had finally agreed to accompany him south to the Holy Land on the promise of rich pickings – the protection of wealthy pilgrims en route to Jerusalem. This, at least, was an enterprise with some degree of honour. Locksley cared not a jot for that, but after Thessalonika, Gisburne had discovered a desperate need for it. He was a common mercenary, fighting for pay, fate having robbed him of the chance to be a knight. So be it. He had come to accept that bitter truth. But he could not ignore the knightly virtues with which he had been raised for half his life – could not simply unpick them from his being. He was not a callow fool or dreamer; he knew the terrifying realities of war. But now, perhaps more than ever, he yearned for his actions to carry some meaning, however slight. To work for something more substantial than the greed or ambition of a warlord. Slaughter – at which he had proved so proficient – had brought such feelings to the fore.

Gisburne had also begun to understand that Locksley had no such feelings, no such misgivings. He had begun to wonder *what* feelings the man had. Locksley had saved his life countless times, often putting himself in mortal danger in order to do so. But while Gisburne had once marvelled at his courage, and felt deeply indebted to his protector, what he could not fight off was the creeping suspicion – and the final, undeniable realisation – that Locksley had done it not for the sake of a valued friend, but simply because he could. It had begun to dawn upon him that Locksley not only had no friends, and no personal attachments, but had no real need of them. He loved only challenges – opportunities to push himself to ever greater extremes.

Gisburne had seen many such men on campaign, those who spurned company and toughened themselves for war, made fortresses of themselves. Armies were filled with them. But, almost without exception, they were in denial. They were building walls in order to protect some frail thing within – to save themselves the pain of personal attachments.

Some could sustain it, but many ended up bitter caricatures of their former selves, or crumbled inward, into the growing emptiness they contained, and became wrecks of men. In Locksley, however, he had encountered something altogether different – a man who seemingly did not see the point of relationships – at least, not meaningful ones. He was a man who loved the void – who gazed into it and saw not the horror of emptiness, but infinite potential. When Locksley looked at other men and women, he saw about him not people, but a source of amusement. Obstacles, challenges, resources. To be used, overcome or tossed aside as part of a grand game that he would play and play until he had won. The irrepressible spirit that men so much admired – a spirit to which despair was utterly alien – was, in reality, an unstoppable, all-consuming force of chaos. Locksley was a man made for war – a man who was emotionally unhurt by it, because he had nothing whatsoever invested in it. Gisburne was not like him and could not be. And during those trying times, in which years of experience are compressed into months, he had invested heavily in their friendship. It was not something he could avoid, nor easily undo. But now he understood the investment was not returned, he realised it made him vulnerable.

Gisburne had encountered such a man only once before: Prince Richard, now King Richard the Lionhearted of England, Duke of Normandy, Aquitaine and Gascony, Count of Anjou, Maine and Nantes, Overlord of Brittany. Like him, there was nothing Locksley dared not do. Locksley had none of the advantages of birth that Richard boasted, but he had a ferocious intellect that Richard lacked. And, Gisburne suspected, he had known the reality of poverty. There was no telling what he might achieve if he set his mind to it – if he lived long enough.

When they fell in with Reynald – somewhat against Gisburne's better judgement – things at first seemed to have come good. The Holy Land was ever turbulent, but it was not at war. There was great wealth to be tapped – they even minted their own gold coins here. The women were bewitching, the food and wine cheap and plentiful, and when the merchants tried to cheat you, they at least did so honestly, offering a smile and a shrug when they did not succeed. For battle-weary soldiers, it was idyllic. And Reynald himself was a knight of noble standing, devoted to the protection of Christian pilgrims. A straightforward task, or so it seemed.

As Gisburne was soon to discover, Reynald's Christian zeal led him into actions far beyond the protection of pilgrims. In the first week that they were garrisoned at Reynald's desert fortress of Kerak, they were sent on a foray to seize three Arab traders their new master had claimed were spies, and their possessions. When one had the temerity to protest, swearing he would petition King Guy of Jerusalem about the outrage, Reynald had him flung from the castle walls as the others watched. The body remained on the rocks below as a warning, its bones picked clean by vultures. As he gazed down at them in disgust, Gisburne realised that what he had taken for a tangle of dead, dessicated shrub and a tumble of stones on the rocks below was in fact a disordered pile of regularly replenished human remains bleached white by the sun.

Slowly, the grim realisation dawned on Gisburne that they had fallen into the service of one of the most odious tyrants in the whole of Christendom. That Locksley had begun to admire the boldness of his methods gave him no comfort. He sensed, for the first time, a kind of madness in this man he called "friend" – worse, a madness that was *drawn to* madness, that revered it, as if driven by some unchecked compulsion to dissemble and destroy.

Reynald, it turned out, was not merely a bully, a murderer and a thief, but a fanatic. As a much younger man, Gisburne learned, Reynald been captured by Seljuk Turks during a plundering raid on Syrian peasants at Marash, and was kept prisoner at Aleppo for sixteen years. The conditions under which he was kept were known only to Reynald, but Gisburne had seen two outcomes of long-term imprisonment of Christian knights at the hands of the Muslims. Some – such as Raymond of Tripoli – had come to a better understanding of their captors, even to respect them. Reynald, however, was of the other type. When his vast ransom was finally paid – one hundred and twenty thousand dinars, so it was said – he emerged more bitter, more unpredictable, and more dangerous than ever before, driven by hatred and a desire for vengeance.

He lost no opportunity to rid the world of Muslims – or separate them from their wealth – even where it took things over the brink of disaster. Just five years before Gisburne's arrival, Reynald had attacked and plundered Saracen caravans, spitting in the face of the delicate truce between Baldwin, the Leper King of Jerusalem, and the Sultan Salah al-Din. Reynald's dogged refusal to relent, even under pressure from his own King, had plunged the Christian and Muslim worlds into war. Reynald himself had joined the fray with characteristic vigour, his ships ravaging villages along the Red Sea coast in acts of unashamed piracy. He then attempted to destroy the Muslim holy places at Medina and Mecca. Salah al-Din vowed he would have Reynald's head. But when peace was finally restored, Reynald's head remained on its shoulders, his lusts for war and wanton destruction still festering within.

They were not contained for long. Early one morning Reynald called his men to arms, saying that a company of Salah al-Din's men had attacked Oultrejordain. When they rode out to face them, they found not a column of soldiers, but a caravan of Muslim merchants with women and children, peacefully traversing an agreed trade route. By the time Gisburne realised what was happening, it was too late: Reynald had sounded the charge. Gisburne watched as all – Locksley included – revelled in the plunder. He packed up and left as soon as he could, dragging a protesting Locksley with him. Locksley seemed to have developed an unhealthy infatuation for Reynald – not as a man, but as a force – which disturbed Gisburne deeply. He knew Reynald himself wouldn't fret over their departure – they were owed pay, and the noble knight cared far more for money than loyalty. The money didn't matter much to Gisburne either – the important thing was, they were alive, and out from under that sick shadow.

At any rate, their service – and the lack of opportunity to put their pay and plunder to use – had made them wealthy. Gisburne had a slew of silver coins sewn into the quilting of an old gambeson – so many, he'd lost count. To the casual observer, it was a spare garment, somewhat worse for wear and much repaired. Until they tried to pick it up, of course, but they never did. Locksley simply carried his wealth in a leather bag – and, when that grew too small, a hood, tied around the top with a length of broken bowstring. It jangled unambiguously every time his horse took a step, in a way that clearly gave Locksley a perverse pleasure, and made Gisburne wince. Against all expectation, Locksley had never had any hint of trouble from potential thieves.

They resolved to settle in Jerusalem for a while, and enjoy the fruits of their labour.

For a time, it was a kind of paradise. Never before had Gisburne realised the extent to which his life had been dominated by the constant need to be vigilant, to make decisions. In combat, it was a neverending strain – one so immediate and all-consuming that one never stopped to think about it. If you stopped to think – if you hesitated – you died. Looking back, Gisburne could not remember a time when he had not been in battle, or preparing for it, or tensed and ready for some other new threat. Now he had stopped, the exhaustion flooded over him.

He welcomed the release. The first three days he slept almost without a break, in their luxurious new lodgings – a cool, airy upstairs room with thick, sand-coloured walls and large arched windows – only dimly aware of the gentle breeze that occasionally billowed the sunlit muslin curtains. Then a bored Locksley came and kicked him out of bed, saying there were better beds to be languishing in, with better company. -

That was Locksley's way. He was restless. Questing. Gisburne knew that this hunger for adventure would eventually make him tire of repose altogether, and he feared its return. But for now, Locksley seemed content to throw his energies into all the delights that the city had to offer. And they were many. Gisburne had become wary of Locksley's friendship over the past months – had fought to detach himself from it, to resist relying on what he knew to be inherently unreliable. This was a new Locksley, one he had never seen before. Locksley during peacetime.

But the plain fact was, in the here and now, he was good company. The crazed fire that Gisburne had seen in his eyes faded, and he became a calmer, more languidly charismatic version of himself – an irrepressible charmer with deep pockets, an unquenchable thirst and a seemingly inexhaustible supply of songs, jokes, and magic tricks. Women fell at his feet; men would have too, given the chance. Gisburne, for once, allowed himself to relax and enjoy the ride, content to let Locksley take centre stage. Of course he could still be infuriating – often impossible – but Gisburne had at least grown used to those foibles.

Meanwhile, on the horizon, storm clouds gathered.

A new power had been growing. His name was Salah al-Din – "Saladin" to the Latins. It was clear to any with half a brain that he would one day challenge the long dominion that the Christians had had over Jerusalem – won through merciless slaughter of its largely Muslim population in 1099. But Gisburne, like everyone here, put all such concerns from his mind. It was easy to do in this city – not because no one talked of it, but because they constantly did. It was gossip. Background noise – like the din of a tavern or the hubbub of the souk. In theory, Muslims and Jews were banned from living within the city. In practice, Arab, Christian and Jew traded, ate, drank, argued and debauched as one. They talked of a day of reckoning, and laughed it off together. There had been nearly a hundred years of stability under Christian rule. None seemed willing to break the habit of complacency. None wished to believed that this state of paradise would end.

The scales fell from Gisburne's eyes in dramatic fashion.

Although neither spoke directly of it, Gisburne had known for some time that both had begun to feel frustrated by luxury. Gisburne, because it was too disordered and directionless. Locksley because it was too staid and restrictive. Locksley's revels had become wilder as time went on – too much for Gisburne. Gisburne's natural response had, in any case, been quite the opposite of Locksley's: increasingly, he absented himself and let Locksley go his own way. Their shared lodgings had become like those of a loveless married couple, each living their separate lives around each other. For a while, that proved a perfectly tolerable arrangement.

Then, the night before the *arrière-ban,* the friendship – or the pretence of it – ended for good.

It ended with Rose.

XXXII

GISBURNE DID NOT know her real name. But "Rose" was what Locksley insisted on calling her. One of the higher class prostitutes in the quarter – and an individual with whom Locksley was obsessed – she looked every inch the classic Arab beauty: olive-skinned, black-haired, full-lipped, fine-featured and curvaceous. Gisburne believed she was actually Greek, though it was hard to know for sure – like so many of her profession, she was evasive about the facts of her own life, and mostly told men exactly what she thought they wanted to hear.

But she was easygoing, coquettish, fun. She would laugh and sing when the situation allowed, with no trace of serious emotion to mar the mood. It was easy to believe she really was enjoying herself. Perhaps she was. Or perhaps she was simply good at her job. Gisburne didn't suppose it mattered much to Locksley – he suspected that to him she was more cherished possession than lover anyway. And he realised, after a time, that it didn't matter much to him either. He liked her company well enough – what little he saw of it. She seemed to have a knack for making people feel at ease. What other physical comforts she had to offer, he didn't know, and maintained a discreet distance in order to avoid finding out. But he had little doubt Locksley was pushing them to their limit.

Rather beyond their limit, as it would turn out.

One night, in late May, Gisburne had been out drinking with Mamdour – a Nubian spice trader who was one of Gisburne's regular opponents at backgammon and chess (Locksley was the most formidable player of the three by some margin, but lacked the patience for such trivial games – especially on the few occasions that he lost). Mamdour was a small, wiry man with a face like a shrivelled fig, who, to Gisburne's eyes, looked at least twice his thirty years, but was nonetheless was able to hoist a full barrel with the ease of an oversized Kent brewer. He also had a glint in his eye and a ready wit that he put to good use in his business negotiations. Before making his connections along the Red Sea and settling in the Holy City, he had sailed a felucca on the Nile, and had a seemingly endless fund of anecdotes and jokes, most of which seemed to be at the expense of his fellow Nubians ("Give a Nubian an empty bowl," he would say, "and he'll look underneath it to try to find his soup.").

Gisburne, his head dazed with drink, had returned late to his lodgings that evening, contemplating the thrashing he had suffered at backgammon, but also the harsh revenge he had inflicted on Mamdour – by getting him blind drunk. Muslims who partook could rarely hold their drink. The tactic hadn't helped Gisburne win at backgammon, but the little man would have a stinking head tomorrow.

He had chuckled to himself as he'd walked up the narrow steps to the apartment. It was a perfect, balmy night. Music and laughter and aromas of spices and grilled meats drifted on the gentle breeze. It was one of those moments when it felt good to be a wastrel.

Then, in the cool of the chamber, he stopped. Everything was perfectly still. A lamp burned. The curtains that opened onto the small balcony blew gently on the breeze, the hangings over Locksley's bed wafting in sympathy. Nothing was out of place. Nothing out of the ordinary. But something was terribly wrong.

His brain told him to turn left, towards his own welcoming bed. To crash down on it and embrace oblivion until morning. Instead, he turned right, and walked slowly, unevenly, towards the thin curtains billowing before the balcony. As he passed Locksley's bed, something caught his eye. A reflection. A glint of something covering the tiles of the floor at the bed's side. He remembered feeling it was out of place before he realised what it was. Before he realised it was blood.

It was a great glistening pool – almost black in the low amber light – stretching at least four feet beyond the bed. As he moved further round, transfixed, his groggy mind spun with the possibilities and what they might mean. That Locksley had been murdered. That he had killed himself. Most shocking of all to him was the thought that came next; how he would extricate himself from this situation, so as not to look guilty. Only then did he realise how successful he had been in detaching himself from the man he had so long thought of as a friend and comrade.

Then the wind blew the hangings about the bed – stained on this side, as he now saw, with crimson flecks and spatters, and a dark, striated smear where a bloody hand had clawed at them – and a worse truth was revealed. Sprawled upon the bed, naked, her eyes staring, was the blood-soaked body of Rose. She had been stabbed, and her throat slashed. It seemed, from the slashes on her arms, that she had tried to defend herself. Her natural beauty clashed with the horrid, awkward pose; Gisburne had seen many dead and dying bodies before – hundreds, perhaps thousands – but somehow he knew, with a kind of wretched despair, that this was the one that would stick forever in his mind.

As he stood, struggling to comprehend the situation and his own response to it, Locksley entered through the balcony curtains, dressed only in a voluminous galabiya that almost hung off one shoulder, an ornate goblet in one hand. He stopped, and for a moment the two stared at each other, the curtains blowing.

"Oh," he said. "You're back."

At first, Gisburne could not quite place the emotion on the man's face. Then the fog cleared, and he recognised it. Locksley looked embarrassed. Not horrified. Not traumatised. Not guilty. Just embarrassed. It was as if Gisburne had walked in on him playing with himself, or kicking the dog.

Locksley seemed to simply wave it away. "She kept shouting," he said, a note of irritation in his voice. And he drank deeply from his goblet, and looked back at Gisburne as if the matter were resolved. "Help me sort this out would you, old man?"

Gisburne made two important decisions in that moment. One was to put as much distance between himself and Locksley as possible. He knew, now, that the man was insane. The other was to comply with Locksley's request. This second decision was by far the more immediate of the two. It was his pragmatic mind working – his soldier's mind. No matter who you were, what your occupation or how many people you had butchered on the field of battle, murder was murder. It mattered little that he himself was guilty of no crime. If this were found out, they would undoubtedly both be tried and executed. He was too close to this for his pleas of innocence to be listened to. And if he fled now, this same night, and the murder was still found out, the accusation would follow him forever, possibly never to be resolved. In some ways, that was worse. He briefly considered going straight to the court of the King, and reporting the entire sordid scene. But, much as he resisted the feeling, the notion of betraying the man who had saved his life did not sit well with him. And so, although it appalled him, he knew the only course was to dispose of the evidence. Then – and only then – would he leave Locksley to his own devices. He would go far away, to England. It had been long enough since he was there, and there were matters to be resolved back home.

This decision emboldened him for what was to follow.

The disposal was surprisingly easy. Locksley said he knew of a place, and putting the wrapped body, covered, in a barrow, led Gisburne not to a remote spot beyond the walls as he had expected, but through the maze of narrow streets into the heart of the Old City. There, he revealed the crumbling entrance to a vast, ancient cellar, part of which ran under the Holy Sepulchre itself. What it had once been, and how Locksley knew of it, Gisburne could not guess, but now it was clearly being used as a local rubbish dump. And so, beneath the very place where Jesus Christ had suffered his final agony, and offered up his greatest sacrifice, Locksley and Gisburne dumped the murdered body of a whore. Without ceremony, the nameless woman known as "Rose" was tumbled into the clutter of objects and stinking refuse that now filled that dark vault, and the stone slab restored to its entrance.

All that night, Gisburne scrubbed blood from the tiles in a strange, numb daze, and made plans for his departure.

The next day – the day of the *arrière-ban* – was burned into his memory, its sights and smells as clear as if they were still before him. He could see it now: himself and Locksley perched around a barrel that served for a table on the Malquisinat, the jocularly-named "street of bad food" – between them, a jug of sweet Judean wine and a dish of spiced lamb and artichokes flavoured with lemon, garlic, almonds and saffron, into which they thrust scooped pieces of flatbread, still hot and fragrant with woodsmoke. It all seemed so perfect.

Locksley was smiling, enjoying the morning, as if everything were just as it always was. He ate and drank with gusto, and joked and gossiped with Mamdour. Mamdour's mood, as always, was playful, if a little subdued. He described how, with Gisburne's encouragement, he had tested the patience of his god by the partaking of wine from Lebanon – his one weakness. Now, he said, Allah was showing his displeasure by having a herd of cattle bellow and stamp and shit in his head. Locksley roared with laughter, and nudged and slapped Gisburne. Mamdour held his head and groaned in an almost theatrical manner. "Oh, it was a bad night..." he said. "A baaaad night!"

The words seemed to burn into Gisburne. His mind was in turmoil. All he could think of was escape. And yet, he found himself putting it off, going through the same motions as any ordinary day – sitting, eating, drinking – as if in denial of the horrors of the previous night. He did not want to believe it had happened, but knew he must act. Knew, in fact, that he was in a state of shock, and that it was only this that paralysed his limbs. But, for the first time in years, he also felt powerless to break it.

It was Salah al-Din who supplied the solution.

All at once, there was clamour in the streets. There was a blast of a trumpet, and a half dozen of King Guy's armoured knights appeared, bearing his banner. Gisburne's heart sank. They had discovered the body. They had found out who was her favoured client and had come to arrest the culprits. He was to end in disgrace, just like Gilbert de Gaillon.

But, at that moment, Christendom had little interest in the petty concerns of Guy of Gisburne.

A knight read out a proclamation from the King himself. They would have to announce this many times today – perhaps had done so several times already. As he did so, the bustle of the street faded until there was silence. It was an *arrière-ban* – a call to arms for all able-bodied men within the kingdom, with immediate effect. As it was read, Mamdour regarded his friends with a pained, sad expression, suddenly understanding that they were soon to regard each other as enemies.

Salah al-Din was on the move. It was war.

In order to function during wartime, one had to put certain everyday concerns to one side. Gisburne's chief concerns were hardly everyday – and perhaps he had been rather too keen to put the whole matter out of his mind. But the fact was, there would be no leaving. Not now. He had to make the best of it. And he would have to bury his feelings about Locksley. They were going to war again. He would need him. What troubled him most was the sense of relief he felt at this – the feeling that somehow war felt a more safe, and more secure place than peace.

War had also brought an unexpected master. Henry, the distant English King – who had a hundred times the shrewdness and sagacity of his eldest son – had elected to buy off the Pope with a hefty pledge of money rather than abandon his kingdom for the sake of some damn foreign crusade. The money was to be used to hire mercenaries, for Henry was not keen to lose his knights to the enterprise, either. Little did he realise, his own son and heir – who had learned the power of money but the value of nothing – would, one day soon, abandon everything, kingdom and all, for the chance to spill Saracen blood in that distant desert.

And so it was that Guy of Gisburne and Robert of Locksley found themselves upon this parched rock, fighting side by side under the banner of Henry II of England.

XXXIII

THERE WAS SOMETHING primal, something animal about the way Locksley drew a bow. It seemed to possess his entire body, every muscle stretched to bursting point, his hands heaved apart across his chest as if ripping it asunder. It was like an act of violent destruction – like watching a bear tear a man in half.

But there was also a curious grace, in that continuous, unrestrained movement. There was no hesitation, no thought, no pausing to aim. The instant the bowstring reached its apogee, it was loosed.

Gisburne had seen it more times than he could count. Still it fascinated and astounded him. And never more so than today.

Locksley flexed – one, long, powerful gesture – not breathing, squinting along the arrow's length, bow and bowstring creaking in protest as if being taken beyond the limit of their capabilities. As he did so, a great clamour welled up to the left of them, amongst their own ranks. Urgent shouts and stamping horses. Locksley did not hear it. He eased back as he drew, giving the arrow height, adjusting for the southerly breeze.

The barbed point of the arrow stopped against the yew bowstave, and was gone.

Gisburne – desperately blinking his desert-dry eyes – saw Salah al-Din flinch, and turn towards the clamour. A figure behind him flung up one arm and fell. The Sultan wheeled around, glaring straight at Gisburne and Locksley's position, and two huge men – his Mamluk bodyguards – leapt in front of him, obscuring him from view.

Locksley howled in frustration. "Find me arrows, boy – I don't care how or where!" But the cowering boy simply pressed his hands over his ears and rocked back and forth, whimpering at the growing noise.

Locksley ripped a Saracen arrow from the flank of a Flemish crossbowman and shot wildly at the Sultan's tent with a horrifying roar, as if willpower alone could drive the bloodied tip to its mark.

But there were other, greater moves afoot – the very actions, in fact, that had turned the Sultan's head just seconds before.

To their left, Gisburne now saw, a party of Christian knights – those few who still had their horses and their lives – had formed up and were preparing to charge the Saracen lines. It seemed a futile act. But before Gisburne had realised what was happening, the tiny remaining force had thundered full tilt down the slope, smashed through the front lines of the astonished Muslim army and beaten and battered its way almost as far as the Sultan's tent.

He felt a kind of visceral thrill shudder through what remained of the army; there were cries of "God wills it!" – every man about him emboldened by the cavalry charge. Locksley gave a great laugh, raising his fist in the air and straining forward like a dog on a leash as if ready to rush down and join them.

Chest-deep in men, stabbed with lance and spear and lashed at with every kind of flailing weapon, the knights' horses were finally overwhelmed. Some fell. Others withdrew, not yet ready to give up the fight. Finally, with a blast of trumpets, Salah al-Din's army, no longer content to simply let the Christians die, surged up the slope with a terrible roar as the knights regrouped and were upon them again.

The clash was terrible. Fresh flights of arrows flew. In the right flank, still dozens of yards from the advancing horde, Gisburne gripped his sword, ready to fight to the last. As he did so, a young knight – his head bloody, and a look in his eye that he tried to fashion into defiance, but which Gisburne knew to be terror – rode between him and the enemy. He drew his blade – then jerked horribly as two arrows struck him almost simultaneously in the neck and chest.

Locksley did not hesitate.

"Time to become a knight!" he hollered, and, dashing forward, hauled the still twitching figure off his mount. Gisburne shuddered as the knight hit the ground heavily, head first, his neck twisting and cracking as he did so. Locksley flung himself into the vacated saddle, and then, in that moment – with all Hell breaking loose and himself a heartbeat from death – took the time to give a wry shrug and say, almost with a note of apology: "God wills it..." With that, he grinned at the big, bearded infantryman, who stared back at him, dumbfounded, and made as if to doff his cap. "See you again, John Lyttel – in this life or whatever follows!" And he was gone, bow slung over his back, sword drawn, plunging down the slope towards the heaving mass of men and blades.

Gisburne – who, in recent weeks, had wanted nothing more than to get away from Locksley – now felt, with a kind of perverse indignation, that he was buggered if he was going to let the bastard leave without him. He wheeled around, his blood fired with a new, crazed energy, knowing exactly what he was looking for, but with no expectation of finding it. But there, no longer bucking but stamping in circles, was a Saracen mount. It had lost its saddle, but that hardly mattered. "If it's got four legs and a mane, you can ride it," de Gaillon would say. "And I wouldn't be too picky about the mane."

Gisburne ran, sword still in his hand, grabbed the horse's reins and somehow scrambled onto its steaming back. He tried to turn the horse with his knees. It went left when he urged it right, and right when he urged it left – but there was no time to take up the matter now. He'd go with whatever the horse wanted.

Ahead of him, infantry and cavalry had become mixed in the mêlée – but to the right, in the rapidly advancing Saracen lines, there was a weak point. Only footsoldiers. He could make a decent mark in that. It was an act of madness – little more than a final gesture of stubborn defiance. A gobbet of spit in the face of a charging, fully armoured foe. But anything was better than nothing.

He spurred the horse. It leapt forward, seeming to go straight into the gallop. And Gisburne rode out, wading into the surging ocean of flesh and metal, an unrestrained cry in his throat, flailing at faces, lances, hands, anything, with a strength he did not know he had.

XXXIV

WHEN GISBURNE CAME to, he was lying with half his face buried in hot sand and grit. He had no memory of what had happened, but his left arm, stretched out above his head, burned as if on fire – and the hand felt wet. The realisation made him start. His right hand went to his head. There was a swollen gash there, on his forehead, now dry and gritty. Something had struck him, although he had no memory of it. Perhaps as he fell; or perhaps it was what caused him to fall.

One eye was open, the other crusted with what he supposed was blood. He blinked, forced the lids apart, and looked at his raised limb. His forearm had been skinned on the upper side. Still wrapped around his wrist, pulled tight, was his horse's rein, now soaked in his blood. It had since clotted and dried, sticking the leather strap to the bloody, sand-flecked crust of his exposed flesh. The remainder of the rein lay on the sand, trailing off to a broken end.

Slowly, the realisation came upon him that he must have fallen, and been dragged. How the rein had become detached from his mount, and what had become of the beast, he could not guess. But it had probably saved his life – what little of it there was left. His left hand, he now understood, was not wet. Not any more. It was cold. Numb. Beneath the dried blood and grey grit he saw it was deathly pale, and drawn into a claw. Tentatively, he flexed the fingers. They moved slowly, with a kind of agonising remoteness, like something no longer fully part of him – something in a dream. As they straightened, a sensation like needles made him wince.

He went to lift himself up, and a sickening pain shot through his left shoulder. It felt like it had been pulled from its socket. Quite possibly, it had. Pushing against the ground with his right fist, he raised himself inch by inch, leaning into the rock at his back. He lifted his head and looked about him. His was just one of dozens of bodies dotted about, both Saracen and Christian, some whole, many mutilated. One, just a yard or so away – a handsome Muslim foot-soldier who could not have been more than eighteen, his staring eyes now dead and glassy – was crawling with scorpions. Gisburne shuddered at the sound of their movements. They mingled with the groans of the dying that drifted on the hot breeze. As he raised himself further, he saw the bodies repeated, over and over. He heaved himself up onto unsteady legs, swaying, gazing about him. Hundreds. Thousands. He could not see to the edge of it.

A movement made him start – an upright figure looming nearby. Not twenty paces away, an Arab passed, steadily picking some small objects from the bodies strewn about – Gisburne knew not what – and placing them in a leather sack. He took not the slightest notice of Gisburne.

He was alive. It made no sense – could only have been by the most bizarre fluke – but he was alive. For now.

Examining his injured arm, he picked at the twisted strips of leather wound round the bloody wrist, his own skin bunched up before it. They resisted, stiffened by blood, stuck fast to his flesh. He knew he had to remove the rein or else lose his hand. And so he clenched his teeth and began to unwind. It pulled away, taking skin and dried blood with it, the pain like a red hot iron raking across his forearm. The cry stuck in his dry throat. Fresh blood gushed. Sweat that he did not know he had broke out on him, making him shudder with sudden violence. But he was free. He threw the bloody scrap to the gore-strewn ground, his heart pounding in his chest, panting with wheezing lungs, and flexed his hand.

Yes, he was alive.

He stared into the west. Behind him, he knew, was the unimaginable carnage of battle, and the victorious army of the Sultan. Ahead, nothing but desert. But beyond it, Saffuriya. And beyond that, Acre. The sea. England. It was an impossible, absurd dream. But the pain had awakened something within him – some spirit that refused to acknowledge impossibilities.

He took a single faltering step, staggered, and swayed. He had no water, no food. Barely the strength to stand. He knew the wise move was to turn around, back to the east – to surrender to Saladin's men, to make himself their prisoner. He at least stood a chance that way.

Then, with a will that seemed to come from some other place, he began to walk slowly into the west.

XXXV

Somewhere in France – December, 1191

THERE WERE THREE knights blocking the fork in the road. Templars. At first, Gisburne thought they must have been from the ship. Yet his common sense told him this was impossible. But for a brief stop in the woods to dress and safely stow the skull – during which Galfrid, on watch atop a pinnacle of rock, had seen not a single horseman for a mile about – he and Galfrid had been riding at the gallop all the way. Their pursuers would have to have taken wing to overtake them, and even Templars did not have that power. Not yet, at least – though Gisburne did not doubt that Llewellyn was working on such a scheme. Then, as they drew up their horses, he spied a familiar shock of red hair and beard upon the central figure.

Tancred's men.

Word had spread fast. Far faster than he had imagined. And somehow, Tancred had anticipated his move – had known, perhaps, that the skull was threatened, and if taken would be transported north. Nothing would surprise him. He was proving himself a formidable opponent; a skilled player of the great game. Perhaps he had such groups of men on every road leading out from Marseille. But now the one eventuality Gisburne had wished to avoid – direct, open conflict with Tancred de Mercheval – was irrevocably upon them.

Galfrid glanced nervously at the wooden reliquary box hanging from the cantle at the back of Gisburne's saddle, then back at the distant trio upon the road.

"Have they seen us?"

"They've seen us."

"So what this time?"

"Remember Paris?"

"Vividly," said Galfrid. "But so will he. And, if you remember, I was knocked off my horse and almost killed."

"You will have learned from that," said Gisburne. He nodded in the direction of Fulke. "But my guess is, this one won't." He drew his sword. Even if they got past, they could not outrun them; they had to put them out of action. "Are you a scholar, Galfrid?"

Galfrid looked at him as if this were the most ludicrous question he had ever been asked. "Yes..."

"You know the battle of Cannae?"

"Of course, but..."

"I'll take the right flank." Then Gisburne's mount reared up at the touch of his spurs, and leapt to the gallop. Galfrid groaned, spurred his horse and thundered after him, Gisburne's pilgrim staff whirling about his head, everything now pinned on the strength of his master's guess.

Gisburne's guess was based on two factors. First, what he had seen of Fulke and knew of such men. Second, a more tenuous fact to which he had alluded outside Paris: *Templars aren't what they used to be.*

For months after the news had reached England, it seemed there was but one word on everyone's lips. Hattin. *Hattin*. It was uttered quietly, fearfully, as if the word itself had the power to infect and spread disillusionment and destruction. It was spoken with shock, and with awe. With anger and disbelief. Amongst ordinary people it was customary, when some disaster struck, to treat the terrible event with a kind of black humour. Thus, it was tamed. Made safe.

But there were no jokes made about Hattin. On that day, the whole Christian world had changed. It had faltered and shifted on its axis. From it, all sensed, there was no going back. The complacent now saw their terrible error. The fearful found justification for their paranoia, and began to see enemies everywhere – in every dark face, foreign custom and unfamiliar tongue.

Twenty thousand men had faced Salah al-Din's army that day – twelve hundred and fifty knights mustered from Jerusalem, Tripoli and Antioch, plus many thousands of serjeants, Turcopoles, mercenaries and regular infantrymen drawn from the local population and beyond. Perhaps three thousand finally escaped the battlefield. Of those captured, some had been ransomed, others sold into slavery. The Turcopoles, as deserters from the Muslim faith, had been slaughtered where they stood. Salah al-Din had, of course, afforded King Guy himself the respect deserved by a king and fellow general. The Muslim leader had sense of decorum. But Reynald de Châtillon, upon whom he had sworn revenge and who spat insults to the last, he personally beheaded. Many across Christendom would have breathed a secret sigh of relief at that news.

Widely known as a humane ruler, Salah al-Din was also a supremely practical man. He had understood that the elite knights taken prisoner that day – some two hundred and thirty Templars and Hospitallers – were far too valuable a military resource to simply release. Ten years before, his army of twenty-six thousand men had been smashed by a far smaller Christian army at Montgisard, and all because of a contingent of just five hundred Templar knights. He had learned his lesson. And so, he had the Templars and Hospitallers taken at Hattin executed. In the space of a day, the Christian military orders had been decimated – almost to a point of collapse.

They had not collapsed. Doggedly, they had fought back from the brink. But in building up their numbers over the past four years, they had perhaps not been so choosy. So it was that a number of dubious characters – many of them ambitious bullies unworthy of the title "knight", let alone the honour of wearing the red cross – had found their way into the Order.

Men who knew force, but not strategy – who believed that victory was found in the exertion of muscle and sinew, not of the mind. Men who had plenty of experience of fighting, but little of waging war.

Men like Fulke.

As Gisburne and Galfrid charged towards the three knights, Gisburne saw that Fulke had learned a lesson. He had ordered the three into a tight defensive formation, allowing no gap between. He would not have his attackers break him this time. It was no surprise to Gisburne that Fulke also put himself at the centre. He smiled, holding his sword high, so close he could see their eyes glint beneath their domed helms, Galfrid now almost level on his left side.

"Hah!" he cried and wheeled suddenly to the right. Galfrid veered left.

Gisburne switched his sword from his right hand to his left and drew it back.

Galfrid, meanwhile, brought the staff round in a sweeping arc. His opponent struck out at him as he passed, but the staff was far longer in reach than the knight's sword. The blade missed Galfrid, struck the whirling staff, but could not hope to stop its forward momentum. It struck him full in the chest with a horrid *crack*, pitching him backwards over the cantle of his saddle to sprawl awkwardly on the ground.

On the right flank, as he closed, Gisburne had seen his enemy's eyes widen in alarm behind the faceplate of the man's helm. The last-minute switch of hands had taken his adversary completely by surprise – and put him at a fatal disadvantage. The knight – right-handed – had limited reach and power on his left side. Gisburne, meanwhile, now had the full sweep of the sword to his left. The knight raised his blade, knowing he could not strike Gisburne, hoping only to parry the blow. At the last moment Gisburne dropped his own, then brought it sweeping upward. It bypassed the knight's blade completely and connected with the faceplate of the helm, striking so hard it jarred Gisburne's shoulder and bent the faceplate out of shape. The knight lost his weapon, reeled backwards in his saddle, righted himself, fighting with the helm which was now jammed upon his head; the faceplate pressed against his cheek, half blinding him, his horse tottering in confused circles.

Fulke, meanwhile, had been so tightly hemmed in by his fellows that he could do nothing to repel the first charge, and sat impotent whilst those about him – those who he thought guaranteed his safety – were battered and unhorsed. The lesson he had not learned – that he should have learned – was something that de Gaillon had already drummed into Gisburne by the age of thirteen: "a good general never attacks his enemy the same way twice."

Galfrid and Gisburne now wheeled around for a second pass.

Fulke roared and waved his sword – a gesture that revealed the terror it was meant to mask. They closed in around him. Gisburne parried a sword blow. Galfrid struck the Templar hard in the stomach, driving the wind out of him like a bellows. Gisburne struck again, sending Fulke's sword spinning through the air. Fulke scrabbled for the mace at his saddle, knowing he would not – could not – be quick enough.

Something grabbed at Gisburne's saddle. The knight with the crushed faceplate had wrestled his helm off his head, and now – one eye half closed, the cheek swollen like a rosy apple – was yanking the box free. It came loose, swung around and smashed Galfrid in the back, knocking the staff from his hand and him out of his saddle. His horse panicked and kicked. Galfrid kept his grip just long enough to slither to the ground.

The tables had turned. It was now two mounted men against Gisburne – and they already had the reliquary box in their possession. Galfrid snatched up the staff, caught the reins of his horse and tried to bring him back under control. But, unlike Nyght, the horse was not used to battle.

The mêlée was messy and confused. Gisburne dodged a swipe of Fulke's mace as their horses barged against each other. He had no helm on his head – the great helm still hung upon his saddle. If just one blow connected with his skull, he was done for. He swung his sword in retaliation, but Fulke parried it. They remained locked for a moment, each struggling until Fulke grabbed Gisburne's sword blade with his gauntleted left hand and held it fast. Gisburne pulled at it, suddenly aware that the knight with the swollen face was advancing behind him, battleaxe raised above his head. Gisburne could not get free, could not move or turn, and Galfrid was still yards distant.

Without warning, the other knight uttered a bizarre choking cry and fell, an arrow in his back. The axe clattered to the ground, and the box – still clutched in his other hand – slid from his grasp. Fulke looked on in astonishment, and Gisburne now saw that a black-clad rider on a dark horse was hurtling towards them, head and face completely obscured by black wrappings, bow in hand – a Saracen bow, short and compact. Gisburne took advantage of the distraction, hauling hard on his sword. It slid from Fulke's grasp, slicing through the leather grip of his gauntlet. He howled in agony, his horse rearing.

The black rider – the same slight figure Gisburne had seen invade their room in Auxerre – leapt from his horse almost before it had stopped, flung down the bow and snatched up the fallen reliquary. Fulke, meanwhile, disliking the new odds, turned his horse about. Gisburne swiped at him as he fled. But the black rider was already back in the saddle, turning away to the north, the box gripped under one arm.

Gisburne looked around urgently, and saw Galfrid – alive and well.

"Go!" shouted the squire. "Don't wait for me!" Gisburne nodded and made off after the departing black rider, already a good half-furlong distant.

Watching Fulke receding along the other fork, Galfrid stooped, tore the arrow from the stricken knight's back, nocked it on the discarded Saracen bow, and took aim.

"Have a souvenir from England," he muttered, letting the arrow fly.

The arrow clipped Fulke's left shoulder. He recoiled, swayed, and fell.

Galfrid shouldered the bow, climbed into his saddle and galloped away after his master.

XXXVI

GISBURNE HAD RARELY seen anyone ride with such
skill, or with such fury. Like its rider, the horse was
slender and small of stature, but long-limbed and
powerful and impossibly swift. Gisburne thought
he recognised the distinctive shape of an Arabian
horse. If that were the case, his palfrey's chances of
catching or outlasting such a beast were zero.

Some two hundred yards along the dry dirt
road, the black rider had darted off into the trees.
Gisburne followed. The trees were not closely
packed, but they were small, and their branches low,
and riding between them at speed was hazardous in
the extreme. Gisburne's quarry seemed to negotiate
them with an almost supernatural ability, ducking
and dodging between the boughs with the instinctual
grace of a deer. Only by following an identical path
did Gisburne manage to stay in the saddle, and even
then he found himself lashed by twigs and branches.
It struck him, then, that the pursuit was futile. He
could only gain the advantage by doing the one thing
he knew he was unable to do – breaking away and
somehow cutting the thief off. To follow doggedly
in the same hoofprints might work if he were astride
a fresher, faster beast, but his mount was already
flagging, already at the limit of its endurance. He

was certain, too, that the black rider's horse was well within his – that he was idling, toying with him, saving his energy.

Then, as he was giving up hope, something happened that he could not have predicted. The black rider slowed, drew up amongst some young oaks, and dismounted. So, he wished to fight. Well, that was something Gisburne was better equipped to deal with, at least. He dropped down from his horse and faced his adversary at some dozen yards distance. The dark figure stood, the box still tucked under his arm, one hip pushed slightly out. Gisburne could see now that the fellow had no sword upon his belt – though weapons of various kinds were tucked about his saddle. What he did have was a matching pair of curved knives the likes of which Gisburne had never seen, their black and silver grips protruding from broad, black scabbards. But so far, he had drawn no weapon, and showed no obvious sign of doing so.

Without warning, he started towards Gisburne. Gisburne's hand went to his sword hilt. The black rider paused, then continued; Gisburne drew the blade, took a step forward. The figure seemed to drop, then spin, and a foot whipped around and kicked the weapon from his hand. Gisburne's hand went for his knife. The foot whipped around again – but this time Gisburne was ready. He caught it, and lifted it, throwing his attacker off balance. The box tumbled away. The black rider landed heavily on his back, was momentarily stunned – and Gisburne was on him. He sat astride the fellow's stomach, denying him the knives in his belt. His foe struggled hard, but, fast as he was, he could not match Gisburne in weight or strength. Then Gisburne grabbed at the wrappings about his captive's face. He would know at last who this was, who kept their face covered and crept about in the night.

Gisburne pulled. The material unwound. "Time for you to show your face, you miserable cow–"

The word *coward* stopped in Gisburne's throat. He sat back in shock. The face of Mélisande de Champagne glared back at him, her eyes fiery, her hair full and wild.

"'Miserable cow'...?" she said. Then a black-clad foot hooked around his neck and flipped him backwards. Gisburne fell heavily, rolled once and leapt to his feet, clutching his bruised throat, his eating knife drawn. But Mélisande was already up, a blade in each hand. They stared at each other for a moment, the only sound their panting breaths – eyes locked, muscles tense. Galfrid drew up sharply some twenty yards distant, and looked in baffled astonishment.

"Do you want to live?" she said.

Gisburne stared at her, frowning, still in shock.

"Yes," he coughed, his windpipe still smarting.

She sheathed both knives in one swift move. "Then follow me."

And she turned and whistled for her horse.

XXXVII

As THEY RODE through the sparse, open forest, Mélisande leading the way, Gisburne found himself going over the events of past weeks. The first sighting in Paris. The intruder in their room. The meeting on the outskirts of Marseille. The dark assassin in the streets. Everything now seemed to take on a different hue.

"We share a common goal with regard to the skull," she had said before they had mounted up to follow her. "Trust me." And for some reason, he did. She had let him catch up with her in the woods, when she could so easily have made her escape. She'd had the chance to kill them, as they slept, and had not taken it. She had, in fact, saved their lives – his, more than once. She had also taken the box, he now realised, only when it was threatened with capture by Tancred's men. He didn't doubt she could take it from them again if she chose to do so. She was determined and capable enough.

He looked at her, several yards ahead now, her coils of golden hair tumbling down her back. The girl who had run wild in the woods and fields. She might well be that same girl at heart, but her methods had clearly moved on. Where had she learned those skills, and acquired those weapons – both of which seemed to point to the empire of Salah al-Din? And to whom, or what, was she now loyal?

The spell was broken by Galfrid sighing deeply beside him.

"Typical woman," he said.

Gisburne stared at him, screwing up his eyes as if the better to comprehend this strange, random statement.

"*Typical woman?*" he repeated, with incredulity and not a little irritation. He looked back to the slender figure ahead of them. "One who dresses as a man, creeps about like an assassin in the night and steals holy relics from Templars? I don't know what kind of women you're used to mixing with, Galfrid, but this is a first for me."

"I just meant..." said Galfrid, looking as if he already regretted saying it, "that it's typical of a woman to be the very last thing she appears to be."

Gisburne huffed at that. "I've met plenty of women who are exactly what they appear to be. Disappointingly so. Believe me, this one is far from typical."

Out of the corner of his eye, he saw Galfrid give a wry smile. Gisburne chose not pursue it.

Something else was taking his attention now. Something he had not expected, and was at a loss to explain. In the hard riding and fierce fight, his body and mail had heated up considerably, and now, it seemed to him, a distinct odour was rising from it.

Gisburne sniffed at his mail again. Not vinegar. But not exactly pleasant. Thick, this time. Meaty. Slightly rank. Something half recognised, but so incongruous it was impossible to place.

"Galfrid...?"

Galfrid looked across at him.

"This latest thing I am smelling. From my hauberk..."

"Lard," said Galfrid, matter-of-factly. "Good for proofing the links against rust. I took the liberty before we left Marseille."

"Lard. Of course. Stupid of me." Gisburne nodded, resignedly. "So, I am to smell like a side of bacon now..."

Galfrid gave a smirk. "She won't mind," he said.

Gisburne chose not to grace that with a response.

"We're here," said Mélisande at last, slowing. She put her fingers to her mouth and whistled, and a whistle answered. Up ahead, Gisburne saw the trees thin out into a clearing, from one edge of which led a wide path. And in the clearing was a large encampment – the very same as Gisburne had seen that night in Marseille. The three wagons were drawn into a horseshoe, and among them were pitched several tents about a central fire. Liveried servants cleaned, groomed horses and served food, while a half dozen knights – in surcoats of green, each emblazoned with a yellow sun – sat eating and tending their weapons. Several had evidently jumped to their feet at her approach, and on catching sight of Gisburne and Galfrid, three went for their weapons. Mélisande stayed them with a hand. "Make ready to leave!" she called. Immediately, activities were curtailed. The fire was extinguished, the horses prepared. All set about striking camp and packing the wagons with well-practised efficiency. "Welcome to my home," she said to Gisburne.

As her people bustled about her, Mélisande squatted by the glowing remains of the fire. Without a word, a servant handed her some meat and a cup of ale – two more servants thrust the same into the hands of Gisburne and Galfrid.

"Eat," said Mélisande. "We leave as soon as the wagons are ready."

Gisburne did so. Judging by the intensity of the activity, that moment would come soon.

"This is the second time we have shared a meal," said Gisburne. "Perhaps this time we can speak more plainly."

"Perhaps." She almost smiled.

Gisburne studied her intently.

"You've acquired some Saracen ways," he said. "Some Saracen skills."

"I spent some time there," she said dismissively. "In the so-called Holy Land. I learned a great deal."

"Such as..?"

"Such as, it is not all so holy." She laughed. "Why? Do you think me perhaps an agent of the Sultan?"

"I think you are a loyal servant to King Philip," said Gisburne. Mélisande said nothing, her face neither confirming nor denying it. "I saw you in Paris. Weeks ago. Leaving the Îsle de la Cité via the Grand Pont." Those were the certain facts. But Gisburne decided it was time to add some conjectural flesh to their bones. "You were at his palace. Preparing for this venture, as Tancred was." He shrugged, and drank. "I've encountered no other agent of the French crown upon my travels, but it is absurd to think the King would not have someone keeping an eye on things. It might as well be you."

"What a nice way to put it." Mélisande smiled sweetly – a smile that somehow seemed to combine perfect innocence with impish mischief, and gave away absolutely nothing. "I also saw you in Paris," she said. "Fighting with Templars. If you wish to continue in this line of work, you really must learn to be more discreet."

Galfrid stifled a snigger.

Gisburne sat forward. "You claimed we shared a common goal," he said. "That goal is to keep the skull out of the untrustworthy hands of this rebel Templar. Correct?"

This time, he saw in her eyes that he was.

"Tancred strays further from the fold every day," she said. "He no longer feels bound by the authority of his own order. His view is that the skull should never have been given up. That it has a power. And perhaps... yes, perhaps he means to take it for himself."

He smiled. "Then as long as the skull is in France, it would seem we are indeed of one mind, and one heart." He thought she almost blushed at that. Then, after a moment's hesitation, he added: "But what about after that?"

She looked into his eyes for what seemed a long time, then stood suddenly.

"You will travel with us from here," she said. "It's best."

"But the wagons are slow," protested Gisburne. "If we are to prevent Tancred getting ahead of us, then men on horseback..."

"...will be easily spotted and swiftly hunted down," she interrupted. "Tancred is already ahead of you. And these wagons are faster than you think."

Gisburne looked at them sceptically.

She sighed, growing impatient. "I am the daughter of the Count of Boulogne. No one will suspect you are travelling with me. And even Tancred would not dare cross a nobleman's family in his own land. It will afford you greater protection."

"Whilst allowing you to keep closer to your prize," said Gisburne.

She smiled at that. "You *are* good," she said. "But don't flatter yourself."

Gisburne hesitated, and Mélisande took a step towards him, her manner suddenly sincere. "You're exhausted. Tancred's men are looking for you, and they know your faces. With us, you pass unnoticed. You can travel in one of the wagons, out of sight – even sleep, if you need to. And I won't be offended if you take turns. To keep watch on your box."

Gisburne knew perfectly well that she could have taken it for herself by now. That she still could, given the men at her disposal. He wondered at it – could not entirely fathom it. And what would happen once they reached Paris, and Gisburne and Galfrid went to break away with the skull, heading for England? That was a mystery. But, Gisburne found, it was a mystery to which he very much wished to know the answer.

"The first wagon is mine," said Mélisande, pulling off her jerkin and throwing it in the back. "The second will be yours. It has space enough for you to be comfortable."

"You know they'll be watching the roads," Gisburne said, as he tethered his horse to the wagon.

"Not these roads," said Mélisande. "And if they're still with us past Lyon, we'll lose them in the Morvan."

Galfrid looked startled. "No one in their right mind chooses to go through the Morvan in winter."

Mélisande smiled, stepped forward and brought a hand up to the squire's face. "And that is precisely why we do it." She turned, removed her belt and knives and hurled them into the wagon. "And now, I am going to make myself a woman again." She pulled herself aboard her carriage. "I suggest you rest. Au revoir, gentlemen." The flaps of the canvas tilt were pulled tight shut and the convoy began to move.

Galfrid stared after her as if in a trance.

"Typical, eh?" said Gisburne, and hauled himself into the back of their wagon.

XXXVIII

The Morvan – December, 1191

BY THE THIRD day, they could see them. Loping along the treeline, their shaggy heads hung low, they wove in and out of the trees at the forest's edge, sometimes disappearing from view, sometimes in plain sight, but always keeping pace, their ice-blue eyes fixed on the travellers.

Galfrid watched them nervously as his horse plodded though the deep snow, the wagons creaking and labouring behind them. "What are they doing?" he said. "Why don't they just attack?"

"They're not stupid," said Mélisande.

Gisburne pulled back his hood and squinted at the trees. "They're waiting for us to die," he said.

"And if we don't?" asked Galfrid.

No one answered the squire's question.

Mélisande had not shrunk from her promise to take them through the Morvan mountains. When her scouts had returned and reported Templars on all the main routes through Burgundy, she had turned the wagons towards the snowy plateau. It was, thought Gisburne, an ideal place for outlaws to hide out. Once someone determined to hide up here, not even an army would root them out. In turn, of course, his hypothetical outlaws would have no passing traffic to rob. This had started in Gisburne's mind as an abstract thought – a mere fanciful train of thought – but as they progressed it began to trouble him, and he started to keep an eye on the trees. Who knew *what* was up here?

Very soon they realised their only company went on four legs.

They heard the howls on the very first day. The snow was heavy and untouched, the going painfully slow. None challenged Mélisande's decision, but she began to look pained and drawn, as if it weighed heavily upon her. Gisburne understood, somewhere within, that those who travelled with her were more than servants and retainers. They were family, just as the wagons and the tents they contained were home.

The wolves brought a new level of anxiety. At first, it was the merely the sound that pulled and shredded their nerves. The long, mournful cries – sporadic that first night, but incessant by the second day – oppressed them. The horses, already unnerved by the deep snow and struggling with the extreme cold, were twitchy and apprehensive. Their fear would also tire them more quickly; Gisburne hoped against hope that the baying would dwindle and fade into the distance when the wolves finally gave up. He had no argument with the beasts; he was happy to leave them be. He hoped they felt the same.

Bit by bit, the howling drew closer. The creatures were tenacious, and were tracking them. By the end of that second day – a day which seemed to last forever – Gisburne knew that some kind of conflict was inevitable.

It was almost a relief when they finally saw them. They were disembodied sounds no longer – not distant, imagined phantoms, but flesh and blood. But that brought new worries. They were real, now; flesh and blood that regarded them as prey.

Gisburne had seen wolves many times, but not like this. These creatures were bigger, leaner, more rangy than anything he had encountered before. The fur that hung about their bony frames was dark and matted, their eyes wild and piercing, each one of them panting in great smoky breaths. He didn't like the state of their coats. It showed they were malnourished; and that meant they were hungry.

Then one of the horses at the back of the convoy, tethered to the last of the wagons, was attacked. Mélisande's knights fought them off, but the horse – its throat and back leg ripped – had to be put down where it lay. They left it, in the hope the hunters would be satisfied.

Perhaps it was the taste of fresh blood that emboldened them. Some time around midday, a shout went up from the head of the convoy. Gisburne and Mélisande rode forward, and saw, up ahead, a half-dozen wolves spread out before them in a great arc. Gisburne watched as one – the largest – crept forward of the rest. The leader. The others moved only when he did, never pushing, never challenging, but all the while shifting formation, as if in response to invisible, inaudible signals. The wolves were now spread across the whole of the valley ahead of them like the jaws of a trap, and the convoy was moving into its maw.

Gisburne suddenly had a vivid memory of Hattin. Of the Christian army marching to its doom, into the jaws of Salah al-Din's trap.

"There's only one way to end this," he said.

Mélisande and Galfrid armed themselves with bows and advanced ahead of the convoy several paces behind Gisburne. "Shoot anything that moves," he said. He had armed himself with a spear. It was meant for just one wolf: the leader. He meant to draw it out. But it would be difficult; the creature was canny to have survived this long in such conditions.

Gisburne stepped forward of the others, vulnerable now. The pack shifted, closed. He spied the leader. Then it dropped flat. He trudged forward, further still from his fellows.

Something dashed out from the right. Galfrid's arrow flew, but failed to hit home. While they were distracted by the right flank, those on the left suddenly closed in. Mélisande felled one with her bow, and on the other side, Galfrid hit another. It collapsed into the snow and lay whimpering. When Gisburne turned to the front, the leader was just yards away, its body low, its steely eyes on him, teeth curled back, drool dripping from its jaws. It was already imagining him as food.

"Come on, then!" he cried, thrusting the spear forward.

The wolf flew at him. Others would try to join him, support him in the kill – but that was where Mélisande and Galfrid came in. At the edge of his vision, Gisburne was dimly aware of the furred creatures closing in, of arrows flying, of yelps as they made contact. Ahead of him, the lead wolf leapt. Gisburne dropped, raising his spear as he did so, the point driving into the wolf's chest as it came down on it with all its weight. It made a terrible screech, thrashing as Gisburne fell back into the snow, lifting the animal up and over his head on the end of the spear. He heard it crash down behind him, felt his spear shake loose.

But it was not yet done. Gisburne turned. In a fury, as if its injuries were no more than a wasp sting, it snarled and leapt at him again. As it did so, he had a vision of Mélisande, a look of horror on her face, the arrow on her bow aimed directly at the wolf leader – and at him. He knew she could not – would not – shoot. The beast's teeth closed around his arm; he wrestled, swung at it, and both fell to the ground.

When he scrambled to his feet, the wolf lay lifeless in a red-stained depression in the snow, his eating knife in its neck. The rest of the pack had stopped. They ducked and padded the ground uncertainly, some whimpering. Gisburne drew out his knife, and advanced toward the nearest of them.

"Go!" he shouted, waving his arms at it. "There's no meal for you here today..." To his amazement, the creature lowered its head, and backed away. The rest followed, melting away into the trees. There was a cheer from the convoy.

Mélisande ran to him. "Are you all right?" Still panting in great, foggy clouds, he confirmed that he was. She advanced towards the bloody animal. "We should eat it," she said. It was a moment before Gisburne realised she was not joking. "Our food supplies are running low. We don't know what game is to be found ahead." And with that she crouched, and with drawn knife cut the hind legs and haunches off the animal with a practised efficiency Gisburne had seen only on the hunt. She wrapped them about with cloth and tied them tight.

"Don't you want to make a waistcoat of the skin too?" said Galfrid.

"Grey's hardly my colour," she said, as if Galfrid's suggestion were utterly preposterous, and went back to her horse with the bloody packages, as if eating wolf leg were the most normal thing in the world.

XXXIX

Up ahead, distantly, through a break in the mountains, Gisburne could see the land fall away, the terrain soften.

"We're through," he said. "Traverse this last pass and we descend to low valleys once more." Beyond, now, lay Auxerre. Then Montargis, then Courances. And Nyght. He would reclaim his horse, and they would strike out for Boulogne, and the coast. Before that, of course, was Paris. He meant to miss out Paris. What Mélisande would think of that, and how they would be reconciled, he was yet to find out. But for now, it did not matter. He felt only relief, and joy.

The members of the party were in high spirits as they descended from the plateau. Even the horses, which had endured the worst hardships of all, seemed to sense better times ahead. The sky was clear, the sun shone, and the snow was thinning. The mountain road directly ahead was completely clear but for a few drifts. Gisburne guessed it was the high winds on this side that had kept the rocks bare – but now, he also saw, the snow was beginning to thaw. He rejoiced at the thought. No more snow. No more ice. He didn't care if it rained from now until Doomsday. They would have rocks and stones and earth beneath their feet once more.

As they descended, laughing and joking, Galfrid shocked all by breaking out in song, in a fine tenor voice. They clapped along as he trilled about summer coming in, even affecting a comic falsetto for the chorus.

Another sound – distant, but distinct, at odds with the merriment – made Gisburne turn. He scanned the mountainside, the horizon, but saw nothing unusual. He raised a hand. Galfrid saw the concern upon his master's face, and his song faltered and died. Gisburne strained to hear against the wind.

The sound rose up again, gusting with the breeze – familiar and unfamiliar.

It was howling. Or rather, it was an approximation of howling.

"Wolves? Again?" said Galfrid.

"Worse," said Mélisande. "Men."

As she said it, one of her outriders came back up the road towards them at full gallop.

"Templars," he said, pointing ahead. "A large party. Heavily armed."

"How many?" said Gisburne.

"Fifteen at least," he panted.

"Did you see red ribbons upon their arms?" demanded Mélisande.

"I don't know," he said, his face flushed. He shook his head. "Possibly..."

"Think!"

"Who else would it be?" said Gisburne grimly.

"Hide in the wagon," said Mélisande. "They won't search them. They wouldn't dare."

With great reluctance, Gisburne and Galfrid followed her advice.

XL

THEY LAY IN darkness beneath the awning of a furled tent, feeling the wagon pitch and rumble on the stony track. Gisburne had insisted they have their horses saddled and packed and tethered to the rear of the wagon; if the need for a quick getaway arose, he did not wish to be caught unprepared. But the reliquary box had stayed inside, out of sight, and now nestled between their heads. Mélisande, sat at the front of the wagon, occasionally called back, relating what she could see. There was indeed a large group, spread across the road. They were Tancred's men, and Tancred was among them. Then her commentary went silent, and Gisburne knew they were close.

Gisburne heard a voice howling in imitation of a wolf, then breaking into laughter. He swore it was Fulke. Galfrid cursed under his breath at the sound; his arrow had struck home, but the bastard wasn't dead. There were shouts, commands, other voices raised in protest. The wagon drew to a halt. Mélisande's voice – clear and strong, with no hint of anger – rose above all others, greeting Tancred respectfully and requesting that they be allowed to pass. Gisburne did not hear the response –

only the low hiss as he spoke. Mélisande's voice sounded once more, asserting their right to do so, and reminding Tancred whose daughter she was. Then he did hear Tancred's words. They ignored Mélisande entirely, and instead addressed his own men. They were to look for a box – wooden, locked with a key, and little bigger than a man's head. If Tancred had not known about the reliquary before, he certainly did now.

Then there were other shouts – evidently as Tancred's men attempted to search the wagons, and were prevented by Mélisande's own knights. Words uttered in anger. Outrage, dishonour. Insult. Then a thud, a crash. A scream from one of the female servants. The sound of metal against metal. Mélisande cried out in appeal – but a moment later the air was thick with the sound of clashing weapons.

Against the backdrop of bitter fighting, Gisburne felt someone enter the wagon. He threw off the awning, sword in hand. Mélisande looked back at him, her face distraught. Gisburne looked at Galfrid. "Do you think there's any point hiding now?" he said.

"None," replied Galfrid.

"Stay here," Gisburne said to Mélisande. Without waiting for a response he took her head in his free hand, kissed her on the brow, and he and Galfrid flung open the wagon's tilt.

The convoy was in chaos. Women screamed and tried to take refuge in the other wagons, whilst Mélisande's mounted knights hacked and stabbed at the surrounding Templars. It had begun as an attempt to prevent them searching the wagons, but had become a confused and bloody pitched battle.

The horses of one wagon were starting to panic and looked as if they might break loose – or break their legs trying. Several of Mélisande's men had already fallen, and one look told Gisburne that they were going to lose this fight.

"Let's try to even these odds," he said, as he untethered his horse from the back of the wagon and leapt onto it. Galfrid followed suit. Gisburne could see neither Tancred nor Fulke in the mêlée, but no matter – there were plenty more heads to swing his sword at. As he looked back, he saw Mélisande, framed by the wagon's tilt, loosing an arrow and preparing another. He smiled to himself, then turned to face the foe.

Gisburne had already struck down two of them when it happened.

Something must have struck one of the wagon's horses. A sword blade or lance. The beast gave a piercing whinny, the wagon lurched violently, then the horse next to it spooked into a blind panic. The creaking contraption lurched again. The brake snapped. Then the wagon rumbled forward.

"The box!" cried Galfrid. "It's in the wagon."

Gisburne turned just in time to see it move off – and Mélisande, still in the back of the wagon, realise with sudden shock that she was now entirely at the mercy of the stampeding animals. It gathered pace rapidly as it headed down the hill. Soon it would not be able to stop, even if the horses wished it to. Gisburne turned his horse about and raced after it, the wind whipping his face, Galfrid close behind. As he did so, he heard an icy voice – Tancred's – bark a command from somewhere far behind him. "After them! Stop the wagon!"

He glanced back – and saw no fewer than six of Tancred's knights in pursuit. But that was not his concern now. As it hurtled down the rough track, out of control, the wagon veered dangerously close to the suddenly precipitous left-hand edge of the road, its canopy flapping wildly in the wind. He could no longer see Mélisande. But just then, one of the fastenings broke free, and the gusting wind caught under the wagon's covering and lifted it clean off. The huge expanse of canvas – as big as a sail – flew high in the air. Its bottom edge brushed Gisburne's head as he rode beneath, missed Galfrid entirely, then, as it fell, wrapped around one of the Templars riding full tilt after them. The horse stumbled, the rider cried out, and both careered off the edge of the road, tumbling over and over down the mountainside, the great awning still wrapped about them.

Now, in the body of the wagon, Gisburne could see Mélisande, clinging on for dear life and working her way to the front. A horse thundered by on his right side. Somehow, one of the Templars had got past him, and was now drawing level with the wagon. As he watched in astonishment, the rider – as foolhardy as he was fearless – leapt from his galloping horse and into the back of the wagon.

He fell heavily. Mélisande heard, turned and took up a whip, lashing the knight mercilessly about the head and neck as the wagon jumped and pitched from side to side. But this one had a fanatical determination. He crept towards her, through the blows, drawing a blade as he did so.

Gisburne urged his horse on, drawing up between the side of the wagon and the sheer rock face towering to his right. One shift in the wagon's trajectory and he might be crushed, but he did not intend to stay long enough for that. He freed his foot from the stirrup, braced it against the saddle, gripped the pommel with both hands, and jumped.

He rolled into the back of the wagon behind the Templar. The knight turned just in time to see a tent pole swinging towards his head. It knocked him flat, sending his blade spinning out and over the precipice. Gisburne leapt on him, hauled him up by his surcoat, and hurled him from the back of the wagon, straight under the crashing hooves of his comrades.

Mélisande had taken the reins – which by some miracle had not come adrift – but the horses were not stopping. Gripping the side of the wagon as he went, thrown from side to side as the wheels rumbled horribly close to the road's edge, Gisburne crawled up to the seat beside her and hauled on the reins as hard as he could. The effort counted for nothing. The wagon's momentum down the incline was driving the horses on. Nothing was going to stop it now.

Up ahead, the road curved sharply to the right, around the mountain; with sinking heart, Gisburne realised the wagon would not make the turn.

A hand grabbed him from behind, and heaved him backwards. He struck out, blindly, as the wagon bumped and lurched, knocking his assailant off him. The Templar cracked his head on the reliquary box and was out cold – but already two more had climbed aboard, and another, at the gallop, was drawing up alongside.

Gisburne looked at the diminishing road, looked back at the advancing Templars, then pulled

Mélisande towards him. "Stay close!" he roared against the din of the wagon. The last of the Templars flung himself from his saddle into the wagon – only to watch in amazement as Gisburne leapt from the wagon and into the saddle the Templar had just vacated. Gisburne hauled Mélisande onto the horse behind him, and with only moments to spare, she leaned over and grabbed the reliquary box.

Their horse veered away, following the road. But the wagon did not. The last thing they saw was the look of horror on the faces of the Templars as – too late – they saw the fate hurtling towards them. Then the wagon, its horses and its ill-fated passengers plunged screaming over the cliff edge.

As they draw to a halt and dismounted – panting, exhausted – Galfrid caught up with both of their horses.

They looked back, but could see nothing and no one. The Templars were spent, or had given up. Mélisande's retinue was scattered and left far behind. Gisburne gazed into the empty distance, worrying at their fate. Mélisande looked up into his face, and read the thoughts there.

"They know what to do," she said, placing a hand on his shoulder. "They'll regroup, make their way back home. But we'll see no more of them this trip."

"Better for them," said Gisburne. He was suddenly all too aware of the destruction he brought in his wake.

"Just the three of us, then," said Galfrid, with his usual air of gloomy fatality. "Our gear is all here. Every bit. But I'm sorry to say we have no food beyond a hunk of bread and a morsel of cheese that have both been a week in my satchel."

"We must find something," said Gisburne. "We've a long road ahead, and no time to linger. Tancred will know where it is we're heading." He eyed Mélisande as he spoke the words, but she was deep in thought.

"Wait!" she said suddenly, and she went to her horse. She delved in her saddlebag and returned triumphant with a brown, bloody package.

That night they dined on wolf leg stew.

XLI

Forêt de Boulogne – December, 1191

MÉLISANDE HAD SAID nothing as they bypassed Paris.
There was no struggle, no protest, not even a sideways
glance. Gisburne wondered at it – wondered what her
royal master would make of this, what her reasons
now were for sticking with them when her task was
done – or, rather, undone. Perhaps there was yet some
other agenda, known only to her. Gisburne couldn't
think about that too much – the politics of it made
his head spin. The fact was she was now one of them,
part of their little unit, seemingly dedicated to the
same task as they. And he was glad of it. Not because
he had wished to avoid a fight over their destination,
but because he did not wish to say goodbye. Not yet.
But her easy acquiescence, welcome though it was,
had sparked another unexpected emotion in him.

Disappointment.

Even though it was better for their mission, better
for him and Galfrid – better, in fact, in every way –
he had felt dismay when they came to Paris, and she
had offered no fight at all. Her defiance was what he
admired about her. What he loved. And he wondered
at its absence.

It felt strange, this backdrop of gloom, when they had taken on so much and emerged triumphant. But the further north they travelled, the more her mood – their mood – had taken on an oppressed air. He fought against it. They were almost home. The trials they had faced so far were surely the greatest they would encounter on this trip. They should be *glad*, not doom-laden. But the truth was, even though he did not believe such things, he, too, could not shake the feeling he was moving towards something dreadful, but inevitable – some fateful and cataclysmic encounter.

The one truly cheering episode had been his reunion with Nyght. He had not been prepared for the emotion of it. It had seemed years, not weeks, since he had seen his beloved horse, and it was not until they turned down the road towards Boussard's smithy that the full significance of the moment struck him. He had been through so much, travelled so far, been so close to death, that the idea he would ever actually see Nyght again had seemed a fantasy. But he had not understood this until it was close to being realised. As they neared, and heard the sounds of Boussard's hammer clanging in his forge, a welter of emotions boiled up in him. Joy at the prospect of what was about to happen. Fear that something would yet prevent it – that something terrible had happened to the animal.

But nothing had. He looked better than ever. And when Gisburne saw him, he had to turn away from his fellows, embarrassed at the tears in his eyes. It was ridiculous, sentimental. But he almost felt that this moment, and the enthusiasm of Nyght's greeting, justified everything else that he had gone through.

He patted Nyght's black, shimmering neck for the thousandth time that week as they rode through the still snowy forests of Boulogne. The going was good, the ice had melted, the roads were mostly clear. Even the sun was shining. The road stretching away before them curved around to the left up ahead, and just before the curve loomed a great oak – or what was left of one. It had, Gisburne supposed, been struck by lightning in years past, and now stood like a strange sentinel – its top half and all its branches quite gone, the thick trunk split down the middle, each half leaning in a different direction, one of them burnt black.

Mélisande suddenly stopped.

She frowned, looked around, taking in her surroundings, sizing them up – recognising them. Only then did Gisburne recall that these were her father's lands. The land of her childhood.

"We are close," she said.

"Close?"

"The Saracens have a saying 'The greatest perils are those closest to home'. I know you feel your journey's nearly done, but I fear the most dangerous part lies ahead."

She raised a finger, pointing along the road. "Before us, past this bend, lies a crossroads. Right is for Calais. Left for Boulogne. And straight on for Castel Mercheval. Tancred's castle."

"Well," said Galfrid. "We'd best make sure we take the right one."

She looked at Gisburne. "You know I cannot come with you to England," she said. Her expression seemed one of deep sadness. Gisburne hoped he understood why, but there was something in her –

something inaccessible, unfathomable – that left him uncertain. He nodded, nonetheless.

"You know, you could leave now," he said. "Go home. Be safe. You don't need to pursue this any further." The words did not come easily – except for the wish that she stay safe. And that desire, he found, overrode all others.

"I cannot," she said. Gisburne waited for more – some explanation, perhaps – but she said nothing. Instead, she geed her horse gently, and they moved off again.

No sooner had they done so than the road turned, and the crossroads came into view. And there, waiting upon it, was a group of mounted men.

Templars. Six of them. Fully armoured – painted helms upon their heads, shields on their arms, couched lances held aloft. Their belts bristled with weapons. Their surcoats shone blinding white against the dark trees. Their horses snorted and stamped in the cold air.

"But of course," said Galfrid. "Bunch of Templars on a road. About time we had that again." He sighed. "If I survive this and live to be a hundred, I'm going to have nightmares ever after about a bunch of Templars on a sodding road."

"It's Tancred," said Mélisande. Gisburne screwed up his eyes. She was right. Not just Tancred's men. Tancred himself – the faceplate of his helm pushed up, his horrid visage staring out from beneath it. And next to him, he now saw, was another familiar figure, his full, red beard flapping in the wind.

"Fulke, too," said Gisburne.

"I wish I'd poisoned that bloody arrow," said Galfrid.

It had taken weeks for Gisburne to come around to appreciating Galfrid's bleak humour, but this time, he was not laughing. These were not any knights. Not any Templars. Not just Fulke's bully boys. This was Tancred de Mercheval himself. Tancred, who had defied both the Temple and the King of France, who had deduced the nature of the box and the man who carried it, who had tracked him relentlessly across hundreds of miles, through snows and mountain roads – and who knew he would be here, today, at this crossroads. When it came to it, Gisburne realised he actually knew very little about Tancred. About who he was, or where he was from. But he understood one thing: for all his fierce intelligence and fanatical zeal, Tancred was simple. He had no fear. He had no doubt. And he would never give up.

"So, I suppose we charge at them full tilt as usual?" said Galfrid.

"No," said Gisburne. "We'll die."

Galfrid grunted. "Best not do that, then."

"No."

"Give me the box," said Galfrid.

"What?"

"Give me the box. I've got an idea."

"Are you mad?"

"Possibly. But that'll be your fault. I was fine before this whole skull thing. So, are you going to give it to me?"

"Of course I'm not."

"Well then..." And he reached down, yanked the box from Gisburne's saddle and spurred his horse.

"No!" cried Gisburne.

"Keep them busy," Galfrid called as he galloped across country toward the Calais road.

"Galfrid! *No!*" But it was too late. Gisburne watched as two of the knights peeled off in pursuit.

"Well, it's an idea," said Mélisande, and with a sudden *Ya!* she spurred her own horse forward. "Divide and conquer!" she cried, thundering off in the opposite direction, towards Boulogne. A second pair of knights took up the chase, and all were swallowed up by the tree-lined road.

Only Tancred and Fulke remained.

Gisburne saw some words pass from Tancred to Fulke. Fulke nodded to his master, and walked his horse forward.

His progress was slow, deliberate. This was not an attack, that much was clear. But what it was, Gisburne was at a loss to say. He was close now; close enough that Gisburne could see his left hand was bandaged, and his left shoulder padded with something beneath his mail. It looked, now, as if Fulke wished to parley. Was it possible? Could it be that Tancred, after all, wished to strike some kind of bargain with him?

Fulke stopped ten yards away, lowered his lance, turned it point down, gripped it like a spear and drove it into the earth. He scowled at Gisburne, turned his horse and cantered back.

Tancred lowered his faceplate. Then his lance. And finally Gisburne understood. Fulke's lance was put there for him. Tancred meant to joust.

Gisburne had never fought in a tournament. He had supported Gilbert de Gaillon many times, had seen how it was done, had trained in the art. But the lance was not his weapon.

He rode up to it, pulled it from the ground, and hefted it under his arm. It felt awkward, alien. He glanced down at the great helm hanging from his saddle – apart from his mail, the only protection he had. But he did not put it on. He had no shield, either.

Tancred began to move – his horse trotted, cantered, broke into a gallop, its hooves pounding towards Gisburne, the lance pointed straight at his heart. He had only moments. Then something struck him, something liberating. He would not play Tancred's game by Tancred's rules. He threw the lance away.

If Tancred was bemused at Gisburne's behaviour, he did not show it. Nor did he show any mercy. He thundered on as Gisburne drew his sword, then spurred Nyght on, straight towards Tancred's rushing lance point.

It was something Gisburne had seen done only once – and not in a tournament, but in battle. At full gallop, he transferred his sword to his left hand, and with his right, pulled a mace from his saddle. He fixed his eye on Tancred's lance point, sword raised, mace ready, guiding Nyght only with his knees. If the lance struck any part of him, he was dead. So his goal would be to ensure that it did not.

At the last moment, he dropped flat against his horse and swung his sword upward. It struck Tancred's lance, caught it between blade and crossguard, and forced it up and away, sliding against the blade with a horrible sound. As Tancred passed, Gisburne sprang up, swung around and lashed at the Templar's back with his mace, making ringing contact with Tancred's helm. Braced for an impact which never came, and hit from behind, Tancred sprawled forward and crashed off his horse, leaving his lance sticking out of the ground at a ridiculous angle.

But Gisburne had miscalculated. Flinging himself around, he had overbalanced. He let go his weapons, grabbing for the reins, Nyght's mane – anything – but to no avail. Nyght slowed, and Gisburne toppled, fell, and rolled along the ground.

His weapons were lost in the snow. And now Fulke was making a charge. He was not so concerned about chivalry. He was not about to offer Gisburne a lance, or wait for him to mount his horse, or even for him to find a weapon. He just wanted to kill him. To stick him like a wild boar.

Gisburne looked around wildly, vulnerable and defenceless. His eyes settled on Tancred's lance. He sprinted for it, wrestled it from the ground, and turned as Fulke was almost on him. Crouched low, he raised the point, the butt of the lance braced against the earth. Fulke's lance sailed past him, uselessly, while Gisburne's shattered on Fulke's shield. Fulke reeled in his saddle, his buckled shield falling, but righted himself, drew his sword and rounded on Gisburne once again. Gisburne did not hesitate. He swung the remaining part of the lance, smashing Fulke in the chest. This time, the big man was unhorsed. He fell with a great thump in the snow, and did not move.

Gisburne turned to see Tancred, his eyes blazing with a cold fire, advancing upon him with sword and mace. He looked around desperately for his sword, for Fulke's, for anything – but it was too late. Tancred, teeth clenched, lips drawn back, whirled his sword at him. Gisburne parried with the broken lance. The sword flew again in a great swooping arc, smashing against the lance, forcing Gisburne back. Tancred spun, swinging the blade round and up, almost taking off the top of Gisburne's head. He had seen nothing like this – no fighting style to compare.

Then he saw the grip. Tancred was holding his sword with the forefinger hooked over the crossguard, which had a loop of steel to protect it. Realisation dawned. He was wrong. He had seen that style before. He looked into Tancred's cold features and saw, somewhere deep within them, the face of a sandy-haired boy – a boy who once inspired him on his first day at the practice ground.

"It's you," he said, his eyes wide.

Tancred hesitated.

"The boy at Fontaine-La-Verte. It's you!"

"That boy is dead," hissed Tancred.

He flew at Gisburne again with a furious barrage. The mace caught him a glancing blow on the temple, sending him spinning. He staggered, tried to regain his feet as Tancred came at him again. Gisburne leapt back this time, and Tancred's blade struck the earth just inches from his feet. Gisburne slammed his foot on it. The blade snapped, sending Tancred reeling back with a roar – then Gisburne swung the broken lance and cracked it across Tancred's skull.

Dazed, weaponless, with blood coursing down his face, Gisburne scrambled away towards the trees.

When he looked back, he saw Tancred following – relentlessly, like a man possessed. Gisburne staggered on, dimly aware of a sound ahead of him – rushing, gurgling. A stream. He stumbled and clawed over rocks, blinking hard, trying to focus, to stay conscious – then stopped suddenly, swaying. He was at the very edge of a cliff, his toes over the precipice. Forty feet below, in a straight drop, the tumbling waters of the stream crashed.

He lurched backwards, but Tancred was on him again. He wrestled Gisburne to the ground, battering him with his bare hands like a demon. Gisburne felt Tancred's bony fingers grasp his hair, then lift his head and smash it against rock. His arm reached out, grasped something: a stone. He swung it as hard as he could at Tancred's head, then got his foot under the Templar's chest and heaved him off. He heard Tancred crash to the ground yards away. Then silence. He lay for a moment, listening to his own rasping breath, barely holding on to consciousness.

A large figure loomed suddenly over him. Gisburne stared up through swollen, blurry eyes.

"Pilgrim..." it growled. Fulke, bloodied and bruised, grinned down at him. "You look like you need a drink..." he continued. And he kicked Gisburne in the ribs, in the head, over and over, edging him closer to the cliff until his crushed body slid over the precipice.

Gisburne felt momentarily weightless. Limbs flailed. Earth and sky spun past. Then he plunged into freezing, tumbling water, with a heart-stopping shock. Some distant, receding part of him realised that his mail was dragging him down. It enveloped him, paralysed him. Rocks battered him as he was carried away by the swift water. He gasped, felt a rush of ice into his lungs. Pain flashed like bright light.

Then all was black.

XLII

HE KNEW HE was in a desert. The absolute conviction came long before he was able to properly comprehend what he saw. As the wide, dazzling plain grew gradually clearer before his eyes, it was confirmed as fact. A vast expanse of fine, near-white sand, almost blinding in the intense sun, rippled into low, regular dunes, its surface ceaselessly shifting, blurring, swirling like a smoky haze all the way to the indistinct horizon. He knew, with equal certainty, that this was the desert west of Lake Tiberias, although it resembled a desolate part of the Judaean desert he had once passed through, near the Dead Sea.

But it possessed a strange purity more extreme even than that. There were no trees. No signs of life. Not even rocks under which hard-shelled creatures might hide, or stunted plants gain purchase with their meagre roots. Nothing to disturb the indistinct surface of the sighing, shifting sea of sand. Nothing except him.

He was walking.

His walk was laboured, as if he were climbing a hill, as if his feet and legs were lead, and the sand displaced with each weighty footfall parted and slid away uselessly beneath him. There was no slope. Just endless, gently rippling dunes.

He knew that Acre lay somewhere ahead, and that he had to reach it. The urgency was almost a physical pain. There was a ship there. A ship that would not wait – his one chance to reach home. As he laboured, seeming to get nowhere – unable to judge his progress in this landscape even if he was – he felt the awful scale of the task weighing down upon him, asserting its impossibility with every step. In his chest he felt a kind of tight panic. It began as a simple fear that he was not moving fast enough, that his feet and legs would not obey his commands – that when he tried to apply more speed, they seemed sapped of strength. But over time – he could not tell how much – it grew and changed, mutating into something more terrible.

He began to doubt his sense of direction. Everything, everywhere he looked, was the same. The sun – directly above, making one tiny pool of his shadow beneath his feet – told him nothing. He did not now know any longer whether he was heading towards Acre, or away from it – if he had, in fact, been putting even greater distance between himself and it since he had begun. He could not remember when that was. He felt the creeping, gnawing terror of the unknowable, the ungraspable, the indefinable – of himself slipping further and further adrift from the world, from his place in it, from anything that could fix him in time or space. From his own sanity. It was the dread of chaos.

The horrors of Hattin suddenly returned to him. In his mind, he knew them to be distant. Yet the sprawl and stench of death left in its wake, and the shouts of the terror-stricken and the dying, seemed all at once to assault him – and with them the horrid possibility that he was, of his own free will, walking back into their midst. That, somehow, they had become an inseparable part of him, and could never be left behind.

The figure jolted him back to the present.

It had appeared without warning. There had been no approach, no gradual reveal. It was simply there, directly ahead, a hundred yards or so distant. Just standing. At first, he could not make out any details. It was evidently a man, tall but somewhat hunched, its head bowed, its back turned to him. As he drew closer, his progress still painfully slow, he saw that it appeared to have its arms wrapped about itself. It was leaning slightly to one side, as if drunk or in pain. The clothes, he could now see, were ragged. Bloody. No, not simply ragged – slashed. And wet. And the figure itself – absurd as it clearly was in this place – seemed to be shivering. Though the distance between them would seem to have been too great to allow such a thing, he swore he could also hear the chattering of its teeth.

A wave of something akin to repulsion passed over him. It was not just the strangeness of the encounter – of this man in the desert, dripping wet and clutching himself with cold, wrong though that was. It was the creeping certainty that this was merely the prologue to something far worse.

Suddenly, he was mere yards away. Close enough, now, to see the cuts and slashes in the figure's bloody garments, and the exposed wounds beneath. Some were as shallow and neat as parted lips. Others were so deep that great ragged flaps of flesh hung loose, and what should have been inside spilled out. But none were bleeding. Not any more. Instead of the glistening red of fresh meat, the exposed tissue was grey as ash, the blood blackened, the skin pallid. The dead flesh of a corpse.

At precisely the same moment this realisation struck, he recognised who it was. Immediately, as if awoken out of a slumber by his own terrible thought, it gave a jerk, and twitched its head, and with a horrid, lopsided gait, began to turn.

The long-dead, milky eyes of Gilbert de Gaillon stared blankly at him, blue-black lips curled back, the elongated teeth in the shrunken gums chattering incessantly.

There had been so many times in his life when he had wished he could restore de Gaillon to the life of which he had been so cruelly robbed. Now that wish had been granted, and it was an abomination. The thing that had once been a wise and noble friend twitched, and stumped awkwardly towards him, one part-denuded arm outstretched, flaps of blue-grey skin hanging, jaw gaping open as if to articulate words. But all that came from the cavernous, wet hole was a gurgling, wheezing groan, and a string of black drool.

Gisburne could not speak or shout. But in his head, he heard his own voice, struck through with horror and revulsion, repeating over and over: *He belongs dead. He belongs dead. He belongs dead...*

Everything merged, became confused. For a moment it seemed he was looking out through the corpse's eyes. Far away, on the horizon, was a horse. Black. Riderless. Nyght. The stallion whinnied and shook his head. If he could only get to him... He tried to cry out – used all the force he could muster – but all that would come was a feeble whisper.

Then, the first of the things rose out of the sand.

Black and shiny, its insectoid limbs thrust out of the hot desert. They unfurled like spiked, obsidian blooms just yards from him, their quill-points planted upon its pale, shifting surface in a splayed circle. Then came another. And another. Seven black, bunched things in all – each unfolding with the same halting, mechanical motion, the same horrid, dry rattle. Then, within each ring of arched, protruding legs, the trickling sand heaved and bellied up. The mounds parted and fell away, and the huge armoured creatures lifted themselves free of the cascading sand.

They were scorpions. But they were also men. Great, gangling arachnids, each the size of a cow, but within them – merged into each black, articulated monstrosity – a strange approximation of human features, somehow blurred and imprecise, as if realised by an intelligence that only half understood what it was attempting to replicate.

They stood as if frozen for a moment, and then, suddenly, were hurtling towards him, legs clacking like dry bones, weird mouthparts gnashing and glinting.

He was running now. His legs were like lead, aching and slow, but would not move faster. The things were gaining – he could hear them uttering a strange *scree scree scree* as their legs pounded the sand – but he did not dare look back. Not even when he felt them at his back, saw their glistening limbs flash about him. He knew only that he had to protect what he clutched to his chest. That was all that mattered. But he realised, then – in a moment of confused panic – that he had no idea what it was. It shifted and moved against him. Then he looked down, and saw it. Cradled in his arms like a baby was de Gaillon's head, eyes wide, jaws snapping, a strange, strangled cry issuing from its tattered throat.

He screamed. There was no sound, but he knew he screamed. Then the world broke apart and he was plunged into edgeless, formless black, filled with colliding voices shouting over and over in endless repetition like a thousand lost souls, their words overlapping and incomprehensible – the ravings of madmen. Febrile fragments of images flashed and swirled in the churning, inky void, thrusting themselves at him before being swallowed up again: stick-thin figures shaking spears; a dancing pattern of fresh gore; huge, amorphous creatures with hunched backs and horns; tiny hands, red with the sheen of blood; flapping, eyeless birds as black as oil. And faces – hundreds of bellowing, idiot faces, pushing in at him – everyone he had ever known, taunting, laughing, screaming.

XLIII

THE FIRST THING he saw was a handprint of blood.

His eyes could barely focus; his head swam. But it was there, in the flickering half-light, stamped upon rock. He blinked, frowned at it. Where he was, he couldn't tell. But he knew he was drifting in and out of consciousness. The dream – the nightmare – had been a taste of Hell. While it had persisted, it seemed a perpetual torment, something from which there would be no escape. His heart still pounded at the memory of it – at the lingering belief in its reality. But now he knew that was not real. And he knew this was.

Thank God.

Through the indistinct haze, he now saw that there were others like it – small imprints of hands, some no bigger than a child's – all in faded colours. And around these, appearing to dance in procession across the uneven surface of the rock, strange little stick figures. Men. Animals. Other things he could only half identify.

They swirled. The room – if room it was – began to spin. He was dimly aware of flames licking at the periphery of his vision. Of a shadow moving over him. A shape, drawing closer. He tried to lift his head, and all turned to black.

XLIV

PAIN. IT SHOT through him, jolted him awake. A stabbing in his side. There was a sound, like bellows – a loud, almost musical wheezing. It was a moment before he realised it was his own breathing. His teeth chattered, his whole body shook. He lacked the strength to stop it – felt distant from himself, disconnected.

He tried to open his eyes. They resisted, felt glued together. Moving his tongue, he could feel it rasp against his palate. The inside of his mouth was bone dry and tasted of woodsmoke.

At his back, now, he felt a hand, supporting him, firmly but gently. Something hot touched his cracked lips. A scalding, salty liquid was spooned into his mouth. It burnt his tongue, but as it flowed down his throat its effect was instant – flooding into his muscles, reviving him like a potion. He sucked at it eagerly.

Then the hot liquor flowed too fast and made him choke. He spluttered convulsively and passed out with the pain.

XLV

A POP. BURNT flesh. He could smell it. A red-hot
needle on his cheek. A hand swiped at it. Not his.
His eyes rolled, would not focus. He felt himself
going again – tried to hold on by counting the
dancing men on the wall. They slid sideways and
upward and out of sight, and exhaustion plunged
him back into oblivion.

XLVI

A CAVE. IT was a cave. He knew it before he opened his eyes this time – must have somehow worked it out during his brief spells of wakefulness. He didn't know how, but the realisation gave him hope. He was connecting things – piecing the world back together again.

When he awoke, his whole face was burning. Urging his swollen eyes to open, he blinked away the sticky rheum, and the flames filled his vision. He was lying on his side, hunched around a small rock, his head only inches from the glowing, cracking logs of a fire. His nose and cheeks were roasting in the fierce heat. He flexed, rolled onto his back, away from the flames. The simple movement felt like a boot in the ribs.

He couldn't feel his hands and feet, and momentary panic gripped him. He tried to move his legs. They answered – still part of him, but numbed and insensible with cold. His feet were ice, his head fire. Every inch in between ached – but that, too was good. It was no longer the raw agony of fresh injury. It was the dull pain of healing flesh.

He took a moment to gather himself, letting his eyes rove around the dark interior. The chamber was the size of a monk's cell, but longer, and easily high enough to stand in. A bear cave, perhaps. But also a cave of men, long ago. Their marks – some faded, some obscured by green moulds or centuries of soot – were everywhere visible through the thick haze of smoke. Parts of his delirious dream flashed back and made him shudder. It sparked off a wave of uncontrollable shivering. He remembered that it was still winter.

As he looked, he realised that the rock on the cave floor, near his chest – a pitted, roughly egg-shaped stone about the size of a human head – had lichen and moss upon it. It had only recently been placed there. He wondered at its purpose. Only gradually did he understand it was to prevent him rolling into the fire as he slept.

Someone had taken care of him. But it was makeshift. His body was swaddled in dirty blankets which, even against the smoke, had the acrid smell of aged damp. But whoever they were, they had kept him alive. His torso – the part that he could feel – was cold and clammy with sweat. He knew now he had to move, get the blood flowing back into his limbs, and learn the extent of the damage inflicted upon him. He struggled to free his hands, extended them toward the flames and forced the paralysed claws of his fingers to flex.

As they returned to life, he shuffled sideways, raising himself up gingerly, bit by bit, into a sitting position against the cave wall. He put his fingers to a spot on his cheek that stung with the fierce anger of a fresh burn. There was a tiny, crusty pit in the flesh. Something had popped in the fire – a stone or pocket of sap – and hit him there.

Now, from where he sat, he could see a sliver of daylight at the cave's mouth. It was just beyond a bend obscuring most of the opening from view. The height of the cave also dipped there. An occupant of the cave could see out whilst still remaining hidden, and anyone entering would have to stoop low to get in. He noted, too, that the smoke did not flow out of the cave mouth, but was pulled towards him by an inward draught, presumably to escape via some fissure above. A natural chimney. If the fissure was long and the ground above it thick with foliage, the smoke would also be dispersed. One could perhaps hide here for months without being detected. He began to appreciate the wisdom of the ancient men who had once made this their fortress.

The smoke caught in his throat; he tried to resist coughing, but could not. Excruciating pain stabbed his side. It was something he'd known before. He hawked up deep, gritting his teeth against the pain that it caused, and spat on the ground, looking for fresh blood. It was clear. That was good. It probably wouldn't kill him, then. Just give him weeks of pain before it healed.

There came a crackle of dead wood being crushed underfoot. The rock chamber baffled his senses; made it seem, for a moment, that the sound came from behind him, deeper within the cave. Then a shadow passed across the meagre slit of daylight at the cave's mouth. Human, a bow across its shoulder. By instinct, his hand went to his sword, but grasped nothing but rotted leaf mould and bits of ancient animal bones. For the first time in his life, there was no sword by his side. No knife. No weapon of any kind. Except... He grasped the rock with stiff fingers, heaved it to his shoulder and, with his back flat against the wall, ignoring the pain, pushed himself up on unsteady legs. The uneven surface of the rock grazed the flesh as his backbone ran hard against it.

A crouched, hooded silhouette turned the corner. He rested the rock on his collarbone – not certain he could even lift it in his current state, but determined to do so no matter what pain ensued. The figure straightened, its face now lit by fire.

Mélisande.

She gave a wry smile. "Don't start what you can't finish," she said.

He let go the breath he was holding – it almost turned to a laugh of relief – and with it the rock. It thumped to the ground and tumbled towards the fire. He slumped as if the stone had taken all his tension with it, allowing himself to slide slowly back down, his back still against the cave wall. He winced as he felt a familiar stab of pain in his chest.

"Well," he said through gritted teeth. "You're the second surprise today..."

She threw down a dead hare and slung a bag off her shoulder. "The first..?"

"That I'm alive."

Kneeling, she unpacked a bundle of grubby cloth from the bag. "You only realised that today?" She peeled back the folds to reveal half a loaf of bread, an onion, dried fruit, a leather flask, some cheese. To Gisburne – suddenly famished beyond words – it was a feast.

He broke off a chunk of bread, and as he tore at it with his teeth, chewing open mouthed, a slow realisation dawned upon him. He'd had no sense of passing time – had let go his grip on the world entirely. "How long have I been here?"

"Three days," she said.

Gisburne stared, his mind flooded with questions – gripped with panic at the sense of lost time. He had to put himself back into the world. But what would he find when he got there? What had passed since he had plunged into that freezing water?

Mélisande turned to him, put a hand on each side of his face, studied his eyes intently, turning his head left, then right. She opened his mouth, looked in, closed it, and gave him a light slap on one cheek.

"A little flushed, but you'll do," she said, and reached into a vertical split in the rock wall. From it she took a soft leather case, unrolled it, checked a variety of small knives it contained, then tied it up and threw it into her bag. "Sorry if the fire was a little fierce. I didn't want it to die while I was gone. It's the devil to get started, with everything so damp."

"Well, I've been marinated and larded – why not cooked?" He watched as she pulled a wineskin from the crack, shook it, and slung it over her shoulder. "How did you get me here? And how did you find this cave?"

"I didn't," she said, breaking off a third of the loaf and stuffing that, too, into her bag. "You did. Must've dragged yourself here from the river." She shook her head, her expression a mix of amusement, disbelief and admiration. "You are a tenacious fellow, Guy of Gisburne." He had no memory of having done so, but knew better than most how the body could fight to protect itself.

She reached into a gap in the rock wall once more, and this time drew out a stoneware bottle. "I followed your trail, then did what I could to hide it. It was bloody, easy to spot in the snow. I scattered it as best I could. A fresh fall of snow finished the task." Uncorking the bottle, she sniffed at it. "Drink," she said, and thrust it into his stiff hand. "It'll help with the pain."

He took a swig. The liquid hit his throat like fire, the cough it induced racking his chest with new pains. "Christ!" he exclaimed. "When you said it would help with the pain, I thought you meant it would *stop* it..."

She almost smiled at that. "It'll also keep the cold at bay."

"What is this stuff?"

"It's called 'marc' – strong drink, from my father's estates. Just don't get it near the fire; I haven't nursed you this far to see you go up in flames. And keep the fire going or you'll freeze. They shouldn't see the smoke unless they're looking for it, and they won't be looking. There's more wood near the mouth of the cave. And your gear – as much as I could salvage."

"Sword?" said Gisburne. She nodded. "Helm..?"

"Yes. Nearly all. The bindings broke and your horse threw it off in the forest. Otherwise it might all be half way to Paris by now."

Gisburne shook his head. Nyght would not go far from his master if he could help it. Although he did not want to think about what fate his horse had suffered. And then there was–

"Galfrid." He tried to sit up. She pushed him back down.

"Captured," she said.

"And the box too, then..." Gisburne's hand went to his neck; the key to the reliquary box still hung around it. With Gisburne half dead at his feet, Tancred had had the chance to take the key, and to finish off his foe. But he had wasted both opportunities. Gisburne felt a grim satisfaction at that. They would never succeed in opening the box, no matter how hard they tried. Not without the key. And that meant he had something they needed. But as the ghoulish face of the White Devil loomed in his mind beside the sweaty, contemptuous visage of Fulke, cool detachment evaporated. He was filled, instead, with overwhelming hatred. His heart pounded, his fingers clenched. He heaved himself to his feet.

"I have to get out there…"

She turned on him. "You must rest! You must stay hidden." There was an odd, evasive look in her eye. She busied herself fastening her bag.

Only then did he fully realise that she meant to leave.

"You're going?"

"It's necessary."

"For how long?"

She did not reply. But previously scattered thoughts suddenly came together. The store of food. Her hasty packing. The information about firewood, about his recovered gear. He felt a creeping dread.

"Are you coming back?"

Still she said nothing.

"Why such a hurry?" he said. His voice was stern. This time, when she remained mute, he gripped her wrist and turned her towards him.

She flashed angry eyes, resisted him with surprising strength, her beautiful face creased in a frown. Then she gave up, let her head fall. "I had a contact inside Castel Mercheval."

Gisburne let her wrist drop.

"A servant. He passed me bread and ale – the food that kept you alive. Information, too."

"Had...? You said *had*..."

"Today..." She faltered. "He was not at the appointed place. I must assume he has been discovered. If so, God help him. And if he has been discovered, then it's only a matter of time before they also find me. So, you see, I must leave you. For your own good."

"But I only just got you back..." The feeling behind the words surprised him.

"You must accept it."

"But you could lie low here. How are they to know..."

"No!" Mélisande shook her head, her patience almost gone. "They will make him speak. Then they will know I am somewhere in this forest. But they don't know about you. Not yet."

"But if he speaks..."

"I told him only I needed food for myself. He could not tell them anything of you even if he wanted to. Now I must move if I am not to bring Tancred down upon you."

Gisburne stared at her for a moment in the fire's dying light.

"What of Tancred? You said you were passed information."

"Tancred believes you dead. You almost were."

"The first of those facts is in our favour," said Gisburne thoughtfully. He took a determined step, meaning to reclaim his sword. He winced, and staggered, steadying himself against the cave wall. "The second, not so much..."

"Tancred will work on Galfrid, get what he can from him. Meanwhile, he has sent for an enginer from Amiens to open your reliquary box. He fears devices that may damage its precious cargo."

"He's no fool."

"Apparently the first two men who touched it collapsed and lost their wits," said Mélisande, giving Gisburne a searching look. "They say it is cursed."

That gave Gisburne a grim satisfaction. But he doubted Tancred – the blessed, incorruptible Tancred, God's right hand – would be put off by such a trivial threat. Gisburne had thought no one would be able to force open the reliquary. But he was wrong. Another like Llewellyn could do it. And when they did...

"Help me," he said, taking another step towards the cave mouth.

"What?"

"Help me get my armour on."

Mélisande actually laughed at that – a strange, strained chuckle. "You're going after your box, when you can't even get your armour on?"

"They can keep the box," he said. "I'm going for Galfrid."

She stared at him, dumbfounded. "Are you mad? You're half dead. You must heal first."

"When does the enginer arrive?"

"Three days, but–" said Mélisande.

"Then I have three more days to heal. After that, Galfrid will become superfluous to them."

Mélisande had seen the tenacity of this man – had seen how he had dragged himself back to life. She nodded slowly, then gripped his hand.

"Succeed," she said.

"You could join me," he said. "We could fight together."

She shook her head. "I cannot." Somewhere out in the forest, a distant horn sounded. She tensed, turning towards the sound, and pulled her hand away. "I told you. They are hunting for me. They will scour these woods until they find me; and once they have done so, they will stop. And you will be free."

"But if they don't capture you..." began Gisburne. Then he saw the wounded look in her eye, and finally understood. "No!" he said. "Not that... I won't allow it."

"You cannot stop it." She stepped further back from him, defiant – but her voice had softened now, was almost pleading. "I am known to them. But you... You do not exist. You're dead. A ghost. The only one who can move secretly against them. If there is anything that can be done now, it must be you who does it."

"I won't have you sacrifice yourself..." He grabbed at her hand, but she wrested it free.

"It's not a sacrifice," she insisted. "It's a tactic. Think. I am of the house of Boulogne. Even Tancred would not dare to cross that line."

Gisburne was not so sure. "One does not negotiate with Tancred de Mercheval," he said.

She smiled sweetly, her eyes fixed on his. "Then you had better come to my rescue."

She threw her bow on the ground and backed away towards the halo of light at the cave's entrance.

"Don't worry, I'll make it look good," she said. "I never submit without a fight – even if it's a token one." Outside, the horn sounded again in the forest

– closer, this time. Another answered it. Gisburne fancied he could hear the distant barking and baying of hounds. Mélisande glanced out towards the forest, then back to him – the look in her wild, sad eyes a mix of defiance, torment and exhilaration.

"Think of me," she said, then rushed forward, kissed him hard on the lips, and was gone.

XLVII

When the yelps and cries had finally abated, Gisburne crept out of the cave and into the forest.

It had been an agony greater than any he had suffered at Tancred's hands. At first, as he had stared in shock and despair at where she had stood a second before, he had cursed the numb, cramped slowness of his limbs – his ineffectual grasping at empty air. Then he thought to charge after her, to take on her pursuers there and then. But he knew that was folly – one that would surely get her killed, squander the advantage she had won for him at such great cost, and in turn condemn Galfrid. So he sat, listening but not wanting to hear, powerless to prevent her plan, his head appreciating its infallible logic, his heart detesting it.

Three days. He had lost three days. When he had finally stepped out of that cave – and felt the blessed relief of fresh, clean air in his lungs – it had prompted an absurd parallel in his mind. He had thought of Christ. The Saviour had been destroyed, was buried in a cave, and rose again after three days. Gisburne laughed at this until he thought the pain in his side was going to kill him – then, unable to stop, he laughed some more. Finally, the hysterical release burnt itself out. He had stared out over the forest for some time after that, flexing his muscles, feeling them return to life, relishing the pain that told him he was alive.

And so he stood, cloaked by an odd calm, surveying his new domain with his tomb at his back. Resurrected. A ragged saviour. But he brought no message of peace; no forgiveness, no promise of paradise. He was a spirit of destruction. An avenging angel.

And avenge he would.

Mélisande had been true to her word. In the cave was the greater part of his gear. His sword, shortsword and knife. His satchel containing coins, char-cloth, fire-steel and flint. And his great helm, still in its leather bag. His hauberk she had somehow managed to remove from him in order to tend his wounds. There was also the longbow – where that had come from, he did not know – and a meagre handful of arrows. It was little enough to work with, but it was a start.

When he descended into the forest, he found parts of it densely packed – sometimes impenetrable. Here and there were clear paths – some evidently used for hunting on horseback, others used perhaps only occasionally by foresters or foragers. At the end of one such path he happened upon a wide, almost circular clearing. All about it were huge trees of unimaginable age, and in its centre a bowl-shaped depression into which a slimy leaf mould had formed. It was, he realised, an old bear or wolf pit. He stared into its dank interior for a while, then walked on.

He had meant to return to the cave, to make sure the fire didn't die. But within him, another flame – which Tancred had failed to extinguish

– was burning with renewed ferocity. He walked obsessively amongst the trees for hours – walked until it was almost too dark to see – feeling the blood flow back into his limbs, getting to know the forest in the broad expanse between the cave, the road, and Castel Mercheval.

Three days. He had three more days until the enginer came. Three days to prepare. Three days for Galfrid and Mélisande to continue suffering at the hands of Tancred. But he would bide his time. There was only one road by which the enginer could come – and he would use that fact, too.

As he walked – as he grew in the darkness – the words of his old mentor came back to him.

"You can't control a battle. Anticipate your enemy's possible moves as best you can. Try to think like him, if possible. Understand, however, that you can never know what a man will choose to do in the heat of battle; he may not even know that himself. But you can limit his options. That is the key. Control the battlefield."

Control the battlefield. That would be his strategy. Other, more heretical thoughts swam alongside it in his head. Thoughts of which he knew de Gaillon would not have approved. But his purpose – his method – was clear. A mounted knight was unstoppable, so unhorse him. On foot, he remained a formidable soldier, so knock him down. On his back, even the strongest knight was at his attacker's mercy. And Gisburne would show none.

He would strike fast. He would give them no opportunity to see their deaths approach. He knew Tancred did not fear death. But even there, he had the advantage. He was dead already.

In the dying light he gazed down at his fingers – still soot-black from the cave wall. How old a relic of ages past this was – whether of those whose hand prints marked the cave walls – he could not tell. It was now commingled with soot from the fires set by Mélisande's living hand. At least, he hoped it was still living. He raised his eyes from his blackened fingertips to the deep shadows amongst the trees.

Three days.

This would be his battleground. Here, he would build the engine of Tancred's destruction. And he knew that destruction must be total – the rogue Templar's vile nest and all in it reduced to ash.

It was time to embrace the forest. Time to put aside all gentility, all restraint.

It was time to become like Hood.

V

TANCRED

XLVIII

Nottingham Castle – October 1190

WILLIAM DE WENDENAL didn't have time for this. It was late, he had eaten and drunk too much, and until moments ago had been in that part of the evening where, the day's obstacles successfully negotiated, it had seemed safe to expect nothing more taxing than a conversation by the crackling log fire with his honoured guest and a slow slide into unconsciousness. But now – thanks to the recent intrusion of one of his serjeants – his head was hot with the business, and he was already feeling the gnaw of indigestion in his chest.

The poacher had been caught red-handed and would hang – that was beyond doubt. But, given the circumstances, it had seemed politic to grant this one an audience. Not that he gave a damn for the thieving wretch, but his guest had taken an interest, and that did matter. Wendenal needed to show every courtesy; his career might well depend upon it. He wasn't happy about it, all the same. Apart from anything else, the encounter would very likely mean him having to speak English, which he hated. And in front of this most esteemed visitor, too. It was just embarrassing.

He sipped his wine agitatedly, his eyes making a fleeting connection with those of the other man, the two of them – until recently engaged in animated discussion – now standing in an expectant – and, for Wendenal, awkward – silence. He felt exposed. On show. As he strode impatiently, his guest – his own goblet abandoned – drifted away from the warming glow of the great fireplace, retreating towards the shadows. He seemed to like shadows, to be at the edge of things. Or perhaps it was his having to be at the edge of things that was the source of his everpresent, smouldering frustration. There was much Wendenal could not know or guess about the man. Some said his whole family was descended from the Devil – a tale that his guest's father had apparently related often, and with obvious relish. Wendenal poked at the fire irritably and watched the orange sparks fly up the chimney. If the granting of this simple request would send the Devil-prince off to bed happy, then he would do it. As far as his own feelings were concerned, though, to make any kind of favourable impression this night, the miscreant's story was going to have to herald the Second Coming at the very least.

There would the usual protestations of innocence, of course. He'd heard them a hundred times before. "I didn't do it." "It was someone else." "I was with my wife." "I was with someone else's wife." Or, occasionally, there would be pathetic attempts to justify the crime, as if the laws of the land were suddenly mutable, and open to negotiation. "I had to do it." "Someone made me do it." "My family was starving." Dangerous notions of that sort had been spreading like a plague of late. But such delusions had always been about, if one knew where to look, festering in corners, ready to infect the desperate and weak-minded. Last Lammastide, one poor wretch even had the nerve to claim God told him to do it – appearing to him in the form of a woman with the head of an owl as he was emptying his bowels in the woods. So, a liar, a thief, and a blasphemer, all in one.

Clearly the man's wits had cracked – and what dark thing had crept in to take possession wasn't Wendenal's concern. That was a matter for clergymen. What was meted out here was earthly justice, and here the flesh was punished without prejudice. That was his way. Even-handed, absolute. When one stood in judgement, sympathy was the enemy of clarity. Anyway, if he were to give credence to every story that came his way, there wouldn't be a single guilty man in the whole of the two shires.

Something unusual in this particular poacher's story had caught his serjeant's attention, however. And, more importantly, that of his guest. Wendenal had known poachers make such claims before, of course – and more often, of late. One couldn't blame them for it when faced with death; the desperate but vain attempt to imbue their lives with some value, to wriggle free of the noose. Part of him admired their tenacity. But the greater part was appalled by the arrogance. By what warped sense of propriety did these stinking, ragged clod-rakers think they had the right to bargain with him, holder of one of the highest offices in the land? Did they seriously believe they could face him as an equal and make him *barter*, as if in some dung-strewn peasant market? When it came to it, none ever had anything of value to offer anyway, nothing to give their life even fleeting worth. This one would undoubtedly follow the same course.

The case was cut and dried: he had been captured in the forest with one of the king's deer shot dead at his feet and would be strung up within the week – tonight, if Wendenal had his way. Strictly speaking, the law required only flogging or a fine for the crime of poaching – but such lawbreakers were, almost by definition, never good for the money, and there had been too many liberties taken in recent months for Wendenal to be satisfied by leniency. But for now, it would do no harm to indulge the whim of his visitor. And, he had to admit, he trusted his loyal serjeant's gut on such matters more than he trusted the wisdom of many of his knights. After all, hadn't he risked his master's displeasure to bring this to his attention?

At the clatter of the guards' approach, Wendenal drained his goblet of wine and slapped it down on the oak table. Fortified by drink and a simmering irritation, he turned to face the doorway and struck a suitably authoritarian pose – catching a last glimpse, before he did so, of his guest hastily retreating beyond the tapestries before being swallowed up entirely by the deep shadows at the far end of the chamber. That was how his friend – no, he did not dare call him "friend", not quite yet – how his *ally* liked to do things. To observe. To take note. To weigh up. So unlike his hothead of a brother, thought Wendenal.

The heavy door clanked and creaked, and the prisoner was brought forward.

The man who stood before him, his hands bound, cut a curious figure – one that Wendenal could not easily fathom. He was tall, dark haired, with fine features, his physique that of someone who had grown up well-fed and – unless Wendenal misread the signs – trained in the fighting arts. (Fed by whom? And trained for what?) His bearing, whilst not exactly noble, was certainly far from the hapless peasant Wendenal had been expecting. Yet, at some point not long ago, the course of this man's life – and his fortunes – had undergone a dramatic change. His appearance was ragged, his hair long and lank, his visage neither properly bearded nor properly razed, his apparel that of one who had been months on the road. (The road from where? To where?) The clothes themselves – inasmuch as they could be discerned one from another – were a strange mix of the exotic and the commonplace, a layering of the richest and the most mean garments. So what was he? Built and equipped for combat, certainly, but clearly no knight. Garbed like one come from the Holy Land, but clearly no pilgrim.

The man stood straight, unmoving, his head only slightly bowed. That he had lived and fought hard was clear. There was no fat on him; his limbs, though not large, were like iron – something beaten and shaped in extremes. Where the tanned flesh was exposed, scars were visible – Wendenal counted at least four, on his forehead, chin, forearm and the back of his left hand. Each had been inflicted by a blade – save the one on his forearm, whose long shape looked like a burn. Most striking of all was his face, which showed absolutely no fear. No anger, no resentment, no defiance. The look – or, perhaps, it was the absence of a look – unnerved him. To allow time to muster his thoughts, Wendenal turned slowly about and paced before the prisoner, searching for some clue in his face. The man's dark eyes – fixed on a point on the stone floor, some yards in front of him – glinted in the firelight like steel, revealing nothing whatsoever. Once or twice Wendenal had seen the look on campaign – the look of a man who had been to Hell and returned, and who had nothing left to fear.

"My serjeant says you know who Hood is," said Wendenal in his careful, precise English. Much as he detested speaking the language, it was still better than hearing someone mangling his native *langue d'oïl*. "So, we make this simple. You tell me what you know, and I tell you whether it gets you a reprieve. If you delay, or say nothing, I assume what you know is nothing."

The man did not respond. For a moment, Wendenal was unsure if he had even heard. "Well? Can you tell me who Hood is?"

"No one can," came the dour reply.

Wendenal gave a snort of exasperation. "As I thought," he said, reverting to his own language. "Pointless. A waste of time." He raised his hand.

"But I am the only man alive who knows the true madness in that mind." Wendenal stopped mid-gesture. "I can find him. I can identify him. I can stop him. And nothing would give me greater pleasure." The reply was in perfect *langue d'oïl*.

Wendenal looked at the man with narrowed eyes. "How can you claim this?"

"I fought alongside him for two years and more. We ate and drank together."

"And yet you say you do not know who he is?"

"I know what he called himself: 'Robert of Locksley'. But I do not believe he knew anything of the village whose name he bore – nor it of him."

Wendenal snorted dismissively. "It's in your interest to maintain that little mystery, of course. Suppose he is exactly who he says he is?"

"Then I am the Earl of Huntingdon. I don't doubt there *was* a Robert of Locksley once. Perhaps there still is. But I am certain it is not he."

Wendenal threw up his hand in frustration. "This is absurd. You say you know him better than any man, then that you do not know him at all. That you have information, and that there is none to have. Which is it?"

"I never met anyone who knew him before. It is as if he stepped out of a void. He is without name, without lineage – outside of history. He is like the biblical plague of locusts – he consumes everything of worth in one place, then, when it has nothing left to offer him, he moves on. Changes his name. His appearance. His voice."

"His voice..?"

"I once saw him conversing with a Scotsman over drink. At the start, you'd swear he was from England's northern shires. By the end, one could not tell the difference between his voice and the Scot's. It was as if he was consuming him. *Becoming* him. As if he could not help himself from doing so. As if he needed others' souls in order to continue his existence." He let his head drop. "Unless, of course, he really is a Scot, and the accent I knew was an act." He looked up again, his eyes suddenly keen and urgent. "This man is a danger. To me, to you, to everything. Just now he is the famed outlaw of Sherwood. That game will last him a good while. Through it he unexpectedly finds himself on a par with kings. He has never tasted that kind of power before. And having tasted it, he will not loose his grip. Believe me when I say he will push this game to its ultimate conclusion."

There was an air of doom in the man's final words. Of apocalypse. Wendenal forced a sceptical laugh – an attempt to hide the extent to which they had disturbed him. "Or he will be brought to justice like any other rogue."

"That would be preferable, yes," said the man, softly. "That's what I offer."

"And only you can achieve this?"

"This man is not like any other rogue."

"So, you are suggesting I simply let you loose to go galloping after him?" Wendenal laughed, his guards joining him.

"It would be a start," said the man, and the laughter stopped.

"This is ridiculous. Just words. Wild stories. Perhaps you should've considered a career as a storyteller rather than a poacher. You certainly seem to have more skill in the former than the latter. But so far you have not given me one hard fact. Not one!"

The man's brow creased in frustration. He made as if to step forward but was restrained by his guard. "He has a cross tattooed on the inside of his left wrist. Like this..." He pulled back the sleeve of his tunic to reveal a small, blue-black symbol, its ink blurred at the edges. "We had them done at the same time. Also his right hand is smooth. No wrinkles or marks. It was thrust into a fire during a skirmish in Sicily. For a time he could not shoot a bow. There were those who said he never would again, but he proved them wrong. He delights in proving people wrong. There is also a star-shaped wound on his right thigh, from a mace blow. Again, he was lucky."

"His thigh..?" said Wendenal, his voice rising as he spoke. The underlying question was clear. The man almost smiled.

"He's not my type." Then, after a pause, added: "We lived and ate and drank together for thirty months. Mercenaries. Through driving snow, heaving seas and parched desert. At Hattin..." Wendenal's eyes widened at the mention of that name. "You get to know a man, whether you like it or not."

"And yet, in all that time, there was not one clue as to who he really is?"

"Just one." His face darkened, as if at some troubled memory. "A name. 'Rose.' It is dear to him. It recurs, over and over. But whether it was a mother, a sister, a wife or a lover..." He shrugged, looking defeated, as if finally acknowledging the paucity of the information. "Perhaps one day we shall know."

Wendenal stared at him for a long time. Part of him wished only to have this man dragged away and flogged. God knows, he'd taken up more than enough of his time and energy. He was arrogant, defiant. Possibly a fantasist. Yet there was something... Something Wendenal could not place. Something that – against all reason – rang true, and that stayed his hand. He mulled over the man's words. *Mercenaries*. That was what he had said.

"He is not a knight?"

The man's jaw clenched. "He is not."

"But then, who exactly are *you*?"

The man's eyes remained cast down at the floor. "I'm no one."

Wendenal had to admit that the man, infuriating and baffling as he was, had a knack for keeping one's interest. "Well, let's see..." With a gesture, he indicated for his serjeant to search the man's baggage, scanning the gear as it was spread before him. "Are *you* a knight?" he asked.

"No."

"Then you're a thief. This hauberk is a knight's property."

"I am no thief!" snapped the man, his eyes blazing. The guards gripped his arms again, and he calmed himself. Wendenal indicated for them to release him. "I am not a knight. I was denied that honour. But the mail is mine nonetheless."

"It's of little interest to me what wager or bartering delivered this into your hands. Only the deserving have the right to wear it."

The man shrugged and nodded. "I'd dearly like to see a world in which only the deserving wore mail. We'd have fewer knights, I grant you, but the quality would certainly go up..."

This was too much. Outraged, Wendenal struck the man a heavy blow across the face. "Who are you to pass judgement on the quality of knights?" he snapped.

The man staggered, straightened, and stood firm, wiping the blood from his lip. "One who has seen the best and the worst of them," he replied. He fixed Wendenal's burning eyes with his own. "Enough to know that apparel may be deceptive. That a man may wear the crown of a king, though there be a more deserving head."

Wendenal stared at him in stunned silence. How was he to respond to this? Was it possible, after all, that this man had some powerful information – that he knew of his allegiances? "Now you add treason to the crime of killing the King's deer," Wendenal said, carefully. "If you thought to talk your way to leniency you're going about it the wrong way." The guards stifled a laugh.

"I merely speak my mind because I tire of doing otherwise," said the man. "But no deer died at my hand."

"Ah. Now we come to the heart of the matter. 'I didn't do it.' Serjeant?"

The serjeant flushed, and stepped forward. "He was caught standing over the body of a stag, his arrow in its eye. Had his horse not been lamed in its pursuit, he would surely have made off before we got to him."

The man gave a sigh of exasperation. "My horse was not lamed in the pursuit, but cut with a knife. As you'd know if you bothered to look." The serjeant glared at him. "And where is the bow I am supposed to have used?"

Wendenal frowned at the serjeant. "Well?" There was certainly no bow among the accoutrements spread before them. The serjeant simply looked embarrassed and cornered, then finally shook his head in defeat.

"A longbow is hard to hide. So, am I supposed to have shot an arrow with no bow, and then hamstrung my own horse?"

"If not you, then who?"

The man reached into his jerkin. All the guards about him flinched. The serjeant gripped his sword – but before he could act, the man had pulled out a broken arrow and flung it to the ground before his captor.

Wendenal fumed in the tense silence, his eyes fixed on the eight-inch length of ash shaft. "Was this man not searched?" he rumbled.

The serjeant flushed, his eyes panicky. "I don't know how he..."

"Never mind," snapped Wendenal.

The man pointed at the broken fragment. "This is the arrow that killed the king's stag." The goose feathers on its fletched end were dyed green, bound with green linen thread. A distinctive touch. "I dare say you've seen the like before, piercing the bodies of men you sent into the forest."

Wendenal did not raise his eyes. "I know from whose bow this arrow comes."

"I saw him. Spoke with him. Moments before your men arrived."

"You saw him?"

"That is how close your men came to the one known as Hood."

Wendenal heard a sound behind him, in the shadows. A clearing of the throat. A low whisper. He nodded, and looked the man in the face.

"Tell me what happened."

XLIX

GISBURNE KNEW TOO late that he was riding into trouble. The stag had crashed to the ground just fifty yards ahead, almost as if hurled from the greenwood. It had been running full tilt, Gisburne realised, and felled whilst doing so. A stunning shot – or a lucky one.

Moments later, a small man in a dirty brown hood had leapt out after it. Gisburne had not paused, not hesitated in his progress. In truth, he had little interest in the man or his business. He would ride on his way and leave him to it. Where Gisburne was riding to, he did not know. He hardly cared. The past few days – days that had robbed him of the last few things of any value – had left him exhausted, his heart empty. Even Marian, who had seemed so warm during these difficult weeks – enough to inflict upon him the curse of hope – had finally said *adieu* with disheartening ease. Now there was only this old horse left. His father's horse. Painful as it was, after so long in the saddle, riding was a comfort. The only comfort. He would, therefore, keep riding until something else presented itself.

As he neared, he saw the man had a drawn knife, but no bow. At that, he felt his neck prickle, and his throat tighten. When the man then turned and gestured in triumph towards the forest, Gisburne knew for certain that he was not alone.

They were around him in seconds – crashing out of the wood, bursting from the leaves and branches like beetles from a rotting log, a dozen rough-looking men. The horse shied and stumbled on the rooty path, almost throwing Gisburne headlong. He overbalanced, gripped the reins and slithered off the saddle in an awkward dismount. When he turned, arrows and blades were pointed at him. He had seen them poaching – in some quarters, a capital crime. They would not let him live.

Gisburne turned about, calculating his chances, when a familiar voice turned his every muscle to stone.

"Well, well, old man – I see you escaped the Devil's horns after all!"

And there he stood, like some kind of vision – inextinguishable, imperturbable, impossible.

Locksley.

"Good to see you. You look like shit." And with that he planted his fists on his hips and threw his head back in a great, raucous laugh.

After Hattin, Gisburne had given Locksley no thought. The man, and his crime, had ridden into oblivion. He existed afterwards not even as a memory, but as a remnant of a bad dream that had no bearing on waking life, and which could now be allowed to simply melt away. His intrusion back into this world – into this place – shook Gisburne to the core. And yet, now he looked upon him, he had the uncanny feeling that he should have expected it. That it was somehow inevitable. But of course... Locksley could not be expected simply to die. Not after *that*. Gisburne did not believe in fate – in lives being somehow arranged

by the cosmos. And yet, as he looked upon this man –
who, like him, had done the impossible, and walked
out of the Hell of Hattin – he felt the earth beneath his
feet, the air in his lungs, the sky above his head, vibrate
with a weird expectancy. A strange feeling of the
two of them being connected forever by that shared,
impossible moment.

Good to see you. That was what he said. He did not
mean it, not as others meant it. Yet it was as hard to
resist as always. Gisburne clenched his teeth, exhumed
a memory from some dark *oubliette* in his brain. An
image of a lamplit chamber; of billowing curtains. And
blood.

"What do you think of my little band of thieves?"
Locksley grinned, as if it were all a grand children's
game. But he had not ordered them to stand down,
and showed no signs of doing so.

"So is this what you do now?" he said, surprised by
the bitterness in his own voice. "Poach deer and rob
poor wretches who have lost everything?"

A flicker of something akin to confusion – or perhaps
it was petulance – flashed across Locksley's features.

"Oh no," he replied with a shrug. "We rob the rich,
too." There was a ripple of laughter from the men.

Gisburne felt an urge to warn them, but did not
know how. What could one say about a man who
did not exist? He recalled an occasion, just before
Thessalonika, when he had asked Locksley about the
village whose name he carried. In truth, he had been
feeling homesick, and yearned for an excuse to talk
of his own home. Locksley was dismissive, moving
the conversation rapidly on. At the time, Gisburne
had thought it typical of Locksley's impatience and
lack of sentimentality – his total, sometimes baffling

absence of interest in things past – and that he had dismissed it because he wished to stay focused on the coming conflict. Now, looking back, Gisburne sensed something more evasive in the response. The uncovering – almost – of a lie. What did he really know of him, after all? There was not a single thing upon which he could rely – no glimpse in any of their conversations, he now realised, of family, of childhood, of anything. As if he had stepped out of a void.

Gisburne looked down at the deer. The arrow that had pierced its left eye bore a familiar green fletching. He poked it with his foot. "Only you would aim for an eye when the body presents a target as big as a barrel."

Locksley grinned. "There must be challenges in life." Then, suddenly, he turned.

Gisburne, too, felt the rumble beneath his feet. Horses approaching at the gallop. The men began to back away into the trees. Locksley looked back at Gisburne and narrowed his eyes as if weighing up his options. Gisburne felt they looked at him now as they never had before – that he had revealed something of himself, and in doing so had stepped outside of Locksley's circle, and into a far more dangerous realm. He was uncertain whether the approaching horsemen meant his salvation, or were hastening his death.

"Time we went," said Locksley with a jaunty smile. Then, pulling a knife, he stepped up to Gisburne's horse and slashed the blade across the back of its hind leg.

There was a horrifying screech as it collapsed and thrashed on the ground, blood coursing from the wound.

"*No!*"

"Sorry, old man..." Locksley shrugged, and became one with the greenwood.

L

WENDENAL TURNED ANOTHER circle of the room, hand clasped behind his back, as the man reached the end of his account. He stopped and frowned when he realised there was no more to come. "Why cripple your horse?" he said. "So you were captured in his stead?"

"To stop me going after him." The man's voice was expressionless.

"If that's the case, why not kill you?"

The man looked oddly pained. "Because," he said, "he wants me to go after him."

Wendenal stared at him for a moment in silence, wondering at this paradox. He gave a dismissive snort. "The portrait you paint is of a man as slippery as an eel. How do I know *you* are not Hood?"

A laugh rose in the man's throat, became a guffaw. "Even Hood is not mad enough to kill the king's deer and then cripple his own horse." The laugh died away, his expression becoming suddenly dark – even, Wendenal fleetingly thought, shot through with – what was that? Grief? "It was my father's horse," said the man distantly. "Old, but... A knight's horse. A destrier. If you had seen it, you would know." Wendenal glanced at his serjeant, who nodded in confirmation. "All I had left of him, but for this hauberk and sword. He is – was – a knight. He served King Henry all his life, with a loyalty that never faltered. Even in... the most difficult of times."

Wendenal knew at once to what the man referred. His father had stood against Richard when the rebellious prince had tried to take the crown from the old king. Richard had failed, and Henry had pardoned his sins. But now Henry was dead, and Richard king. This ragged man's ill fortune was beginning to make some kind of sense. The man straightened and looked Wendenal in the eye. His voice was firm, resolute.

"My father's lands were taken from him to be sold. Money to pay for more sides of bacon for Richard's crusade. My mentor – Gilbert de Gaillon, the finest man I ever knew – was killed by him for standing up for what was right and good. Richard took my birthright, hastened my father's death. And I have, with my own eyes, seen him preside over such acts of outrage that common mercenaries were shamed. If there were a means to end this cruel king, to put right this injustice... by God, I would take up its banner here and now."

Wendenal affected an incredulous and grave expression. "You dare speak of the King this way, when you know your life already hangs by a thread?"

The man held his gaze. "I do so because you are William de Wendenal, High Sheriff of Nottinghamshire and Derbyshire, and I know your true feelings for Richard."

Wendenal's guest took this as his cue to step from the shadows. "I think we can dismiss the guards, now," he said. The guards hesitated, and looked to

Wendenal. He gave a curt nod. As they filed out, the guest walked up to Wendenal's prisoner, who stood a full head higher than he, and lingered for a moment, looking up at him, his wine goblet still in his hand.

"Do you know me?" he said. The man looked deep into his face, frowning. "Let me simplify matters. I am John. Prince of England. There are other things – duchies and the like – but that's the main one. I nearly had Aquitaine once. And then there was Ireland – but the less said about that, the better. I am also brother to Richard the Lionhearted. Lucky me. Now, perhaps, you can tell me who you are?" He raised his eyebrows and gave a wry smile. "It seems a fair exchange." Wendenal marvelled at the easy charm that he knew he himself lacked.

The man looked from Wendenal to John and back, for the first time flustered. Then he bowed his head in what seemed genuine humility. "Gisburne," he said. "Guy of Gisburne." Then he added, awkwardly. "We met once. A long time ago..."

"Indeed?" smiled John.

"If my words caused offence..."

"They did not," said John. He unfolded the fingers of his right hand and examined the gold rings upon them.

"Well, Guy of Gisburne," said John. "If de Gaillon was your mentor, then you were once destined to be a knight, were you not...?"

Gisburne lowered his head again – but this time Wendenal thought it looked more like shame. "I was robbed of that opportunity by his death. His disgrace..."

John's eyes narrowed. He nodded slowly.

"So. Another thing lost to you, courtesy of my dear brother." Gisburne, his eyes still downcast, said nothing. John turned suddenly. "Sir William, will you release your prisoner to me?"

"As you wish, my lord." It was a startling request, but not one Wendenal felt inclined to refuse. He was happy to have him out of his hair. Though what John wanted with this strange, shabby character, he could not imagine.

The prince sauntered over to the fireside, took a sip from his goblet, and set it carefully down on the hearth. "We thought we had found someone with information about Hood, Sir William. You feared he would disappoint us. But I see we have found much more than was promised."

He wandered back to Gisburne, and before Wendenal knew what had happened, struck his bare hand across Gisburne's face with all his strength. Gisburne staggered, his expression one of shock.

"What my brother took from you, I now give back, Sir Guy of Gisburne," he said. "Be a true knight, and courageous in the face of your enemies."

His face red from the blow, Gisburne stared wide-eyed at the prince, as if unable to comprehend this shift in his fortunes.

"You came late to your manhood, Sir Knight," said John with a smile. "We must ensure you make the most of it."

LI

Forêt de Boulogne – December, 1191

SINGING WAS THE usual way Lucatz the Enginer kept
his spirits up. It didn't really matter what the tune
– anything was grist to Lucatz's mill. A ballad. A
hymn. A bawdy song, if there was no one about.
Then, he would raise his voice to the heavens until
it cracked with laughter at the fate of the squire
and the randy milkmaid, or the bibulous monk and
his ass.

Today it was different. Today, he made do with
murmuring under his breath, or kept his lip buttoned
altogether. Not that he couldn't do with his spirits
being raised. For the past few hours he had been
lashed by freezing rain, and in that time had also
discovered that the urgency with which he had set
out had made him forget to pack either his leather
cloak or a change of clothes. He was also peeved by
the need to travel so far at such short notice, and
unnerved by his destination: Castel Mercheval.

He'd had dealings with its lord before – that,
presumably, was why it was he who had been
summoned. Lucatz had designed and built many of
the siege engines (technically *counter*-siege engines,

but he hadn't pressed the point) that bristled Castel Mercheval's battlements. Trebuchets, ballistas, mangonels. Mechanisms for delivering boulders, dead bodies, scalding sand and gravel and a variety of hot, noxious or flaming liquids. He had even persuaded Tancred to let him experiment with a "scorpion". Tancred's own inspiration – a kind of ballista meant to fire a spinning, seven-bladed star the size of a meat dish – proved beyond his capabilities to realise, despite Tancred's chillingly intense explanation of the necessity for, and holy significance of, each one of those seven blades.

Why the master of Castel Mercheval required quite so many devices, beyond feeding his own obsession, Lucatz could not guess. But he wasn't one to complain. At least, not at first. It had meant two years work, after all. But then there had been the other mechanisms – the ones meant for restraint and torture. Even these weren't normal. They were for special kinds of torture – things he had never seen before. It was a world that was alien to him, and he liked it that way. At Castel Mercheval he'd been forced to think about it too much, for too long, and in far too much detail. Death and pain at a distance he could cope with, but that... And there had been Tancred himself. And his torturer – that odious man. With any luck *he* had since died. Lucatz imagined him having been eaten up and spat out by one of his own devices, rebelling against the tasks it had been called upon to perform. By the end of it, Lucatz had crept away, far wealthier, unsure quite what he had contributed to the sum of human happiness, and sincerely hoping he would never see or hear from the White Devil again. He still did, from time to time, in his nightmares.

He supposed he should be flattered that such a forbidding master thought him the best man for this job. And the pay would certainly be good. Tancred was generous in that one way – though even as he thought it, the words forming in his head, he felt their ghastly incongruity: *Tancred. Generous.* Like a cat was merciful to a mouse in not killing it straight away. Well, this job was straightforward, at least. And it would not bring him up against *those* things – *that* man. But at this moment he'd swap all the world's money and respect to be home by his own fire with a mug of hot, spiced cider.

This forest also made him nervous. Maybe for some bumpkin, this place was bliss, but he hated the stillness of it – yearned for the human stink, and noise, and bustle of Amiens. The open countryside around the city was perfectly fine, too. It was peaceful, but still orderly – nature shaped by honest human toil. But this...

He felt anxious when completely separated from the influence of man. The dark and disorder of this forest – the thick, unrelenting profusion of it, evident even in the wintery ghosts that now loomed resentfully on every side – oppressed him. There were no human voices to be heard here, and probably only slinking, lank-furred creatures to hear his (the thought made him shudder; he pictured weird whiskered things with long, moist, snuffling noses and matted coats like wet blankets). God knew the sound of a human voice would be a welcome thing, even if it were his own. But something in the forest's mute, brooding presence kept him silent. Thus, no sound accompanied his passing but the wheels of the wagon and the hooves of the horses, the cold drip of the rain and the groan of the trees in the bitter wind.

As the forest had gone on and on, he had begun to understand the source of his disquiet. This ancient, dark place offered nothing distinct, nothing known or knowable. Just shadow. Who knew what it hid? This was a thought he had struggled not to acknowledge – to keep at bay, in dread of what his imagination might summon up. For it was not just the rational fear of announcing himself to bears, or wolves, or outlaws that made him bite his tongue. It was a deeper terror of foul things that had no place in God's creation, that crept in through the dark places – whether in the mind or the forest – and filled up those potent, waiting shadows with their unearthly, infectious forms.

He shook his head, drips flying from his hood. Think of something else... Work. Processes. Yes, that was it. In his mind – for perhaps the third time that journey – he began to make an inventory of the contents of the wagon. The long wooden chest containing his tools. A small cauldron of pitch and a number of pitch sticks. The second smallest of his anvils. Several lengths of rope, gauges various. Ditto chains. A barrel of hinges, catches and sundry parts. A box of nails and rivets. Parchments, quills and black gall ink. A leather apron and gauntlets. Lenses. A wide, segmented case containing jars of a variety of powders and solutions, mostly combustible or caustic.

A sound turned his head. Something falling in the forest, echoing weirdly amongst the wet trees. He sighed, shuddered and turned back. Well, anyway... There was hardly any eventuality for which he wasn't prepared. He'd packed in haste, starting with the things he knew he was likely to need – but in the end had simply loaded almost everything he had. It was quicker and easier to bring the lot. He certainly didn't want to be found wanting. Not after this long trek, and with the eyes of Tancred and his knights upon him. The thought of those eyes – Tancred's eyes, that face – chilled him to the bone.

Another sound made him start. A crack. One of his horses shied and whinnied. This was not something falling. It was something moving. A branch snapping under its weight. The horse settled quickly – they were placid beasts – but as it did so, something on the winding path ahead came into view. A dark, vertical shape in the road.

Lucatz felt his throat tighten. It was a figure. Or at least, a kind of figure. It stood motionless, strangely hunched, its limbs twisted and uneven and – now he could see – unnaturally long. His first thought – to reach for his knife – died in him as he stared.

It was not human. He did not even believe it was alive. It could not be. Steeling himself, he urged his animals on. As he neared, the weird shape resolved into a crude construction of branches and twigs, bunched and lashed together to create a life-sized mockery of the human form. The horses balked before the primitive mannequin before he had need to stop them. He supposed he should have been relieved. Had it been a man in the road – a man bent on his destruction – he might now be fighting for his life.

Yet somehow – and this was the irrational part of it – this was worse.

In asking himself who had put this here, and why, he had begun to reach horrible conclusions. He had begun to believe, with creeping unease, that it was put here for him – that the horrid form was a symbol for what was to come; a warning of some imminent, terrible fate.

Close by, to his right, there was a creak. A groan of wood. Another crack. Startled, his eyes flew to the trees.

And there, in the flicker of a moment, he saw it. Dark and bat-like, as big as a man, it flapped its leathery, winged body and was gone. Most horrid of all, however, was the blackened human face that grinned from its head. His mouth dry, his heart pounding, Lucatz had a brief moment to stare into the vacant shadows beyond the spiked branches before a great weight smashed into him with the force of a horse's kick.

The last thing he remembered as he fell was the smell of damp wood. Then all was black.

LII

ALDRIC FITZ ROLF looked out from the rain-slicked battlements of Castel Mercheval and saw the Devil.

A moment before, the dark opening at the edge of the trees – the one shaped like a ragged, screaming mouth – had been empty shadow. Just the same familiar, blank space that it had been all day, and – but for the passing of a bird, or rabbit, or the long, lean figure of a fox – for countless days before that. Thrusting out in front of the yawning hole, and largely the reason for it, was the great grey-brown slab that some called Arthur's Table – a flat outcrop of rock punctuating the higher ground some fifty yards left of where the winding dirt road emerged from the woods.

To Aldric it had always resembled a listing raft rather than a table. In summer, the hectic foliage of the forest even seemed to be breaking upon it like a great green wave.

Now, its surface shimmered in the slanting rain. Aldric had been glancing at it in the grey daylight, thinking abstractly about the gripes in his stomach, and was turning away to make some comment upon it to Bertrans, his fellow watchman, when the fleeting vision had appeared; tall, hooded, with no visible face, but – he realised only after it had gone a second later – a pair of tiny horns upon its head.

"What the Hell was that?" he said. Frowning, he nodded towards the place. "There..."

Bertrans scanned the forest's edge and laughed. "You're jumpy today," he said. "Nothing living that I can see, except us up here in this piss-poor weather."

Aldric squinted at the dark spaces again, his eyes stinging, rain running from his helm in cold rivulets that crept down his neck. "There was something..." he said. "Beyond the rock. No question."

Bertrans studied him with narrowed eyes. "What did it look like?" All dismissiveness was now gone from his tone. Bertrans knew Aldric was no fool.

"A man, or..." Aldric's voice trailed away. The wind gusted, making the whole facade of trees sigh and shudder – and even Aldric doubted his own judgement. He gave a snort of agitation and turned from the forest.

Bertrans coughed and spat. "Might've been a deer. They don't normally come so close, but sometimes when the weather's bad they're forced down..." He stopped abruptly.

Aldric had turned away to look out across the castle courtyard, seeming to have heard a strange sound from that direction – oddly familiar, but one he couldn't quite place. "Forced down...?" he said, urging his comrade to finish.

But when Aldric looked back at him, the man seemed paralysed in some kind of agony. As he watched, Bertrans's eyes seemed to bulge out of his head, his face growing purple, his throat rasping as if constricted. At first, he thought it must be one of Bertrans's jokes. "Are you all right?" he asked with a laugh.

Only as Bertrans fell did Aldric see the arrow. It had hit where his neck joined his shoulders, entering the muscle just above the right shoulder blade and emerging above the left side of his collarbone.

Stiff as a board, Bertrans tottered forward with a strange, shuffling gait and, before Aldric could act, pitched head-first off the walkway.

He dropped behind the parapet, his back to the stone near where Bertrans's crossbow still leaned, hearing its owner's body hit the ground with a sickening *thud*.

"Alarm!" he cried. "*Alarm!*" The effect was instantaneous; the ordered chaos of the castle's bustling interior instantly transformed. As one, the castle's knights, soldiers and servants going about their daily tasks changed direction like a flock of birds in flight. Some broke into a run, others dropped what they were doing and returned the way they had come. Many scaled ladders and steps to their positions on the ramparts and towers. Inner doors were secured. Horses prepared. Siege weapons were brought to readiness. It was a drill they had performed a thousand times under their master's iron regime – on a daily basis, sometimes at night, and in all weathers. Tancred believed in total battle readiness, and strict discipline. The penalties for those who failed in their duties – who failed God – were harsh. In Tancred's world, there were no half measures. No mercy to which one could appeal. No ambiguities. There were those who respected him, many more who hated him, but none who did not fear him.

Then, from the great square keep, came Tancred himself – his armour on, his sword buckled, his surcoat gleaming white; Aldric had not once seen him otherwise attired – followed closely behind by Fulke and Ulrich. The expressions of the two men – one flushed, the other pale – were something between trepidation and outrage; that of Tancred, as cold and implacable as the stone of his castle. That they had been questioning the squire and the woman was beyond doubt, but whether the pair had given up any information was another matter. Above the urgent clamour, as he cocked and loaded his crossbow, Aldric heard Tancred's voice, like metal against rock. "Who called it?" A serjeant pointed up to where Aldric was crouched.

Then, from Aldric's left, along the rampart some dozen yards, came a harsh cry and the heavy clatter of a crossbow falling onto flagstones. It was Engenulf. Aldric had heard the same hiss he'd heard before Bertrans's death, and now made the connection. An arrow. He turned to see Engenulf motionless, a look of near comical astonishment on his face, the arrow pinning his bleeding right hand to his breastbone. Before he could blink – and in stark contrast to Bertrans – Engenulf crumpled like a rag as if his bones had been sucked out, then slithered over the edge of the walkway to the courtyard below.

Tancred had reached the wooden steps to the rampart now, but something Ulrich said stopped him. Aldric did not hear what it was – just the low rasp of his voice – but the man's hand was extended in a gesture of caution. Tancred did not even look at him. "God will protect me," he said, and advanced up the steps like a wraith.

It occurred to Aldric then to attempt to locate the position of their attackers before Tancred arrived and questioned him on the subject. He raised his head with slow caution into the space of the nearest crenel until the edge of the trees was revealed to him. The attackers – whoever they might be – were clearly keen shots with a bow, and their number as yet unknown. Aldric had no wish to be next. But it was something more than self-preservation that drove him. His chief desire, at that precise moment, was to live long enough to plant the head of Bertrans's killer on a stake.

What he saw, as Tancred's footsteps approached, raised as many baffling questions as it answered. He had primed himself to be sensitive to the subtlest signs – unusual movements, things out of place, glints of metal or muffled sounds of command from amongst the trees. In the event, no such sensitivity was required. In full view, on the flat slab of the great stone, stood a single figure – tall, hooded, as dark as Tancred was pale, a bag across one shoulder, a bow held flat across his thigh, arrow nocked upon it, ready to be drawn. Aldric cursed his stupidity – his doubt. Had he trusted his first instinct, Bertrans and Engenulf might now be alive.

"Tancred!" boomed out a voice from the rock.

Tancred stepped forward to the parapet no more than a yard from Aldric. His lip curled, and Aldric heard him utter a single word: "Gisburne..." Without hesitation and in one swift movement, the stranger raised and drew the bow and loosed the arrow.

It whistled past Tancred's ear. The master of Castel Mercheval did not flinch, nor did he make any attempt to conceal himself. If the bowman wished to kill him with a second shot, there was little anyone could now do to prevent it. But Tancred showed no hint of fear. There were those who said that if he were face to face with the Devil himself, he would walk straight up to him, sword drawn and ready to fight. Now Aldric knew that was true.

Tancred's fearlessness, irrational though it may have been, shamed him. He rose to his feet, crossbow raised, and saw that several yards along the battlements Gaston – a serjeant, similarly armed – had done the same. Their adversary was well within range – close enough that mail would not save him – and the second arrow that Aldric had expected to see already upon his bow was not there. The bow itself was lowered, his other fist now raised as if it contained something of great import. Some time in the past few moments, Aldric now noticed, the stranger's shoulder bag had also begun to drip blood.

"He was supposed to be dead," hissed Tancred.

Fulke, still a yard behind him, flushed red. "I thought..." His voice died away.

Tancred's mouth twisted into a snarl of cold contempt. "You *thought*..."

Aldric caught Gaston's eye, and without a word both levelled their weapons at the stranger. If he attempted to reload – even if he tried to run – they could pin him. Yet this man, whose gaze was now locked with Tancred's, seemed equally oblivious to the possibility of death. If man he was.

For a time they stood in charged silence, face to face across that expanse of stone, moat and mud, one seeming the demonic twin of the other – black angel versus White Devil. Aldric swore he could see

Tancred's already stony eyes harden as he regarded this shadowy reflection. But what had passed between these two, and what type of being this dark shade – this Gisburne – really was, he could not guess.

A thousand thoughts rushed through his mind in those moments. He had believed the miss with the arrow an accident. Now, considering the bowman's precision in taking out Bertrans and Engenulf, he was convinced it had been deliberate. But if he was Tancred's enemy – and knew he would receive no mercy in return – why spare him? What did he now hope to achieve against Tancred's knights, and these impregnable walls? And if he had come to the rescue of their recent prisoners, why announce himself in broad daylight, rather than sneaking in at night?

"You wait for your enginer in vain," the voice from the rock rang out again. He took a step forward. Aldric and Gaston tensed. Reaching into the bag, he threw before him what appeared to be part of a mutilated limb. It bounced on the rock, leaving behind a splatter of red that slowly dissipated with the rain. The stranger then extended his arm. Hanging from it, Aldric could see a string or fine chain, and at its end, spinning and glinting in the dim grey light, what appeared to be a key. "Only this will open the box," came the grim cry. "If you want it, come and take it."

Tancred stared down at the dark figure, eyes narrowing, jaw clenching. Aldric did not want to know what was going through that head. The master of Castel Mercheval looked up at the grey, empty sky as if seeking something in it, then back to Gisburne.

"Kill him," he said flatly.

Aldric squeezed the trigger. The heavy crossbow leapt in his hands. At the edge of his vision, he was aware of Gaston doing the same. The two bolts – fired almost simultaneously – drove into Gisburne's chest, knocking him off his feet. He slammed onto the wet rock and lay motionless, the patter of the rain the only sound, the stain of red running off the angled surface.

"Get the key," Tancred said, and turned and walked away.

LIII

"GALFRID?" IT WAS too dark to see, but Mélisande knew it had to be the squire. She was certain there were no other prisoners in here but the two of them, but already exhaustion and disorientation were causing her senses to play tricks. There were rats – that much she knew. She could smell them, had heard the scrabbling and scratching, had even felt them move against the soles of her naked, cold-numbed feet. But then, some time during the previous night, twisting and writhing out of the gloom, she had seen translucent snakes with human eyes. She had understood later, when clarity returned, that she was beginning to lose her grip. How much further Galfrid was down that path – and what horrors he was seeing around him in the dark – she could not imagine.

Water dripped. The dank, clammy walls of this unseen chamber stank of waste, of decay, of the dying breaths of past inhabitants. Somewhere high above, through the meagre slit of some unseen window, the wind resonated weirdly. Its reedy rise and fall was like the howl of a starving wolf, but incessant, neverending – the plaintive exhalation of some unearthly creature doomed never to draw breath.

She had fatally misjudged her adversary. She had felt a wild confidence in her plan when she'd left Gisburne – fully justified in dismissing his words of warning. Her father was the Count of Boulogne, after all, connected to some of the most powerful people in Europe. And few families had such strong links with the Templars as the house of Boulogne. The dynasty had supported the Templar cause from the very beginning – with money, with land, with knights. It had even provided two Kings of Jerusalem. What she had not appreciated was just how far Tancred had drifted from the powers that supposedly ruled him – his Grand Master, his Pope, his sanity.

When she was led through the gate of this strange castle, the life she found inside seemed to bear little relation to the knightly order she knew. That, in itself, had unnerved her. Then, when she had stood before her captor, hands bound behind her, and voiced her outrage – invoking her family name, her loyalty to the French King, and had finally thrown at Tancred the fact that she knew personally the Grand Master and Lord of Cyprus, Robert de Sablé – he had simply stared, devoid of all emotion, and told her that God no longer recognised de Sablé as Grand Master, and that the King of France had no right to receive his gift.

Only then did the truth become clear. Tancred really did mean to keep the skull for himself.

Her blood ran cold. There was nothing with which to bargain. She had threatened him then, saying her father would send an army if she was harmed. Tancred had remained unmoved. She was a heretic, he said. An enemy of God, most likely tainted by exposure to Saracen ways. Her father could send a thousand men to crush him if he liked. A million. He would see her punished, nonetheless. God willed it.

But first, a simple question. He said he would ask it only once. After that, should her answer prove unsatisfactory, another would take over. *He* would not ask anything of her – would not even speak. He would simply cause her pain. But Tancred's question would remain, and she could answer it at any time, should she so wish.

It all sounded so reasonable, so ordered. She almost laughed.

Then Tancred fixed her with his dead eyes, and asked her the question.

"How does one open the box?" he said.

Her mind reeled. He did not have the key, but might yet get it. And he had an enginer coming. He could undoubtedly get the box open. But still something about the operation unnerved him. There was more he felt he needed to know – something about it that he feared. He feared failing God.

That realisation felt like triumph.

So, she smiled that sweet smile, and leaned forward as if to whisper in his ear. He leaned towards her, his mask of a face passing horribly close to hers.

"Very carefully," she said.

Without another word, she had been dragged to this dark place. And then the other that Tancred had spoken of appeared. Until then, she had thought Tancred the vilest creature she was ever likely to meet. But she was wrong.

She could hear him now, in the dark. His shuffling feet. His rasping breath.

She strained to listen for other signs of movement – from Galfrid – but could hear nothing. She didn't know how long it had been since he had spoken. Only when he groaned, now, could she be sure he was there. And even that had stopped.

There were no manacles here. No chains. That had been the first surprise. The restraints upon her arms – presumably attached to rope, and from which she was suspended in mock crucifixion, arms outstretched, toes barely touching the floor – were broad and made of soft, padded leather. They did not cut, or chafe. It was almost as if they were made for comfort. This fact – this collision of opposites – alarmed and disturbed her for reasons she could not place.

Her restraints also removed from her any ability to make sound other than by speech. Speaking was what they wanted her to do. So she would not do it. Eventually, when the need to assert her presence – to confirm her existence – became too much to bear, she began to talk to herself, to break the silence of the void. She had done this only when she thought they weren't there. Then she had heard him – her gaoler – shambling in the darkness, and knew she was not alone – perhaps had never been. She had cursed her stupidity, then, reviewing all the words that had spewed out of her mouth.

How he was able to move about in this pitch black – to do whatever it was he was doing, with the scrape and clank of metal – she could not guess. She told herself that all these things had been contrived to dishearten her, to break her spirit. Telling herself that did not lessen their effect, of course. But she knew nothing about the box, and resolved to offer them nothing else. She would remain silent, no matter what. Tancred could not be allowed to know her mission – her real mission.

The reliquary box, meanwhile, had been placed in the centre of the chamber before them. She knew this because sometimes it was illuminated by a single, shaded candle that lit the box itself and nothing else. That was Tancred's idea – to confront them with the source of their suffering, the symbol of their guilt. At first she had fixed her eyes upon it. It was the only visible point of reference in the entire chamber, an anchor for her drifting perspective. But it was not itself anchored to anything. Its dim image seemed to float in the formless black, to advance and recede, to tip and sway. She could not even tell if it was placed on the ground, or upon a table, or hanging on the end of a rope. Sometimes she seemed to see other shapes within it – once, a grinning skull-like face of such leering intensity that she had to close her eyes.

Then there was the time when their host – not Tancred, but the other, whose domain this was – moved closer to the candle than he had meant, and his face had been revealed. It was partly in shadow. But for a fleeting moment, in the candle's sickly yellow light, she saw it clear.

Out of all the terrible things that now surrounded her, this – the face of their silent captor – was the most disturbing of all.

He was out there now. He had taken Galfrid down once today – if it was indeed day. She had heard the sounds as he had worked upon him, then the grunts as he heaved him back up. Galfrid himself had not even cried out this time. It would be her turn next.

*   *   *

TANCRED DID NOT believe in torture. He believed in punishment. An eye for an eye – or for an offence against a pilgrim. A head struck off, a tongue torn out. Evil had to be destroyed without hesitation. Rooted out. If there was a limb that was infected – literally or morally – Tancred would not balk at personally hacking away the offending part. Was it not Matthew who said: "And if thy right hand offend thee, cut it off, and cast it from thee: for it is profitable for thee that one of thy members should perish, and not that thy whole body should be cast into Hell"?

Like Reynald de Châtillon, Tancred would also not hesitate in having someone thrown from the battlements in order to make a point. Unlike Reynald, however – whose example he regarded as the worst form of moral depravity – he did not do it because he enjoyed it. The idea was abhorrent to him. Contrary to what many believed, inflicting pain gave him no pleasure. Nor did it repel him. It was neither here nor there. And that was how it should be. Those who did gain pleasure from it, he regarded as weak. He felt the same, in fact, about those who gained pleasure from anything.

Tancred did what he did because it was right. It was necessary. Others spoke of doing things for their beliefs, but to Tancred the whole notion of "belief" was something that belonged to the morally and spiritually inferior. Tancred did not act as he did because he believed. He did so because he *knew*. Because God told him so – and God was infallible. These certainties were more real and immediate to him than any matter of mere flesh. Of course, God could be merciful, but mercy was not Tancred's calling. He knew better than most that mercy was the enemy of moral clarity. It was the thing that stayed the hand when there was greatest need to strike. Evil did not respect or listen to mercy, and was not worthy of it. It exploited it, depended on it. And God had need to be wrathful from time to time: to smite, to punish. It was then that Tancred served as His right hand. His agent on earth.

Despite his contempt for the corporeal world, Tancred also abhorred deformation of the flesh. Those who were born imperfect were corrupt – their bodies warped by their spiritual deficiencies. But those who deliberately mutilated the flesh for their own ends were something worse: defilers of God's work – men who inflicted their own corruption upon the bodies of others. Like those who had crucified Christ. Wounds inflicted as direct punishment for a misdeed, injuries as a result of misadventure, scars of battle – all served a useful purpose. They were reminders, warnings. But he would play no part in torture that left its mark upon the flesh.

Fortunately, he had occasionally encountered men who were more creative in their approach – and he was pragmatic enough, when instructed to do so, to have employed them to achieve necessary ends.

One such man was Fell the Maker.

It was Fell who shambled out there in the darkness like some blind cave creature. Fell who administered methods of persuasion which gave even Tancred de Mercheval pause.

He knew exactly how far a bone could bend without breaking. How much a joint could be twisted and stretched without lasting damage. How long a body could hang suspended by its limbs – to the point of unbearable exhaustion, and no further. How much extreme heat or cold a body could take, how long it could be denied air without dying. None of these methods left marks upon the victim – not visible ones, at least. That was Fell's great skill, his contribution to human wisdom. Fell the Gentle, some called him. By the end, his guests would tell their interrogators everything. Anything.

Yet he himself asked nothing of them. He did not engage directly with them at all, except through his various devices. He never spoke. There were sounds, but to Mélisande, they seemed more the snuffling of some animal. The snort of a cow. The grunt of a pig.

Mélisande had seen and withstood many physical hardships – more than most men could stand. But what terrified her now was not the threat to her body. It was not the anticipation of pain, or the fear of death. It was the slow realisation that, to Fell, she was dead already. An object without significance or meaning. A piece of meat. To suffer and die – that was a known quantity to her. It might even be just, and heroic. It was the Christian way. But to cease to have meaning, to no longer have any connection to this world, to be nothing... That was true terror.

There were shouts from outside. Among them, a distant voice, echoing strangely, which she felt sure was familiar. It was *him*. It had to be him. She heard Fell grunt in the darkness – the first time she had been aware of him responding to anything outside of this dismal, lightless world. She could not tell if it was an expression of alarm, or a kind of laugh. But her heart leapt. The breaking of the spell – the sudden piercing of this weird, hermetic domain – had spurred her. A momentary thrill of reconnection. She was not yet lost. Not yet abandoned.

No sooner had it begun than it ceased. Cold silence. Mélisande heaved on her bindings, trying to raise herself up, bracing herself for the things she knew Fell would have in store. But also stirring her spirit, her muscles, trying to remember – to prepare.

The shouts outside... She was sure now that it was him. It had to be.

"He's coming, Galfrid, I know it," she said, not caring if their gaoler heard her. "Just a little longer... A little longer..."

But Galfrid – if Galfrid it was – said nothing.

LIV

TANCRED DE MERCHEVAL had reached the third step of the wooden stair when Aldric's voice stopped him.

"My lord..." Tancred turned.

He was not used to being stopped or summoned. It did not please him. There had been a time when he had been a dutiful servant, what he would now call a "lackey". He had jumped to all commands, had respected all in authority. His superiors had been many – his knight, his Baron, his Count, his Duke, his King. Then his Temple Master, the Grand Master, his Holiness the Pope. For years he had done their bidding without question – even with good cheer – safe in the knowledge that he was promoting the cause of order – of good – in his small corner of the universe. He had been an optimist, but not a blind one. He was well-read in philosophy, and had arrived at his point of view based on both his own experience and the accumulated wisdom of the ages. He fervently believed that if each performed their duties well, in however small a way, then all their small efforts could come together to create something wonderful. A better world, in which each contributed his carefully-shaped stone to the construction of the great cathedral. In this way, the honest peasant toiling in the field was as worthy of respect – and as important to the harmony of the cosmos – as any prince or bishop.

Young Tancred was well liked, and well rewarded for his services, and proved himself a bold and fearless fighter. But while he had always revelled in the physical challenges, discipline and camaraderie inherent in training for combat, he was nonetheless troubled by the use of force. As a good Christian, he questioned it constantly. And yet, he also saw the necessity – the goodness – of protecting those who could not protect themselves. And had not Christ himself violently ejected the money-changers from the temple? The young Tancred respected his Saviour all the more for this moment of pragmatism – of humanity. It seemed to him a guiding principle; violence was always regrettable, but sometimes necessary, if the cause was just. That meant it should always be questioned, the justice of the cause weighed up. Many there were who admired the combination of valour, wisdom and moral rigour in one so young. Admission to the Knights Templar had followed naturally.

Then he had been struck down. For days, he had been as one dead. But he did not die. God would not let him.

Afterwards, everything changed. He had suffered wild swings of mood. There were bursts of terrible anger – at himself, at mankind, and yes, even at God. He admitted now that he had been raving – a temporary vessel, in his weakened state, for the whims of the Devil. But he had resisted. He had seen his foe up close – felt his cold fingers clutch at his soul – and he had wrestled himself free. He had been reborn. He had also begun to realise the terrible folly that had afflicted him his whole life.

Compassion no longer troubled him. God had freed him from its tyranny. And he saw now that it was those such as him – such as he had been – who were the problem. The reasonable, the merciful. The "fair". The world was not reasonable or merciful or fair. They simply allowed the Devil to have his way.

Friends drifted away, but it was no loss. He did not need them. They were a distraction from his new purpose. He heard some whisper, darkly, that he had changed, and knew this was true; but he was glad of it. He'd been blind, and now he could see. That was all there was to it. They said he had lost his good humour, that he had turned to stone. But he was glad of that, too. He found nothing to laugh at in the world. Laughter was delusion, and stone was strong. Incorruptible.

Gradually, he understood that many of those he had admired and served were not worthy of his respect. One by one the idols fell. Everywhere he looked he saw flawed humanity, corrupt flesh. He cut it away. Discarded it. It would infect him no longer.

A Templar was bound to no king – only his superiors within the Order: his Master; his Grand Master; the Pope. For a long time, Tancred had continued to do his duty by them.

Of late, he had come to know that even they were fallible. Weak. Now God spoke directly to him, what need had he of them? They were the reason for the disaster – the punishment – of Hattin. But it was also at Hattin that he had been awakened from his long slumber. Now, while they were distracted by their quest for redemption in the Holy Land, he could get on with the real tasks.

He had finally risen to where he belonged. Nothing now stood between him and his work. Nothing stood between him and God. And he took orders from no one.

It was the note of incredulity in Aldric's tone that stopped him, that inspired a strange, uneven frown on his pale brow.

"What is it?"

Aldric – still staring out over the battlements – opened his mouth to speak, but no word came out. He simply stood there, mute, gaping like a fish.

"Well?" snapped Tancred.

Aldric stared at him, dumbfounded. Somewhere nearby, someone on the parapet muttered "My God..."

Tancred hissed in boiling rage as he charged back up the rampart. In most of Christendom, a man who cursed in the name of God might be fined or flogged; here, far harsher rules were observed. Tancred would personally rip out the tongue of any guilty of even the mildest blasphemy. Aldric had seen him do it. But this time, before he could act upon it, he was stopped in his tracks – his attention seized by what was happening on the rock.

Slowly but surely, Gisburne was rising to his feet. At first, Aldric had thought it the last gasp of a dying man – the final flourish of defiant spirit before it departed the flesh. But as Gisburne rose, the two crossbow bolts still sticking out of him like the appendages of some black beetle, he seemed to gather strength. To rally. To grow.

Aldric – the hair on his neck standing on end – could feel the shock and disquiet of every man watching along that rampart. Finally, the twice-killed apparition stood fully upright – a bizarre, impossible figure – shoulders thrown back, hands clenched into fists at his sides, crow-black hide coat whipping about him in the winter wind. As if in sympathy, the sky darkened, the leaden clouds seeming to press down upon those below.

Tancred's face was now twisted into a bitter mask of anger and hatred. But there was something else – something that Aldric had never seen upon that warped visage before – something which, for the first time, made the grim master of Castel Mercheval seem vulnerable.

Disbelief.

Gisburne's eyes scanned the parapet, fixing on Tancred. He raised his right hand, its finger pointing at his adversary as if he were passing judgement, or casting a spell.

"Your men believe there is a curse upon that box," he called, his voice echoing off the castle wall. "They're right. It's me."

At the words, a shudder seemed to pass along the battlements, as if all upon it had been struck by an icy blast.

"Shoot him!" spat Tancred. "Someone shoot him down!" But no one now had a crossbow cocked, half the men still in a state of petrified shock. Tancred wrestled Gaston's weapon from him, made to draw the string, then flung it down as the better option dawned upon him.

"Scorpion!" he yelled, pointing a bony finger at the gatehouse tower. On its battlements, the operator of the scorpion – a huge sniper crossbow that was Lucatz the Enginer's crowning achievement – jumped out of his stupor. At the cry of alarm, all main weapons had begun to be readied, and the scorpion – lighter than its fellow war machines – stood ready to fire. But its operator had been standing idle, apparently transfixed by Gisburne's uncanny resurrection. It was a failing for which the man would later pay.

Now, in haste, flushed with mortification, he swung the weapon around upon its axis, the point of the arrow projecting over the parapet like the sting of some huge insect. Aldric saw him steady himself and take a deep breath.

The bolt flew. Its aim was good. But the man behind it had been too slow – Gisburne was now moving, stooping to snatch up his bow. The bolt roared through the empty air, striking a yew tree at the forest's edge with a great *crack*, its still-green, spiny leaves shuddering at the impact, the iron point splitting the bough and sending splinters of wood and fragments of bark flying.

The dark, hooded ghoul on the rock straightened. "See you in Hell, Tancred," he boomed.

And with that he turned and ran – yes, *ran* – until the dark maw of the forest swallowed him.

LV

THE PARTY OF mounted knights and serjeants thundered out of the castle gate – the knights in the white surcoats of the Templars emblazoned with the red cross, the serjeants in their blood-red livery.

Fulke had been quick to volunteer himself as their captain. He needed to win back some favour from his master, and riding down this wretch – bringing back his head this time, so there could be absolutely no doubt – seemed the best way to do it. They would flush him out, surround him and pin him with lances. It would be just like hunting boar. Except, of course, that a boar didn't come back at you with a bow or sword. But Fulke had thought of that. Before their precipitous departure from Castel Mercheval, he had spoken privately with the crossbowmen among the serjeants – all of whom were trained to fire from horseback, and at a gallop if necessary – and promised five deniers to the one who could bring down the miscreant without killing him. With their quarry disabled, Fulke would run him through until his lance was red with his blood. Then he'd have one of them perform the messy task of decapitating the corpse, and would ride back triumphant, Gisburne's head held aloft. In his mind, he could already hear the cheers of the jubilant garrison. He would get them to like him if it was the last thing he did.

Soon after Gisburne's dramatic resurrection and disappearance, they'd noticed a thin column of smoke rising from the forest, to the southeast. One of the foresters was certain he could tell the location of the source. When pressed by Fulke, he admitted he had not passed that way in months, and could not vouch for the state of the paths, but a glance suggested it was the place they called the "wolf glade", not far off the road. He knew these woods, as he put it, "better than he knew his brother's wife" – a quip he would not have made within Tancred's hearing, if he valued his testicles.

And so, with a great clatter of arms, armour glinting, Fulke had ridden out onto the forest road at the head of nine knights and six serjeants, helm thrown back, red hair and beard flying. Of course, Fulke's version of "riding at the head" included two serjeants as outriders just ahead of him. He was a knight, not a fool.

They had not ridden far along the tree-hemmed road when a cry went up from one of the serjeants. A horse, riderless, and apparently rooting for sustenance in the verge. As they drew close, they could see it was a cart horse. In the next moment, as the road curved, the serjeant at the head – a stocky fellow named Theobald, or Theobard or some such name – spotted another part of the puzzle, and called back to Fulke. Up ahead was a wagon, seemingly abandoned by the side of the road.

It could only be the enginer's wagon. Fulke urged them on with a triumphant curse, and they flew towards it at a gallop. As they neared, they could see some of its load was scattered, and parts of the wagon itself apparently missing or destroyed. Fulke was just trying to understand what had wrought such destruction upon the cart when Theobald's head snapped back. His whole body flipped up in the air and was flung backwards off his mount, smashing upside down into the side of the other serjeant's horse, which he was desperately trying draw to a halt before it struck. It looked to Fulke as if a great hand had plucked at Theobald as he rode, pinching him about the neck and tossing him in a somersault. His body crunched to the ground, head first, then rolled over, head lolling limply. Fulke drew up suddenly behind his serjeant, several of the men behind him careering into each other with much protest.

Fulke had not paused to allow the crossbowmen to ready their bows – something they could not do whilst riding. Effectively defenceless against a man with a bow, they now struggled to prime them as they pulled their horses in a circle and scanned the trees for targets. But they found none.

Then Fulke saw it. It was almost invisible against the backdrop of dark trees, but stretched across the path between two adjacent trunks – the exact height of a man's neck, if the man were on the back of a courser – was a rope.

That Theobald was dead was beyond doubt. Fulke – furious that first blood had been to his adversary – wheeled his horse around in tight circles, his sword drawn, shouting obscenities at the mute ranks of trees.

Just then, one of the serjeants – Fulke didn't know his name – called out. In the dead foliage at the side of the road, close to where the wagon had been abandoned, was a gap – the opening to an old path. This, he said, was the old path the forester had meant – he was sure of it. The wisps of smoke, still just visible above the trees, lay directly beyond. Around the opening lay freshly-broken twigs. Fulke bravely permitted the serjeant to dismount and investigate on his behalf. He peered along the path, and called back to report that he could make out bits of the ill-fated enginer's cargo scattered along it.

The path was far too enclosed for horse and rider – barely wide enough for those on foot to go more than single file. But Fulke roared in triumph nonetheless, sheathed his sword and leapt off his horse, dragging a poleaxe from the side of his saddle and tucking a mace into his wide belt. He had his man. He knew where he was, and which way he had gone. And he had fifteen armed men to this one. Those were the kind of odds he liked. This was going to be a slaughter – one he would relish.

"You and you – stay with the horses!" barked Fulke. "The rest, with me..." All but two dismounted, and loaded themselves with every kind of weapon. One of the mounted men addressed Fulke then, asking if it was not wise to remain mounted, and perhaps find a different route in. Fulke glared at him, and spat on the floor in contempt. He would deal with that one later. Now, without hesitation, he turned and plunged into the forest.

Once inside, Fulke ordered two of his serjeants to scout ahead. The path was eerily quiet – no birds, just the creak of shifting boughs in the wind and the steady drip-drip of rain and meltwater from the leafless branches. Along it, strewn with apparent carelessness, were all manner of strange, discarded objects – soaked scraps of cloth, a small hammer, a leather belt, several iron rivets in a pile, a freshly broken jar with stinking, acrid contents.

One of the serjeants hissed back to Fulke, pointing ahead. All tensed and readied their weapons. As they drew closer, Fulke could see the path opening up into a clearing. And he could hear a sound – muffled, indistinct, but unmistakably human.

Fulke, advancing slower now, joined the serjeants who had stopped at the edge of the open glade. He saw what they saw, and froze.

It was just as the forester had described – an almost perfect circle that had, at some time in the distant past, been painstakingly cleared, and was now surrounded by a ring of ancient oak trees, each one of huge size. Almost dead centre of the clearing, a fire burned, smoke spiralling up into the grey sky, some of the logs as yet unmarked by the flames. They could only have been placed there minutes before. About it were scattered various objects – some, simple tradesmen's tools that Fulke recognised even at a distance; others enigmatic, glinting with metal and glass.

And beyond, tied upright to one of the largest of the trees, was a man.

Fulke had not expected to find such a thing. For a fleeting, irrational moment, squinting at the gagged, partly obscured features in the low light, Fulke thought it was Gisburne himself; that he had been cheated of his prize by some mysterious interloper, who had, perhaps, captured the villain in the hope of reward. In the next moment, he was castigating himself for his stupidity. This could not be the same man. He was stocky, short, his clothing common. He was also the source of the sounds, the wailing and whimpering. His eyes widened as he saw the knights and serjeants, and his volume and urgency rose.

Fulke urged the nearest of his serjeants on. The man took one step, then did not move, apparently reluctant to come out from cover. "Pathetic coward!" breathed Fulke, shoving him forward with the point of his poleaxe.

The serjeants advanced slowly, warily into the open.

All looked about them, senses keen, weapons drawn, loaded, ready – the only sounds the crack of the fire in the damp, the whimper of the bound man, and the constant creak and drip-drip-drip of the surrounding trees. Fulke did not like it here. There was an almost unearthly stillness which made even those sounds seem weirdly muted. He gripped the poleaxe tighter, and wondered at this glade's ancient purpose. Perhaps once some pagan place, he thought, trying to suppress the shudder he felt pass through him.

Beneath the sharp tang of woodsmoke, the place smelled of damp and mould and rot. Then, as the wind gusted, something else hit his nostrils: tar or pitch. The wind changed, whipping the smell away again. Then there was something else – faint, but distinctly there, at the back of it all, wafting now and then. Something he had only smelled on the hunt, or in battle. Blood. Fresh blood.

There was death here, he was sure of it.

It was not the man against the tree. He was very much alive. Fulke realised, slowly but surely, as they advanced step by step across the damp and spongy floor, that this could only be the fabled enginer from Amiens. If he got Gisburne and brought back the enginer in one piece so the box coud be opened, that would be triumph indeed. He felt a surge of confidence. Gisburne had not killed the enginer after all – had not even maimed him, as far as he could see. He was not as ruthless or invincible as he had made out. And the enginer must know from their garb that he was now saved.

So, why was he whimpering harder, and shaking his head at their approach, his eyes wider than ever? Fulke drew up level with the crackling fire and paused. On the ground now, half hidden, he could just make out a large circle of tiny stakes in the ground. He vaguely wondered if a tent had been pitched there, when one of his knights nudged him, and gestured towards something else on the ground, just beyond the fire. A thick, dark plank of wood, about the length of a man's arm and a forearm in width. It bore a simple carved design, and on one side were broken, black iron hinges. The lid of a box. Fulke recognised the design. The mark of Lucatz, the enginer. He even believed, now he thought about it, that he might have seen this very piece of wood before. It was the lid of the box that contained Lucatz's tools. Except now, it had a loop of string attached to one end, like an apron. And embedded in it were two crossbow bolts. Crossbow bolts bearing the fletching of Castel Mercheval.

So that was how the pig did it. He was no demon, not invincible. Fulke gave a gruff laugh of satisfaction and took a step forward. The enginer whimpered louder through his gag, trying to speak, shaking his head with ever greater urgency. Fulke stopped and stared, his meaty forehead creased in a deepening frown as realisation began to dawn.

There was a creak behind them. A snap. Fulke turned, just as something big and bloody – some creature – came rushing at them through the air.

His men reeled about, threw up their arms and drew back to avoid being struck by the thing, shoving and trampling each other in their panic. Those now at the back – Fulke and his serjeants – were barged roughly. They staggered back, fighting to maintain their balance. The earth gave way beneath their feet.

Fulke plunged into darkness, bouncing off a flailing figure. His head grazed against wood. A hand clawed against his face. His body jammed against something, fell again awkwardly, then suddenly stopped. Disorientated and confused, it took him a moment to understand what had happened.

He was in a pit of spikes. A bear trap. The realisation almost made him laugh. He had set out on the hunt, and had instead become the hunted. The trapped beast.

He did not know if he was injured. He only knew he was somehow hanging sideways, unable to turn, his legs trapped, his beard and hair full of twigs and mouldering leaves, the taste of blood in his mouth, the reek of pitch in his nostrils. About him, half glimpsed in the dark – and closer than he would have liked – was the writhing and groaning of the dying, the hot smell of torn flesh.

With supreme effort he heaved against the stakes – they would not move – and twisted around as far as he could. It wasn't much – just enough to see daylight, once he'd blinked away the blood and loam in his eyes. There was shouting above. At the edge of the pit, one of his knights knelt, reaching a hand towards him. "Here!" he cried. "Quickly!"

It was Rogier de Grosbois. Thank God... He'd always liked Rogier. Not like the others, giving him the evil eye behind his back. He would reward him richly for this. They would drink together, and reminisce about it for years to come. He strained to reach out his free arm. Somehow, he reached the hand, and clasped it tight. Rogier smiled.

Then – barely audible – came a high-pitched whistle. A *thunk* of impact. Rogier de Grosbois gave a strangled cry, and fell dead into the pit, eyes bulging, an arrow in his ribs.

Shouts. Another whistle. Another impact. The cry was shrill and piercing this time.

Fulke roared in anguish to any who would listen. To show them he was still alive. To give them a chance to show their loyalty.

From above he heard only the pounding of feet as the remaining knights and serjeants fled back into the forest.

LVI

It HAD BEEN wise to leave that open space. Or, rather, it had been deeply *un*wise to enter it. Now, as the remaining knights and serjeants ran back along the path, some of them began to understand that entering these woods at all had been a terrible mistake.

Their suspicions were confirmed just yards into the thicket. The serjeant named Renaut stumbled over a length of rope, which he was sure had not been there on the way in. His crossbow fired uselessly into the branches above and he stumbled to his knees as a pair of knights – Gilles D'Arconcey and William de Clomot – pushed past. There was a clunk, and a long *zzzzzzzzzzzzip*. Renaut feared the worst. Others tumbled into the back of him. As he lifted his head, he saw a huge wooden spar – the shaft of the plundered wagon – swing out of the dark thicket and across the path as if on a great hinge. Its great weight smashed into the two knights, who'd both been running full tilt. D'Arconcey was knocked flat on his back and lay stunned before Renaut, but de Clomot – who had stopped dead as if against a stone wall – somehow remained upright. The shaft swung back, and de Clomot with it, weirdly suspended. Then Renaut saw the row of crude iron spikes that lined the shaft. And the blood. Stumbling on the rope had triggered the trap. But it had also saved him.

There was a scramble to head back the way they had come. This path meant death. All knew they needed to get off it – to find another route out. But the thicket that pressed around appeared too dense to pass through.

Renaut had not been the last to get away. Behind him was Odo – a big man, less fleet of foot than the others, but harder to stop once he got moving.

He never got that chance. Renaut heard a curse, then a crash, and glanced back. Odo had fallen and was scrabbling for his crossbow on the damp, mouldy earth, a look of terror on his face. "Something's got me!" he cried. "Something's got my foot!" Renaut stopped, conflicting impulses fighting within him. Then a dark shape rose up from the damp undergrowth. Renaut raised his crossbow, realised it was no longer primed, fought with it – too late. He saw the glint of a poleaxe as it was swung, and heard the thud as its spike hit Odo in the back. Then, before Renaut could call to his fellows, the shape had gone, swallowed up by the thicket. Mouth dry, heart thumping, he pounded along the path and ran into them huddled at the clearing's edge.

"I saw him!" he hissed in a hoarse whisper. "Back there. Odo..." He realised, as he said it, that the man now also had Odo's crossbow. He primed his own, hurriedly; then, before any of them got the idea into their heads to go after him, added, wild-eyed: "He melted back into the bush – like he was part of it."

Richard de Saulieu stepped forward, his expression stern. "He's just one man. He can't be everywhere. And we know he's behind us now." He scanned the perimeter of the clearing. Part way around, to the right, was an opening in the undergrowth – the entrance to another forest path. "There..." He pointed. "We take that and double back to the road. Then we'll get the hounds and flush him out like a beast."

Without another word, he dashed across the open space and disappeared. The others followed close behind, running low, starting at shadows, Thomas Le Maupas guarding their back.

No sooner had they plunged down this path than Renaut heard another stifled cry behind him. It was Thomas.

Renaut felt sick. Thirteen men had walked into this forest – nine knights and four serjeants. There were now only three. He knew they had put themselves in a trap, that Fulke had wasted his fellows' lives. But he trusted de Saulieu. And de Saulieu was right – their enemy couldn't be everywhere. They were now on their way out of the catastrophe.

Up ahead, just past de Saulieu, he saw grey open sky. The end of the path. They were close to the road now, and to their waiting horses.

De Saulieu pushed a branch out of his way. There was a creak, and then something no bigger than a cat swung down from the trees and struck de Saulieu in the head. He snapped back suddenly at the impact, helm spinning off into the twiggy undergrowth, blood and teeth flying through the air. After a moment, his knees buckled and he crumpled in a heap. The last of the knights, Bernard de Pouilly, stepped forward to help his friend, bemused, unaware quite what had happened. But as the shape swung up past Renaut's face, he understood.

Renaut's first instinct was that the thing swooping over the forest path was some kind of bird. Something big – a raven, perhaps, or a buzzard. Now, as the black object slowed and began to swing back, he saw. The enginer's anvil, suspended on two lengths of thick rope. He called out to de Pouilly in alarm. De Pouilly turned from his fallen comrade to Renaut, looked up, and – too late – saw the great block of iron hurtling back towards him. It smashed his face like an egg.

Renaut ran, then, crashing off into the undergrowth, away from the path, trying desperately to cut through to the daylight of the road. Twigs and brambles scratched his face and tore at his clothes as he waded through the impossible tangle, his crossbow still clutched in his hands, still primed. Behind him, now, he heard another movement. He hoped it was one of his fellows – one who was not yet dead – but he did not stop to look back. He panted and thrashed, the footfalls crunching behind him, gaining on him, speeding along the path he himself had cleared. Tendrils wrapped around him, grasping at him, holding him fast – he realised with horror he had blundered into a thick, impassable briar.

He remembered the crossbow. He fought against clinging, woody stems, surcoat ripping, and turned and levelled his weapon at the fast advancing black shape.

The bolt was missing, fallen in the chase.

He heard a bow shoot – not his. Something thudded into his chest. Then all went black.

Renaut's last moments on earth were spent hanging in a dead thorn bush like the prey of a butcher bird.

LVII

ALDRIC HAD BEEN one of those ordered to stay with the horses. Fulke didn't like him, he knew. He never had. Well, that was fine. Aldric didn't think much of Fulke, either.

He and his fellow serjeant – the one named Arnaut – had remained mounted at Aldric's insistence, keeping the horses ready and together, waiting, listening. Until the screaming started.

In many respects, Aldric had been glad to stay put, even with the crumpled corpse of Theobald – which had been propped against a tree – staring at them. He didn't trust Fulke's instincts as a commander, and the circumstances screamed "trap" to all but the most dimwitted. They had been stopped, forced to dismount, and led down what Aldric had no doubt, based on what he had seen so far, would be a well-prepared path. Prepared for them. How much damage a single man could ultimately inflict on so large a party was open to question, but the simple fact was they were doing everything their enemy wanted them to do. Aldric was instinctively opposed to doing *anything* his enemy wanted. His enemy wanted him dead. He might not be able to stop him in that endeavour, but he was buggered if he was going to help it along.

That Fulke was aware of this fundamental tactical wisdom was beyond doubt. Fulke was not stupid, not really. But he had the heart of a coward, and like all cowards feared most of all that this fact might somehow be revealed. He would never act cautiously – even when caution was wise – if it risked making him appear hesitatant or afraid. And so he and his band had voluntarily given up their greatest advantage – their horses – and plunged into the close quarters of a fighting ground chosen by their adversary, where the effectiveness of their numbers was reduced and their enemy invisible.

Fulke wouldn't care too much about that; he tended to be impatient with tactical thinking. Anyway, having led the charge into the undergrowth, he would surely then send others ahead to take whatever manner of death was coming their way. To Fulke, that's what soldiers were for – to place between him and imminent destruction. Decoys. Mobile shields.

The man Aldric had been saddled with was not so happy to be left behind. Arnaut was a hothead. One who charged wildly into danger, mistakenly believing he was showing courage, when in fact his actions merely marked him out as impulsive and reckless. At least, they did to Aldric. There were others who were taken in by it, who admired Arnaut's spontaneity, his boldness. Aldric, however, recognised both as products not of courage, but of fear. He flung himself at things because he did not have the nerve to approach them cautiously – because if he did stop to think, he would falter and crumble. Aldric supposed that when you had examples such as Fulke to follow, there would always be such men. Arnaut had not yet fought in a battle – not a real one – but Aldric had a bet with himself that when battle came, Arnaut would be the first to charge, and the first to bite the sod. And, of course, Fulke would let him.

Having to stay out of the fray had frustrated Arnaut almost to the point of frenzy. He had cursed and complained while Aldric bit his lip. Then came the cries of the men – the sounds of agony, of terror, of defeat. To Arnaut, this confirmed the folly of them sitting here on their arses, doing nothing. To Aldric, it confirmed the exact opposite.

At first, Aldric was successful in restraining Arnaut – even getting him to curb his restless pacing on his mount, which was making the others edgy.

In the event, it was a horse that finally tipped the balance.

These horses – all trained for battle – were not easily spooked. But upon hearing the muffled shouts from the trees, one – the handsome black courser that Fulke had laid claim to in some recent confrontation – had suddenly got some strange idea into its head. It had bucked and reared so violently that it had lost its bridle and broken away from the rest before bolting – not along the path and away from the cries of the men, as one might expect, but crashing straight into the tangled, twiggy shrubbery between the closely packed trees.

Somehow, its break for freedom had triggered the same impulse in Arnaut – or rather had broken the last bit of restraint that was holding him back. Perhaps the notion of a riderless horse heading into battle when he was not was just too much for him to bear. All Aldric knew was that suddenly Arnaut had drawn his sword and had leapt down from his saddle.

"You can sit here and do fuck all, if you like," he bellowed with a manic look in his eye – something between fevered excitement and abject terror. "I'm going to do something!"

Yes, thought Aldric. *You're going to die.*

Aldric knew – because he was not an idiot – that dismounting was a terrible idea. But Arnaut either did not know it, or, like Fulke, did not care, and perhaps could not help himself even if he did. And he was not going to stop. Stuck for an alternative, knowing they must stand fast, and stand together – more so now than ever – Aldric threw himself off his horse in an attempt to restrain him. Before he could even get close, Arnaut had charged off, disappearing into the spiky thicket with a frenzied crashing and crackling of twigs.

The sounds stopped as suddenly as they had started. There was a brief silence, before Arnaut emerged from the bushes again. Aldric was struck by three different notions at this unexpected return. He was amused that the spirited hero had been defeated by a thicket; he was relieved that, at last, he seemed to have seen sense; and he was momentarily bemused that Arnaut was walking backwards. As he was still thinking these thoughts, Arnaut keeled over, and crashed like a felled tree, and Aldric saw the crossbow bolt, half its length embedded in Arnaut's left eye.

Then, storming out of the woods, came the black shape of the man Aldric had killed.

Terrifying in appearance – his face blackened with soot, and now streaked with rain – he strode forward, wild eyes fixed on Aldric, inexorable in his steady advance. He stepped over Arnaut's body, flung away the discharged crossbow, and raised a second, ready drawn. Aldric – staggering backwards, realising he had only seconds before the bolt was placed and loosed – scrabbled for something, anything, to hurl at his assailant. He hauled at a warhammer strapped against a chestnut palfrey's saddle, but the spike snagged in the bindings. The horse turned, was gashed by the weapon's point as Aldric fought to tug it free, then kicked and leapt sideways. The binding snapped. Aldric sprawled, righted himself – his attacker now only yards away – and got ready to fling the weapon. But as he swung it up, the man loosed his bolt. It smacked into Aldric's shoulder, jarring bone and sending him spinning. He crashed flat on his back, winded, his left arm numb.

He remembered having no pain in his shoulder, just a distant awareness of the hooves of the chestnut slamming down near his head, and the bolt's steel point, now protruding from his back, scraping against a stone in the mud.

The man drew his mace and stood over him. Aldric made no further attempt to move. He knew he was dead, that there was nothing to be done. He braced himself, and – mustering what little defiance he had left – looked his killer square in the eye.

"Do it, then," he said through clenched teeth.

The man stood poised for a moment, weapon raised, then peered closely at him.

"You are one of the men who shot me," he said. "From the battlements."

Aldric frowned. The very last thing he'd expected was a conversation. "Yes."

"Tell me quickly – the man and the woman you have prisoner. Do they live?"

"Yes.

"*Will* they live?"

"Probably. Unless..."

"Unless?"

"You know the kind of man Tancred is."

"What kind of man is he?"

"All is black and white to him. Once they have no useful purpose, he will kill them. Although perhaps they now have one..."

The dark face frowned.

"You. He can use them to draw you. Throw one from the battlements as an example. Cause the other pain, to exploit your weakness."

"My weakness?"

"Compassion," said Aldric. "You have friends."

"Do you think that a weakness?"

"Tancred does," said Aldric. Then he thought for a moment, sighed deeply, and shuddered at the pain it brought. "But compassion is never a weakness." He was suddenly struck by the absurdity of his situation, of taking part in a philosophical debate whilst he lay bleeding in the mud, about to have his head – the head in which such fine thoughts were formed – smashed in by a mace. "You probably should've killed him while you had the chance, all the same," he added, pragmatic to the last.

To his amazement, the man laughed. "As he should have killed me," he said. "We'll both have that chance again before today is out."

Aldric's head swam, the pain in his shoulder suddenly asserting itself. He groaned.

The towering figure leaned in. "What's your name?"

"Aldric. Aldric Fitz Rolf."

"I am Gisburne," said the man. "Guy of Gisburne."

Aldric wondered if this was some strange affectation of his attacker – making a proper introduction to those he was about to kill. His head fell back on the mud in defeat. "Just get it over with."

Gisburne stared down at him. "We're settled," he said. Then he threw the mace into the bushes and turned to walk away.

Aldric heaved himself up onto his one good elbow, and stared after the retreating figure in disbelief.

"Get a new master, Aldric Fitz Rolf," the man called over his shoulder, and disappeared back into the forest.

LVIII

GISBURNE WALKED SLOWLY back to the clearing, hearing the groans of the men in the pit as he approached. The dead deer – red raw where he'd hacked off one hind limb to stand in for part of the enginer – hung harmlessly on its length of rope, swaying gently as it turned back and forth. He had suspended it from a long, high bough that projected partway across the western edge of the clearing, and launched it from a cleft in the main trunk. He'd eat it later, if he still lived. He hoped for company at that meal.

In truth, it had never been close to actually hitting Tancred's knights. But it didn't need to. All that was required was the fleeting belief that it would – that brief moment of panic. The fact that it had spattered them with fresh blood as it swung added to the effect.

He heard de Gaillon's voice in his head – the voice that was now always with him. "Overthrow the mind and the body will follow." To which he sometimes would add: "The opposite is not always the case..." Gisburne had proved both points today. He had seen strong men give up the ghost and die when they felt there was no hope, and those with no breath in them rally by force of will. He had been one of those men.

He paused by the still-glowing remains of the fire, scooped up the earthenware bottle, released its cork and took a swig. The harsh, warming liquor flowed through him, making him shudder – a pleasant kind of pain.

He stepped forward to see what he had caught.

There were three men; more than he'd hoped. And Fulke was one of them. Well, that was something. It made the half-day it had taken to dig out the pit worthwhile.

Two were dead, or as good as – one impaled through the abdomen, another with terrible injuries to his face and a wooden stake driven clean through a thigh. But Fulke – who had more luck than he would ever deserve in life – had, by some miracle, managed to entirely avoid the stakes. He had toppled sideways, and was now wedged between three stakes, one of which had managed to pierce and pass under his mail. He hung now suspended, flailing uselessly like a beetle stuck in honey. His face was grazed and bloody; smears of fresh pitch marked his beard and face and stuck to his hands.

As Gisburne stared down at Fulke, the big man suddenly became aware of him. He struggled to free himself with renewed urgency, grunting furiously as he did so. It was no good. Gisburne waited until he had given up, red faced and panting, before addressing him.

"You look like you need a drink," he said. And he poured the remains of the bottle of marc over the stranded knight. Fulke howled as the alcohol hit open wounds. Gisburne tossed the bottle away and left Fulke to huff and wail with his dead and dying fellows.

He walked towards the enginer, still tied to his tree, who had soiled his drawers. Gisburne could see the terror in the enginer's eyes as he approached, could hear the whimper behind the gag. Stopping before him, he drew his shortsword. The man's eyes widened, and his head shook.

"I'm sorry," said Gisburne, then raised the weapon – and hacked at the bonds about the ancient trunk. The enginer collapsed onto the wet forest floor as the ropes gave, and stared up at his captor, amazed.

"Run away," said Gisburne.

The man fled into the forest.

Gisburne stood for a moment, contemplating the destruction surrounding him. But he was not done yet. As he turned, a sound amongst the trees – as of something large, on the move – made him tense, and a black shape pushed out of the spiked bushes. Gisburne let his shortsword drop to his side, and his blackened face lit up in unrestrained delight.

"Nyght!" His horse came to him, and gave him a hard nudge with his nose, as if in reproach. Gisburne sheathed his shortsword and put his arms about his horse's shimmering neck. "Don't be angry," he said. "I'll take better care of you next time..." And he turned to head back to the path, Nyght following closely by his side.

As he walked back past the pit, a familiar voice rang out. "Listen!" It was Fulke, his voice suddenly conciliatory. "Friend!" From those lips the word sounded ridiculous – pathetic. "Listen! I have no love for Tancred. I can help... I have information. About your friend, and the woman. I can help you get inside. I know a way... One that no one else does..."

Gisburne paused by the pit, looked briefly at the smiling, crimson face of Fulke leering up at him, kicked the still-glowing embers of the fire into it with the toe of his boot, and walked away.

He heard the *whoosh* as the alcohol ignited. Then the crackle as the pitch caught. Nyght whinnied beside him, but stayed calm. At the same moment, Fulke let out a desperate shriek as he saw his fate, the flames already biting his clothing and beard. The men trapped around him cried out for help – from God, from man, from anyone – as their flesh, too, began to burn.

Gisburne plunged back into the forest, the roaring flames leaping higher from the pit behind him.

Tancred would also hear the screams of his men, and would know he had already lost.

LIX

TANCRED DID NOT wait for his men to return before unleashing his wrath. He had heard their screams – heard them perish one by one – but it was God that told him of their miserable failure. They had erred, let down both him and their Maker, and so he had no compunction about the terrors he would bring down upon them and their foe. He would rain down fire and destruction until either his enemy's body or his will to live had been utterly obliterated.

For the past hour, the trebuchet atop the southeast tower had flung huge rocks amongst the trees, cracking boughs and pounding into the underbrush. The mangonels on the gatehouse and battlements had thrown hot coals and flaming bales which left high, arcing trails of black smoke in their wake. And both had hurled great jars that exploded in plumes of flame as they burst against the earth and the trunks of trees. At Tancred's insistence, the scorpion atop the gatehouse had joined the barrage, firing one bolt after another – some flaming – into the forest's midst. For him, war was total, even against just one man. Their target had been a circle of some several hundred yards about the thin column of smoke that marked the clearing. That smoke had darkened and thickened as the cries echoed in the forest. Tancred ordered his men to target the sounds. They did so, athough he could see the reluctance in their eyes. The fear. He knew the source of it, even if it did not touch him: they feared they were slaughtering their fellows, murdering them.

He had put them right about that. At worst, he said, they were putting an end to their agony. And all was to be bent to their main purpose, no matter what the outcome. If he had to burn the entire forest down, and everything in it, he would. Better ten good men were sent to Heaven than one agent of the Devil went free.

Now, the smoke from their adversary's fire had been completely obscured, the rough circle of once-thick forest around it smashed and broken, thick with smoke and – even in the rain and damp – glowing with flames. Tancred strode back and forth along the southern battlements over the main gate – now hot as Hell with the fires of the engines – urging his men on. He did not do so with words of encouragement. There were no words, and encouragement was not his way. Instead he paced at their backs like a restless corpse, glaring at them, lips curled back from his teeth in an unconscious sneer, the distant, leaping flames of the forest reflecting in his cold, dead eyes.

Long ago, Lucatz the Enginer had advised him – as tactfully as he knew how – never to allow the siege engines to remain primed. With the exception of the counterweight trebuchet, they should be readied only immediately before firing. It would not only reduce their effectiveness, but could also cause strained ropes and wires to snap with a lethal whiplash, or even cause the whole device to implode. Tancred had listened patiently, unmoved and unmoving, as Lucatz had explained. Then he said simply: "Make them stronger."

Lucatz had stared at him for a moment, too timid to challenge the suggestion, then set about the task. But Tancred had seen the reluctance in him, too. The same weakness. None of them understood as he understood. Evil could strike day or night. Its agents were among us, looked like us. He had to be ready at all times. And when he struck, he had to do so with a hammerblow.

The creak of ropes, the clack of ratchets, the clatter of wood against wood and the distant thump and crackle of destruction had become merged almost into a melody, when a cry went up from the watchmen. Tancred flew to the parapet. A single chestnut courser – one of the serjeants' – had emerged from the maelstrom via the road, and now galloped towards them, its reins hanging before it. Clinging about its neck was a single ragged figure, doubled up in agony, blood clearly visible even upon the familiar scarlet livery.

"Open the gate!" roared Tancred, and marched to the wooden stairway, his red cloak flying. This was the only living thing to have emerged from the forest. The man's life was, of course, irrelevant – but he would have the soldier's report before he died.

Tancred heard the great gates clank and squeak as the guards threw off the bar and heaved them open to admit the rider. He sensed that it was not yet over; that there would be more of Gisburne before the day was out. Part of him relished the idea. He wished to face him again. To look him in the eye as he met his doom.

As he alighted in the bailey from the stairway, he saw two servants struggling towards the dog compound near the stables, a great trough of steaming offal swaying between them. Behind the compound's wooden bars, the hounds yelped and snapped.

Tancred stopped the servants with a hand. "No," he said. Rooted to the spot, the two men stared back, terror written over their faces. "Not yet. Keep them hungry. We may have need of them." Visibly relieved, the men set down their burden, wiped hands on greasy thighs, and hurried away. There were those, long ago, who had seen fit to point out that having a pack of dogs so close to the stables would spook the horses. Tancred had replied he had no use for horses that were spooked by dogs. They would become hardened to it, or they would be released from his service. By implication, it was clear to his questioners that the same applied to them.

When Tancred turned, the horse was already through the gate, its rider slumped flat against it, his body hanging half way down its flank.

Tancred recognised Aldric's horse – he knew his horses far better than he knew his men – but as it drew to a halt before the stable block beneath the west wall, he sensed that something was awry with its rider. It was not Aldric, or anyone he immediately recognised. And, as a small knot of knights and soldiers gathered around to offer help, or to hear what they could from him, and the limp figure slithered further from his mount, the bloodstained surcoat rode up to reveal another beneath. Black.

There followed an explosion of unleashed fury. As it slipped and fell, the figure righted itself with sudden and unexpected grace, hauled at the saddle, and swung with ferocious speed at the surrounding throng. Blood and spit and shattered teeth flew as a sword struck one full in the face. Another collapsed as the blade swung back and came crashing down upon his collarbone, slicing six inches into his torso. A third was slashed across the throat and fell to his knees in a foaming crimson gush.

All of this happened before anyone could react. Now they reeled back, grasped for weapons, or remained paralysed – easy prey for the flashing blades.

Gisburne – Norman broadsword in one hand, Saxon shortsword in the other – first targeted those who would fight back. The sword flew from a knight's grip, its ringing, spinning blade catching a serjeant upon the cheek. A cocked, loaded crossbow was battered sideways and went off, its bolt splintering a guard's shin.

The circle drew back around him, Gisburne's targets dwindling, until the remaining soldiers all stood about, staring wide-eyed at the demonic figure and the slaughter he had inflicted upon them. One of the guards, at a safe distance from the invader's blades, levelled his crossbow.

Tancred's hand pushed the bow down, its bolt discharging harmlessly into the ground. The crossbowman stared in bemusement as his master thrust him aside and advanced into the circle, drawing his sword. Gisburne locked eyes on Tancred, and gripped his weapons tighter – and for an instant, Tancred could swear he saw a smile flicker across that face.

The Templar found himself almost glad at this development. What Gisburne had hoped to achieve by this astonishing, foolhardy action was a mystery, but part of him – the part that was still human – could not help but admire the man's boldness and tenacity. He knew it was the Devil that gave Gisburne strength, but there was a certain purity of purpose that Tancred found... pleasing. Tancred realised, perhaps for the first time, he respected purity above all else – even when it was the purity of evil. There was a clarity – an honesty – in its utter lack of compromise. They were two sides of a coin, Gisburne and he, their interdependence – their conflict – an inevitability. Yes, this moment had been ordained. The two of them, face to face. He felt a strange satisfaction at what was to come next.

"God wills it," he said, and swung his blade.

LX

GISBURNE'S STRATEGY HAD been a gamble. A precarious balancing act, in which he had attempted to read the mind of his opponent – his deluded, insane, barely human opponent – and judge exactly which pieces in the game could be given up or put at risk. Each piece had its purpose, its place – and its moment when it became redundant.

His thinking had gone like this: Tancred would not kill Galfrid and Mélisande – at least, not until he had used them to draw him out, and acquired the key to the box. And then, he gambled that Tancred would not kill him until he had the relic in his hand. In fact, he was depending on it. This was the most unpredictable part of the plan, depending on the notion that he, Gisburne, was the only one who understood the box, and that Tancred might feel the need to extract further knoweldge from him in order to open it safely.

At the moment, sadly, it was looking very much like Tancred wanted to kill him.

Gisburne parried the first blow with his shortsword. There was a spark as the blades hit; a splinter of metal flew and struck Gisburne on the cheek. He stepped over the body of one of his victims and leapt back, the surrounding men falling back around him. They were an audience now – the horror of the slaughter now turning to a kind of baying bloodlust. A lust for his blood, the usurper's blood.

Tancred fought with speed and grace – went at him with a series of astonishing moves, his body spinning, the blade flashing at him almost faster than Gisburne's eye could follow. He sidestepped and parried, deflecting the blade, trying to protect his own. No one wanted to use their precious sword to parry another. But it was better than dying.

Tancred's technique was unlike any other, except for that of a sandy-haired boy all those years ago, at Fontaine-La-Verte. This much he already knew to his cost. It broke all the rules. Tancred had the wrong grip. He used both short edge and long edge of the blade – the "back" and the "front" – with almost equal vigour, in spite of everything Gisburne had ever been taught. He even had the audacity to turn his back on his opponent as he whirled his blade about him.

Before, Gisburne had found he simply did not know how to fight this man; there was nothing familiar with which to engage. This time, he simply fell back. Gisburne would not be tricked into playing by another's rules. Tancred flailed and slashed at him, growing furious with frustration as he stumbled and backed away, the baying crowd jeering around them. They cheered as Gisburne fell against the wooden stairway. Tancred's sword flashed close to his head, and embedded itself at an angle in the newel post – almost splitting it. Tancred hissed like some nocturnal creature, and heaved it free – but Gisburne had already leapt to his feet and was half way up the stair. Tancred pursued him –

and Gisburne smiled. *Try your little dance on the stairs, you prancing bastard,* he thought.

Tancred could not. Forced to fight frontally, his technique stripped away, he suddenly became a conventional opponent. Vulnerable, mortal. Gisburne pushed his advantage. He bore down on his foe, using his extra height, slashing at Tancred's head while his own was beyond his opponent's reach. The White Devil – for the first time on the defensive – flung himself to one side, stumbling on the wet wood of the steps, one foot almost slipping between the treads. Gisburne pressed on, landing a kick on the side of Tancred's head. He fell sideways against his own sword hand, the blade clattering against the stone wall. Gisburne swung his foot again and caught the Templar across the mouth. Blood splattered on the stones.

Tancred roared in anger, grabbed at the foot and missed it, then swung his blade full force at Gisburne's legs. Gisburne flung himself back and fell hard against the treads, losing his shortsword. He was scrambling up the steps as Tancred swung again, his blade biting. Had he worn the full hauberk of a knight, the mail about his legs might have turned the sword point. But he did not. Tancred's sword cut through Gisburne's long leather boots and snicked the front edge of his shinbone. He cried out between gritted teeth, and the leering faces cheered their approval. Tancred immediately changed tactic, targeting Gisburne's feet and legs. They were his weak point – impossible to defend at this angle. And now Tancred had realised it, and meant to cripple him.

Gisburne clawed faster, backwards up the stairway, his blade connecting awkwardly with Tancred's. The gathered men cheered at the turnabout – more, it seemed to Gisburne, in a kind of poisonous anger than with any fervour. That was what Tancred bred here. There was no passion – only hatred.

Suddenly, he felt cold stone beneath him. He was on the parapet.

He stood, knowing he had only moments to decide his course. Behind him was the southwest tower. Ahead, advancing now, the grim, glaring visage of Tancred de Mercheval. Once at the top of the steps he could resume his lethal assault. Gisburne turned and ran for the tower, smashing his sword pommel into the face of an astonished guard and sending him sprawling off the walkway. A second guard literally leapt off, out of Gisburne's path, rather than get in his way.

Gisburne raced up the internal ladder to the fighting platform at the top of the tower, where the larger of the mangonels was positioned. As he emerged, a man-at-arms flew at him with a mace, and Gisburne ducked, felt the man nearly tumble over the top of him, then heaved him over the battlements. In another moment, Tancred would be up the ladder's steps, his sword whirling at him in unstoppable arcs. The confined arena would favour Tancred; there would now be nowhere for him to hide from Tancred's spinning blade. Doubtless, Tancred would now be considering the folly of Gisburne's move and relishing his demise, knowing he had the advantage of the battlefield.

But Gisburne meant to make it his own. Looking about him, Tancred's feet already audible upon the rungs below him, Gisburne saw what he was after. He'd known they would be here: a row of large demijohns by the side wall, beyond the mangonel, and at the front, three large copper vats on wooden pivots, positioned over chutes in the stonework. Gisburne threw down his sword and set his shoulder against the first of them.

As Tancred loomed up the stair, Gisburne had already dislocated the first vat off its pivot. Ignoring the stab in his side, the sickening ache in his shoulder, he heaved it over onto its side, its gallons of oil flooding the floor of the tower battlement. Then over went another, and the third. The thick, viscous liquid gushed past Tancred's feet and cascaded in a black waterfall down the trap door. It fell past the connecting ladders, and on down the spiralling stone steps – coated the interior of the tower, and glugged and oozed out of the tower doorway as it went, creeping out along the battlement walkway. Tancred stared in perplexed rage at the glossy slick, then back at his opponent. He placed one foot forward, and it slithered sideways.

Gisburne shot him a look of vicious glee. "Spin on that," he said.

And, as Tancred swiped at him in fury, lost his traction and grasped at the strut of the still-cocked, creaking mangonel, Gisburne lunged forward and booted him in the balls. Tancred doubled up and went down like a Parisian whore, his blade skittering away from him. Gisburne fell on top of him in the black morass, grabbed him by the surcoat and wrestled him onto his back. He slithered, recovered his sword, and – still holding Tancred by a handful of stained silk surcoat and oily mail about the scruff of his neck – struggled to his feet, his blade poised high above his head, ready to strike.

This had not been part of the plan. But killing Tancred now did not seem such a bad idea.

The reptilian, expressionless eyes in that oily, bloody half-and-half face flicked sideways. Then Tancred gave a kind of hoarse cackle. For a moment, Gisburne did not know what it was. But as it grew, he realised. It was laughter. So unexpected, so horrid and so utterly alien was the sound issuing from that scar-like slit of a mouth, that at first Gisburne could only gawp in dumbfounded revulsion. Then his eyes followed Tancred's line of sight. Upon the gatehouse tower, he saw the scorpion turned upon him, its operator's eyes wide, its huge, spiked bolt pointed at his heart.

Tancred, still chuckling, narrowed his eyes as if to say: *Let's see if you can survive* this *one...*

Gisburne hesitated, for a moment looking like he might accept Tancred's unspoken challenge – might put the marksman's mettle to the test – and to Hell with the consequences. His eyes dropped to the demijohns, only yards distant. If he could just grab one of those...

Then a bellowed cry made him turn.

"Gisburne!"

It came from the bailey. There, down below, a man-at-arms gripped a bloody, near-lifeless Galfrid. Next to him, bare-footed and bound, stood Mélisande, and behind her, the grinning Ulrich held a blade across her white, exposed throat.

He will exploit your weakness. That was what Aldric Fitz Rolf had said.

Gisburne's sword faltered and fell, the castle echoing to this wholly new sound – a sound its denizens had never before heard: the dry, hollow sound of its master's jubilant laughter.

LXI

A CIRCLE OF knights had gathered about the box. But it was not this that held Gisburne's attention. It was the fact that, a little way beyond, Mélisande was being tied to a stake and surrounded by dry, bundled brushwood. That, and the bizarre vision that lurked near her.

The box had been placed on a stout table in the middle of the bailey's open courtyard, and those gathered – all of Tancred's remaining knights – now stood around it, hushed and expectant, the only sound the scratching and yelping of the still-famished dogs in the cage by the stable block.

At Gisburne's left hand, some distance from this group, was a wooden pallet – it did not seem fitting to call it a table – large enough to hold the body of a man. The wood was worn and pitted, its surface stained almost black over the years, by uses Gisburne did not want to guess at. At one end, a row of thin blades, pincers and other unidentifiable tools lay in a neat row.

Spread out on the ground on the other side was a motley collection of gear, mostly Galfrid's: clothes, knives, a mace, Gisburne's pilgrim staff, sundry personal effects. It had all been picked over and gone through in search of the key, and any other possible clues that might enlighten them about the box, and now lay discarded. It was no longer needed. Gisburne had wasted no time handing over the key. He wanted this over with. And so they had gathered, eager to see their hard-won prize – to gaze into the face of the Baptist.

They had not harmed him; had not even threatened to do so. All the threats had been directed at Galfrid and Mélisande. And there was only one question they wanted an answer to. A simple question, repeated over and over.

Gisburne had resisted, but it was a token, a delaying tactic, and no more. As he had stood there – his hands bound in front of him, his arms gripped from behind by a guard with foetid breath – they had pushed Galfrid forward, his hands similarly bound. He bore no mark, but his body was clearly unable to take much more of whatever it was they were doing to him. He had taken two steps and collapsed. As they had hauled him up, and he had again almost crumpled, Gisburne had appealed to them. "For mercy's sake," he'd said. "Give the man his stick so he can stand upright at least, and face his punishment as God intended."

Tancred had narrowed his eyes at that, but nodded to his serjeant, who had thrust the pilgrim staff into Galfrid's hands. They then manoeuvred him to the pallet next to Gisburne, where he stood, head bowed, silent and impassive.

Both Galfrid and Mélisande were to be punished, Gisburne had been told – not for their own sins, but for his. They had been in his thrall – that much was clear – and now only he had the power to ease their suffering.

Tancred gestured to Galfrid. "This man would not reveal the truth," he said. "So we will reveal his flesh." Meaning they were going to skin him alive. This, Tancred called "fitting punishment". He pointed at Mélisande then, away behind the group. "This woman put two of my loyal men in the cold earth. So she will burn." He turned to Gisburne again. "Only you can redeem them. Answer the question and they will receive a swift death."

Gisburne had looked at Mélisande as Tancred spoke these words. She seemed largely unharmed – surprisingly so – but her features were drawn, and her eyes filled suddenly with such despair that he felt his heart would break to look at them longer. He tore his gaze away. There was little point trying to fathom Tancred's warped logic – far less trying to reason with it. He knew he would have to give him what he wanted.

It was then that the bizarre vision – the one he heard them call "Fell" – stepped forward.

He was big. Not merely corpulent, but unnaturally broad in the hips and shoulders, giving the impression that his stocky legs were too far apart to connect to his body. They stuck out from the long, stained smock like the legs of an ox – like the limbs of some monstrous half-cow dressed up in an approximation of human clothing. The smock – as big as a tent, and caked with filth and gore – hung to his knees, but was stretched tight across his stomach and his huge, bovine barrel of a chest. His arms were short, and ended in pink, filthy, sausage-like fingers, twice as thick as any fingers should be, while his large, domed head seemed sunk into the great bulk of his shoulders, as if there never had been any neck. When he walked, it was with a stiff, awkward rocking of his whole body, as if on legs that would not bend. At each effort Gisburne could hear the moist, laboured rasp of his breath.

But it was not any of these things that finally made Gisburne shudder. It was the fact that his features were entirely obscured by a veil – a ragged piece of grimy muslin draped over his head and face. Gisburne could see from the expressions of the knights that he was not the only one to regard this creature with awestruck revulsion.

He had been overseeing the tying of the bonds around Mélisande – he apparently knew how to tie them in such a way that the body would burn before the rope gave out – and now stepped forward to examine the tools on the pallet. He huffed and snorted over them, lifting one long bladed knife close to his face and turning it over.

Tancred raised a hand. "No," he said, his eyes fixed on Gisburne. "The woman first..." Fell gave a strange rasping squawk – was that annoyance? Disappointment? – returned the blade to its place, and shuffled away.

Tancred, his hands clasped behind his back, walked in a tight circle between Gisburne and the horseshoe of knights, then turned to face him.

"How... does... one... open... the... box?" he said, articulating each word with slow deliberation.

Upon Gisburne's answer depended a life. He appeared to struggle within, looked momentarily defiant, gazed at Mélisande, then let his head fall in defeat. "With the key. Just with the key," he said.

"And you swear before God, on the lives of this man and this woman, that to do so will not damage the skull?"

Gisburne let his eyes flick up to the pleading face of Mélisande – pleading not, he thought, for him to save her, but to resist Tancred at any cost. Then to Galfrid, who stood like a lifeless dummy – like a straw-stuffed pell upon which knights practiced their swordplay. "I do swear it," said Gisburne. "Before God. On the lives of my friends." And with a great sigh, he bowed his head once more.

Galfrid already appeared half dead. But, when he had collapsed and been hauled to his feet to be stood next to Gisburne, something odd had occurred. Gisburne had, for a fleeting moment, caught Galfrid's eye. And Galfrid had winked.

Tancred gave an almost-smile, and nodded to Ulrich, holding the key in his outstretched hand. Ulrich took it, leered at Gisburne, then approached the box.

"Carefully," said Tancred. It was not in his nature to trust. The gathered knights watched in silence as Ulrich tentatively located the key in the lock, and slowly turned it. It clicked. The lid released, and sprang up a quarter inch. Ulrich turned, grinning in triumph, then lifted the lid and peered in. There was another click, a strange *thunk*. Ulrich seemed to start at it, every muscle tensed.

"Well, Ulrich?" said Tancred. "Is it there?"

But all that came from Ulrich was a long, drawn out wheeze. He swayed, and staggered back stiffly, then collapsed like a board at Tancred's feet, a tiny crossbow bolt sunk deep between his staring eyes.

In a fury, Tancred turned on Gisburne. "I think you have misunderstood the nature of your situation," he hissed. He nodded at the guard with the flambeau, who advanced on Mélisande's pyre.

It seemed he would have his witch-burning after all. Then he turned his back on Gisburne. "Get this out of the way!" he spat, kicking Ulrich's lifeless body.

"And I think you have misunderstood yours." Gisburne's voice rose clear and strong. Tancred stopped at the words. They no longer had the tone of a defeated man. Nor of an emptily defiant one.

He narrowed his eyes, looked upon Gisburne almost with pity. "A man should know when he is defeated," he said.

Gisburne raised his head to meet Tancred's cold gaze. "The line between victory and defeat is fine," he said. "And the outcome today is yet to be decided."

"Decided!" Tancred gave a scornful laugh. Some of his men echoed it dutifully, emptily. "By whom? You? Look around. You are captured, your precious box and its key taken." Yet, for the first time, there was the hint of uncertainty upon his features.

"But you didn't capture me," Gisburne spoke slowly, deliberately. "I rode into your castle of my own free will. To bring you the key." He paused for a moment, allowing a faint smile to creep across his lips. "So you would open the box."

The cold anger in Tancred's eyes suddenly gave way to doubt, then a terrible realisation. As he stood, one of the knights hunched over the reliquary called out, nervously.

"My lord – why is it... clucking?"

Tancred turned. It was true. From somewhere deep within there came a rhythmic *tic-tic-tic*. Slowly, almost subconsciously, the knights closed in around it.

"What is this?" demanded Tancred. There was a note of panic in his voice now – almost hysteria.

"The box is about to destroy itself," said Gisburne. "Tell me how to stop it – or the girl dies."

"You'll kill her anyway. And there is no way to stop it. You have only moments to safely remove what's inside." His eyes glinted with a demonic fire. "*Hurry!*"

Tancred roared and pushed past the knights to the box, the *tic-tic-tic* suddenly gathering momentum. He grabbed a mace from one of his men, raised it... then froze, uncertain, caught between action and doubt. An almost unknown emotion seemed to flood over him. Fear.

"Close your eyes," Gisburne whispered to Galfrid.

LXII

IT WAS FEAR of failure that gripped Tancred. Fear of losing what God had promised him. Because God could not be wrong. God could not be mistaken. And yet... *And yet...* For an instant, he had felt that terrible uncertainty flicker within him – the self-questioning that he had once seen as a virtue, and which now was utterly alien to him. But it was a flicker, and no more. In another instant, he had conquered it. Conviction once more filled his soul and gave strength to his arm. He raised the mace high.

As he did so, the box shuddered and jumped. Then it jolted with sudden violence, ringing like an anvil struck by a hammer. A burst of white powder exploded outward and upward, covering Tancred and his knights and forming a cloud that settled slowly about them. They coughed, choking on the dust. Tancred – white as a ghost, caked in the stuff – wrenched back the lid of the box.

Empty. It was empty. "No..." he uttered in disbelief. "No!"

The prisoners would pay now.

Before he could turn, he heard the first cries of pain. Around him, it seemed the white dust was now rising off his men in coiling trails, like wispy, ephemeral phantoms – as if their spirits were fleeing their corporeal shells. But it wasn't dust. It was smoke. He blinked hard – then he too began to burn. At first, it stung his eyes, then his skin. The stinging became a fire. Then he was plunged into the flames of Hell.

Quicklime. Burning him, eating into his flesh and that of his men. They began to panic. Blinded, steaming and smoking – the quicklime reacting with their hair, skin and clothes, still wet from the rain – they clawed at their faces, writhed on the ground, ran wildly into each other, some with weapons drawn, inflicting terrible wounds. Their flesh peeling, their lungs on fire.

The last thing Tancred saw was Gisburne, free, sword in hand, and his own clutching fingers, blistering, bubbling, being consumed.

LXIII

To those watching, it must have looked like an outbreak of madness. Or some act of sorcery. Gisburne did not waste his advantage. He smashed his head backwards, feeling his guard's nose crack. Galfrid raised the pilgrim staff. Gisburne grabbed it, and both men pulled. This time, Galfrid got the blade. He swung it about, felling his guard, then killed Gisburne's, a fire in his eye that Gisburne had not seen before. Gisburne dropped, cut his bonds on his guard's sword, then took up the weapon.

Barging past the chaos of staggering, screaming men, his arm over his face, he headed for the pyre – for Mélisande. He was dimly aware, as he skirted around the still swirling cloud, of Galfrid – far less debilitated than he had allowed his captor to believe – smashing his way past Tancred's stunned, crippled knights, towards some other, unknown goal, and then disappearing from view.

Almost at the pyre, a figure loomed suddenly before him. The guard with the flambeau. Resolute. Defiant. In his left hand he gripped a warhammer, his eyes fixed on Gisburne.

Gisburne did not hesitate. But instead of defending himself, the guard – in a last act of perverse malice that could only have been inspired by Tancred's example – threw the flambeau upon the piled brushwood. Gisburne's blade sliced across his temple with a sound like a knife on a whetstone. The guard's helm went flying. Part of his skull went with it, trailing blood. He dropped like a rock. But the flames leapt – the oil-soaked wood sizzling as it caught and flared.

Without pause, Gisburne waded into the fire, clambering up the crackling bundles and hacking at Mélisande's bonds. He cursed the grim care with which they had been tied. Fell had done his job well. But in another moment, both he and Mélisande were diving free of the fire. Gisburne – his left boot still smoking – scrambled to his feet, looking about, ready to fight. A crossbow bolt zipped from somewhere on the battlements and struck the ground nearby. It was too chaotic for the guards to easily pick them off without hitting their own, and the courtyard was now enveloped in a haze of swirling smoke from the blazing pyre – but it might not be so for long. Mélisande snatched up the discarded warhammer, and the pair of them darted towards the stables – the nearest shelter from the eyes on the battlements.

As his back slammed against the stable block, Gisburne saw where Galfrid had been headed.

Directly ahead, some little way off, the weird, bulky figure of Fell tottered towards the supposed safety of the keep, hooting and snorting in alarm. Pursuing him with a look of grim resolve – but limping badly, Gisburne now realised – was his squire. Fell saw the keep's gate was shut, wailed in protest, and changed direction like a frightened animal, heading now towards the dog compound, just yards from where Gisburne and Mélisande now stood.

It was not a wild or random move, but a tactic. He meant to release the dogs. Galfrid's progress was slow and painful – it seemed for a time even the labouring Fell would outpace him – but Galfrid had plucked up a mace. With clenched jaw, he hurled it wildly at the receding figure, just as Fell neared the abandoned feeding trough. It connected, bouncing off Fell's veiled scalp with a sickening *crack*.

Fell stumbled over the bucket of oil that had been used to douse the brushwood, sending its contents splashing everywhere. He staggered forward several more steps, tripped on the edge of the trough and crashed into the stinking offal, great bloody gobbets of it slopping up and out and slapping down upon the wet earth. It turned beneath his great bulk, tipping him and the rotting flesh out in a slimy, thrashing heap. He rose like some antediluvian creature from a swamp, groaning and wheezing, dripping gore, his hands waving awkwardly before him.

Gisburne realised he was blind. The offal in the trough had soaked his veil, and now he was blind. With one thick-fingered fist he groped at it, pulled it from his head and let it fall with a wet splat.

Gisburne recoiled at what he saw. A round, hairless face, its bulging, red-rimmed eyes – like a deep sea fish – blinking in the daylight, the near-lipless mouth, in a permanent "O", ringed with peg-like teeth. It almost seemed the distorted, overgrown face of an infant.

Galfrid had stopped his pursuit; seemed to have made eye contact with Mélisande. Gisburne sensed movement at his left side. He turned and briefly saw the look of grim resolution upon Mélisande's face before she turned, strode to the dog compound, swung the warhammer and – without hesitating – smashed the lock containing the dogs. The gate burst open, grey dogs exploding from it. Fell gave one final, rasping screech before the hounds enveloped him, ripping and tearing without discrimination at whatever flesh they could find. Mélisande and Galfrid merely looked on until the dogs had rendered Tancred's fallen torturer and the contents of the trough indistinguishable from each other.

Thus was Fell the Maker unmade.

Gisburne's hand on Mélisande's wrist broke the spell. He hauled her in the direction of the main gate. She resisted.

"The skull..."

"Forget the skull," he said.

Mélisande looked at him in disbelief, saw that he meant it, and did not argue.

As they made their way past the stables, two men – a man-at-arms and one who looked no more than a stable lad – literally ran into them. Gisburne shoved the guard away, swung his sword upward with both hands and caught him under the chin. He spun and fell onto the straw of an open stall. The stable lad whimpered and ran.

Mélisande dropped to the floor. At first, Gisburne thought she had been injured. Then he saw she was taking the boots off the feet of the guard and pulling them onto her own feet. In the mayhem he had entirely forgotten she was barefoot. She looked up at him with a raised eyebrow.

"A woman must have her shoes," she said, and leapt to her feet.

From the edge of the stable, they could see the gate was heavily guarded. A row of knights and serjeants – some red-faced, eyes streaming from the quicklime – stood before it. Three of them were armed with crossbows. They would not get near it before they were cut down.

"There's another way," he said.

"Where?"

"There!" He pointed to the wooden stairway – the very one on which he had fought Tancred – a short run from where they stood. It led to the battlements on which were the mangonels. And wound around the mangonels there was rope.

Mélisande stared up at the ramparts. "I will if you will," she said.

A *whoosh* cut the air, and a stifled yelp came from somewhere in the bailey.

The second sound he knew must be one of the dogs. The first he had heard before, out on the rock at the forest's edge. Up on the battlement above the gatehouse, the scorpion was back in action, its sniper winding the mechanism for another shot.

But it was not aimed at them. Gisburne looked around, peering through the smoke, trying to follow the scorpion's line of fire – and spied Galfrid, crouched and barely hidden behind the overturned trough. Sated by their feast, the hounds had dispersed, and now, driven to a state of high excitement by the smoke and flames and the cries of the injured, they raced and leapt wildly about the place. All of them but one, which was pinned to the ground by the great scorpion bolt just a yard from Galfrid's hiding place.

Gisburne turned his attention back to the battlement. There were few men up there, but that might not be the case for long. And the remaining men of the castle, although without their leaders, were starting to regroup.

"We have to get up there. But if we show ourselves..."

At that, Mélisande darted from their cover – not towards the stairway, but straight towards the fire. The scorpion shot again, the bolt splitting the burning stake in two as Mélisande hooked a flaming bundle from the fire with the hook of her warhammer, doubled back, and hurled it into the open stall of the stable. The fresh straw crackled and flared. Flames leapt immediately, creeping up to the thatch above.

"That'll give them something to think about," said Mélisande, slumping back against the stable wall.

They waited the moments it took for the fire to take hold of the block. Then, with the heat almost becoming too much to bear at their backs, the thick, choking smoke billowing about the whole of the castle's interior, Gisburne made a break for the stairway.

Two men-at-arms stood between him and the steps; Gisburne flew at them out of the fire and smoke. Both braced themselves, swords drawn, and in a move that was more instinct than decision, Gisburne ducked and threw his entire body at them. It caught them completely by surprise, bowling them over, one smashing into a rain barrel. Gisburne regained his feet, parried the other who was up as swiftly as he, whipped his blade around and caught the man's forearm. The guard howled, dropping his weapon, but the other was up now, and coming at him. Turning, knowing he was not in time to save himself from the guard's blow, Gisburne braced himself for the impact – then saw the man's face suddenly transform as a blazing wad of thatch, sticky with pitch, was thrust at him, setting his tunic alight.

Mélisande drew back the warhammer from the man's chest, ready to strike him down. But it was not needed. The man ran off, screaming, his flight fanning the flames up and over his face, and igniting his greasy hair. He tumbled over the empty oil bucket, his falling body setting fire to the pool on the ground. One of the dogs, which had been cavorting in the oily puddle, was instantly set alight, and with a yowl catapulted into two more, both of which ignited and spread the flame further still, the smell of burning hair and singed flesh left in their wake.

Gisburne and Mélisande were up the stairs now. From up here, the castle already looked like a vision of Hell, filled with smoke and flame, crazed and burning creatures, blinded and fallen knights, still writhing in agony, and red-faced men of all ranks dashing with water in vain attempts to quell the fires. Gisburne tried to find Galfrid in the pandemonium, but there was now no sign.

And several down below had seen Gisburne and Mélisande. Crossbow bolts zipped past as they ran along the walkway, crouched low, heading for the gatehouse. One who had not seen them – his weapon still trained upon the bailey, seeking a target in the choking smoke and the slew of bodies – was the guard behind the great scorpion. As Gisburne neared the door to the gatehouse tower steps, some of the men down below shouted up to the guard in warning. He frowned, strained to hear what they were calling against the clamour, and finally – still unclear as to their meaning – turned his great crossbow in the direction of their frantic gestures.

But it was too late. Gisburne was on the fighting platform. At the last moment, the scorpion wheeled hard about, the tensed arm of the mechanism knocking Gisburne's sword from his hand. He did not stop, wrestling the man to the ground before he could fire. Suddenly, the man had a knife in his hand, its point catching Gisburne's left shoulder. Teeth clenched against the pain, he caught the man's wrist. The two locked and wrestled, the knife hovering over Gisburne's face and neck.

A kick from a borrowed boot sent the knife and its owner flying.

Mélisande took up the position behind the scorpion as Gisburne again grabbed the guard and hauled him to his feet. But this one was not yet done. He shoved at his attacker, the two stumbled, and Gisburne fell backwards onto the arm of a mangonel. He felt it shudder and creak beneath him. Then the guard was at him again, teeth bared, arms outstretched like claws.

Gisburne flung himself to one side, hauled the guard across the huge bucket at the end of the mangonel's arm, and pulled its lever.

There was a sound like a tree trunk snapping, and a heavy *thunk* that shook the tower.

Too shocked to scream, the sprawling figure of the guard was flung in an impossible arc, his amazed expression rapidly receding as he spun and crashed down, far out into the forest.

Gisburne and Mélisande now owned the gatehouse and its weapons.

Pulling the hooked end of the rope from the mangonel's winding mechanism, Gisburne tried to judge its total length. It looked long enough. It would have to be. The other key ingredient was exactly where he expected to find it. Against the wall, beyond the mangonel, was the row of great demijohns, standing on sacking and surrounded with straw, the exact twin of its counterpart in the oil-slicked southwest tower.

He smiled to himself, and blessed the uncompromising uniformity of Castel Mercheval's strict regime.

There was little doubting Lucatz's expertise, but Tancred's choice of enginer that day had been unfortunate. Back in the forest, Gisburne had not only plundered Lucatz's wagon, he had discovered an unexpected bounty in the terrified enginer's brain. It had needed no effort to shake it loose. Lucatz, fearing for his life and desperate to earn himself some favour – or perhaps dissuade Gisburne from his course altogether – had volunteered all manner of startling facts. His stuttered warnings told of the state of readiness of the fortress, about its many lethal devices. Barely able to believe his luck, Gisburne had built a detailed knowledge of the castle's defences. His plan, such as it was, had formed around it. He knew that the gatehouse offered no access to the tower or the battlements from the ground. The main towers along the curtain wall had stone steps spiralling most of their height – but at the first sign of attack, the guards would have drawn up the wooden connecting ladders to isolate them from both the ground and the adjacent walkways. This was meant to hamper the progress of attackers who managed to scale the walls, denying them access to the bailey below. But Gisburne contrived to work it against them – to block their enemy's advance, to stop the castle's soldiers getting to their own battlements. The only access to the south curtain wall from the ground was now via the two wooden stairways that stood between the main towers and the gatehouse. These, too, could be removed by the castle's defenders if need be. Now Gisburne meant to destroy them.

He hauled out the demijohns one by one, scanning the bailey for signs of Galfrid. He could not – would not – leave without him. But there was no sign.

Mélisande turned the scorpion. On the rampart, a crouched figure scurried. A guard had ascended the wooden stair near the southeast tower, and now advanced on them, crossbow raised.

Without a second thought, she fired.

The bolt skewered him in the midriff, sending him sailing backwards over the battlement like a game bird stuck with an arrow. More were ready to follow. Near the southwest tower, the blazing stables were keeping the frantic occupants busy. But the same was not the case on the other side of the gatehouse. Beneath the southeast tower, men were gathering, their hard eyes fixed on them.

Within a moment of the scorpion firing, another crossbowman was already rushing up the steps, hoping to take advantage of the delay in reloading the weapon. And Mélisande – still winding the mechanism – could not hope to fire in time. But then, half way to the gatehouse, the advancing guard suddenly stiffened and tumbled down into the bailey. Gisburne and Mélisande looked around in shock. Down below, another cried out and doubled up, a crossbow bolt in his thigh.

Someone was firing at them. Gisburne looked around, trying to guess the sniper's position from the angle of the shots – and finally saw him, crouched at the corner of the keep. Galfrid. Gisburne's heart leapt – a rush of relief and triumph. He signalled, gesturing towards the neglected wooden stairway to his left, near the southwest tower, hoping Galfrid would somehow see and understand. Galfrid looked up, loosed another shot, then darted out towards the southwest wall and dived behind a barrow.

He had understood, Gisburne was sure of it. All he had to do now was get himself up those steps and to the gatehouse, and then...

Gisburne turned his attention back to the other stairway. Three more men – two of them knights – had now climbed the steps and were heading towards them. Mélisande would not be ready – and even if she were, could not hope to get all three. With nothing else to hand, Gisburne raised one of the precious demijohns high above his head, ran at the tower battlement, and heaved it at them with all his strength. It hit the first of them full in the face, knocking him flat. As it fell, it struck the stone rampart and burst apart in a great eruption of flame. The fire splashed like water, dousing all three men and spreading along the walkway. They shrieked and thrashed. One rolled off, plunging to the ground in a roaring fireball.

It was time to finish the job. Gisburne heaved another demijohn, and swung it up and over the tower battlement.

It flew, bounced on the wooden steps, cracking a tread in half, bumped down three more, then tumbled off the side of the stairway. The men below leapt back in a circle as it hit the mud with a heavy thump – and by some wild fluke, remained intact. Useless. Gisburne stared in disbelief. He heard several of the men laugh in relief. Saw them turn to mount the steps. Then there was a creak as the scorpion turned.

"God wills it," said Mélisande, and fired.

The bolt struck home. The jar exploded in a bright orange fireball, igniting the entire stairway – covering it and all the men around it in sticky, liquid flame.

No one, now, could challenge them from that quarter.

On the other side of them, beneath the southwest wall, the stables were now a roaring inferno. But the wooden stairs were still intact. Gisburne prepared another demijohn of Greek Fire, his eye on Galfrid's head, which bobbed up from behind the barrow.

"Come on, little man," he muttered. "Almost there..."

The smell of roasting flesh gusted into Gisburne's nostrils from the bailey and made his mouth water involuntarily. He tried to put the thought out of his head.

Galfrid dashed out from his cover. But as Gisburne watched, another shape – small, incandescent – bowled out of the swirl of smoke ahead of his squire. A dog – on fire, and running more out of blind, agonised reflex than any coherent thought in its addled brain – scampered wildly towards the southwest tower, smashed into the wall by its doorway in a flurry of sparks, and collapsed in a smouldering heap. For a moment, it simply lay there. Then, like the roaring flue of a volcano, the entire tower erupted in flame.

It was dazzlingly bright, deafeningly loud. Every figure still standing in the bailey fell or threw themselves to the ground. The heat from it seemed to turn the day to blistering summer. The demijohns of Greek Fire atop the tower also exploded. Flames burst from the tower's top like a great bloom, raining down on the wooden walkway, and engulfing it.

It had ignited the oil. The oil that Gisburne himself had spilled. He had wanted this – but not yet. Not with Galfrid still inside.

He looked down to see Galfrid, halfway to his goal, stopped dead and gazing on in shock. The stairway was destroyed. There was now no way for him to reach the battlements. The squire's wide face looked up towards him. Gisburne saw his shoulders fall, his head shake silently from side to side. Galfrid's eyes then turned towards the gate, then back up to his master.

"Go!" he shouted, drawing a sword from his belt. "Go quickly..."

Gisburne saw two serjeants, weapons drawn, charge at Galfrid from the direction of the gate before everything in the bailey was obliterated by billowing black smoke.

Mélisande, distraught, was wrestling to prime the scorpion when a great *crack* resounded from the blazing tower and the whole stone edifice upon which they stood seemed to sway. Gisburne grasped her wrist and pulled her from the weapon. She relinquishd her grip easily, knowing it was hopeless.

Then he wrapped the mangonel's rope about them both, and hurled himself and Mélisande over the battlements and to freedom.

The mangonel's ratchet clacked as the rope unravelled – far faster than Gisburne had hoped. It stopped short some ten feet from the ground. They bounced once, twice, then released their grip and dropped to the mud.

As they scrambled across ditch, and ran away from the castle walls – now silhouetted behind them by the glare of the fire – there was a sound like a thunderclap, and a deep roar that shook the earth beneath their feet. They fell to the ground and looked back. A crack had appeared the full height of the southwest tower, its walls split asunder by the fire's heat. As they watched, another crack burst open between the tower and the wall with a deafening explosion of dust and shards of white-hot stone. The uneven black gap widened. The entire tower seemed to list, then fractured like glass, collapsing with a stomach-churning rumble, its stones sliding into the ditch in a great heap of smouldering rubble.

With the flames roaring higher, the heat almost unbearable upon their faces, Gisburne and Mélisande turned and fled into the forest where Nyght and the other horses waited.

LXIV

Wissant, France – Christmas Day, 1191

GISBURNE AWOKE IN darkness at the click of the latch.

"Don't move," she said, closing the door behind her. "Go back to sleep."

Gisburne had no inclination to move, but he had never intended to sleep. He had flung himself down on the bed fully clothed, and had lain there listening to the sigh of the sea and the shrill cries of gulls, intending for that delicious repose to last only a few minutes. That had been the previous afternoon.

"Where have you been?" he croaked, still barely awake.

"It doesn't matter," she said, and began organising her gear. "It'll keep till morning." Gisburne let his head fall back, but lay resolutely awake.

They had got some strange looks when they had first arrived here. It was hardly surprising. Gisburne – desperately tired and now unsteady on his feet – had almost fallen through the door. It had crashed open, the wind blowing rain and dead leaves about the interior. A startling enough figure in his rough horsehide coat and rusted mail, he was now also bruised and bloody, his clothes stinking, muddy and scorched. As they had walked in, the landlord almost choked on his beer. Three other people, supping quietly by the fire, had left immediately. Gisburne would have had a wry smile at that had he not been so exhausted. Why they were afraid of a man who had so clearly been beaten, slashed and burned to within an inch of his life and now stood ready to crumple with near terminal fatigue, he could not guess. Perhaps they simply thought certain kinds of people brought trouble in their wake. They might be right about that. But if there was one thing he didn't want just now, it was a fight.

"We want lodgings," said Gisburne. "For tonight, at least. Maybe longer. A room of our own." He leaned in towards the landlord. "No animals."

The landlord – a thin man with thin hair plastered over his pink shiny scalp – nodded slowly. He had managed to calm himself after the initial shock of their dramatic entrance. Gisburne guessed that he'd seen a lot in his life. The man looked from Gisburne to Mélisande and back again. She was dressed in the same clothes she had worn since her capture at Castel Mercheval, but now with a hooded tunic of Gisburne's – far too big for her – thrown over the top and belted at the waist. Whereas before, in her own clothes, she had easily passed as male, the addition of the oversized tunic somehow had the effect of accentuating her femininity, and the landlord kept peering at her, dipping a little at the knees to better see under her hood.

"My squire," said Gisburne. "All right?" He slapped two coins on the table top.

The landlord simply shrugged and nodded. He wasn't about to argue. Not with a man who looked like this, and not with business the way it was. He looked like he didn't care whether Gisburne had a goat dressed in a cassock and called it his wife, just as long as he could pay.

Wissant had been Mélisande's suggestion. The town was only a few miles from Calais, but the contrast could not have been greater. Once a great port, it was now in steady decline; Calais's gain had been Wissant's loss. But it had its advantages. Neither the Templars nor anyone else would expect them to be heading here. And the accommodation was cheap, with few questions asked.

He heaved himself up on the bed and watched Mélisande's shadowy figure moving about in the darkness. It was warm – the room had no fire, but was against the chimney breast, which filled the small, low-ceilinged chamber with radiant heat – and he was feeling drowsy. He knew his body was close to collapse from the extremes it had endured; it would take days of sleep to recover. But not now, not here. Not with her. He wondered what she was doing. It looked like she was packing again. Why was it she always seemed to be packing?

She glanced at him. "I told you to sleep," she said. "It's the middle of the night."

He shook his head. He wanted to tell her it was a waste, but he wasn't sure how. He wasn't even sure himself what he meant by it.

She raised one eyebrow at him. "You don't need to keep watch on me. If I meant to rob you, I'd have done it by now."

A smile stirred in him, but never quite formed on his lips. "It's not that," he said.

She smiled sweetly, then sat on the bed by him, dumping her leather bag next to her. "There is a ship bound for England in the harbour," she said, "ready to sail on the morning tide. It's all arranged. You need only be on it, and you will be home again."

"And you?"

She smiled a sad smile, her head to one side, but said nothing.

So, it really was over. He sighed and let his head fall – a great sigh of gratitude and relief. And yet it was tinged with sadness. Sadness at having lost Galfrid. Sadness, too, at the realisation that he would soon be losing Mélisande. This part, he did not wish to end. Not yet. Mélisande was still an enigma. Still intriguing. Still exasperating. Still fascinating. She had helped him, at the risk of her own life. Was still helping him. Why would she do such a thing, if she was indeed in the service of King Philip? Unless, of course... But no, he did not dare think that.

She knelt on the bed and pulled a package of cloth from her bag, and unfolded it on the covers. Gisburne stared at the contents in amazement. "Roast goose," she said, then produced a flask and two wooden cups. "And wine. The good stuff." It had not quite the opulence of their first meeting, but he felt a pleasing warmth at the memory it evoked. It touched him that she had gone to the trouble.

"How did you..?" he began. But she just gave him that look – *Don't ask, and I won't have to lie...* "You seem to have made a habit of bringing me food." It was a habit, he knew, that would end today.

She filled the two cups. "You know what today is?" she said with a smile.

He frowned. What did she mean? What could today "be"? Cold? Long? A Wednesday?

"It's Christmas," she said with a laugh, and knocked her cup against his. "Merry Christmas, Guy of Gisburne."

He smiled, drank the good wine, and hungrily began to eat.

"So," she said suddenly. "You never did tell me..." He sensed what was coming. "The skull..." She didn't need to say any more. But he felt it was time. And she had earned this.

Gisburne shoved a piece of goose breast in his mouth, then, without taking his eyes off hers, reached down and hauled his great helm onto the bed. She looked at him in bemusement. He upended it, and out tumbled something bundled in black leather. Its wrappings fell open as it rolled. Mélisande's eyes widened in amazement, her face lighting up with the glint of gold.

"It was never in the reliquary," said Gisburne, still chewing. "It was always here." He shrugged. "What better place to put a skull for protection?"

Mélisande put her hand to her mouth, began to laugh, then raised the skull before her, gazing into its bejewelled eyes with her own. "But the box..."

"Misdirection," he said. "I learned it from someone I knew in Jerusalem. Someone who was good at conjuring tricks."

Mélisande laughed, pulled a face at the fixed expression of the Baptist and laughed harder still. Gisburne – grim-faced, serious Gisburne, his resistance quite gone – found himself sniggering, then laughing, and finally giving in to a wholehearted guffaw, until both laughed so hard it seemed they might never stop.

With tears rolling down their cheeks, almost incapacitated with mirth, she slapped him on the chest as if somehow this might stop it before she expired. He gave her a good natured shove. She slapped his chest again – harder this time – then roughly grabbed the back of his neck and pulled his lips to hers.

The laughter stopped. They kissed long and deep before she finally pulled away.

"Well, Sir Guy," she said in a hoarse whisper. "Is there still enough about you to properly celebrate Christmas? Or are you all spent...?"

In response, he pulled her to him and kissed her hard on the mouth, his hands sliding around her warm, lithe body. She moaned, returning his kisses, pressing herself against him, wrapping him with her limbs. He felt all restraint slip away. He was done with denial – with duty. The mission was finished. By some miracle he was alive. And tomorrow, she would be gone. Only now did he realise how little he relished that parting. Only now did he realise he wanted nothing more than to forget the past and the future, and lose himself in this moment – in her.

She drew away suddenly and sat astride his lap, her hands upon his chest. Gazing down into his eyes she gave a husky laugh, and rotated her hips slowly. "I see," she said, with a raised eyebrow. "There is life yet..."

And with that she peeled her tunic over her head, and threw it over the Baptist's watching eyes.

LXV

WHEN HE STIRRED next morning, she was gone.

Gisburne – half awake, his head pounding – sat bolt upright.

Her gear was missing. His was still stacked neatly by the wall – a gap where hers once stood. For a moment, he felt a deep sadness. Then panic gripped him. He leapt out of bed, naked, and snatched up the great helm. Empty. He flung it down in frustration, searched agitatedly through his gear, his discarded clothes, the thick bedding. Finally, he slumped down on the bed, clutching his head in disbelief. As he did so, his heel knocked against something heavy, which rocked against the floorboards. Bending down, he peered beneath the bed, and there, staring back at him from the shadows with an unblinking gaze, was the skull. With a snort of a laugh, he hauled it out, hefted it in one hand, and sat contemplating it for a moment. The gold and jewels glinted in the morning light.

She had not taken it, although she'd had every chance. He had been dead to the world that night. Mélisande could have ridden out of the room on a bull, holding the skull aloft and singing *Veni Creator Spiritus* and he probably would have known nothing about it. But she hadn't. Why not? He looked into the skull's ancient eyes, and gave a deep frown. *Why not?*

Perhaps he would never know.

There had been no goodbyes. She had left exactly as she first came to him – as a silent shadow in the night. He looked around the room. Now there was no hint of her left – just the empty space in the bed, and the fast-fading scent of her upon him. The task was done. His mission all but over. But all he felt was a curious sense of desolation.

"You've caused an awful lot of trouble, John," he said, addressing the yellowed bones. "I just hope it's all been worth it."

Minutes later he was stepping out into the fresh, bright morning towards the ship bound for home.

LXVI

Sherwood Forest – January, 1192

THE SNOW HAD never quite left northern England.

For several days, the going had been hard, but as his horse plodded on, Gisburne thought of his final goal – now barely a day distant. By tomorrow, he would be rid of it at last. He would relish the relief it brought.

The forest was vast and deep, its silent trunks – ghostly with frost and ice – like the pillars of some limitless cathedral. He knew this place. But a fresh fall sat heavy in the trees, wrapping everything with a magical unfamiliarity. Now and then, it slipped and slumped to earth somewhere between the trees, or crackling ice fell and splintered with a sharp tinkling. Somewhere, a crow called, its harsh cry muffled by snow – the only other sign of life in this brooding, vaulted expanse.

Entering Sherwood again had evoked strong memories. Of his father, hunting with King Henry one summer, long ago. And him, as a young boy, being permitted to ride with him. It had been thrilling at the time, and a little terrifying. He had been told tales of wild boar and how vicious they could be

– more dangerous than a bear, some said. He had never faced one, and wasn't sure he wanted to. But, at the same time, he hungered for the challenge. Looking back, it seemed an idyllic memory.

There had been a boy there, younger than he, about whom there was much fuss. The King himself clapped the lad on the shoulder and ruffled his hair and gave him tips on how to ride with the hunt. Guy had seen King Henry several times before and found him a gruff and forbidding figure. Never had he seen him show affection.

"That," his father had said, "is Prince John. Go up and say hello. Like I taught you."

Guy did so. Under the watchful eyes of all, he walked his pony up to John, gave an awkward bow in the saddle, and said: "My lord."

"Hello," said the prince, "I'm John. Who are you?"

"Guy," said Guy nervously.

"We can be friends if you like," the boy had said. "I'm probably not going to be king."

Henry had given a hearty but sardonic laugh at that. Only later did Gisburne's father have the chance to explain why. "It is hard for kings to have friends," he said. It seemed it was not so easy for princes, either. After the meeting, John was whisked away, and but for glimpses at a distance, Guy never saw or spoke to the prince again. Not, that is, until another eighteen years had passed.

It was John to whom he now journeyed.

The prince had been much occupied in the north, of late. Here, in his lands, John was struggling to maintain order, to bring unruly barons into line. Gisburne did not know precisely who – his interest in politics was basic, and pragmatic – but he had little doubt that many were the very same men who had smiled down upon the young prince that day, and sworn undying support to the crown.

It was always the same. When there was unrest, out came the petty grievances, the secret ambitions. At any one time, Gisburne calculated, there were at least a dozen nobles who thought they had more right to be king than the King himself – or who simply wanted to have a crack at it, right or not. And there were hundreds who felt they were owed something more, or who would take it anyway if the opportunity arose. Often, they would hide behind supposedly honourable motives. Most would change sides at the drop of a hat. He did not envy John the task of containing this nest of wasps.

What had made things significantly worse, of late, was a growing feeling of defiance against all authority. It was always tougher in the north, where a spirit of independence prevailed. But it had been fuelled to furnace heat by the actions of Hood. Some resented him. Many admired him – even professed to love him. Some even called him a saint. But all, in some small way, felt spurred on by his example. Spurred on to pursue what many vaguely termed "freedom", but which was in reality merely mischief, and disorder. As he rode through the vast swathe of forest, Gisburne was keenly aware that this was now Hood's domain. He sighed deeply, then turned and spat to rid himself of the taste in his mouth.

A cry up ahead made him start. It was an odd cry – human, but hoarse and hard to place, oddly dulled by the surrounding snowfall. Then he saw. Up ahead, on the path, was a distinctive shape, dark against the white – a small figure, hunched, head covered, thin arms waving in the air in despair. An old woman.

"Thieves! Outlaws!" she wailed. "Robbed! Oh, 'elp me!"

Gisburne drew his sword, and picked up the pace. As he neared and watched her – seemingly oblivious to his approach, clasping her head in despair – he began to wonder how she came to be out here, in the middle of nowhere, with no sign of wagon or horse. Had this old crone really walked miles through the snow from the nearest hamlet? Or was she just some old witch who lived in the woods? Somehow, neither seemed possible.

As if in response to his questions, she cried out again. "My ass! My poor ass! Taken!" Then, with another cry – rough as a crow's – she collapsed in the snow.

Gisburne drew up, and leapt off his horse. But as he did so, a sense of unease suddenly gripped him. There had been no tracks on the road he had travelled. And now, he saw there were no tracks beyond where she lay. Just a single line of footprints leading from the trees. Gripping his sword firmly, he knelt by her. "Oh, 'elp!" she wailed. Then he turned her over, and the toothless, stubbly face of a man grinned up from her cowl. "My poor ass!" it said gruffly, laughing.

Gisburne leapt back – but all around, the forest seemed to come alive. From every shadow, every opening, every crook and crevice in the thicket, figures emerged – rough-clad, grim-faced, armed with everything from rusty pitchforks to longbows.

Outlaws. Thieves.

Gisburne judged there to be no fewer than forty. And at least a dozen arrows aimed at his heart. He took a step towards his horse, and every bow tensed. Gisburne's homely feelings of familiarity for his surroundings distorted, became something uncanny. He felt the rush of *deja vu*. The steady creep of inevitability.

Then, somewhere deep in the forest, he heard a crash. A crackling of twigs. Hooves. They pounded closer. Gisburne stared into the dirty faces of the men. They were smiling, and he already knew why.

The "old woman" rose to his feet. "'E's comin' fer ya!" he cackled, pinching Gisburne's cheek with his grimy fingers.

Then, from the forest's edge, burst a horse and its rider. Snow flew from its feet as it stopped and reared, its hooves biting the frozen earth. The horse – a mare – was as white as Gisburne's was black, and from its back a familiar figure beamed down.

Hood's appearance had changed. His beard was darker and more full, his hair longer. Somehow he had acquired the bearing of an aristocrat. But it was his attire that struck Gisburne.

He was clothed in garments entirely of green: a two-thirds length tunic, tight at the waist, with flowing cloak on top, fashioned with lining of the finest fur – all of one piece – the matching hood lying back from his locks and laid upon his shoulders. His hose were of the same green hue, caught at the calf, with jangling spurs of gold beneath.

Gisburne gazed up at the otherworldly vision in horrid amazement. *So, this is how it ends,* he thought.

Hood regarded him with no hint of surprise. It was as if they had parted company yesterday.

"Hello, old man. Well, here we are again." He gestured dramatically with a broad, white toothed grin. "How do you like my merry men?"

Gisburne looked about him. The sea of grim faces cheered and guffawed their sly, gap-toothed guffaws, shaking their swords and scythes. It was raucous. It was leering. But not what he'd call "merry".

Hood circled about his victim as Gisburne had seen wolves do. Wolves, he thought, also looked like they were smiling.

"Nice horse," he said, and patted Nyght upon the neck. Nyght shied away. Gisburne, too, winced at the contact, as if it was somehow infectious, corrupting. "And feisty! Better than that other old wreck you had."

The one you killed, thought Gisburne bitterly.

"I keep that old wreck about me," said Gisburne, and spread his arms wide to reveal his surcoat. Hood frowned, looked him up and down and finally made the connection.

"You used his hide!" he chortled with delight. His men joined the laughter. "Well, waste not, want not."

"I did it," said Gisburne, "as a reminder. Of him. Of my father. Of you." The last was spoken with undisguised bitterness. There was a murmur of disapproval from the crowd.

"Well, I'm flattered," said Hood with a great grin, and bowed low. And he looked like he meant it, too – as much as the man who called himself Hood, or Locksley, ever did. *Typical of him,* thought Gisburne. *It doesn't even cross his mind that he might have done wrong.*

"What do you think of him, eh, Rose?" said Hood into his horse's ear. She stamped and tossed her head. *Rose...* Gisburne shuddered at the memory.

"Rose?"

Hood stopped, and looked down at him, eyebrow raised.

"Just who is *Rose*, Robert?" said Gisburne earnestly, looking him right in the eye. For a moment, he saw something he had never seen in the man's eye. Uncertainty. Quite clearly, the emotion did not sit well with him. He frowned, gave an unconvincing snort of a laugh, and then his eyes flashed with an anger so venomous that Gisburne thought he would be killed on the spot. But as fast as it came, it faded. Hood threw back his head and laughed once again. "Never mind *that*," he said with a broad smile. "Who's 'Robert'?" He and his men guffawed as one. Hood turned about on his horse, as if bathing in their laughter.

"Now, *Sir* Guy – as I believe it now is – we have to rob you."

"The gambeson?" said Gisburne grimly.

"You still have that?" marvelled Hood.

"Different gambeson. Different coins. Same trick." He pulled it from his pack, and flung it to the ground. It landed heavily in the snow. One of Hood's men dashed forward and dragged it away.

Hood smiled. "You always did like those old tricks."

"Now, once again, you have taken everything I value."

"And you shall go upon your way," said Hood. "You have my word on that. But as one knight to another, I have to say I'm disappointed. That you give it up so easily, I mean."

Gisburne felt his blood boil. *As one knight to another...* He fought to contain it. *Stay calm. We're nearly through this...*

"It puts me in mind of some other old tricks. Conjuring tricks. You remember? The left hand distracting from what the right hand is doing?" Gisburne felt a creeping unease. Hood brought his horse up alongside Nyght. "You see, one might almost think that you offer it up in order to distract from something else."

Then he grinned, leaned down and unhooked Gisburne's great helm from his saddle.

Gisburne felt his heart leap into his mouth. He tried to mask his alarm – gave an unconvincing laugh. "But it's just..."

"I know what it is," interrupted Hood, coolly. "And who it is. And why it is here." He pulled the black bundle from the helm and let the wrappings fall away. His men gasped as he held the gleaming skull aloft, turning a circle on his horse. Then he lowered it, contemplating it in his hand for a moment, its dead eyes staring into his. "We'll take its gold. And its jewels. They're a king's ransom. As for the bones... Well..." He stared at it as if examining a horse's teeth. "Never did much care for the name 'John'." His men guffawed again. "But perhaps we can find some monk who'll have them." And he tossed the skull one-handed to the fake old woman, who threw it to a young lad, who lobbed it to a man with a patch on one eye. And so it went, all hooting with raucous laughter as it was passed about.

He had lost. After all this – after all the battles and hardship, and now just a handful of miles from his journey's end – he had failed in his quest, lost his prize. To a thief. No, not merely a thief. To Hood. He found himself mentally calculating the odds of wresting it back, but there was no chance. Perhaps he could get to Hood, maybe even kill him. But he would be dead a dozen times over before he got another yard.

"How did you know?" he stuttered, struggling to grasp what had just happened. Not even Galfrid had known where the skull was kept – and even if he had worked it out, he would never have betrayed him. He was sure of it. Then there was Mélisande. He hoped with all his heart she had not. But he feared the worst. Bit by bit, he felt his world crashing about him.

Hood walked his horse up close again, cocked his head on one side and smiled down at him. It was, thought Gisburne, the way a wanton boy looks at a puppy when deciding whether to pet it, or kill it.

"Don't you see?" he said. "It was always meant for me." Then, lowering his voice, he leaned in until he was close to Gisburne's ear. "Payment. From the King of France. In support of my cause." He patted Gisburne affectionately on the shoulder. "And you were the one who delivered it. For that, I thank you."

Gisburne stared at him in disbelief – at the grinning, taunting face just inches from his, at the exposed flesh around his collar, its veins pulsing with undeserved life.

In one swift move he pulled his eating knife and whipped his arm back, ready to plunge the glinting blade into Hood's neck.

Hands gripped him, held him fast; the knife fell into the snow. His arm was twisted. Another inch and it would break. Bows creaked all around him.

Hood straightened, held up a hand – a rare gesture of restraint. "No need," he said, matter-of-factly.

They relinquished their grip.

Gisburne staggered, his head spinning. All the memories of past weeks were somehow shifting in his head, like the parts of a mechanism, a trap; moving into a shocking new alignment, forcing him to reassess everything that had happened. He did not want to believe it was true. But he knew Hood too well. He didn't trifle with such games. He was not subtle.

And it had an incontrovertible logic – a horrid, sickening, terrible logic. It explained why the French made so little effort to stop him. Why Mélisande had not taken the prize when she'd had the chance. Why she had helped him. He thought of her, over and over. How much of what she had said and done was a lie?

He felt the white, freezing forest crushing in on him. Within moments, his success had become failure, and then something far worse than failure. He had done his enemy's bidding. They had meant for the skull to go to England, and he had done exactly what they had wanted. Had fought and killed to ensure it would happen. And the best part – the real genius of the plan – was that King Philip's hands were clean. He could deny everything – could truthfully claim that he never clapped eyes nor had his hands on the skull. It was simply a tragic loss. And he would not need to point fingers at those who had allowed it to happen – would perhaps even find political capital in defending the Templars to the hilt – but if anyone were to look for evidence of bungling, it would be the Templars who would come up wanting.

Yes, it was a plan of rare genius. And it was he, Guy of Gisburne, who had executed it.

"It was really quite a feat," said Hood cheerily. "I seriously doubt there's another who could have done it." He grinned broadly, then, and pressed a hand against his chest. "Present company excepted, of course." His men chortled gruffly.

"I've been a fool..." said Gisburne, shaking his head. Then he turned on Hood. "But you are a greater one. Do you begin to realise what you're dealing with? Philip doesn't care for your 'cause'. He wishes only to bring ruin to England. To watch it burn. You honestly believe you can bend such a power to your own purpose?"

"Why not?" came the cheery reply. "I'm Robin Hood." And with that, Hood laughed loudly, and spurred his horse. It reared, and leapt, and disappeared amongst the great trees on pounding hooves. A glittering shower of snow fell like a curtain from shuddering twigs and branches, Hood's laughter echoing in the forest beyond.

When Gisburne finally turned around, Hood's men had melted away as if they were never there.

LXVII

Nottingham Castle – January, 1192

GISBURNE STOOD IN silence before John.

The prince had been staring into the fire, his expression unreadable, for what seemed an eternity. Gisburne had said his piece, related the facts. That was a simple enough task, in principle. But even with all he had been through – all the hardships he had endured – this had been the hardest thing he had ever had to do. His very being seemed to rebel against it. He felt his throat tighten as he spoke, as if it physically recoiled from putting the calamity into words. It vividly recalled that time with de Gaillon. When the knight had discovered him doing wrong, and he had felt his whole life slipping from him. The feelings – those sick feelings, not of failure exactly, but of letting down the one person he most respected, of feeling unequal to their high expectations – had a horrible, unwelcome familiarity.

The chamber in which he now stood was the very one in which he had faced William de Wendenal a year before. The chamber he had entered as a pitiful wretch – a penniless criminal facing the noose – and had left a knight. Little had changed in that time – except for the addition of a small table, on which stood a wine jug and goblets, and a chessboard, part way through a game. In his numb, distracted state, Gisburne vaguely wondered who John's adversary was.

The situation was now wholly reversed. This time, he should have entered in triumph. A hero. But instead, all was crashing about him in flames. How he would leave this place today, he could not guess.

Finally, John spoke. His words were steady, precise. "Tell me again what Hood said. About the skull. Word for word."

Gisburne did so. Each word was like a tooth being drawn from his head.

John nodded slowly. When John finally turned back to him, Gisburne was shocked by the expression he wore.

He was smiling.

"Well, I think we should toast your achievement, don't you?" he said. And, with a nonchalance that baffled Gisburne almost to the point of fury, he wandered over to the table and filled two silver goblets.

Gisburne stared at him, then at the goblet that the prince thrust into his hand. Was John mocking him? Was this his idea of a joke? If so...

"Oh, don't look so miserable," chided John, flapping a hand at him. "What was it you told me Gilbert de Gaillon said? About victory and defeat? I forget exactly how it went. But then, he said so many things..."

Gisburne remembered. The difference between victory and defeat. *You're more tired after a defeat – but both can kill you...* De Gaillon had simply meant that sometimes they were not so easy to distinguish. That they were, in part, a state of mind. But losing the hard-won prize to Hood – that was no mere state of mind. That was real. An irrefutable catastrophe. A disastrous turn, just yards from the final goal.

"But I thought..."

"You thought you'd failed because you did not bring me the skull," said John, and took a drink.

Gisburne could not see how it could be otherwise. But once again, John waved away his bewilderment.

"The skull... Well, it's not really important."

Gisburne gaped at him.

"I mean as a thing. An object," added John. "Do you see?"

Gisburne did not. Not for one moment.

"I'll not lie – its loss is a shame. I would like to have denied Hood that prize. And I do so like shiny things." He spread his heavily ringed fingers before him, then dismissed them with a sigh of resignation. "But you have brought me something of far greater value. Evidence of a direct connection between King Philip and Hood."

John paused to allow the point to sink in. Gisburne drank deep, blinking, still struggling to see through the fog.

"You see, I had begun to suspect that Philip was financing revolt in this land, but had no proof. Now, I do. Thanks to you."

My God, thought Gisburne. *He knew. He knew all along Hood meant to take it...*

"Sometimes, Sir Guy, knowledge is more valuable than gold. And personally I'd rather rely on knowledge than faith." He gave a sardonic smile. "I am, of course, aware that this puts me at odds with most of humanity. But certainly this is vital information to have in one's arsenal. Especially now that I am in negotiations to form an alliance with Philip."

Gisburne stopped, his goblet half way to his lips.

"Don't look so shocked, Sir Guy," protested John. "Victory, defeat, ally, enemy. In the real world, these things are so rarely clear cut. And, believe me, I have no illusions about Philip..." John toyed with the chess pieces as he spoke. "He is obsessed with reclaiming those territories in France that belong to the English crown. It has long been his hope that one day, England – embroiled in its own internal strife – would take its eye off Normandy, and Aquitaine, and all the others. Now we know he is not merely hoping, but working towards that end – by promoting chaos in the realm. He perhaps thinks me some kind of ally in this endeavour, since I hate my brother. But I will not see this nation fall." He held the white king before him between thumb and forefinger. "Nevertheless, it pays to keep your enemies close..."

Gisburne suddenly recalled other words of de Gaillon's. *The ultimate enemy is not the one who stands opposite you on the field... It is the chaos that threatens to overrun us when our guard is down.* Much as it troubled him – all this deception, all this ambiguity, all this dissembling – something now began to emerge, bright and clear, out of the murk. A guiding light. John was not like de Gaillon. But he had something in him that was indefatigable. And like de Gaillon, Gisburne now understood, he was not bound by rules – rules were inflexible, imposed from without, and therefore for the weak. He was bound – guided, rather – by principles. And who, in the whole of England, would have guessed that?

The words of Albertus also came to him now. *It is said the skull has the power to bring down a tyrant.* He did not believe in the magic powers of relics. He had marched behind the Holy Cross at Hattin and saw where that led. But perhaps, after all, the skull had laid bare the true tyrants – the agents of chaos. Perhaps it would also hasten their fall. And perhaps he, in his own small way, had helped.

"Do you play chess, Sir Guy?" John returned the white king to the board.

"A little," said Gisburne. In truth, he hadn't played for years – not since Hattin.

"It's becoming very popular, I understand. Apparently, people see in it the confrontation between Saladin and Richard – the black king and the white. I see it rather differently. More broadly, if you like. The struggle between the dark and the light – between the forces of order and the forces of chaos. But then, in life, things are not so black and white. It is not so clear which is which. And sometimes they go in disguise." What was this? Was John still trying to justify the deception over the Baptist's skull?

"We are brought up to believe in evil as a pure and everpresent force, inspiring evildoers to evil deeds. That might work for a monk contemplating matters in a cell, but men like you and I know better. No one ever really believes themselves to be on the side of evil. But not everyone can be right. Of course, everyone thinks what they're doing is for the best, but beware of people who say so. Who come clad in white, meaning to save you. That's where the worst offences lie." He turned from the board suddenly.

"I have heard from Glastonbury Abbey some news of a rather startling discovery there," said John. "The monks were digging in the grounds and unearthed an ancient skeleton of great proportions, buried with his weapons in a log coffin. By his side was a woman, still bearing flowing blonde hair. A lead cross buried with the pair confirmed their identity: King Arthur and his queen, Guinevere." He gazed into his wine, thoughtfully. "As you may imagine, this has caused quite a stir."

Gisburne was uncertain what to make of the news. "Do you want me to look into it?" he asked. John waved dismissively as he sipped at his goblet.

"Oh, it's beneath a man of your talents," he said. "What is most significant about this 'discovery' is that it comes just when the good monks of Glastonbury find their pilgrim traffic is flagging. I'm sure they would claim some kind of holy miracle – of a prayer being answered just when they had need. Others – those of a cynical frame of mind – might offer a more prosaic explanation." He smiled to himself, then turned to face Gisburne. "But it's not the truth or otherwise of the story that concerns me. Let people believe whatever tripe they like. They probably will, anyway, whether you let them or not. No, it's what lies behind it..." His expression had once again become dark. "Don't you see? It comes in answer to a need. To the ghastly emptiness at the heart of the realm. How it reflects England's hunger for a king?"

John turned away once again, continuing in strange, rather distant tones. "Richard will not return. That is my belief. My... hope." Gisburne felt his mucles tense. These words were treason, even when spoken by a prince. "Even if he did..." He shrugged, his words trailing off. "If the people knew the truth about my brother, they would not want him back. But he remains the distant answer to their problems, and they will brook no alternative. Indeed, they turn him to a saint in his absence..." He laughed, mirthlessly. "A saint!" He fell silent for a moment. "Meanwhile, England is without a king – a realm ready to slide into chaos. And Hood – his supposed champion – is hastening its plunge into the abyss." He turned and fixed Gisburne with an intense stare. "I honestly believe that only you and I fully understand this."

Gisburne nodded slowly.

"There is another thing. One of the brothers of that Abbey – a monk named Took – recently spoke out in support of Hood."

"A *monk*?"

"Took has radical notions about property – of the kind that monks tend to entertain from time to time."

"But... supporting a thief?" That seemed beyond the pale, no matter how radical he was.

"He believes that Hood provides hope in a time of need, robbing from the rich to provide for the poor."

Gisburne gave a dismissive, humourless laugh. "Hood cares nothing for the poor!"

"I told you – it's not the truth or otherwise of the story that matters. Word of him spreads. It has its own life. He is becoming a legend. You know that it is already becoming common practice to call any outlaw a 'Robin Hood'? Now, that is real power, when one becomes enshrined in language."

"Just words," said Gisburne dismissively. "A stolen name and a stolen reputation."

"Words have the means to imprison a man," said John. "Even a king."

· Quite suddenly, he turned his back on Gisburne.

"But... I have a dilemma. I admit I've been avoiding the matter, but recent events have brought it to a head. Clearly, if you continue doing... what you do... you are unlikely to remain a secret for very long. That is a problem."

"To put it bluntly, it is no longer fitting for me to have a landless knight in my service. There is only one solution that I can see..." Gisburne had been half expecting it. His failure in the closing moments of his quest had made it seem inevitable. John's reassurances had eased his mind, but he saw now that it was a momentary respite, to soften the blow. He watched in numb silence as John went to a small wooden chest, and removed something from inside. A final gift, he supposed. A parting gesture. Then once again, he would be a knight without allegiance. Without purpose. He did not blame John. The prince had treated him fairly in all things. Instead, he cursed his ill luck. It had dogged him his whole life, since the fall from grace of Gilbert de Gaillon. He thought he had found a master who was de Gaillon's equal. He knew now that this would never be achieved.

"It's not much," said John. "Less than you deserve." Gisburne was barely even aware of holding his hand out to take whatever trinket John was offering. There was simply the cold weight of metal on his upturned palm, and then his fingers closing about it – a half familiar shape. He frowned and held it up before him. It was a large, iron key.

"It's no castle, I'm afraid," John continued, his voice carrying a note of genuine apology. "But I must tread carefully, even now. Especially now."

He turned and let his eyes roam across the chessboard. "The time will come for us to reveal our strategy," he said. "But it is not yet. Richard has his white knight in Hood – the supposed saviour of the realm, about whom people publicly fawn. But you are this realm's true protector. My black knight." He picked up a piece from the board and turned it in his fingers. "It will be a hard road. The outside world will know nothing of what you do. You will receive little reward, and no adulation. You will be misunderstood, resented. Even hated. What is best for this realm is not what is best for the barons. They will misrepresent and distort you as they do me. I cannot promise that your story will be that of a hero; perhaps one day, but not yet. The truth doesn't always come out. But that is why we fight. And you will be their champion. A knight of shadows."

He turned to face Gisburne once more, his eyes gleaming with a strange intensity.

"Do you accept this?"

Gisburne gripped the key in his fist. "I do," he said.

John breathed out, as though in relief. "I know this has been difficult for you. Being a thief. Being..." – he hesitated – "being like Hood. But it is different. We are fighting a war – fighting for a cause. What you do for me is different, just as killing in a war, for a just cause, is different from murder."

Gisburne thought of Hood the thief. Hood the murderer. Yes, it was different. He would make sure it was.

John turned away, then, to the frost-crazed glass of the window, and gazed at the frozen world beyond.

"I do believe it is finally beginning to thaw," he said distantly.

Gisburne breathed deeply, his body filling with renewed vigour – a hardened determination. This would be his mission. He felt muscles and sinews tighten, the spirit burn with a fierce heat, the will become tempered like steel.

And there was something else – a softer emotion. One he had not known for years. An almost overwhelming, child-like joy.

For the moment his eyes had settled upon the key, he had known exactly what it was.

Epilogue

Village of Gisburne – 13 January, 1192

GUY OF GISBURNE rode along the winding, high banked lane, lost in thought, his head pounding from the night before.

For a long time he had been riding with little thought for his surroundings. He was weary – exhausted by the demands of his quest, worn down by the weeks of travel, dispirited by its conclusion. De Gaillon was right; you felt more tired after a defeat. He kept telling himself that it had not been a defeat – that it had achieved exactly what was needed. And perhaps it would even help bring Hood to justice. That was something for which he heartily wished. But he knew the resources of that man – resources drawn from a seemingly inexhaustible well – and doubted that his end would come so easily. And there were other things, too. Things left unfinished.

There was Tancred. For the sake of all that was good, all that was reasonable, he wished the world cleansed of him. Whether that had indeed been achieved, he had not heard one way or the other.

There was also Mélisande de Champagne. Of her, he had thought a great deal. He told himself she was a mere fact of his mission, a temporary alliance – another piece on the chessboard which could now be disregarded. But he was not yet skilled enough in the art to make himself believe that lie.

Then there was Galfrid. His heart shrank at the thought. That was his defeat, his loss. The rest was simply incidental damage – the scarring of battle. But that... He knew what Gilbert would have said: that in order to win, one had to be prepared to lose something. But that did not make it feel any better.

He sighed heavily and looked around him, seeking solace in the quiet of the land. For a long time he had been travelling through the sparse, rolling landscape typical of these parts, dotted with gnarled trees and outcrops of mossy, grey rock. The road itself followed the high ground. To his left, for much of the way, the valley had fallen away in a gentle slope down to a tumbling, icy river, swollen now by the thaw. Its roar had been his constant companion for the greater part of that afternoon. Across the bleakly beautiful panorama a network of dry stone walls spread like grey-green veins, and here and there a lonely cottage leaned into the wind. The snows of recent weeks had here quite gone, and the brisk breeze had whipped the bare ground dry. The sun came and went with alarming rapidity – solid clouds hurtling across the cold blue sky, their pattern of huge shadows sliding across the open fields and moors, plunging them into cold, grey darkness before bursting back into light moments later.

Over the last league, the landscape had begun to soften, becoming flatter, more sheltered by trees, the stone walls replaced by thick hedges. He half recognised these roads now, as one does in a dream – at once familiar and unfamiliar, muddled by memory. It had been a long time since he had travelled this way. Years. He had been a different man then. The last time he had expected to do so, just over a year ago, he had got only as far as the priory at Lundwood. There, the monks were caring for his dying father, cruelly cast off his land by Richard's edict. There, too, had been Marian.

He shook his thumping head to rid himself of that thought, then winced at the way his tender brain seemed to bounce in his skull.

The blame for the state of his head lay squarely at Llewellyn's door.

At their reunion in Nottingham Castle the week before, Llewellyn had greeted him heartily. True to his word, and without prompting, he drew out the promised bottle of potent, ecclesiastical brew – but not before he had plied him with just about every other kind of drink, some from lands Gisburne had not even heard of, and at least one that Llewellyn had described as "an experiment".

As was evident from their surroundings that night, Llewellyn liked experiments. Gisburne gazed around the workshop in the bowels of the castle – a larger and far richer version of his temporary accommodation at the Tower. It was a cluttered treasury of outlandish devices both real and imagined, some complete, many only half realised, others no more than pinned sketches on scraps of material or parchment. Often there was a strange beauty in their intricate design, in the iron, wood, bronze and ivory of their construction. Some featured stout springs or heavy tubes cast in metal, evidently intended to launch lethal projectiles. Others had structures as fine as fishbones – one, stretched with some gossamer-thin, near-transparent material and shaped like a bird. The purpose of many of these things was lost on Gisburne – and, perhaps, on anyone but Llewellyn himself.

The current experiment, in particular, seemed to have taken the esteemed enginer into the realms of the bizarre. In the centre of the pockmarked square table was a wooden stand, and upon the wooden stand something that loosely resembled a human arm, fashioned from dozens of shaped plates of metal, all hinged, overlapping and interlocking in a manner that brought to mind the body of a wasp. It was as if the limb had lately been wrenched from such a creature – but grown of iron and steel, and of outlandish size.

This was not in itself the strangest part of the scene, however. All about it there were drawings of insects and crawling sea beasts, and upon a platter, in various states of preservation or dismantlement, numerous large beetles, hornets and other armoured creatures – some, Gisburne recognised, native to the Holy Land, and perhaps further afield. A dung beetle, locusts, gigantic cockroaches, the likes of which he had never seen before. And spiders – of such size he hoped never to meet in life. Amongst all of them, however, it was the more modestly proportioned scorpions that caused him to shudder.

"Lunch?" said Gisburne, sipping tentatively at Llewellyn's "experimental" brew, and finding it not only palatable, but surprisingly conventional – something like cider, but, by Gisburne's reckoning, some hundred times stronger.

Llewellyn cast him a weary, unamused smile, as if it were the hundredth time that day he'd heard the joke – though quite who visited him down here, Gisburne could not imagine.

"The crabs and lobsters, I did eat," he said. "The Moors partake of locusts, I have heard, but personally I shan't be turning to them for sustenance. Only for inspiration..."

Gisburne turned his gaze to the hinged shell upon the wooden stand.

"That?"

"That."

"What is that?"

"It is the future of warfare," said Llewellyn.

Gisburne stood, studying it more closely. "So, we are to become like crabs and beetles, scuttling across the battlefield?"

"Have you never tried to crush an earwig underfoot, only for it to still be quick and vital after three tries? Have you never eaten lobster, and not had to attack it with all your strength to release it from its shell, though it be a fraction of your size? They are great survivors – armoured by the Almighty since creation. We have much to learn from this wisdom, if we only care to look. Imagine if you could walk right up to your foes, knowing their blades – and even their arrows – could do you no harm."

"Don't think I haven't thought about it," said Gisburne. He picked up the strange carapace, feeling its weight, testing its complex, interlocking plates and joints, and shook his head slowly. "Little wonder that it's becoming a rich man's game."

"It's too heavy," sighed Llewellyn. "And awkward. The articulation needs work. You see, it's all a question of the right steel – making it strong enough to resist a blade, yet flexible enough to be workable. But if I can make it flex just the right way, and make it lighter..."

"I could test it for you," offered Gisburne, feeling the extent of its movement.

"You could," said Llewellyn, standing and taking it from him with a suddenly proprietorial air. "When it's ready..." He placed it carefully – almost lovingly – upon its base once more. It was, Gisburne thought, like one child relieving another of a cherished toy before it becomes damaged. "Don't worry," said Llewellyn, his back to his guest. "I will keep you informed of my progress. God knows you're going to need all the help you can get to preserve your life in the months to come."

Gisburne smiled and raised his glass. "To beetles and lobsters, and all their creeping kind."

Llewellyn raised his own, and they both drank.

By the time they moved on to the monkish brew that evening, Gisburne was already flagging, and they had only managed about a quarter of the bottle before he gave up the ghost. Llewellyn had stoppered up the remainder and presented it to him.

Gisburne had worked his way through most of it on the night before this final day's travel, as compensation for the dismal lodgings in Bradford. All day, he had been regretting it, nursing a thick head that not even a bitter Yorkshire wind could blow away. The worst hangovers of all were born from drinking alone.

Quite suddenly, Gisburne found himself at a turning so familiar it made him stop. A winding lane struck off to the left by a broken oak tree – a tree he had played in as a child. He geed Nyght on, suddenly impatient for what lay ahead.

And then, as the lane turned, he saw it: a picturesque stone house – modest in size, but well-proportioned, with arched windows and a square tower at its western end. The house in which he had been born. The house in which his mother and sister had died. The house Richard had stolen from his father, and John had now restored. Gisburne was suddenly overwhelmed by a feeling he never thought to have again.

He was home.

He urged his horse into a gallop.

As the hooves pounded the road, memory tugged at him, and he did not resist. For a moment, he was a child again. The small boy being chased by the wife of Godwine the farmer, for robbing apples from their orchard. Slightly older, and stealing his little sister's cake, and blaming it on the dog – then, later that week, almost breaking his arm as he'd tried to ride off with a visiting knight's colossal destrier. Not long before he was due to leave for Normandy, pushing yeoman Robert's boy in the mud and relieving him of the silver penny his uncle had given to him for his name day.

Then there was the time with Gilbert de Gaillon. The time when everything changed.

He WAS THIRTEEN. One year into his apprenticeship with Gilbert, and already grown in confidence. Life with Gilbert was good – his master was firm, but fair, and the training, hard as it was, easily within his capabilities. Many knights treated their squires like common slaves who simply had to put up with whatever was thrust upon them, no matter how mean or cruel. Some seemed to consider that good sport. De Gaillon, however, took his responsibilities as a mentor seriously. He was not only the boy's master, nor simply a trainer in the arts of combat. He was also a teacher, preparing his young charge for life. And when he spoke to Gisburne, he did so as he would anyone else, making no allowance for status.

This was almost unique among the knights Gisburne had encountered. At first, he valued it highly. Then, he began to take it for granted. Soon, he was becoming cocky.

It came to a head one night in the summer. It had been a good day – one of those in which everything, even the weather, seemed to work in one's favour, and at the end of which one's muscles had the satisfying ache of hard work well done. He had served de Gaillon his meal and was finally eating his own, seated by the camp fire along with several of the other squires. Nicolas, an older squire who Gisburne greatly admired, was talking loudly to his fellows. Nicolas was tall, broad shouldered, with hair as black as pitch – a son of a wealthy family. His uncle was a Count, and had sent him the gift of a new knife as a reward for his good conduct in a recent tournament. He wielded it like a sword in the flickering light of the fire, and joked about how he could eat two meals at once now he had two eating knives. It was a beautiful piece of work – its handle carved in bone, with all manner of inlays and glittering ornaments. All marvelled at it.

But it was not this that occupied young Gisburne's mind. It was Nicolas's old knife, sticking upright out of a slab of bread.

It was an object Gisburne had long coveted. The handle was of black wood; two elegantly shaped parts, held in place either side of the tang with flat rivets. The blade – about a palm's length – was simple, but satisfyingly shaped and proportioned. Sharpened on one edge, flat on the other, and thick at the base, giving it good strength and weight, the whole gently tapering to a fine point. There was nothing in the way of decoration upon it. It was not ostentatious – probably not very valuable. But in Gisburne's mind, it had a simplicity that he had seen in no other – and every part of him wanted it for his own. Now that Nicolas had his fancy new knife, he could see no earthly reason why that should not be so.

That night, he crept into the tent where Nicolas lay sleeping. It was a mad undertaking. Nicolas was five years older than he, and twice his size – if he caught him in the act, he would skin him alive. But his lust for the prize drew him on. He had expected the theft itself to be a challenge; in the event, both knives were left lying in plain sight by their owner's snoring head. As he plucked up the blade, he saw that Nicolas was dribbling in his sleep like a baby. He left the tent chuckling to himself in a delirium of triumph.

Then the whole world collapsed around him.

In the dying light of the fire, watching him, half-dressed as if just risen from his bed, was Gilbert de Gaillon. Gisburne's limbs froze, his face suddenly burning hot. His mind spun, seeking excuses. Explanations. But there were none. He was utterly exposed. De Gaillon's eyes, glinting in the firelight, dropped to the knife in the boy's hand, then came back up to his face, the unrelenting gaze boring into him as he stood, mute and useless. Gisburne expected some dreadful retribution – a beating, a barrage of unbearable admonishments, total humiliation before all his peers, perhaps even to be sent packing back home, a miserable failure. An exposed thief. But none of these things happened. What did happen was worse than all of them. De Gaillon narrowed his eyes for a moment, then, without a word, turned and walked away.

Gisburne stood, suddenly powerless, for what seemed an age. He was shocked and sickened – more horribly alone than he had ever felt in his life, although what had caused it was just this: that he was never alone. There were always others' needs, others' feelings, others' judgements. He had always pushed them to one side – disregarded them, been impervious to them. He had believed himself somehow indestructible. Now, he felt like Adam, suddenly aware of his nakedness, his weakness, his sin. For a moment he hated de Gaillon for forcing this self-knowledge upon him, wanted to rail against him, beat his fists against his chest. But somewhere beneath it, even then, he knew he would only be railing against himself, and that it was part of himself that he hated. To have disappointed his master – to have failed him... It was its own punishment. The worst feeling in the world.

Biting his lip to hold back the tears, he crept back into Nicolas's tent and placed the knife exactly as he had found it. Then, wretched and shamed, he crawled into his bed and sobbed himself into a fitful sleep.

Gisburne walked on eggshells the whole of the next day. He felt sick. His hands shook. His bowels couldn't keep a grip on anything. He had restored the object to its proper place – but nothing could put things back as they were. Nothing could undo the knowledge of the crime. So, he busied himself around his master, not daring to look him in the eye, waiting for the moment when the subject would be raised. But de Gaillon said nothing of the incident that day. Nor the day after that. Nor any day that week, that month, that year. He simply carried on as if nothing had changed, and Gisburne – trepidation gradually turning to relief, and then being forgotten – did the same.

But everything had changed. It was years before Gisburne fully understood the wisdom of his master's actions that night, but when he finally did, he loved him all the more for it. For trusting him to find his own way forward. For understanding that defeats are often better teachers than triumphs. For believing in him, and making him realise that mistakes do not have to define a man. Gisburne's attitude towards stealing – and towards himself – changed forever that night. No one hates thieves like a reformed thief.

There was an unexpected coda to the story, two days after the abandoned theft. Gisburne was scrubbing the tack for his master's horses when a voice behind spoke his name. He turned, and felt his heart drop out of his chest. It was Nicolas. In his hand, he clutched the sheathed, black-handled knife.

Nicolas had never spoken to Gisburne directly before, except to cut him down to size in front of the others. Gisburne was about to confess all and throw himself on the other's mercy when he realised that Nicolas – who could be a bluff and boastful sort when with his fellows – had not a look of anger or hatred, but a sort of embarrassed, sheepish smile. "I know you always liked this knife," he said. "And now I have two..." He thrust the knife towards Gisburne. Gisburne, stunned and silent, took it from him. Then Nicolas laughed, and ruffled Gisburne's hair roughly, and was gone.

For a time, he had considered throwing the knife into the river Eure. Denying himself this thing, of which he was so unworthy. Then he thought what his master would do. De Gaillon detested self-flagellation, and would probably just think it a waste of a good knife. And so, the knife had stayed.

AS NYGHT SLOWED to a trot, Gisburne let his fingers go to its haft. The knife had served as a constant reminder of those times. Of that night, and of a gift freely given. But it was something else – something less tangible – that had helped keep him true. Ever since, whenever he had been faced with a harsh decision or moral dilemma, he had found himself wondering what de Gaillon would think – had asked himself how the old man would judge his actions. De Gaillon had become a constant guiding presence in Gisburne's eventful existence – even more so in death than he had been in life. He had become his conscience. Gisburne did not know if there was some realm from which de Gaillon now looked down upon him. But that mattered little. His mentor lived on in him. De Gaillon had, in a sense, made him. It was, he now realised, perhaps the closest thing to a personal God he was ever likely to get.

Gisburne threw himself down off his horse and tied the reins to the bar above the stone trough – the place he had tied so many horses as a child, and from where he had once attempted to steal one. As Nyght drank noisily, he stood before the low, wide door, hardly daring to move.

Through the waxed linen of the downstairs windows, a dim light glowed. Smoke curled from the chimney, and the smell of roasting beef and onions wafted on the air. Someone was here. Either John had also laid on servants, or... For a moment, it crossed Gisburne's mind that the whole thing was an elaborate joke. But no. He could not believe that.

As he approached the door with tentative steps, key in hand, sounds of movement came from within. The clank of a pot. The jangle of a knife or spoon being set on a wooden table. He stopped by the door, wondering why he was at such pains to move silently on what was supposed to be his property. As if to assert his ownership of the place – to confirm that the key, and by extension he, did indeed belong here – he went to put it into the lock. Before key and lock could meet, the door opened.

"You took your time," said a familiar voice.

Gisburne stared, wide-eyed, at Galfrid. The little man stood, bedecked in a slightly stained apron, ladle in one hand, savoury aromas flooding past him on the warm air, expression as inscrutable as ever. He gestured back towards the interior with the ladle.

"There's a stew on the go if you're hungry. I couldn't get any..." But there he was stopped. Gisburne flung his arms around the little man and clutched him to his chest. "You're not dead!" Gisburne laughed, and slapped both hands on his squire's back, overcome with joy and relief. Galfrid, dumbfounded, simply stood, arms stuck out either side of him like a scarecrow – ladle in one, fresh air in the other – not having the first idea to do with himself.

Finally Gisburne released Galfrid from the rough embrace and stood back, still clutching him by the shoulders, still laughing. "You're not dead!" he repeated, giving his squire a gentle shake as he did so. He could hardly remember a time in his life when he was more glad to see anyone.

Gisburne looked him up and down. Galfrid's face had a couple of new scars, but otherwise he appeared whole – none the worse for their trials. The vigour of Gisburne's greeting had clearly taken him completely by surprise, however. He looked stunned – and, Gisburne thought, maybe even emotional behind that implacable front. "You're all right..." he said. Then, more cautiously. "You *are* all right?"

A pained expression passed across Galfrid's face for an instant, as if recalling a memory that would rather remained buried. Gisburne thought of what he must have suffered at Castel Mercheval, considered asking him more directly, but then rejected the idea. Galfrid's face changed again, and he nodded, almost casually. It would take time, thought Gisburne. Let him come to it when he's ready. And he smiled, and let his hands drop.

"Well, er... You'd best come in then," said Galfrid awkwardly, clearing his throat. "You must be hungry." And with that, he disappeared inside. Gisburne followed, dipping his head under the lintel as he went.

The low stone doorway opened straight onto a wide hall. At one end, a familiar fireplace was hung with pots, about which Galfrid now bustled like an old woman.

"There's wine here – not Prince John's, the good stuff, mind. Or ale if you prefer. I paid over the odds for that. He could see I wanted it in a hurry. Tricky bunch, these locals – the awkward bugger nearly didn't sell it to me at all. But an Englishman's house isn't a home without ale. Anyway, I've cleaned up a bit, as best I can – it was left in a bit of a state. Hopefully it's as you would wish it." He thought for a moment. "As you remember it."

It was exactly as Gisburne remembered it. A little smaller, maybe. But that was a trick of age. Even the few sticks of furniture his parents had owned – both had had simple tastes – were still here. Gisburne went over to the heavy wooden table that dominated the centre of the room, sat at the bench, and ran his finger over a crudely carved letter "G" on one corner of the thick tabletop – still visible despite years of use and polish. His father had given him a hiding for doing that. How old must he have been then? Fifteen? Fourteen? No – he was already in Normandy then, under de Gaillon's tutelage. He could only have been twelve, at the most. It seemed inconceivable to him that so fragile a relic could still exist from all those years ago – years that had seen him traverse so much of the earth that his childhood had seemed another world. But here it was.

A frown knotted his brow. "Galfrid, I..."

"It's all right." Galfrid held up a hand in protest. "You did what you had to do. And much more besides." For perhaps the second time since Gisburne had known him, there was no trace of irony or cynicism in his tone. "I knew the skull was never in that box." Galfrid looked him in the eye. "You had it all along, didn't you?"

Gisburne nodded, felt oddly ashamed at the deception. But Galfrid waved the thought away. "You came back for us. At Castel Mercheval. That you did not have to do." He shrugged, turned back to his stew, perhaps embarrassed at his own words. "Admittedly, you may have come back more for the wealthy, feisty, beautiful, unmarried Countess, but still..."

Gisburne smiled to himself. Memories of Mélisande flooded his mind. Every time he thought of her – and it had been often – something tugged at his innards. She had deceived him. But then, he had deceived her. It was a fair exchange, he supposed. A normal part of his new life as Prince John's agent. But she had also saved him – had also, surely, done more than she'd had to. And there was certainly no deception that last night together. She had wanted him. And, whatever deceptions surrounded them – and there were plenty – there was something more honest in that one encounter than any he'd known before. For a time, he had attempted to rationalise it – told himself she had merely been a surrogate for Marian, as had many women before. He had felt guilt over some of those liaisons. Guilt at misleading them, guilt at misusing his feelings for Marian. He had felt a pang of guilt over Mélisande, too – but for entirely opposite reasons. He felt guilty because, that night, Marian had not entered his thoughts once. He had not wanted her, nor a dismal substitute for her. He had wanted only Mélisande. For herself.

Never before had he encountered a woman who knew his world – who really understood it, had experienced it. The possibility had never crossed his mind. There were so many things that he could never begin to explain to Marian, that he wished to speak of, but could not – things that Mélisande could simply read in his face, without a word being spoken. To be able to share one's life to that extent... But could a woman such as she – one who went her own way, and would not be owned – ever belong to just one man? How and when their paths might cross again, he did not know. But cross they would. And the mere thought made his heart beat faster.

A jug clunked down before him on the tabletop, brimming with beer. "You look like you need a drink." Galfrid placed two silver-rimmed horn cups side by side and filled them both. "Let's start with the ale."

Gisburne smiled. He knocked his cup against Galfrid's, and drank. Perhaps it was the homeliness of the surroundings, or the relief at seeing his friend alive – Gisburne didn't really care. He only knew, as the foaming, malty brew hit his throat like a blessing, that this beer was the best he'd ever tasted.

"Hmm," said Galfrid, smacking his lips critically, the ridge of his nose wrinkling in a frown. "It'll do. Could be better. Especially for that bloody price."

Gisburne's eyes narrowed. "The locals... You said they were 'tricky'?" He vaguely wondered if any of the locals he had terrorised as a child were still alive.

Galfrid grunted in assent. "They've been keeping their distance, mostly."

"But why? They all loved my father. My mother, too. Do they know who it is who has taken possession of the place?"

"They do know, yes..." Galfrid shifted on his feet awkwardly. "It is..." He looked as if he did not wish to continue, but pushed on, regardless. "It is because of Gilbert de Gaillon. His reputation."

Gisburne felt a sudden fury rise in him – had an urge to fling his cup into the fire. But he'd had enough of that anger. He'd had it for years now. It was time to throw it off. He drank again, until the cup was drained, then slapped it down and sighed deeply.

"If I have to fight for a hundred years – if I have to defy King Richard the Lionheart himself – I will not rest until the name of Gilbert de Gaillon is restored. That is my sole quest."

"*Our* quest," said Galfrid. "There are no sole quests any more." He held out his cup. They knocked brims. "Which means we only have to fight for fifty years apiece."

Gisburne gave a snort of laughter and shook his head. "You really are the most extraordinary fellow, Galfrid." Galfrid shrugged, and gulped his ale. Gisburne studied him with a kind of wonder – the strange, impossible little man. "You haven't yet told me how you escaped Castel Mercheval."

Galfrid's eyebrows raised. "In order to learn that secret," he said, "you will have to get me very, very drunk indeed." He held up a finger. "But I warn you – if you think you can drink me under the table..."

"I have seen the underside of this table often enough to develop a keen strategy in that regard," said Gisburne. And he filled up Galfrid's cup until it overflowed.

"One thing..." he said, as Galfrid was raising the cup to his lips. "Tancred?" It was a question that had been on his mind since that day.

Galfrid's grave expression gave him his answer before the squire even spoke. "He was burned," he said. "By flames. By quicklime. It near took the flesh off his face." Gisburne thought he saw Galfrid shudder as he spoke the words. "But it appears he is not yet done with this world. Either that, or the hereafter refuses to have him. He lives. Against all odds." He paused and drank. "The Templars have disowned him. He goes his own way now. I hear his strength returns, and his will is stronger than ever. But as for his sanity..."

Galfrid didn't need to say more. Gisburne nodded slowly. "Well, it would appear that rather than rid the world of a pestilential evil, I have in fact turned it into something far worse – a hideous, twisted monster now bent on my utter destruction."

"I'll drink to that," said Galfrid, resignedly. They knocked cups once again. Gisburne drank, and stared into the fire. He thought of the pieces now in play. John. Richard. Mélisande. Philip. The Templars. And now Tancred. Especially Tancred. He had surely not seen the last of him.

And yet somehow, deep in his bones, he knew that whatever might pass in what remained of his life, his ultimate fate lay not with the crazed Templar, but somewhere in the great forests to the south.

One day, when the circle closed upon his nemesis, he would become a hunter of Sherwood again – but this time, with a far more deadly prey.